I0778553

CHASING MEMORIES

ADRIELLE MADDOX 2

CHASING MEMORIES

MONTANA WAKEFIELD

Bink Books YA
Bedazzled Ink Publishing Company • Fairfield, California

978-1-960373-03-8 paperback

Cover Design
by

Sapling
Studio

Bink Books
a division of
Bedazzled Ink Publishing, LLC
Fairfield, California
http://www.bedazzledink.com

To Cazz, the world was a little brighter when you were by my side. Your birth changed me in ways only a mother can understand. I will love you forever. And mama, being your daughter was my greatest gift. Your example of selfless love and support built the foundation of who I am. I didn't get to share this with either of you, but you live on in my heart, and with every word I write.

Acknowledgments

My father once said, in regards to creativity, "Open the door and enter, you'll be amazed at the wonders that lie beyond." This story came in a flash, so quick I could only grasp a blur of colorful feathers and the characters' fearless pursuit of truth and freedom. I opened the door and stepped into the world of Adrielle Maddox. I've discovered the characters are flawed, impulsive, funny, and heartwarming. Writing their story has been my salvation and one of my greatest joys. I am so very grateful to those who have helped me share this with you.

Bedazzled Ink Publishing, a huge thank you to all of you. Casey, you are a gifted editor. Liz and Claudia, thank you for believing in me and in this story. Betsy, I won't forget your tenacity to see this in print.

Monet, you encouraged me when all I could grasp was a glimpse of the story and the colorful "Feathers." Mauve, you were my first editor, when no one else would read my pages. Thank you both for sacrificing your time with me as you were growing up, so I could pursue my love of writing.

Malcolm and Roman, you bring me so much joy. I can't wait to share this with you. And Stan, of course Stan. You are my joy at the beginning and end of every day. Thank you for sharing your life with me.

I've learned the secret of life is never losing sight of what's important and holding on to it. And that's you, my family and close friends. We journey side by side through joy and sadness. We are each other's witnesses, support and memory keepers. I treasure you all.

If I had one wish, it would be to bask in that love for eternity.

I'd also like to thank my readers, present and future. Without you, there would be no point in writing any of this down. I hope this story encourages you to pursue your dreams.

Chapter 1

Florida—Present Time

A BLINKING RED news band flashed on the screen. Above it was Angelo's face, vacuous and disoriented. Too stunned to settle into chairs, Coco, Liz, and Dave stood transfixed.

"Caucasian male. Early twenties found wandering by the pier . . . Anyone with information contact the authorities."

The call to action was followed by a number posted under his headshot.

"What's happening?" Adrielle mumbled, the time-travel haze still dulling her senses.

"Holy caramels," Liz said and punched the number on her phone.

Dave clamped a hand on her wrist. "Careful there. Don't forget he's not human."

"It can't be him."

"Might be. If they start probing, they'll never stop."

"What do we say?"

"As little as possible."

"She's not stupid," Coco said.

"Yeah, I wouldn't say he lives in the fifteen hundreds with Michelangelo," Liz said.

Dave pinched the bridge of his nose. "Oh god, I'm getting a migraine." He pressed his fingers to his skull.

Adrielle stood motionless, watching the disaster unfold. The disorientation from crossing the time barrier was dizzying.

"What was the emergency?" Coco asked in a stern voice, worry and annoyance etched on her face.

Adrielle winced. Coco had been dead against Adrielle going back to check out a time travel breach.

"Michelangelo and Leonardo were using Angelo's feathers. Or trying to."

"Hmph. That was worth the risk of compromising the present world?"

Coco had a point, Adrielle turned back to the news. "Why are they showing Angelo's picture? This doesn't make sense. Are they asking who he is?" Panic soared through her. Something had gone terribly wrong.

Everyone was watching her with scared expressions.

Dave wagged a finger. "You can't cross the time continuum without consequences." He may as well have said, *Adrielle, this is on you. Why did you return to the fifteen hundreds when we all just got back?*

"I didn't do this," Adrielle said.

Liz shot Dave a sideways glance and gave Adrielle's hand a squeeze. "Adrielle's new position upholding the Achaean Act and stopping time-travel . . . is complicated."

Adrielle swung her gaze back to the TV. Despite Liz's defense, Angelo's mug shot was a punch in her gut.

"It's awful, but no one could have predicted this," Liz said. "He's one of us. As congealed to us as caramel in Ben and Jerry's Karamel Sutra."

"Unfortunately, there's no telling what else may have gone wrong," Dave said. "Maybe it's a trap."

"A trap?" Adrielle snapped.

Dave snatched the remote. "There has to be another news segment."

"Give it back," Liz said, swiping for the remote.

Dave clicked through the channels and stopped on the weather channel.

"Breaking news: the hurricane is headed this way. Some predictions show the storm could increase to a CAT 3 or 4, bringing winds in the 130-140 mph range. If you live east of the I-95, Authorities have ordered homes to evacuate. It's going to get rough. For those of you riding out the storm, stock up on water and non-perishables." At the end of the announcement, two thirty-something anchors with movie star smiles assured all was well.

Dave grunted. He amped up the volume and studied the projected hurricane paths. "Storm surges are four to five feet above normal. They're right, hurricane Isaac could easily turn to a CAT 5."

"Why aren't they evacuating everyone then?" Coco asked.

Liz pointed at the TV. "Exactly. Don't let their polished smiles fool you. They're groomed to sell ratings."

"Do we have flashlights? Batteries?" Dave's voice was thick with alarm. "We could have long-term power outages."

"How about candles?" Coco reached in her top dresser drawer and pulled out two white pillars. She sat them on wrought iron stands and turned triumphantly back to Dave. "Matches too."

Liz grabbed the remote. With one click the two anchors disappeared.

Dave turned to the TV. "Hey—"

"Shh." She dodged Dave's swipe. "Let's get back to Angelo." She surfed until Angelo's face popped on the screen.

The red banner on the screen was more of the same—a request to call.

Liz turned to Adrielle. "Let's go get him."

Adrielle nodded in agreement.

"Now, everyone," Liz said. "Let's go."

Liz's urgent command shattered Adrielle's remaining travel fuzz. An unsettling sensation overcame her. Was it a foreboding of bad news? Or insecurities heightened by her new powers? Seeing Angelo on the screen sent her into a panic. Maybe Dave was right, and this *was* some sort of trap. But from whom? Domenikos was sealed away in the scepter diamond.

"Quick, call the number," Adrielle said.

"And say what? That he's an alien with superpowers?" Dave said as he paced around the room.

"What could be worse than the world learning there's an ancient species co-habiting the Earth?" Adrielle said. "They'd fear an invasion. Think it was an alien attack. We need to slow down. Think this through and come up with a solid plan."

Dave swung his gaze to her. "I agree."

"Calm down, everyone," Liz said. "We're getting all hyped."

"What do *you* suggest?" Dave snapped.

Liz shrugged. "Break him out."

"Break him out? He's not a prisoner," Dave said.

Liz's frown deepened. "We hope."

"Let's just bring him home. The rest we'll figure out once he's safe," Adrielle said.

"I'm down," Coco said, ducking into her closet.

Adrielle punched the number into her cell and muted the phone. "I'm going to tell them we'll be by to pick him up. Try to say as little as possible."

Coco reappeared wearing a shiny black raincoat and purple rubber boots. She tossed an orange trench coat to Liz. "Adie has her own. Sorry, Dave, no extras."

Dave glanced out the window. Rain was pelting onto the glass. "I'm fine," he said, then turned up the collar on his denim jacket and buttoned it up.

Liz checked the coat over, her eyes widened at the outdated style. "How old is this? The lapels are seventies, I think. Extra wide with thick stitching accentuating the curves."

Coco laughed and exchanged a look with Dave. "It was Layla's. You've become such a Diva since Florence."

Liz shrugged.

Adrielle paced to the window. She strained past the riveting water and wondered what might be lurking. "The storm's a hellion, but it's a relief not to see the murmuration."

"And the call?" Liz asked.

"Oh. He's at the Daytona Police Department. They found him wandering by the pier, disoriented. I said he was a friend. That we'd be by to pick him up."

"We should go," Coco said. "The rain is coming down in sheets and our wipers need replacing."

"WE DO NEED wipers. I can't see a thing," Adrielle said. No matter how fast they set the wiper speed, the blades didn't offer relief. Florida heat had rotted the rubber.

"Slow down. You're veering off the road," Dave yelled. He pressed his fingertips to the dash.

"Chill." Coco leaned forward and hunched over the steering wheel.

"I can drive," Adrielle offered.

Coco shook her head.

"Now the glass is steaming up." Dave, sitting uncomfortably forward, turned the defroster on high. "Watch out!" he squealed, as something dashed across the road. He grabbed the steering wheel and cranked it left. Coco wrenched the wheel right to compensate. The car whirled out of control.

"Hold on!" Coco slammed on the brakes.

Adrielle grabbed onto the seat. The car spun and spun.

"Oh my god," Liz shrieked. She dug her nails into Adrielle's thigh and slammed onto the back of the front seat.

The car finally stopped on the shoulder. They sat speechless, panting.

"What was that?" Coco managed, her voice a thin wheeze.

"A dog," Dave said.

She turned to Dave. "Did we—"

Dave shook his head.

Coco exhaled. "Where did it come from? Jeez. It's the freeway." Her hands were shaking so hard she could barely hang on to the wheel.

"Why don't you let me drive," Adrielle said.

"No. I'll slow down."

Rain pelted onto the roof. Cars were stopped along the shoulder. Swells of water made stretches harrowing, and the half hour drive stretched to over an hour. Adrielle imagined each of them were wallowing in their own version of dread.

The car rolled to a stop at the police station, and they clawed their way out, traumatized from their spinout.

Adrielle's legs quivered as the group dashed across the parking lot. Swirling winds pried their coats open and drove water into every crevice.

Adrielle paused at the entrance. The sign above said, "Daytona Beach Police Department." Never in a million years could she have imagined coming here under these circumstances. She sucked in a breath and opened the double front doors.

A barrage of chatter and ringing phones replaced the howling winds outside. Water sloshed onto the entry mat as they wiped their foreheads and shook their hair and clothes.

Dave unbuttoned his jean jacket and slipped it off, exposing a clingy soaked t-shirt. He'd taken the brunt of it. Without a raincoat, he was drenched before he'd even left Palm Coast. Lacking a place to hang his jacket, he folded it neatly over one arm as though nothing was out of the ordinary.

An officer behind a wall of glass glanced up and down again.

Adrielle led the way to the front counter. "Hi." The officer looked up at her. "We saw the news segment about the unidentified guy and called. They said to pick him up here."

Without a response, the officer pushed a clipboard across the counter and gestured to the crowded waiting room with the flick of his chin.

Liz took the clipboard. They slushed their way to the reception area and settled in the corner.

LIZ STARED AT the clipboard through fogged-up glasses.

She reached into her pockets for something to dry the lenses, then searched her purse. She remembered Dave used up her tissues in Florence and made a mental note to replace them. She pulled out her Burt's Bees lip balm and uncapped the tube. Why were her lips so dry when every inch of her was wet?

Without a dry cloth, she wiped the water droplets with her hands and pushed the frames onto the bridge of her nose. Better.

She glanced around the station. An officer was processing a shifty-eyed guy by the front, his hands cuffed behind his back. Liz lowered her eyes to the clipboard.

Name. Contact info. Reason for coming—all standard stuff. But there was nothing ordinary about waiting at the Daytona Beach Police Department. This was the last place Liz thought she'd ever be. She scribbled all their names. The question read: *Reason for being here? . . . To pick up a friend.* How detailed should she get? Her friend happened to have time-travel superpowers. *Unbelievable.* Liz inhaled a deep breath and resigned herself to filling out the forms.

FIFTEEN MINUTES LATER, a female officer with a badge on a lanyard called out their names. "Adrielle, Coco, Liz, Dave." They stood up and followed her through a metal door to a back area.

Another door led to a small cinderblock room where Angelo sat at a metal table, his head resting on his hands. He was casually dressed in jeans and a faded blue T-shirt—both looked out of place on him. Adrielle was so relieved he was safe and in one piece, she bolted into the room and threw her arms around him.

Angelo stiffened. Adrielle released her hug and studied him. He raised his eyes and stared blankly up at her. He didn't recognize her?

His gaze washed over all of them without a flinch.

Liz pushed past the officer and pressed her face into Angelo's until they were nose to nose.

"Ange, it's me. Liz. Remember? Italy?"

He stared blankly at her too.

Liz clamped her fists on her hips. "Oh, for God's sakes, Angelo. *The Book of Feathers?*"

Angelo blinked, a detached vacuous look in his eyes.

Adrielle's chest tightened with angst. She felt sorry for Liz. After their time in Florence, Liz had elevated him to Dave's rank of BFF.

Adrielle studied Angelo closely. This wasn't him. It had to be an imposter. A Madame Tussaud's resemblance of him.

"Fried Lizard guts." Liz pointed to Adrielle. "Take another look at her. You *have to* remember *her*."

Angelo swung his gaze to Adrielle. After a moment, he shook his head. "I've never seen her before."

Adrielle winced. This was a nightmare. Weren't Achaeans supposed to be timeless? The *inter-travel subconscious* compensated for any lapses in memory during time-travel and adjusted for deficiencies in the new time period. What could have gone wrong?

"Uh, I'll give you guys a moment," the female officer mumbled and disappeared into the hall. The click of the door latch reverberated to a drowning silence.

Everyone gathered around Angelo. "Are you kidding?" "You have to remember." "Look closely." "Florence?" "We worked on the *Book of Feathers* forgery." "What is happening?" "Adrielle?" "Isn't he supposed to be immune to this kind of thing?"

Adrielle tried to squelch her panic. They expected *her* to have answers.

A single resounding question banged around in her head: If Angelo had lived thousands of years and his memory was wiped clean as easily as chalk on a chalkboard, what hope did any of them have?

Chapter 2

Florida—Present Time

AFTER A SHORT interview, the attending officer skimmed over the required forms and released Angelo to them.

Feeling triumphant, they rushed out of the building. They had Angelo back. Perhaps fate had smiled down on them, but nature warned otherwise. In the short time they'd been at the station, the storm had intensified. Violent wind gusts slammed into them like defensive tackles. Icy spray whipped at their faces. They clutched their jackets and hurried to the Jeep. The doors were almost ripped off their hinges as they struggled to get inside.

At Dave's insistence, he drove, while Coco sat shotgun. Angelo sat in the back, sandwiched between Adrielle and Liz.

Adrielle shot glances at Angelo. He looked so lost she wanted to cradle him in her arms.

Liz was studying him too, her face so close to his she was almost nuzzling him. Liz met Adrielle's eyes. She looked as though she wasn't sure it was really him.

Maybe he was an imposter someone had sent to throw them off track. Off track from what?

Liz folded her hands on her lap and looked straight ahead, her expression unreadable.

"Turn on the radio," Adrielle said. A little music might cut through the tension and settle her jumbled nerves.

Coco surfed the stations but all she got were storm warnings. An evacuation was in full order for most of Palm Coast.

Due to rising water, sections of the freeway were coned off, confining traffic to one lane. They crawled bumper-to-bumper for a grueling couple of hours before they reached their exit. Dave turned off the interstate, his tense body poised over the steering wheel. He drummed the wheel with stiff fingers as he navigated the less travelled side streets back to their home. They were overflowing with water and cluttered with branches and debris.

The sign for their street, Palmetto Drive, was lying in a neighbor's lawn.

"Wow," Dave said, as he rounded the corner to Layla's two-story home. He pulled into their driveway and slid the car into park.

Instead of feeling relief, Adrielle was consumed with rising dread. What could she do to restore his memory? The attending paramedics in Daytona had checked Angelo's vitals and told them they believed he must have hit his head, resulting in a concussion. They'd advised taking him to his family doctor.

Doctor? Did Achaeans even have doctors? No, she couldn't chance having anyone study Angelo too closely.

They clamored out of the vehicle.

Adrielle studied Angelo's reaction. He had been here countless times, yet he soaked up the details of the façade and landscaping with no sign of recognition. And he hadn't said a word.

The grandfather clock in the front hall chimed six p.m. They wordlessly stripped off their coats and boots and ambled into the kitchen.

Layla often had a pot of something cooking on the stove. But today, there was no welcoming savory aroma, only the smell of Lysol and potpourri.

"What's up?" Liz said, giving the kitchen the once over.

Adrielle shrugged and headed for the fridge, determined to portray confidence. Affixed to the fridge door with a palm tree magnet was a note. She read it out loud:

> *Gone to North Carolina to visit my sister. Elsa's not doing well. With the hurricane, thought it prudent to leave ASAP. Not sure how long I'll be. You can reach me at my cell.*
>
> *P.S. The house is clean. Fridge is stocked and plenty of snacks in the pantry. Be safe.*
>
> *~ Layla*

It will be ok, Adrielle told herself, re-affixing the note to the fridge. Though the storm was worrisome, they had bottled water, candles, and food.

"We've got the house to ourselves," Adrielle said, forcing a smile. "We should stay put till we know what to do."

"I'm game," Dave said. "My parents are on a cruise."

"Cruise? In this weather?" Coco said.

"Mediterranean."

"Oh."

"Count me in," Liz chimed, digging into her large handbag and pulling out her cell. "I'll text my parents."

Adrielle sighed. A courtesy text would let them know she was safe, but reality was, since Liz's parents' divorce, they were seldom concerned about her whereabouts.

"It's settled then," Coco said, heading upstairs. "We'll hang in my room."

"Let's set up a movie," Dave said, motioning for Angelo to follow.

ONCE UPSTAIRS, ANGELO stood in the center of the room and hesitated before choosing a place to sit.

"Hang on," Dave said, reaching into his overnight duffle bag. He tossed Angelo dry sweats and a t-shirt and pulled out a pair of flannel pajamas for himself. He turned to Coco. "Should we . . . uh, change here or—" He motioned to her adjoining bathroom.

"Change wherever you want. There are dry towels in the bathroom." Coco ducked into her closet and changed into her Lululemon yoga pants and a sweatshirt. Angelo hadn't said a thing the entire trip home. She felt sorry for him. Losing one's memory was possibly one of the worst things to ever happen.

She walked back into the room, and Dave had flicked on the tube and was surfing channels. Angelo looked uncomfortable. He stood there, watching Dave, and clutching onto his dry clothes. It broke her up.

"I'm going downstairs to check on the others," she said and ran down the stairs and into the kitchen. Adrielle and Liz had assembled a tray of chips, popcorn, and left-over pizza.

"What's wrong?" Adrielle said, searching her face.

"Nothing. I see you raided the pantry," Coco said, turning away. She didn't want anyone to see how upset she was.

"You can't forget this." She added a bottle of Coke Zero to the snacks and helped herself to a glass.

"Wouldn't be a party without it," Adrielle said.

"Party?" Liz turned to her.

Coco met Adrielle's eyes and saw her deliberation. "Soooo, what are we doing, Adie?"

"What?" Adrielle looked surprised. And scared.

"You're stalling."

"What do you mean? I'm not—"

Coco paused. "We really doing this? Watching a movie with everything going on? We can't keep him here, like he's our pet."

"Our pet? Why would you say that?"

Adrielle looked hurt. Coco shook her head and raised herself onto the island. "Look. I know what you're thinking. Pretend everything's ok and that he belongs."

"He *does* belong," Liz said, clearly affronted. She pushed her glasses up her nose and planted her fists on her hips.

Coco rolled her eyes. "C'mon. I hate to be a buzz kill, but this isn't your average slumber party."

"Ok, fine. I need time to figure this out," Adrielle said.

"You? More like we. *We* need to figure this out." Coco lifted herself off the island. "Us. Remember? We're all in this together. If there's one thing you should've learned by now, it's that you couldn't have gotten this far without everyone's help."

"I know. I get it. But I'm the one responsible." Adrielle slapped her hand to her chest.

"Responsible? How's that?"

"I have the mark of the traveler on my back. I'm the one that's supposed to know what to do."

Liz raised an eyebrow. She took the lid off the dip and dunked a chip, then stuffed the whole thing into her mouth. She frowned in concentration as she crunched. "Guys, let's give it time. I don't like this any more than you do, but maybe . . . just maybe, it's temporary."

"Fine." Coco said, pulling the chip bag out of Liz's reach. "I don't want you to stress eat. It's taken you months to get fit and lose the weight." She looked from Liz to Adrielle and back. "We should decide on *how much time*."

Adrielle shrugged. "Angelo hasn't said two words."

"It's awful. They're supposed to be changing into dry clothes and setting up a movie, but Angelo's just standing there. Standing." Coco slapped her hands to her forehead. "He doesn't know what to do."

"Bet Dave's stalling too. Hoping that if they pick a documentary, something will spur a spark," Liz said.

"Hmmm . . . Might not be a bad idea," Coco said.

"Okay. Let's give it through the night. Maybe things will look brighter in the morning," Adrielle said.

"And if they aren't, then we do something about it," Coco insisted.

Adrielle and Liz nodded in agreement. If Angelo's memory didn't return, Coco knew none of them had a clue what to do.

ONCE EVERYONE WAS fed, dry, and comfortable, they relaxed into watching a car-chasing who-dun-it mystery Liz had chosen.

Outside, record-breaking winds howled and roared. Under ordinary circumstances, Layla's eighties home offered a safe haven, but Liz worried. Shaking windows coupled with a rattling roof made it feel like they'd taken refuge in a tin can. She winced every time a tree branch slammed against the house. She exchanged a look with Dave.

"How old's the roof?" Dave asked, moving his sleeping bag further away from the window.

Adrielle scooted closer to Coco in the bed.

Debris banged against the side of the house and the room went dark.

"There goes the power," Coco said, picking up the box of candles and matches on the bedside table. Only pale moonlight filtered in from the window.

"It's late," Dave said, consulting his wristwatch with the glowing hands. "Ten. We should turn in anyway."

"Liz, you okay on the floor?" Coco asked.

"Snug as a bug." Liz pulled her sleeping bag up around her chin and brushed off cookie crumbs. She glanced at Angelo and Dave on the floor next to her and smiled. To be honest, she'd missed this. All of them under one roof. She hadn't felt this at home since Florence, where they'd all slept in Michelangelo's guest room.

Until this moment, she hadn't realized how much she'd actually *loved* working on the forgery with the gang. Solving the mystery of Domenikos. She sighed deeply and braced against a deep sense of loss for the past. And for Francesco, the love of her life, who unfortunately belonged back in the Renaissance. She missed him and his affections more than she'd thought. He'd been so devoted to her.

Liz turned onto her side and squirmed to get comfortable. Her stomach rumbled with hunger. Staying a size 4 was an excruciating sacrifice. Did she really want to go through this agony her entire life? She fell asleep counting and recounting calories.

LIZ AWAKENED TO rain pelting against the windows and roof. She sighed.

"Spit it out," Coco said, striking a match. She lit a candle, and soft candlelight illuminated the darkness. It flickered and cast long shadows against the wall.

"I've missed that smell," Liz said.

"The sulfuric smell followed by melting wax?" David asked, sitting up.

"No, Florence. I can't get it out of my mind." Liz rumpled her sleeping bag around her. "That time was magical. All of us working together on that forgery. And *The Book of Feathers*." She sighed. "All those spells. Things turned out pretty wonderfully, I'd say." She sucked in a slow shuddery breath. "Adrielle, I have to admit, translating the text was amazing work. And Coco—who knew you were such an artist? Even Angelo contributed. Remember guys?" She giggled and swiped at a tear. "All those silver feathers for the quills when we were running out of time? That's something I'll never forget. A hundred silver plumes falling on Leonardo's lap." She snapped her fingers. "Just like that." She sighed again, the memory vivid in her mind. "I can still see their faces."

Liz turned to Angelo, hoping for a sign that he remembered too. But Angelo continued to lay on his side, only rustling in his sleeping bag, his rhythmic breathing steady.

Perhaps they were all hoping for a miracle, as Michelangelo would say. For the impossible.

"Wait a minute—that's it!" Adrielle said, sitting up. "There has to be something about his amnesia in the *Book of Feathers*."

Chapter 3

Florida–Present Time

LIZ STOOD UP and flashed her iPhone light on the wood floors. She was almost to the door when Adrielle, Coco, and Dave called out, "Where are you going?"

"To get the book," she said, glancing back at Angelo who lay in his sleeping bag, asleep. "Adrielle's right. The answer's gotta be there, if it's anywhere."

"Whoa. Where do you think the book is?" Adrielle said.

"In your room."

Dave jumped to his feet. "I'm going with. You disappeared the last time you went downstairs for baked chicken, and it still haunts me."

Adrielle laughed. "That's not going to happen again. Domenikos is safely imprisoned in the diamond scepter. And secondly, *C'est ici.*" She pulled the large book from underneath her pillow.

Adrielle laid the *Book of Feathers* on Coco's dresser. A candle on either side gave off a soft glow as the others huddled around.

Under other circumstances, Adrielle may not have let them look on, for it was forbidden for a layman to set eyes on this sacred text. But her new responsibilities included being the sole protector of the book, and she reasoned she was the only one who could read the ancient *Achaean* text. To the others, the odd-looking characters made no more sense than hieroglyphics—the vivid illustrations interspersed with the text, wouldn't give enough information to cause any harm. Besides, they'd already seen it when they helped her create the forgery, which enabled her to fool Domenikos and entrap him.

Adrielle raked her hands through her tangle of white hair. As she scrutinized the spells, each new page sparked hopes of finding answers to Angelo's memory loss.

Outside, the wind continued to howl and whine. At first, Adrielle found the raucous sounds of the storm disturbing, but as she become more immersed in the book, the sound was little more than an unpleasant noise.

A SUDDEN CRASH shook the walls. Coco took one of the candles and rushed toward the sound coming from Layla's room. She pulled back the paisley curtains and strained to see past the rain-splattered windowpane.

A powerline had smashed to the ground, missing the house by inches.

"Close call," Liz yelped behind her. Dave and Adrielle clipped at her heels.

They ambled back to Coco's bedroom, Coco leading the way. She stopped in the doorway. Angelo was stooped over her dresser, holding a candle close to the open book.

THEY ENTERED QUIETLY and watched Angelo for a few minutes. Liz finally walked to him and placed a hand on his shoulder. Angelo looked up at her.

"Can you read that?" she asked.

He nodded and turned back to the book. Liz felt a jolt of joy. For the first time, she saw a hint of recognition in his eyes.

Liz struggled to refrain from kissing every golden curl on his forehead. She turned to the others and grinned.

Chapter 4

Florida Present Time

"BUT YOU SAID you could read the text? How can you not remember anything else?" Liz asked.

"Sure, I can read it. But I don't get it," Angelo said, turning the thin pages.

He raised his eyes to Liz, then looked at each of them until he locked onto Adrielle. The green streaks in his eyes had lost their spark.

"What is this, some fairy tale book?"

Adrielle felt jabbed in the gut. She blinked back tears.

Liz went to Coco's bed and sat on the edge. "Holy shamolee."

After a few moments, Liz sat up a little straighter. She looked at Adrielle, raised her hands as if she were about to say something, then folded her hands into her lap. She shook her head. "I don't get it."

The others exchanged looks of disappointment and bewilderment. How could Angelo not remember any of their shared experiences?

"Angelo, are you sure none of this means anything to you?" Adrielle said, walking to him.

He shook his head. "Nope. Should it?"

Deflated, Adrielle sank onto the bed next to Coco.

With not much else to say, everyone returned to their sleeping places.

Adrielle lay awake, searching for answers, until the light of dawn filtered through the window.

"We should get something to eat," Dave said. "Under the circumstances, I don't think any of us can sleep."

"Good idea." Liz forced a smile.

They took both candles and made their way in the dim light down the stairs into the kitchen. Liz usually made coffee the morning after Friday movie night sleepovers. She'd gotten into the habit in Florence, after watching Salai, Leonardo's assistant.

"No power means no coffee," she said.

Coco opened the fridge. "We should have cereal and milk before it sours." She sat the milk jug on the island.

Dave found the granola and fruit loops in the pantry and sat them alongside the milk, then took a banana from the fruit bowl.

Adrielle busied herself with bowls, spoons, and mugs. How could she eat? She was angry for not knowing what to do. For not sticking by Angelo after the forgery exchange in the cave. She'd gone back to her life in Florida, focusing on trying to keep things as normal as possible, and lost track of him. She wondered now if Haden was okay. Why hadn't he contacted her?

Why was she so troubled? She'd gone about her life assuming they had theirs. After all, Angelo was a grown man—or Achaean, and so was Haden. But then something terrible had happened to Angelo. Was it possible they were all victims of circumstance? Or was there a greater, darker plan in motion?

Adrielle felt the same crushing and overwhelming force as before. It made it difficult to think of anything else. Why was it back now?

After some thought, she was convinced dark workings were behind the apparent goings-on. But how could she get to the bottom of it?

She ate her breakfast quickly and helped wash the dishes.

Now what?

"See you guys later," she said, striding out of the kitchen. She had to think.

Chapter 5

Florida—Present Time

"DINNER'S READY." COCO'S voice barreled through a sleepy haze.

Liz yawned; she'd been having the most delicious dream about Francesco. She rubbed her eyes with the heels of her hands and rummaged through her sleeping bag for her glasses. Adrielle's journal lay open beside her. She'd fallen asleep reading of Adrielle and Haden's planned marriage, and how it never transpired.

Liz sighed; those were different times.

Where was Haden? They'd rushed back to modern times so quickly she hadn't discussed what happened to him with Adrielle.

Clearly, Haden loved Adrielle. And when in love, you did everything to be with that person. So why hadn't anyone heard from him? Didn't anyone else wonder?

Adrielle had recounted that final battle with Domenikos—how Domenikos lunged at her and stabbed Haden in the side when he intercepted his attack. Then he'd fallen over the cliff. But then what? Surely, he'd been able to save himself. Had he popped into another time epoch? After all, he'd survived thousands of years. If he hadn't tapped into his time-travel powers, he must have broken the fall by using his feathers, the way Adrielle and Angelo had. But nobody had seen him as they watched from Michelangelo's studio.

Liz picked up the book and pressed it to her chest. She was determined to get answers. This was a love story if she'd ever read one: Adrielle's unfinished love story.

Two brothers: Haden and Angelo in love with one girl. Adrielle, the beautiful mistress. An evil villain: Domenikos. It didn't get any better than this.

Liz walked into the kitchen with the book clutched to her chest. A candle flickered in the center of the island with Adrielle, Coco, Dave, and Angelo sitting around it. She paused.

The smell of melted wax reminded her so much of Florence, Italy she felt a physical gut-punch. They'd shared many meals under Michelangelo's roof.

Good times. Only Leonardo, Salai, and Michelangelo were missing from this dinner table. And of course, Francesco.

She blinked back tears and realized the others were watching her.

"What?"

"The way your melancholic smile touches the corner of your lips . . . and your eyes have that knowing far-away look. Everyone else see what I'm seeing?" Dave said.

Everyone nodded.

"At this very moment, you look exactly as Leonardo painted you." He chuckled. "I still can't believe it . . . Liz, the Mona Lisa."

"She's still our Lizzie. Look, we've saved you a spot." Adrielle motioned to the empty stool by Angelo.

Swept away by emotion, Liz wiped the corner of her eyes and sat down.

"You okay?" Dave mouthed from across the table.

She nodded, still trying to recover from the swell of affection for her friends. She fanned her hand for much-needed air.

"It's this. Adrielle's journal," she said, revealing the book she had clutched to her chest. She placed it on the island and reached inside her handbag for a Kleenex.

Chapter 6

Florida–Present Time

WHILE THE OTHERS settled in Coco's room for the night, Adrielle headed across the hall to the bathroom, a candle lighting her way.

She sat the candle and chronometer on the vanity, turned on the faucet, and undressed.

It was quieter here. She stepped into the tub. The cool water felt soothing, and she relaxed.

She soaked for a long while and stepped out of the tub, water dripping down onto the mat.

The door burst open. Angelo stood frozen, his eyes pinned on her naked body.

"Get out," Adrielle screamed. She yanked a towel off the rack and wrapped it around her body. Then locked the door with a trembling hand.

She'd never felt comfortable in her own skin and now he'd seen her.

She studied her warrior's crest in the mirror. The quarter-sized crest glimmered in the candlelight. A red, black, silver, and pale green feather, interlinked in the shape of a wreath—each color rich with meaning and obligation.

In the heat of the battle, feathered wings had sprouted from her back and saved her from the terrifying fall. What did it mean to live up to its expectations?

She was a leader. Half Achaean, like Domenikos, her twin. She had to tell Coco Domenikos was their brother. It would be a difficult conversation.

Domenikos said time travelling was an innate part of being Achaean. She disagreed with his tactics but could see his side. The ban on time-travelling her father imposed, the *Achaean Act,* handicapped Achaeans from their natural state. But it was wholly necessary for the survival of the human race.

The weight of upholding the Achaean Act was a heavy burden for any and every Achaean. She sighed. Perhaps it *was* better for Angelo to forget.

Adrielle slipped her chronometer over her head, committed to find answers.

Chapter 7

Florida—Present Time

THE KNOCK ON the door startled Adrielle. She straightened in bed and sat the *Book of Feathers* aside.

"Come in."

The door creaked open, and Angelo poked his head in.

She was surprised to see him. He'd barely said two words since the police station. Adrielle motioned him in.

He looked tired. He absorbed the room as he took slow steps to the foot of her bed. His gold curls shimmered in the candlelight.

Adrielle hunched her knees to her chest. "What's up?"

He shifted his weight from foot to foot and inhaled a long breath. "I'm sorry about earlier. I didn't know anyone was in the bathroom."

Adrielle's cheeks grew warm. "My fault. Forgot the lock."

"Can I?" He motioned to the bed.

"Sure. Sit down."

Angelo sat on the edge of her bed. "Are you okay?" he asked. The intensity of his expression surprised her.

"Of course. You?" She wrapped the chain of her chronometer around her fingers.

He shrugged. "I—uh . . . Liz expects us to be friends. Were we? I can't remember. But I feel this pull to you." He let out a rush of air and leaned in. "Can you explain why?"

Adrielle's chest tightened. She couldn't begin to describe their relationship, much less understand it. "We were friends."

"Only friends?"

Adrielle turned away. His longing for the truth made her uncomfortable. She gathered her hair into a messy bun and snapped on a yoga tie from her wrist.

What could she say? They were lovers in a past life? That for reasons not yet clear, she was marrying his brother, Haden. Did he even remember Haden? Or that he was Achaean?

She glanced down at her chronometer. It had stopped. If it weren't against Achaean law to disappear into another time period, she would.

Adrielle raised her eyes to him. "Angelo, what do you remember? How did you get to the police station?"

Angelo shrugged. "I was on the beach, a storm brewing overhead. It started to rain and by the time I reached the pier, the wind was blowing so hard I could barely stand. The officers parked on the side of the road called out to me. Said there was a hurricane, and I should take shelter." He looked pointedly at her. "They began firing questions and I couldn't even tell them my name."

A fresh wave of grief swept over her, and she placed her hand on his sleeve. "That must have been awful."

She heard a gasp on the other side of the door.

"Lizzie, are you spying on them?" Coco asked.

"We can hear you," Adrielle said, breaking into a smile.

Liz burst into the room. Coco peeked in and hesitantly entered.

"I heard voices. That's all. Voices," Liz said, looking from Adrielle to Angelo.

Dave tore into the room. "We've got a leak." He was drenched, his hair and pajamas dripping onto the floor. He slid his bangs off his forehead and shook wet fingers.

"Were you outside?" Liz asked.

"Nuh-uh. The attic. There's a large hole in the roof over Layla's room. The wind must have blown the shingles off. Or maybe a tree hit and made a hole. I don't know. "But we've gotta patch it right away."

"I'll help," Angelo said, standing up. As they rushed out of the room, Angelo glanced back and met Adrielle's gaze. The look in his eyes said this conversation was not over.

Chapter 8

Florida—Present Time

ANGELO AND DAVE found wood and extra shingles in the attic. They carried the supplies outside and propped the ladder against the eave.

"I'll go up," Angelo said. "You support the ladder at the bottom."

"You sure? A wet roof is dangerous enough, but the wind . . ."

Angelo nodded. "We need to patch it right away."

Angelo climbed onto the roof, wood and shingles tucked under his arm. He wrestled to keep his mind on task, but his mind drifted as he worked. He couldn't go on indefinitely, trapped in a house with people he knew nothing about.

He had the impression Adrielle was withholding information. Without recollection of their past, or solid evidence to back this up, he wasn't sure how to approach her. She was so cautious around him.

Possible conversations rolled around in his head, but none seemed right. He couldn't afford misunderstandings. Anything he said could clam her up even more.

Adrielle had evaded his question about their relationship and sidestepped it altogether. That wouldn't get him the truth or help get his memory back.

One thing was clear: Adrielle was going to have to open up about everything, whether she liked it or not.

"This fix will keep the water out until we can find a more permanent solution," Angelo said, looking up at the dark sky.

Dave shrugged. "It's all we can do."

Angelo took one end of the ladder and motioned for Dave to take the other. Everything seemed to be temporary. "C'mon, let's head inside."

DAVE AND ANGELO entered the kitchen to find the girls chatting around the kitchen island.

"Everything patched up?" Coco said, standing from her stool.

"Yep, should hold until Layla gets a roofer here," Dave said. He caught Adrielle and Liz's exchanged looks as he and Angelo slid off their coats and wondered what they'd been discussing. Despite the warm ambiance the candlelight gave, the tension was high.

"Thanks, you two. I'll get towels." Coco slipped past them and returned a few moments later. "Here." She tossed them each a towel and sat down.

"Come sit. Liz has put dinner together," Adrielle said.

"The best," Liz said, smiling broadly up at Angelo. "Cold pizza and warm soda."

"Fantastic. I'm starved," Dave said, taking one of the two empty seats on either side of Liz. He motioned for Angelo to take the other stool and sensed Angelo's hesitation as Liz looked expectantly at him with a big goofy smile. Obviously, it was making Angelo uncomfortable.

Liz hadn't said why she was so doting toward Angelo, but he knew she'd grown quite fond of him during their time in Florence.

Angelo took the stool next to her and they ate by candlelight.

"While you two were braving the storm, we were reminiscing. Laughing at all the stupid things we did in school," Liz said. "Remember when we ditched P.E. and got caught?"

"Yeah." Dave turned to Angelo. "We were sitting in the schoolyard under a large oak tree when the senior class came out the back doors to use the track. Mr. Snavelovski, our gym teacher, sent us to the office and we had detention every day after school for an entire week."

"What about you, Angelo. Do you remember anything? Anything at all?" Liz said.

Angelo shook his head. He cleared his throat, "Wish I did." He scrunched his napkin into a ball and tossed it onto his paper plate.

"Don't worry about it. It'll come back to you," Dave reassured with a small pat on the back.

LAYLA'S HOUSE ONLY had two bathrooms, so they got ready in shifts. Coco went into her adjoining bathroom and Adrielle used the bath in the hall to change into her pajamas. By the time she came out, Angelo was waiting for her. His expression was serious.

"Hope I didn't make you wait," Adrielle said.

"Not at all," Angelo said. "Actually, is this a good time to talk?"

"Uh, sure. Let me put these away."

Angelo followed her down the hall and waited by the door as she stashed her laundry into the hamper.

"Come in," Adrielle said, sitting at the end of her bed.

Angelo stepped into her room. Instead of sitting, he perused her bookshelves loaded with books in French, Spanish, and Mandarin. He took slow measured steps to her music stand and rifled through her handwritten music sheets. He picked up her old acoustic guitar and strummed a chord.

Adrielle gasped. "You play?"

Angelo shrugged. "I guess. Actually, I don't know. That came out of nowhere." He smiled broadly, the spontaneity and genuineness reaching to her core.

Adrielle laughed, and Angelo put the guitar down clumsily.

"I fool around with it, mostly," Adrielle confided. "I've picked up some chords and a bit of finger picking from YouTube. I've always wanted lessons but we couldn't swing it."

"And the songs?" he asked, tipping his head toward the stack on the music stand.

"Oh, you saw those huh? My attempt at making sense of things."

"Ahh." He paced over to the *Book of Feathers* lying open on her bed and picked it up, then sat down beside Adrielle. He laid it on his lap and searched the pages. His eyes skimmed over the words.

"Why can I read this?" he asked, turning to her. Adrielle was stunned. His eyes had an intensity she hadn't seen in him since before the eclipse.

A searing jolt stung her back. The crest of feathers. *Damn,* it hurt. A tiny whimper escaped her.

"You okay?" Every trace of Angelo's smile vanished.

She was about to say yes, when the searing deepened. It felt like a branding.

Adrielle turned away from Angelo's probing gaze. She'd hadn't decided how to handle this.

What good would it do to tell him he was Achaean? A different species co-existing with humans? What would happen if Angelo knew he could time travel? If he remembered how? Wouldn't it be better for him to build his life from this point on like a human? Especially because time-travel was forbidden, and it was her duty to uphold that law.

Angelo took her hand in his. He leaned in and whispered in her ear, "There are things you aren't telling me, Adrielle."

She turned to him.

His face was taut, questioning. "Why are you studying this book full of spells and ancient rituals?"

Adrielle swallowed past the knot in her throat. There was no way to dodge the question. His assessing gaze was unraveling her.

Adrielle pulled her hand away and leapt off the bed. "I've got to go." She wasn't ready to unload the entire Domenikos Achaean war on him.

She reached the door, and Liz was standing there with the journal in her hands. Adrielle didn't know how long she'd been there. Or what she'd heard.

"I think I've found something," Liz said. "And for the record, I think you should tell him everything."

Chapter 9

Florida–Present Time

ADRIELLE RAN PAST Liz and ducked into the hall bathroom. She locked the door and ripped her pajama top off and studied the crest in the mirror. It was searing now.

The crest looked alive. The four feathers shimmered, but the black feather was the brightest of all.

Black is for truth, Astraia had said. Angelo wanted the truth. If she told him, there was no going back.

A loud rap at the door disrupted her thoughts. "Adie, let me in." *Coco.*

She didn't want her to see this. Adrielle slipped her top on and opened the door a crack.

"What do you want?"

"Oh no you don't." Coco stuck her foot in the door. She pressed inside and closed the door behind her. "What are you doing? Liz told me Angelo's asking questions you refuse to answer."

"Shhhh. They'll hear you."

"Adrielle Maddox, what is going on in that head of yours? Tell him everything."

Adrielle pressed her lips together.

"I know that look. What are you afraid of?"

Adrielle shook her head. "I'm not afraid. I'm just not sure it's best."

"For whom? Angelo deserves to know who he is. What he is. We all do."

Coco was adamant. What if she knew Domenikos was her brother? Would she want to know the most evil, vile, creature—the one responsible for them growing up without parents, was her brother? What good would it do to know that?

Adrielle fiddled with her watch. She was the new Achaean leader, and it was her choice. No one else's. She wasn't ready to make that call.

"I'm not sure it isn't a mistake."

"You're not alone in this. We're here to bounce ideas off. Let's go over our options. Option one: Let Angelo live in ignorance. But remember this whole thing started when *you* wanted to find *your* purpose in life. So why shouldn't

Angelo? Is he supposed to live the rest of his life oblivious? Adrielle, he has a purpose too. You can't keep him in the dark forever." Coco tucked a stray strand of hair off Adrielle's face. "Option two is to tell him the truth. See where that takes us."

Chapter 10

Florida—Present Time

AFTER MUCH DELIBERATION, Adrielle called a meeting in Coco's room. Adrielle arrived with the *Book of Feathers*. And Liz with the journal.

The sleeping bags were cleared off the floor, and Coco and Dave sat on either side of Angelo. Adrielle and Liz sat across from them, forming a tight circle.

Coco lit two white candles and placed them in the center.

The air was thick with tension. Adrielle lay her book in front of Angelo, where everyone could see. And Liz did the same.

"And here we are," Dave said. His quick side-stares to Angelo were full of worry.

"You okay, bud?" Liz asked. "The stress of meddling with history overwhelming you?"

Dave nodded. "Yep. This reminds me of the *Knights of the Round Table*. Only . . . two of our knights are missing. Anything can happen from this point forward."

Liz squeezed Dave's hand. "Things haven't been the same without Kate and Veda."

Dave wiped his eyes. "This circle represents something special. All of us may not remember King Arthur's round table, in the Arthurian legend. But here we sit, gathered around these special books, much like King Arthur and his knights. We are all knights. Each with purpose. Here in this moment in time, with equal status. Whether we like it or not, we're in this together." He looked up and met Adrielle's eyes. "Together, we're part of something bigger than each of us. And we have individual roles to play. Even you, Angelo."

"Especially Angelo. Wait and see what I just uncovered," Liz said, tapping the journal. She broke into an impish grin.

Angelo looked pointedly at her. His expression said to get on with it.

The grandfather clock chimed midnight. Blustering winds continued to howl and angry rain pelted the window. Coco's jasmine oil diffuser mingled with melting wax, seemed to transport them to a holy place.

"Is this what these books are about? A legend?" Angelo asked in a curt tone.

"No. This is no legend. This is real," Adrielle said. His dismissive tone set her off. She opened the *Book of Feathers*.

"In the beginning, long before humans roamed the Earth, there was an ancient race called Achaeans. This is their sacred book. It entails their history and sacred spells, among other things." Adrielle brushed her hand gently over the thin pages.

Angelo's expression was unbelieving.

"Achaeans can look like humans, but they aren't. They've lived on Earth for tens of thousands of years and have special powers."

"What kind of powers?" Angelo said after a few moments.

"Well, for one, they can time travel." Adrielle's breath hitched as she waited for his reaction. Angelo was watching her with a thoughtful expression. A pang of alarm slammed her. She hadn't considered he might not believe her. She'd thought it would all come back once she told him. She felt the burning need to help him understand the depth and importance of their Achaean heritage.

Adrielle pointed to a detailed ink drawing of an Achaean in bird form in the beginning of the book. "Look. Achaeans in their natural state look like large birds. They have strong wings, so aside from travelling through time, they can fly."

Adrielle turned the book for Angelo to get a better look. She paused while he read the text and studied the pictures. He looked up at her and shook his head. "This sounds like a myth."

"It isn't," Adrielle said as she tried to control her anger. "Achaeans survived epochs and horrific battles. There are still a few here among us."

Angelo leaned back onto his hands. "This is what you've all been keeping from me?"

Liz and Dave exchanged a look. His disbelief seemed to hurt them as much as it did Adrielle.

"It's true." Adrielle sucked in a long breath and met Coco's gaze. With the raise of her chin, Coco urged her on.

"So, you may not believe it yet, but these Achaeans are pretty special. I imagine they survived by travelling through time. But it's forbidden now."

Angelo chuckled. "Humor me. Why should I believe you?"

"Because it's true. A long time ago, their leader, Aaron, fell in love with a mortal woman. She helped him realize time travelling endangers humans. And because of his love for her, Aaron made a new rule, the *Achaean Act*, which forbade time travel. It was the only way to save mankind."

Dave lifted a finger. "Angelo . . . consider going back in time and changing even the smallest thing. It could alter history. In some cases, changing the timeline . . . well, if this happens, some of us might never be born."

Angelo appeared to be considering this.

"There was a rebellion," Adrielle said. "Some Achaeans felt this law encroached their freedom, while others understood the dilemma. There was a revolt and the leaders, including Aaron, were slaughtered. Only a few survived."

"Where are they now? The survivors?" Angelo's attention was back. "What do they have to do with us? And why do you have their book?"

Everyone fell silent. Adrielle saw the disappointment on their faces. They'd hoped by explaining Achaean history to Angelo, he would remember. But only curiosity was reflected on his face, not recollection.

Liz raised an eyebrow and nodded to urge Adrielle to continue.

"Angelo, I'm the enforcer of the Achaean Act. It's my duty to make sure no one transgresses."

"But you're human. Shouldn't that be an Achaean responsibility? Why isn't the book in the hands of an Achaean?" Angelo said.

Adrielle wasn't ready to explain she was half Achaean. Not now, when she hadn't even told Coco yet. Eventually, once he got his memory back, he would know.

"In time, you'll have all the answers. For now, know that long ago, this book was entrusted to the leader of the Achaean army. His name was Haden. Does the name mean anything to you?"

Angelo shook his head. "Nope. Should it?"

A sense of loss overcame Adrielle. This was a failed conversation. She raised her eyes to him. "He's your brother, Angelo. Haden is your brother."

Chapter 11

Florida–Present Time

THE CANDLE ON the floor flickered, casting long shadows onto the walls. Wax dripped down and pooled onto the holder.

Angelo's inability to remember his brother jarred Adrielle. These were bonds that shouldn't be broken.

For years Adrielle blamed everything in her life on not having a mother. Coco had been her salvation, holding her together during her darkest thoughts. The possibility of not having Coco in her life, of not remembering her, was devastating.

Adrielle looked at the others for some kind of response.

They appeared as shaken as she was. Even Liz, who minutes before was about to explode with new information, stared at Angelo in disbelief. She pressed her lips into a thin line and remained silent.

All Adrielle could do was wonder where this all came from. How a life's slate could be wiped clean like that, robbed of everything that defined them.

"Are you saying I'm Achaean?" Angelo asked.

Everyone nodded.

"I have a brother? Haden?"

They nodded.

"Where is he—this Haden?"

"No one has seen him since the eclipse, when we fought to overcome Domenikos," Adrielle said.

"Domenikos?"

Adrielle gave a weary sigh. They could tell him things, all sorts of things, explaining everything they knew, but they couldn't turn on the switch to help Angelo remember. "He's the leader of the rebellion," she said in a quiet voice.

Adrielle could feel her friends support, urging her on. Their insistence that this would lead them down the right path. But Adrielle wasn't so sure. Too much detail could overwhelm him.

Coco's sharp gaze cut through, and Adrielle squirmed. She hadn't told her Domenikos was their brother.

"If I'm Achaean, are you saying I can time travel?" Angelo said.

"Yes." they said in unison.

Angelo's eyes had a spark of curiosity, and Adrielle felt hopeful.

"Walk me through this. How do I go about it?"

"It's forbidden," Adrielle said. "So . . . there's no need to go through the particulars."

"That's convenient," Angelo said.

Adrielle was taken back. She wasn't about to break the rule to show him.

"So where are my wings? You said Achaeans have wings."

Everyone shifted and looked uncomfortable.

"I don't know how they appear or why. They just do," Adrielle said.

"Show him, Adrielle," Liz said, after a pause.

Adrielle stared at her mortified.

"Adrielle had a feather poking out of her back. It's a crest now," Liz continued.

Adrielle gave Liz a sharp side-ways glance. The last thing she wanted to do was show him her back.

"Go on," Liz urged, "it may be what he needs to spur his memory."

"No." Adrielle shook her head.

"Is that what I saw, when—" Angelo stopped.

He had seen her in the bathroom.

A new wave of embarrassment assaulted Adrielle. Her crest tingled and stung. Overcoming her modesty, she stood up. This went against her logical mind, but the burn of her crest revealed what she had to do.

Adrielle turned and fumbled to unbutton her shirt. No one had seen her back since the tip of a feather first appeared, the night Josh was killed. The night Kate saw it. She missed Kate, she was so willing to give of herself, despite what anyone might think of her.

Adrielle lowered her shirt.

Everyone gasped. Adrielle tugged her shirt back up, but Angelo grabbed the fabric.

"The feathered wreath is brilliant. The colors shimmer in the candlelight. Is it a tattoo?"

"No, of course not. It's ingrained in my skin. The mark of the traveler. Each feather represents a seal judgment." Adrielle started pulling up her blouse, but Angelo stopped her.

"Let me see it," he said. "There's something intriguing about it."

Adrielle fought every impulse to button her blouse. She lowered the fabric and exposed her entire back.

Angelo was so close she could feel his breath on her skin. He brushed her crest with his fingertips and a searing jolt cycled through Adrielle.

Angelo yanked his hand back.

"What is it? You okay?" Dave asked.

"I felt a shock," Angelo said. "And I saw the flash of a silver bird."

"You saw that too?" Adrielle said as she turned around and searched his eyes.

Angelo nodded. "It appeared and disappeared before I had a chance to—May I?" Adrielle nodded. She turned back around and braced for impact.

Angelo touched the crest again. Once more, a current of electric heat cycled through Adrielle. He held his hand on her back and heat intensified as he stroked the silver feather.

He finally removed his hand. Adrielle yanked her shirt up and faced him. He was studying her with renewed curiosity. She waited impatiently for him to say something.

"Oh boy," Liz murmured.

Dave leaned into Liz. "What was that?"

"I don't know. Call it love. Destiny. But whatever it is, it can't happen," Liz said.

"What?" Coco and Dave said at the same time.

"I'm not kidding. This connection between them . . . it's that thing I uncovered," Liz said. "I hate to be a buzz kill, especially when it comes to feelings, but Adrielle can't be with Angelo."

Adrielle was horrified at the insinuation.

"Why not?" Coco said.

"The journal explains she needs to accept Haden's invitation for marriage in order to have access to *The Book of Feathers*. If she goes with Angelo now . . . whew." Liz swiped at her forehead. "It changes history. And there's no telling what might happen."

Chapter 12

Florida—Present Time

"It's a good sign he saw the silver bird. It's the color of his feathers. Maybe we're onto something." Liz said.

"Or maybe it means he's going to conquer Adrielle. Don't forget, silver is for conquest," Dave said.

"I don't think so. If only I could piece together the clues," Liz said, squinting at Dave's hair. "Your hair is knotted. Stop raking your fingers through it."

"Hmmmh." Dave licked his fingers and smoothed it down.

"Let's review," Liz said. "After Angelo saw the crest and touched it, he was visibly jarred. Adrielle left in a hurry. And Coco rushed after her. Then Angelo used a lame excuse and left too. No one seemed to want to talk about it. So, it's up to us to figure it out."

"It's up to all of us."

"Fine. It must have been strange for him to see the bird, just by touching Adrielle. And what was that between them?" Liz said.

"Maybe he's going to conquer Domenikos?"

"Why would he have to? Domenikos is safely imprisoned in the diamond center. He can stay there forever, as far as I'm concerned," Liz said.

"There's no forever," Dave said.

"Well, I think it's a good sign. Maybe touching the crest awakened something."

Dave held up a finger. "I've been considering that too. But why didn't Angelo remember more?" He raised his chin defiantly.

Liz picked up Adrielle's journal and stroked the snippet of the red feather she used as a bookmark. It had come from Adrielle's back and like the other feathers in Adrielle's crest was a vibrant hue, deep and rich. Aside from making Liz feel powerful, the softness of the barbs brushing against her fingertips always soothed her.

As Dave paced and muttered, she was having an internal conflict. All she had to do was tap into its powers. Use it to travel back to the Florence and relive the eclipse. Then stick by Angelo like glue. Then she'd know what happened to him.

"I'M TELLING YOU, when Angelo touched me, it sent an electric shock."

"It can feel like that, when you're crazy for someone," Coco said.

"This was different."

"We're out of our league. Call that witch lady."

"Witch lady?" Adrielle asked.

"Yeah—the one with the scepter."

"Monika?"

"Yes." Coco was animated. "We need her advice. She's the one that started this whole thing."

Adrielle shook her head. "That was Domenikos."

"What eva. Summon her."

"She's not the type you summon."

"I get it, she's scary. But with Haden gone . . . wait, we could travel back and—"

"Redo the whole forgery thing?"

"Yeah. Stick by Angelo and follow his memory train."

"I can't believe you, Coco. It goes against the rules and who knows how *that* would turn out second time around. I barely made it out alive the first time."

Coco shrugged. "Just saying."

"Fine, I'll *summon* her." Adrielle opened the *Book of Feathers* and turned to a summoning spell. "Quick, close the door."

"I'd rather keep it open."

"Not exactly the response I was after."

"What if the spell backfires? Or something worse?" Coco said, looking over Adrielle's shoulder at the spell.

Adrielle looked up at Coco. "It's straightforward enough. Looks like all I have to do is read it out loud, insert Monika's name, and concentrate on her appearing."

"But can you handle it?"

Adrielle sighed. "Which is it? Summon, or no?"

Coco shrugged.

"Let's try. What choice do we have?"

Coco closed the door and returned to Adrielle's side.

"Here goes." Adrielle read the spell out loud and looked up startled as pops and hissing came from inside the walls. The wall studs, and ceiling joists bent and twisted. Coco squeezed her eyes shut and clung onto Adrielle's hand.

The door swung open, and Dave and Liz ran in, their footsteps slapping hard against the wood.

"What did you do?" Dave yelled. His gaze dropped to the *Book of Feathers.* "My god, you cast a spell?"

Angelo ran in behind them. "What's going on?"

Though the windows were shut, shrieking wind blustered and swirled around them.

"Adrielle's hair is whirling like spun cotton candy," Dave yelled.

Dave and Liz clasped onto each other as the wheeze and whistle groaned around them like a vexed dragon awakening from a deep sleep.

Angelo's attention locked onto the book. His third eyelid closed.

"Look," Liz exclaimed. "Maybe Angelo will be back to himself."

"But will the house survive?" Dave shrieked.

"Shhhh, let her concentrate," Coco said.

Adrielle turned back to the spell. Just as she resigned to the fact that the house would splinter into a zillion pieces, the chaos ceased. Adrielle took several relieved breaths in the sudden stillness, then looked around. Monika was nowhere in sight.

In the center of the room, inches away from them, stood Astraia, looking angry.

Chapter 13

Florida—Present Time

ASTRAIA STOOD IMMOBILE; her wide black wings spread behind her.

"What are you doing?" Astraia hissed. Her attention went from the *Book of Feathers* to Adrielle.

"I'm summoning Monika," Adrielle said, straining to mask her confusion, shock, and fear.

"Monika?" Astraia said. "What are you up to?"

Her menacing voice sent Adrielle shivers.

Astraia saw Angelo and strode toward him. She clamped a firm hand on his shoulder.

"What the—?" Angelo squirmed, but Astraia's grip held firm.

"What's happened to you? Do you not recognize me?" Astraia studied him with a puzzled look. "How is this possible?"

"Haaaaa—heee—he has amnesia," Liz stammered, taking several steps toward Angelo. Astraia stepped between them.

Dave winced. He cupped his hands around his eyes and seemed to be bracing for what might come.

Astraia glowered.

"My bad." Liz took baby steps back and clutched Dave's hand.

"Ouch," Dave said.

Coco pressed against Adrielle. Her attention was pinned on Astraia.

"He has no memory," Adrielle said. "I was summoning Monika for guidance."

"Guidance?" Astraia shook her head. "You're our leader?"

Angelo stepped in front of Adrielle and tucked her behind him.

"This is impossible. Angelo, it's me," Astraia said.

Adrielle fought to retrace the spell words in her mind.

Adrielle raised a finger to attract Astraia's attention around Angelo's body. "Uh . . . I might know what the mix up was."

Angelo shot Adrielle a warning look over his shoulder. Adrielle stepped around Angelo, and Astraia strode to her.

"I wasn't trying to summon you. I was concentrating on the black bird on her shoulder. I wasn't specific enough for the spell, obviously," Adrielle said.

"Obviously not," Astraia said, standing very tall. "If you can't do the spells, you shouldn't dabble with the power."

"*The Book*'s entrusted to me," Adrielle said, her anger flaring. She straightened. "If you'll excuse me, I'll try this again."

Adrielle paced over to her bed. Astraia returned to studying Angelo's face.

Adrielle looked over the spell. Once she was certain of the steps, she closed her eyes and recited it, concentrating on Monika's flowing purple robe. Her red pointy fingernails. The reflection of her diamond scepter.

A rap shook the room so hard, the friends stumbled to keep their balance. Only Astraia and Angelo stood unshaken.

A blinding light flashed and sparked in the corner of the room. It swelled until the entire room blazed white.

Adrielle blinked and waited for her vision to adjust. The old woman's silhouette came into focus.

"Summoning me in this manner is an invasion of privacy," Monika said, her voice gruff and irritated.

"Please, I need your help."

The bird on Monika's shoulder squawked. It flapped its wings, flew to the ceiling, and hovered there.

Monika's gaze swept around the room. "Oh, I see. Come back here, Arnadella. It's all right."

The bird flew onto Monika's shoulder and tucked its head under its wing. Monika caressed the bird with one long stroke, then she ruffled its black feathers.

"Astraia, your sister is still angry at you. I'm afraid she may never get over her permanent bird form," Monika cooed.

Liz and Dave mouthed, *"Sister?"*

Astraia straightened. "She brought it onto herself."

Monika seemed undaunted. She directed her attention back to Adrielle. "Go on."

Her crinkly hands tightened on the scepter's golden rod. The diamond in the scepter's head was large and dazzling. Brilliant shards of light escaped from the facets and danced throughout the room. Adrielle felt a draw from the stone and turned away to avoid falling into a hypnotic state.

Was she the only one affected? Adrielle studied Angelo's reaction. He appeared shocked and terrified all at once.

"Something terrible has happened," Adrielle said, fighting to keep her emotions in check. "Angelo's lost his memory."

Monika raised her arm and silenced her. She turned her steely eyes on Angelo. She beckoned him with red pointy fingernails.

He approached slowly, cautiously, and stopped a safe distance from her. It struck Adrielle as odd he kept his gaze averted from the bird.

"What is your name?" Monika asked in a throaty croak.

"Angelo."

"Is that all you are known by?"

Angelo shrugged.

"What do you remember of your life?"

"Nothing. But I feel a strange pull to Adrielle." Angelo turned to look at her with an intensity in his gaze. An earnestness.

Monika also turned to study her.

"Angelo, the pull you feel to her is involuntary." Monika turned to address Adrielle. "You feel it too."

Adrielle nodded.

"His gestures, his way of moving, are still there," Monika said, "But everything else is gone. His memories, his way of analyzing his environment."

Monika half closed her eyes. She stood motionless, only the whites of her eyes showed for so long, it looked like she'd fallen asleep.

"Nothing of this world caused it," Monika responded as if no time had passed. She turned her attention back to Angelo. "Place your hand upon my scepter. Touch the diamond."

Angelo placed his hand on the stone and appeared to be struck immobile.

"What do you see?" Monika roared.

"I see myself standing in front of you. Watching a red feather floating down a prism. I am asking for help to find Adrielle. How is this possible?" Angelo jerked his hand off the stone. He searched Monika's eyes, but she said nothing. "Explain how I now remember coming to you for help?"

"Ahh, good. Good, Angelo." Monika nodded. "You remember at least one memory. So, there is still hope."

"Still hope?" Liz said, her voice trembling.

Monika glanced at Liz. Liz sidled up to Dave.

Angelo turned to Adrielle. "This memory means we are connected in some way. And that makes me happy. Judging by how shaken you are, you must care for me too." He turned back to Monika. "Thank you. For whatever just happened. This is the first intense emotion I've felt since they found me."

"This diamond has tremendous powers," Monika said. "Hidden in its many facets, are gateways to the past. Placing your hand on the stone enabled me to find a joint memory I had previously shared with you, Angelo."

Monika turned to Adrielle. Her dark eyes burned into her. "He remembers it now, only because I revealed this memory to him. But his other memories may not be so easily regained. It is possible he may never get them back. They could have been destroyed as though they never happened."

"How is this possible?" Adrielle asked, shocked.

"Domenikos," Monika said.

"How. Is. This. Possible?" Adrielle asked, trying to control her anger. "He's imprisoned in the diamond forever."

Monika chuckled. "Nothing is forever. You, most of all you, must know everything is in constant motion. Domenikos must have uncovered the pathway to the Time Vault inside the diamond."

"There's a pathway?" "Inside the diamond?" "Is it possible?" Liz, Dave, and Coco murmured at the same time.

Adrielle rubbed her temples at a growing migraine. She inhaled a long breath and fought to keep calm. "I thought his entrapment meant he couldn't hurt anyone."

"Ahhh . . . that's where you are wrong," Monika said. "Those who wish to do evil will find unthinkable ways."

Adrielle let out a long sigh. She glanced at Angelo, who seemed to be taking this calmly. "Well, you said there is hope. What can I do?"

"The Time Vault has been compromised. From inside the diamond, you must find the key tunnel to the Time Vault and seal the entry. Once you've restored the data—"

"Hold the brownie." Liz strode up to Monika. "What is the Time Vault?"

Monika held out a hand, and Liz stopped inches from her palm.

"As life unfolds, memories are created and stored inside the Time Vault," Monika said.

Dave raised his index finger. Monika turned to him.

"Are you saying it's like one big data storage?" Dave asked in a squeaky tone.

"Holy shit," Liz said, exchanging a look with Coco.

"Domenikos must be in the Time Vault erasing the backup disk," Coco said.

"Not just the backup, everything," Dave said.

"To be clear . . . isn't travelling down the time-tunnels not that different from time travel?" Adrielle said.

Monika cocked an eyebrow. "Time-tunnels are backdoor gateways to the past. From there, memories can be accidentally or intentionally destroyed. Same as time travel. Once destroyed, they are abolished forever."

"Sweet Jesus," Dave said.

Adrielle felt the heat of everyone's stare. This shortcut went against the Achaean Act. She exchanged a look with Astraia, but her expression was unreadable.

Knowing the diamond contained time tunnels changed everything. Was it safe for Monika to have the diamond? How did she acquire so much power?

Adrielle decided this was not the time to challenge Monika, but she needed to keep a closer tab on her. "Okay. Let's go through this. Is it possible to enter the diamond and not change anything, but restore what's been damaged?"

"Yes. But no one has attempted this before. You may unintentionally change history. Humanity as we know it," Monika said.

Dave slapped a hand to his forehead and sighed deeply.

"I'd be breaking the rules. Bending them, for sure." Adrielle scanned the room for reactions. Everyone was watching her expectantly. "Is one life worth risking multitudes?" Still no reaction. She glanced at Angelo and felt a stab of emotion. And a sting in her crest.

"How could I not try to save him?" she asked Monika.

"You do not need my approval," Monika said. "You are the Time keeper. But know this: it is the only way to save him."

"Holy schmoley," Liz cried out.

Adrielle gave her a side-glance. Liz's opinion was clear. Her opinion was always clear. Adrielle glanced at Astraia, who stared at her stoically. She turned her attention back to Monika. "How do I access the Time Vault?"

"I will open the entry. Somewhere inside the diamond, you will find the pathway."

"Can Domenikos escape?" Adrielle asked.

Monika nodded deeply. "Once the conduit is open, anything can get in or out. The pathway must be sealed quickly."

Dave approached her and placed both hands on Adrielle's shoulders. He glanced at Angelo and looked pointedly at her. "You can't do this. You'll be doing exactly what Achaean leaders tried to avoid."

"Dave, it's the only way." She turned to Monika. "I accept the challenge."

"We're coming with you," Liz said, and jabbed Dave in the side as he opened his mouth. "We're your support team, remember? We can help."

"No. It's too dangerous," Adrielle said. "What happened to Angelo could happen to any of us. Maybe all of us."

"We're already at risk," Coco said. "Think of how easily Domenikos killed Veda and Kate. Domenikos won't stop until he hurts everyone."

"Of that we are certain," Monika said. "The extra help may warrant the risk. But beware: you can become entrapped."

"Entrapped?" Dave squealed.

"Yes. The diamond facets contain billions of pathways, knotted and twisted like a maze. Most lead somewhere, but some end as abruptly as they begin. Tread carefully. Enter and exit through the same facet or you will become lost."

"It's decided then," Liz said, stuffing the journal into her handbag. She pulled her handbag strap onto her shoulder and released a deep breath. "We're going."

Monika raised the scepter.

Dave pointed to the diamond. "I can't believe we're going in there. Is she going to shrink us?"

"Wait. Wait. Wait! *Where* is Haden?" Astraia said. "He should be in on this decision."

"Haden. Of course. I haven't seen him either," Adrielle said.

"You can locate him from inside the diamond center. Everything is visible from the inside," Monika said.

"Then I'm coming too," Astraia said, crossing her arms.

Adrielle wasn't sure she could trust her. She winced at the stabbing pain from her crest, reminding her, Astraia's intentions to find Haden were sincere. Astraia held the same black feather mirrored in her crest. The black feather of truth. Adrielle gave a resigned little smile. "Fine. We're all in then."

Dave shuddered, his gaze going to the black bird on Monika's shoulder.

The bird seemed to terrify him. He leaned into Liz and whispered loud enough for them all to hear. "Having her tag along is like one of Domenikos' minions shadowing us."

Astraia shot him a threatening glance.

Adrielle turned back to Monika. "We're ready."

"Once you enter the Time Vault you have twenty-four hours to exit," Monika said.

"What?" everyone squawked.

"It's a built-in default."

"What happens after—?" Dave stuffed his fingers in his mouth.

"Twenty-four hours. That's it." Monika raised her scepter high. A violent column of air more powerful than the hurricane arose. The force whipped against Adrielle's skin until she couldn't move her lips and sucked them into the diamond.

Chapter 14

Inside the Diamond Center

THE SCEPTER HIT the ground with thundering force, followed by an unearthly stillness.

Dave put his finger in his ear and wiggled it. "Nothing. The pressure's changed. I wish they'd pop."

Adrielle took a head count. Coco, Angelo, Liz, Dave, and Astraia. Everyone had made it.

Adrielle looked around. The diamond walls were a myriad of cuts, sleek and severe. The facets severed the light like a glass prism and reflected all the colors of the rainbow. Adrielle sucked in a deep breath. Thankfully, they could breathe.

"It's beautiful," Coco exclaimed, reaching to touch one of the walls.

"Don't!" Adrielle warned. "We don't know yet what could happen by touching the surface."

Coco yanked her hand back.

Adrielle tread to the diamond's edge. She couldn't see through the thick walls of the crystal. "Each one of these facets is an entry way to somewhere." She inspected the surface, overwhelmed by the vastness of possibilities. "There's no way to know which facet holds the portal to the Time Vault. I have no idea."

"Maybe there's something in here?" Liz offered, digging into her handbag and pulling out the journal. Her triumphant expression changed to disappointment as she flipped through the pages. "I don't understand. I've read most of the journal and don't remember reading anything about the Time Vault. Or the portals inside the diamond." She continued to look through the journal.

"If only I had the *Book of Feathers*," Adrielle said.

"You left it in a safe spot, I hope?" Coco said.

"Of course," Adrielle said annoyed. "If I had it, I could see if it mentioned the Time Vault. But I don't remember seeing anything about it either."

"That's an idea," Dave said, pulling out his cell.

"Social media Dave? Really? I doubt there's reception." Liz pulled out her phone. "Nope."

Dave went to his docs and opened a pdf.

"You're going to read?"

"*She* is." Dave passed Adrielle his phone.

Adrielle glanced down at the screen. "My god! You scanned the *Book of Feathers*?"

"Technically, I took photos of every page, compiled them into a pdf, and ran the OCR software on the document," Dave said. "OCR is set up to read languages, but I think it can match character strings in a search."

Adrielle was both relieved and angry. "You shouldn't have access to the book."

"Aren't you glad I do?" Dave grinned.

"What?" Liz and Coco asked. They peered over Adrielle's shoulder.

"Holy caramels. You're a genius," Liz shouted.

"Or this could be our downfall," Adrielle said.

Liz nudged Adrielle. "Go ahead, search. See if it says how to get out of this glass box and into the Time Vault."

"I don't think bringing the book was such a great idea," Adrielle said. "Domenikos is here too. If he sees the real spells, what was the point of the forgery?"

Adrielle swiped through the pages and felt everyone's eyes on her. "It's going to take a while."

"Or not." Dave said, taking his phone back. "Now how do you spell *Time Vault* in Achaean?"

"Seriously?" Adrielle said.

Dave smiled. He had a smug look on his face.

"Guys?" Coco said.

Adrielle typed Time Vault in Achaean, thanking the gods the language didn't have fancy stuff like diacritics. A list of possible matches appeared followed by the number of occurrences.

"Uh, guys!" Coco said a notch louder.

"Wow. This confirms everything Monika told us," Adrielle said.

"Hey! Guys, over here!" Coco yelled. "Why is no one listening?"

"What is it?" Adrielle looked up. Coco's face was so close to the crystal barrier it was almost touching. "Careful, don't get too close."

"Come, look. I can see our house in Florida." Coco moved her face side to side. "Changing your angle gives a clearer pic. I can hear it, too. The wind is still blowing." She closed her eyes and held up a finger. "Wait. We left the radio on. There's an epidemic."

"What?" Adrielle said, rushing to her.

Coco slid away from the wall and Adrielle took her place.

"Closer. Almost touch the surface," Coco said.

She studied their house. "It looks like it did when Monika had me look into the diamond scepter, the night of Josh's murder."

The others exchanged whispers.

"Quiet!" Adrielle hissed.

Behind the sounds of her friends, she could hear the drone of a thousand voices. She closed her eyes to concentrate. The sound was the whistle of the hurricane funneling through the diamond. She focused and singled out the radio report.

"It's incredible. I can hear the news report of the hurricane. But I also hear voices. Terrified screams of multitudes. More and more people have lost their memories. Blocks of their lives gone—just like that." She felt sick. She wrapped her arms around her stomach. "Why would he do this?" As she asked, she knew why. Because he could.

"Is it real? Is that even possible?" Liz asked.

"Anything you imagine is possible," Astraia said. She was in human form now, her arms and legs wide at her sides. She looked like a warrior.

Chapter 15

Inside the Diamond Center

Adrielle felt the tightness of panic in her chest. That indescribable mix of anxiety and hopelessness. The same fear was reflected on each of their faces.

"We can't let this be a setback," Adrielle said, standing straighter. "I won't let the broadcast be our vision for the future. Let's keep our spirits high. Listen up. *Everything* is still at play. Let's concentrate on the positive."

Angelo placed his hand on Adrielle's shoulder and gave a squeeze. "Well said. I don't remember much about you, but I admire your attitude. I sense a strong backbone."

Adrielle felt a rush of warmth where Angelo touched her. She pushed it out of her mind and turned back to the wall.

As she changed her perspective in tiny increments, prisms of colors diffused around her. By shifting her visual field, she uncovered the faint opening to a tunnel. "I found something. An opening. It must lead somewhere—maybe another epoch."

Coco went her side.

"Stand back. Our house is a different color. The landscaping's missing. Cars look older, too." Adrielle took a quick breath. "Seventies models."

Coco moved closer.

"Wait. Someone's getting out of a car and unloading groceries. It's Layla. My god." Adrielle gasped. "She looks thirty years younger."

"Let me see," Coco said.

Adrielle moved aside. "Right here. From this angle."

Coco crouched into the same position. "It can't be her. She looks forty. Maybe thirty. Wow, she was pretty."

"I wanna see," Dave and Liz cried at once.

They each took a turn looking.

"Fascinating," Dave said. "Can we really be watching history as its being created in the past? The true past?"

Coco shrugged. "That was her car. The photos are in her album. Way before Adie and I came into the picture."

"Hmmm. I wonder what would happen if you went back to the time when you met Angelo?" Liz blurted out.

Everyone turned to her and her face turned beet red.

"If we could find the spot . . ." Liz pushed her glasses up her nose and examined the tunnel closely. "Wait—"

Dave chewed his thumbnail.

"Ugh. Spots. I hate it when my glasses are smudgy." Liz took her glasses off and wiped the lenses with her t-shirt, then slid them back on. "Better. As I was saying . . . maybe, Adie, if you were in touch with Angelo before he lost his memory—back when he was a full-fledged Achaean." Liz turned to him. "Sorry Ange—"

"Ange?" Dave mouthed.

"I don't mean to make you feel bad." Liz continued, "It's just that . . . I think maybe then, you'd get answers. You might even be able to remember everything. And everyone." Liz glanced at the others then back at Angelo. "I feel terrible you don't remember any of us."

"Let's deal with the Time Vault first. We need to find it fast," Adrielle said. Unless Domenikos had escaped as they were zapped inside, he was somewhere around. And she wanted to be ready for the confrontation.

"I agree. We never got to the bottom of that twenty-four-hour warning," Dave said.

"The timer started once we got into the vault. Right?" Liz said.

Adrielle glanced at Astraia, who was watching them without a comment.

"I think the key might be to concentrate on joint memories," Liz said.

"Let's come up with a game plan. Once we find a location, we know we can see a different timeline by varying the perspective. Let's see if I can go further back in time by inching closer." Adrielle put her face as close to the diamond surface as she could, without touching it.

Her visual field went in and out of focus. She shifted her angle through the prisms slightly. "There's another tunnel further back." Moving in micro-movements, she looked through the tunnel like a set of binoculars. "There are trees. More trees. Ughh. All I see is green." She backed away and rubbed her eyes. Maybe she'd been wrong, and this wasn't the way to push further back along the timeline.

She leaned back in. "I see the lake now. The one a few blocks away, where Layla said they picnicked every fourth of July. And there's the canal leading to the beach. But no houses. This was before they were built. It worked." She turned to the others, feeling a sense of accomplishment. "I went to Palm Coast before it was developed."

"Nice job," Liz said.

Dave held up a finger. "I have a plan." He scrolled through the *Book of Feathers*. "I want to do a word search for *Time tunnels*. Or *Accessing the Time Vault*. How do I spell that in Achaean?"

Liz pulled out a notepad and pencil and handed it to Adrielle.

Adrielle scribbled it down and handed it to Dave. "Here you go. You and Angelo work on that, while the rest of us search through the surface walls. See what else we can find. We don't really know what we're looking for."

"Use your powers, Adrielle," Astraia urged. "You have a built-in *truth meter*."

"I'm not sure what you mean."

"You've earned the crest of the traveler," Astraia explained. "It comes with certain powers. Start using them."

"I don't understand what they are yet," Adrielle admitted.

"Listen to your inner core. *Really* listen. You'll know when you find the right path."

Astraia had one thing right. She wasn't tuning in to herself or anything else.

ADRIELLE WAS STARTING to feel desperate. They'd scoured the prism walls until their eyeballs ached. There had to be a better way. Hundreds of thousands of tunnels lead to more tunnels. If everything could be seen from inside the diamond, as Monika said, this could take them several lifetimes.

"Any luck?" Adrielle asked Dave.

"Not yet. But look at Angelo, he's a natural."

Angelo looked up from Dave's phone. "I've typed in: *Time Vault, Time tunnels, accessing your memories*, and any other words that might help in Achaean. I'm following up on the links."

"Keep at it," Adrielle said. She felt slight guilt at allowing everyone access to the book, but they were all on the same side. At least most of them. She found herself watching Astraia, who was also carefully inspecting the diamond surface.

Adrielle drifted back to the diamond wall to continue her search. She rubbed her eyes. The brilliance of the light burned.

AFTER SOME TIME, Adrielle stepped away from the wall. "You may be onto something, Astraia. I'm not accessing my powers in here. I'm trying, but I can't seem to tune into anything. I've even tried using the chronometer to travel back in time, to see if I could go."

Coco looked shocked.

"If I wanted to, hypothetically," Adrielle added. "I can't go anywhere. I think we're trapped, unless we can find a way out."

"The same goes for me. No luck morphing into my bird form either," Astraia admitted.

"Hang on. I might have something," Angelo said, glancing up from Dave's phone. "It says here, the only way to access the time vault is to enter a tunnel into your own past. Somewhere along the length of it. The point where you're most vulnerable is where you'll gain access to unlock your memories."

Adrielle felt a spike of nerves. "We need to find a tunnel into our own past? Not just any tunnel?"

"Correct." Angelo re-read the passage. "I think it means finding the exact memory point where you faced your greatest challenge." He looked excitedly at Adrielle. "If you take that path, it must lead to the entrance of the Time Vault. But it doesn't say how to open the vault. Or how to get inside."

"Slow down. One thing at a time," Adrielle said.

"I have a thought," Liz said. "While you're looking, try visualizing the memory when you were the most vulnerable. I have a hunch if you do, the tunnels might be clearly visible."

Coco turned to Liz. "Just say it. You mean that Adrielle should think about the fire, because of her nightmares."

"Mmmm. That's good. But I'd go even deeper."

"Deeper? What could possibly be deeper than that? The fire consumed Adrielle's entire life."

Adrielle considered her other fears. Sure, the fire seemed to be what affected her entire life. But there was a deeper, darker, power at the root. *Domenikos.* She let out a moan. Meeting up with him and trying to pawn off the forgery as the authentic *Book of Feathers—that* was crazy scary. The scariest thing she'd ever faced. There had to be earlier times she'd had conflicts with Domenikos.

"Adie! You okay? You don't look so good," Coco said.

Adrielle glanced at Coco, who had that motherly worried look. She still didn't know Domenikos was her twin. That familiar guilt-knot tightened. Coco had always wanted a brother, and she actually had one.

Liz let out a long, drawn-out sigh. "If it was me . . . I'd focus on Angelo."

Dave snapped his fingers. "Right. If we could find his tunnel, he'd have a good shot at his memories."

"Technically, yeah. That's the end game," Liz said, and paced around the small space. "I was wondering if Domenikos is messing with everyone's memories. Remember the newscast?"

Dave nodded.

"It might go deeper than Angelo. My bet is—and this is only a hunch going on personal experience," Liz said, beaming. "*Love* holds the key."

Dave's expression was incredulous. "Jeez, how do you come up with this stuff?"

"Hear me out. What else causes a roller coaster of emotions? I'll bet there are more crimes of passion than planned homicides," Liz said, looking sad and swiping away tears.

"All right, all right. There's no need for that." Dave wrapped an arm around her. "You get so carried away sometimes."

"All the strawberry shortcake in the world couldn't make me forget Francesco." Liz turned to Adrielle. "So, Adie, I'd go to the point where you first fell in love."

Liz was insane. Adrielle turned away from Angelo. *Had she been in love?* She closed her eyes. She couldn't remember loving Angelo. But there were passages in her journal that suggested something had happened. But she'd married Haden instead. As hard as she tried, she couldn't remember why. Had Angelo really been the love of her life? Or had she fallen in love with Haden?

Adrielle concentrated on her feelings for Angelo. An intense pain pierced from the crest to her heart, making it hard to breathe. She put her finger on her heart and pressed firmly. An onslaught of memories flooded her mind.

The first time she'd seen him, she was a little girl, and he was a silver bird. His feathers gleamed in the sun as he flew outside her bedroom window. She saw him sometime later, in his human form, in her father's den. There were others present at the time. She knew that her father was the Achaean leader, so it must have been a conference of great importance because the room was brimming with commotion.

The memory morphed to a picnic along a shoreline. She and Angelo were sitting on a blue herringbone blanket, sharing crescent almond cookies. She wasn't sure how old Angelo was, because he didn't seem to age. But she was about fifteen. They were happy, watching the waves roll in. The memory was so intense she could feel the sea mist on her skin and hear the lapping of the waves.

Adrielle felt a soft touch on her shoulder and the memory stopped. She turned, surprised to see Angelo, his eyes moist with tears.

"What's wrong?" she asked.

"The almond crescents," he said in a sad voice.

Adrielle realized he'd experienced the same memories too.

A joint memory had to be the answer. It could mean a joint tunnel. Then they'd be able to access the Time Vault together.

Adrielle took Angelo's hands. "Concentrate." She turned to the diamond barrier. She squeezed her eyes tight and hoped like mad this worked.

"No, you don't," Liz said. "We're coming with you."

Chapter 16

Inside the Memory Tunnel

ADRIELLE HEARD LIZ say they were coming with them as a tremendous centrifugal force sucked her and Angelo from the diamond. Freefalling down a dark tunnel, Adrielle clutched Angelo's hand. Her heart thundered in her chest.

Adrielle stopped falling and opened her eyes. They were on the golden seashore, sitting on the same blue blanket as in her memory.

She felt mentally detached from the scenery, as if they'd been placed inside the picture in their minds. A crushing wave of memory hit her. Angelo squeezed her hands, and Adrielle felt overcome by a crippling combination of joy and sadness. The look on his face confirmed he was feeling it too.

The small rocks under the blanket poked through as they watched the waves roll in. The blue of the water was bluer than she had remembered and surrounded them on three sides. A peninsula.

Why were they here? What year was this?

On the blanket was a basket of almond crescents. Adrielle felt her chest for her chronometer. It was gone. No chronometer to go by.

The sun had a low slant to it. The shadows of the rocks to their right left a long imprint in the sand.

"We made it," Adrielle said, pushing away her fear. She gave Angelo's hand a squeeze and watched him closely for an initial reaction.

He turned to her, with agony in his eyes. "Don't marry him, Adrielle. You don't love him. You love me."

The pain in his voice ripped at her. She sat frozen, listening to his breath grow shallow.

He leaned into her. "We can get around this. I love you." He pressed his forehead to hers.

Adrielle suppressed a shiver. Nothing else mattered but the two of them. Their heartbeats bound by love. She closed her eyes. She loved Angelo. This was real, as real an emotion as she'd ever felt. She'd give anything to be with him, but it wasn't possible.

Overwhelmed by crushing sadness, she released a slow breath and gazed out onto the ocean. A slant of light hit the surface of the water and reflected a rainbow of colors along the surface. How could beauty and pain exist at the same time?

"The diamond. We made it out," she finally said.

Angelo stared blankly at her.

Panic rushed through her. He didn't remember even that. What if he never got his memory back? Everything about him, present and past, she remembered now. All the things she'd forgotten in present day Florida.

Adrielle wrapped her arms around his neck and pulled him in until her forehead touched his. He smelled like her jasmine shampoo and clean sweat.

She searched his eyes, and he looked questioningly at her. The green flecks of his irises were vibrant. She'd grown to love his truth. His dedication and loyalty. Integrity. He possessed an endless list of attributes.

It hit her, this experience was not unlike time travel. Her memory bank was replenished. But why was she the only one that remembered the diamond, and their mission to find the Time Vault?

She clutched his hands. His fingers were trembling. "Angelo, listen carefully. *What* exactly do you remember?"

"I remember when I saw you for the first time. I knew my life would never be the same." He leaned in and brushed his lips against hers.

His kiss was warm and passionate. The kiss deepened and it was the most powerful feeling Adrielle ever experienced.

"I love you Angelo," she said, swept into a tide of longing. This was not possible.

Angelo pulled her closer. "It doesn't have to be this way. I can protect you." His heart was pounding against her chest. "Love me. Not him. Stay with me."

Love was not supposed to be this painful.

"Want me," he begged, in a quiet whimper, knotting his hands in her hair.

Adrielle felt the wet warmth of his tears on her neck. There would never be another. Not ever. She bit back the words and held them in, as he crushed his mouth onto hers, and she tasted the salty dampness of his tears.

Chapter 17

Inside the Diamond

"THEY VANISHED?" LIZ said, her eyes pinned to the diamond wall. "Aren't we all in this together?" She turned to Dave and Coco.

They looked like they weren't sure if the question was rhetorical.

Astraia stood a few feet away.

"Well? Any theories?" Liz said.

"They need to revisit their relationship, for Angelo to regain his memory," Astraia said flatly.

"Is *that* what the book says?" Liz felt her anger rising. She spun to Dave, hoping for answers.

"What if Domenikos shows up? What do we do then?" Liz said.

A flash of fear crossed Dave's face. He shrugged. "I don't know. I can't read Achaean." He looked at Astraia, who kept her distance.

Great, their lives were in the hands of Astraia. And that was terrifying.

Chapter 18

Back in Time–Inside the Memory Tunnel

THEY LAY TANGLED in each other's arms until well past twilight. The coolness of the earth seeped through the blanket and leached their warmth. Adrielle shivered. Angelo wrapped his body around hers. His body could warm hers, but nothing could heal her heart. It had been crushed when her father had explained her fate was sealed the moment she was born.

"I should go," Adrielle said, not wanting to leave Angelo's embrace. This would be the last time they'd be together like this.

"Don't go. There has to be another way." Angelo's voice cracked with emotion.

Adrielle sat up. "There isn't." She'd gone over this a thousand times in her mind. "We're running out of time. The upheaval is approaching. I promised my father I'd marry Haden for the welfare of us all."

"That is absurd. How is that a solution?"

Angelo's eyes become shiny. She shrugged. He wasn't wrong. She'd wondered that herself. But when she'd objected, her father had been adamant.

"Haden is the head of the Achaean army. The protector of the *Book of Feathers*. He will protect me."

It sickened her that she was saying what her father had said all her life. She stood up, her legs feeling numb. "I don't have a choice."

She turned away. She wouldn't let Angelo see her cry. She ran along the shore, her feet pounding the cold sand. Her balled-up hands pumping at her sides. Icy wind carved through her. The growing distance from him tore at her heart.

The future was terrifying. A future without love. Without Angelo. Adrielle stopped and looked over her shoulder. Her breath caught in her throat.

There he was. Standing on their blanket. Watching her exit his life. He believed she was making a mistake. She memorized this moment, the last taste of happiness she would ever feel.

Adrielle swept her tangled hair off her face and turned away from him. She ran. Hot tears burned down her cheeks. She had broken him, the strongest bravest soul she'd ever known.

Only when she was out of Angelo's sight, did Adrielle stop. She leaned against the rock face to catch her breath. The jagged rock soaring up the side of the mountain pricked her back. Crashing waves pounded against it.

She felt sick. Angry for not standing up to her father. She bent over and braced her hands on her knees. Her whole body convulsed. She threw up until there was nothing left inside but acrid bile.

Maybe he was right. Maybe they *could* fight this thing together. But *maybe* wasn't an option. The human race was at stake.

Adrielle waited until her legs could carry her once more. She looked up at the starless night.

Chapter 19

Inside the Diamond

LIZ SAT INCHES away from the diamond surface. The colorful reflections were brilliant. Beautiful. Staring into the prism of light, she could almost believe anything was possible.

She wondered how Adrielle and Angelo's journey down the time tunnel was going. And then she thought about Francesco and her sacrifice of leaving him behind.

She'd tried to explain to him why she had to go, said she was from a distant future. A faraway place that wouldn't exist for hundreds of years. But it was no use. Francesco couldn't understand that any more than she could understand why he'd fallen in love with her. She sighed a heavy regretful sigh. It didn't matter now. He was in her past.

"What are you thinking?" Dave asked. He was sitting cross-legged next to her, staring.

She shrugged.

"Don't give me that. I know you," Dave said.

"It's just—" She met his gaze. "He made me feel like I mattered."

"Oh. You're homesick for Francesco." Dave wrapped one arm around her and pulled her close. "You matter to me."

Liz smiled back. Dave was sweet. A nerd by anyone's standard, but sweet. She laid her head on his shoulder and released a slow shuddery breath.

"Want to talk about it?"

Liz shook her head no. She finally finds love, and whammo, pressures of the universe conquer and divide. "It sucks my only chance at love is back in the fifteen hundreds." She pressed the heels of her hands into her eyes to stop the tears.

"C'mon, you don't know that. Love could be right around the corner."

"It's not. It won't ever be the same. Like it was with him." She'd bet if she found her memory tunnel, it would be dull until she'd met him. Francesco was lively. He made her laugh. She looked up at Dave, and he was studying her.

"I never told you. The day Francesco commissioned the painting for me, he was ecstatic. He said he had a surprise. I thought it was another dress."

She gulped, swiping away her tears. "Remember how he showered me with silks?"

Dave nodded. "How could I not? The silks were luxurious."

"Well . . . he showed up at Michelangelo's with a basket, and told me to close my eyes, which I did. And then he blindfolded me. I couldn't help but laugh. No one had blindfolded me since the third grade." Liz chuckled. "Anyways, he twirled me around and around until I lost my balance." She stood up and twirled.

"Careful," Dave said, "you're awfully close to the edge."

"Francesco caught me as I went to fall. And then he led me outside, blindfolded, if you can imagine, through the streets of Florence. I thought we were going to his workshop to see his seamstress."

Liz closed her eyes and embraced the memory. She could still feel the crispness of fall biting at her cheeks as Francesco led her through the narrow, cobbled streets. The sweet smell of merchants' carts full of fresh produce. Liz laughed, twirling and envisioning that magical moment.

"Watch out!" Dave cried, as Liz stumbled onto the diamond wall and went through it like butter on hotcakes.

Chapter 20

Adrielle–Inside the Memory Tunnel –Back in Time to Ancient Achaea

THE SEVERAL MILES from the beach to the edge of the city stretched agonizingly long. Adrielle ran, her fists thrashing at her sides, her feet pounding dry sand. Her legs quivered as she reached the wall surrounding the city of Achaea. The sun had gone down some time before, and she felt uneasy.

She approached the barbican cautiously. They were on the brink of a rebellion, the tides of treason upon them. Being the daughter of the powerful Achaean leader came with heavy baggage. Her life was at stake.

Around every corner in Achaea, shady dealings were in progress. A lingering glance had the same effect as daylight on an intrusion of cockroaches. And the truly frightful thing was some rebels didn't scatter. The infestation was ripe for the uprising.

Adrielle was familiar with the stirrings of anarchy. Part of her upbringing included time travel, to visit ancient cities on the brink of war. Though it was forbidden, her father made an exception for her, as long as she went as a spectator.

She'd witnessed Caesar fall from his great rule, betrayed by loyal advisors. She understood now, more than ever, how necessary this training had been and appreciated her father's foresight. He'd often said, "With great power comes great risk."

She reached the gatehouse where four guards flanked the large portal gate.

Averting her eyes, Adrielle gave the guards a quick nod and passed through. She glanced over her shoulder and headed toward the city center, to her family's home.

The air was crisp and cool. She rubbed her arms and glanced toward the north end of town, where Haden's castle presided on a hill. Its stone turrets and bastion seemed to reach out of the earth. They soared skyward and cast looming shadows onto the town site below.

As the head of the Achaean army, Haden's responsibilities were tremendous. Achaea boasted it was the place of refuge for all Achaeans. Soon, keeping harmony in this city proved impossible.

Overhead, the silver bird circled. Despite her recent revelation that she wouldn't be marrying Angelo, he was fiercely loyal to her. He followed her back from the beach, his powerful wings carrying him the distance. He'd stayed far enough behind to possibly believe she was unaware of his surveillance, but he was there whenever she looked up.

Adrielle could only imagine what Angelo was feeling. The heavy mantel of responsibility was crushing. So was the guilt for not choosing him.

Them.

Adrielle entered the gate through the stone wall surrounding her home. She glanced up at the sky, and Angelo was hovering in the distance, a tiny dot in the sky. He waited a moment, then disappeared.

Adrielle stared at the nondescript building that was her home in Achaea. The exterior walls were made of granite, one foot thick and two-stories high. No windows. This was not the average building from these times, made of mud and a tile roof. This was a fortress, loaded with security measures and minimal comforts.

Adrielle was riddled with excitement and anger. This was her birthplace. She missed her family. But she resented her role as the Achaean leader. Being the liberator to unify both societies, mankind, and Achaean, was an excruciating sacrifice.

If she were free, she'd be pledging her love to Angelo, instead of choosing duty over love.

Hashing over what-ifs would get her nowhere. She hoped in time, Angelo would realize they each had a role in this great scheme.

Many were opposed when her father decided to marry Adrielle's human mother. Some believed crossbreeding Achaeans with mortals was blasphemy. The union produced three offspring—the first ever in the history of the world. And this threatened their family. Ultimately, her father lost his life. She wouldn't let this happen to her.

Adrielle walked through a tall arched doorway that opened to an atrium. New memories awakened as she gazed at a long hall that lined the perimeter of the walls and led to the interior rooms. Each room had a window, and a door opening onto the central courtyard. The large gathering space housed a garden and a well for fresh water.

The olive oil lamps were burning brightly in her father's study. Adrielle felt a flutter of excitement. Would she see him? It wasn't customary for him to be there, this time of night. If he was, it might be a good time to discuss the impending coup.

Muffled voices floated onto the hall. Adrielle hesitated. Who could be with him this time of night? Domenikos? She felt her legs quiver. She'd never admit she was afraid of her own brother, but she was.

Since childhood they'd avoided each other. They were always on opposing sides. No matter what Adrielle did to try to assuage the situation, even if only for their parents' sake, Domenikos reciprocated with a satirical kind of savagery Adrielle couldn't condone. He was at the core of every malevolent act she'd ever experienced.

The light from the oil lamps spilled out into the hall. Careful not to be seen, Adrielle crept closer. She strained to see through the crack in the door. A long black cape hung on a peg on the wall. Haden.

Thank God, Haden. Adrielle felt a rush of relief.

Another quick peek revealed he and her father were bent over *The Book of Feathers,* in deep concentration. Over what?

Adrielle stepped away. She pressed her back to the wall and closed her eyes. Visions of their wedding night assaulted her mind. Seeing Haden stirred unexpected feelings.

"It's the only way," her father said.

"I can protect her—" Haden said, his voice husky.

"You can't. He is too strong." Her father's voice was grave and dry with an urgency in his generally calm demeanor.

Who posed such a threat? Domenikos? When he slept under this same roof? Did they already know?

"I'll lead you through the plan once more. Even the slightest deviation could mean her life. You understand? Her life!"

The room fell silent, then rustling pages.

"Here. This spell will take her back. Everything must be done exactly as I say. Understand? Breathe no word of this to anyone."

Adrielle couldn't breathe. Her mind was reeling. The smells in her home. The voices. All of it, conjured up a long-forgotten past and painful memories.

It was impossible to navigate the complexities of three different time epochs simultaneously: what was about to happen, what was presently happening, and what had already happened in the past.

This was insane. The future hadn't happened yet, but she had full knowledge, access, to all her memories from Florida. She was hyper aware her friends were waiting in the diamond center, hoping she'd restore Angelo's memories and access the Time Vault. And this meeting between Haden and her father—it had actually occurred thousands of years ago—every single detail unfolding as it had in her original time era.

Adrielle was finding it hard to breathe. Her life here, in ancient Achaea, felt like this was the *real* present time.

No. She had to keep her mind straight. This was a viewing. That's all. An alternative to time travel. She was in a time tunnel. *To restore Angelo's memories.* She had to remember this at all costs. This phenomenon of multi-unfolding time epochs was stranger than déjà vu.

Adrielle rubbed her temples. In the next few hours, her father would be tortured. Murdered at the stake. She swallowed. She hated knowing this without being able to stop it. She had to steel herself from painful emotions.

Did she have powers in this time tunnel? She didn't seem to inside the diamond. Could she travel unnoticed to see where Haden had gone after the eclipse? Or find out where he was now? Maybe he'd have answers.

She was determined to uncover what Domenikos was up to. But not without Angelo's memory fully restored. She couldn't risk it. This was the mission. To make Angelo whole again.

She was at an impasse. She was tempted to run into her father's den and tell him everything. About Domenikos. His treason. His planned coup. And his murder. But after hearing her father's voice for the first time since her veiled amnesia, after being propelled through time to present day Florida, she knew he'd be against it. Of course he would. It went against his Achaean rule. It contradicted everything he'd fought for.

Despite her father's efforts to maintain an armistice between mortals and Achaeans, the savage war raged on. He'd raised her to take his place. She was his protégée. He'd given the blood sacrifice with his life, and now she was the one who'd bear the sacrifices needed for his vision of peace to thrive.

Her love for him was crippling. Yet she'd grown up in Florida resenting she hadn't known him.

Long forgotten smells and sounds awakened a deep-rooted anger. She resented not sharing her life with him. No father-daughter dates. No fatherly advice. No shoulder to cry on when she was the brunt of ridicule because of her lack of pigment. She'd been robbed. The hole in her gut wrenched with longing.

ADRIELLE WAS ALREADY awake when morning sun blared into the center courtyard and into her window. For hours she'd wrestled the starless night for what to do.

She'd lain in bed, listening to her parents' debate that lasted most of the night. Their muffled voices drifted up from the central courtyard. Adrielle couldn't make out all the words, but she caught enough of the conversation to get the gist. Surprisingly, their voices brought a calmness she'd never experience. She had been filled with angst for most of her years in Florida.

Eva, her mother, begged to stay behind with Aaron, but he didn't deem it safe. After much deliberation, they agreed Eva and Coco would be transported safely to an unknown future sometime before Adrielle, so they'd be settled when she arrived.

The three of them would be transposed into a much younger age, so the integration would be easier. It was decided then, Adrielle would be younger than Coco. She seven, and Coco eight. That way Adrielle could benefit from having an older sister, and Coco could shield her from forthcoming onslaught for her differences, until she was ready to take the lead. The inter-travel subconscious would take care of any social deficiencies, automatically adjusting to the future society. Adrielle got out of bed and peeked out her window. Her parents sat at the dining table across from one another, their fingers interlaced. Seeing the two of them in love brought a rush of emotions.

They were her family. Her parents. All she'd ever longed for, during the years growing up in Florida. Instead, her family had consisted of Coco and Layla.

A bowl of untouched apricots, figs, and goat's cheese stood between them. They didn't look in agreement about the plan and were still working out the details.

Adrielle turned away from the window and dressed quickly. A simple linen dress that came down to her ankles and leather sandals with ties that wrapped around her calves. She stepped out into the hall about to join them, when Angelo appeared out of nowhere. He pulled her back inside.

"We need to talk," he whispered with a fire in his eyes, his words coming out rushed. "I remember everything now. And I think I've found the portal to the Time Vault."

Chapter 21

Liz–Inside the Memory Tunnel
–Back in Time–Florence 1504

FALLING INTO A time tunnel was not at all like time travelling using Adrielle's feather. When Liz had used Adrielle's feather and unintentionally ended up in London, or in Florence, there was no time lapse. She was just there. But this time, when she lost her balance from twirling and melted through the diamond wall, she fell into a long tunnel, spiraling along it into the past.

She was twisting and falling in darkness until something slammed against her. The contents of her stomach swirled as the ground raced toward her. She pressed one hand on her belly and another on her mouth, concentrating on keeping the contents in.

The spicy aroma of a farmers' market assaulted her, the smells identical to her memory. Her vision confirmed she was in Florence, Italy.

Everything lusciously the same, as though she'd never left. Her stomach cried out in hunger at the smell of freshly baked bread. She inhaled the aroma and absorbed the same azure sky she'd dreamt about. Fluffy clouds floated by, and she got lost in the moment. She was happy. Gloriously, insanely, happy.

Anything was possible here. It felt strange, knowing this place felt most like home, though her real life was back in Florida.

The sound of vendors haggling back and forth with customers reminded her some things never changed. Peddlers were just as noisy and annoying as she remembered. Bartering was one thing she hadn't enjoyed, and the vendors saw her coming. They doubled the price of produce, whenever she asked. Maybe they'd seen her as a foreigner with a ferocious appetite. Some things did change. She wasn't that person anymore. Food didn't control her.

Liz pulled on the waistband of her cargo pants. Size two and still ample room. She felt a sense of accomplishment. She pushed her weight out of her mind and took in the sights.

Colors were so vivid. She was here, really here. Excitement flooded through her. With some luck, she'd see Francesco in less than an hour.

Liz went to tuck her purse strap over her shoulder. *Freaking hot chili peppers. It wasn't there.*

This couldn't be happening. Was she back in Italy without her handbag? Without Adrielle's journal? She was naked without it. Without Dave. No Adrielle, and no Angelo. Gawd, how could this have happened?

She gnawed on her nails. Flakes of her OPI nail polish chipped and peppered her clothes. *Her manicure.* She assessed the damage and shoved her hands into her pockets. She needed her stuff. She'd look a mess when Francesco saw her.

A mob of people pointed at her. *I must look like an alien.* She licked her fingertips. She smoothed down her curls and stood up. She yanked at her short t-shirt revealing her pierced navel.

This wasn't good. *Breathe. Get a hold, Liz. You are an explorer.* A capable woman. A woman in love.

Francesco. He'd have her dripping with Florentine silks in no time.

Sweet and spicy smells tickled her nose. She moved quickly past the keyed-up spectators to study her surroundings. The corner store, with baskets brimming with vegetables and spices. Wait. There was that familiar merchant and his wife stocking the produce. Yes! It was all coming back.

She'd come here with Salai to gather spices for his famous stew.

She began to form a soft plan. Michelangelo's home was less than a mile away. She dug in her pocket, pulled out her Burt's Bees ChapStick, and smeared it on her lips. She'd go there first, to get a lay of the land. Surely, they'd be happy to see her.

DAMN THAT LIZ. Dave was sick with worry. He'd warned her about getting too close to the surface. So had Adrielle. Twirling and twirling with her eyes closed. What was she, a schoolgirl? And now she was gone. He pressed his hands to his head.

He leaned in closer to the surface and peered. It was as smooth and reflective as glass, seemingly endless. No sounds were coming out either. No cries for help. Tension squeezed at his chest. Had Liz vanished forever? "Liz?" he whispered. His eyes welled with tears.

He spun around. Coco was in her own world, inspecting the glass surface. Unbelievable. Lizzie was gone, and she was oblivious to it.

"Watch out, you might fall through," Dave warned, his voice cracking.

"I'm not an idiot," Coco said, without looking up.

He turned to see what Astraia was up to and— "Ahhh!"

She was right behind him, with a nasty frown. Her arms crossed.

"Where . . . did . . . Liz . . . go?" Astraia's voice was as gruff as her expression.

"She was twirling. And tumbled," Dave admitted.

"Tumbled?"

"Yes. Tumbled." He extended his arm. "Right through that wall. Like butter."

"To where?"

Dave shrugged.

"Where?" Astraia asked in a tight screech.

"Florence is my best guess."

"Florence?"

He nodded. "Couldn't possibly know without going myself."

Astraia's eyes narrowed. "Get her."

"I, uh." He looked at where Liz had disappeared. "That's ridiculous. I couldn't possibly—"

"Figure out how. *Now!*"

Dave winced and braced for retaliation. "I don't know how."

"Are you saying Liz is gone?" Coco said. She started toward him, looking angry. Her gaze went back and forth between them.

Dave could only nod.

Coco pressed her lips into a thin line.

Dave gave her a resigned little smile. "I'd fix it, but I'm drawing a blank."

He pulled on his shirt collar. He couldn't concentrate with Astraia breathing on his neck. He covered his eyes so he couldn't see her.

There was a reason her sister was permanently perched on Monika's shoulder. Had Astraia used a spell to turn her into the black bird? For, like, ever? *Stay calm. Calm.*

"Dave." Coco's voice was closer. He opened his eyes.

Astraia was fuming. *Shits about to get real.*

"Most likely . . . Liz was thinking about Francesco. Her first love," he said, hoping to appease Astraia. "Hang on."

He fought to envision the last engaging memory he could remember. The day he met Liz for lunch. Florence, 1504. He was in the square. He'd just found out about her engagement. Liz's news was a surefire way to get trapped. *Damn.* Despite the dangers of meddling with history, it was fun being a part of it. Savoring it.

Concentrate. He balled up his fists and squeezed harder until his fingernails cut into the heels of his hands. *Nothing.* He inhaled deeply, his heart racing now, trying to bring up smells of ripe fruits and vegetables. Sweet red peppers. He opened one eye. Astraia's expression was unreadable.

Oh c'mon. None of this was working. *Silks?* He envisioned luxurious Florentine fabrics. So soft to the touch. The colors—so vibrant. He eyed the diamond surface. Maybe he could lean just a bit to see if he saw anything.

Something rammed into him like a raging bull. He lost his balance and hit the wall. The diamond surface dissolved as he went through it. And kept going. And going . . .

He was free falling, spiraling into a dark tunnel. Twisting. And falling. Rotating . . . Déjà vu. Had he dreamt this before?

He remembered he'd secretly wanted to be a diver. If only he weren't afraid of heights. He tucked his legs into a pike as he'd imagined a million times and tumbled forward. Back. Reverse. Down. Down. Down. OUCH! A bludgeoning force slammed into him, head on.

Dave opened his eyes. His face was pressed against the ground. He was in the market, sprawled on the pavers.

Everything looked the same as that first day when they'd gone back in time. He picked himself up and dusted off his pink polo shirt and Khakis.

Coco appeared next to him out of nowhere. She summersaulted onto the ground like a gymnast. And then came Astraia—a perfect 10.0 landing.

A crowd gathered. Instead of cheers, spectators pointed. Their faces aghast and frightened. Most made the sign of the cross.

Goodness. This isn't good.

Chapter 22

Adrielle—Inside the Memory Tunnel
—Back in Time to Ancient Achaea

ANGELO HAD A tight grip on her arm. Adrielle searched his face. He was disheveled, his cheeks rosy and flushed. His curly hair tousled.

Adrielle inhaled his scent, and she felt a strong connection to him. Memories of them together rushed in her mind and she grabbed onto the doorframe for balance.

Angelo shook her gently. The green pigment of his eyes was hypnotic. "Did you hear me?"

She nodded. "Yes. Your memory's back. All of it?"

"I think so."

"My god. That's awesome," she said, but felt ambivalent. It meant he didn't need her anymore. She hadn't wanted to admit how much she liked having him around, memories or not.

She was reliving emotions she'd forgotten. She had a second chance.

"What's up?" Angelo said. "Is this about yesterday? At the beach? Because that's a conversation we had many years ago."

He was right, it was ancient history they couldn't alter.

"You said you found the portal to the Time Vault?"

He winced, disappointment flashing in his eyes. He lifted his hands off her arms and stepped back.

Life with Angelo would be magical, but she couldn't cave to her own desires. She wore the *Mark of the Traveler* now.

"There are black holes running pathways throughout the universe similar to these memory tunnels," Angelo said. "We entered this tunnel at a point where both our lives crossed. But there are other entry and exit points all along it," When I followed you yesterday, "I saw a break in the sky. A tear."

"Where?"

"Overhead to the left." He pointed. "I didn't want to investigate it alone; in case it was a trap, and I couldn't get back. We should examine it together."

Adrielle shifted her focus to the atrium below her bedroom window. Her parents were no longer there. She felt the sting of frustration. She'd wanted to speak to them. This might be the last time she saw them alive.

Adrielle was determined to find a solution to Domenikos' havoc. She stepped out of her room and saw Coco.

This version of Coco from the past had the same flair for fashion she had in modern day Florida. But instead of a short hip haircut, she wore it in two long braids interlaced with flowers, and curling down to her waist. The look was whimsically romantic.

"Breakfast?" Coco said, appearing happy to see Adrielle. "There are fresh figs and apricots from the market."

"I'm on my way out." Adrielle glanced over her shoulder. Angelo lagged behind, staying out of sight.

Coco's face crumpled with disappointment. "Are you going to see Haden?"

"A little later, maybe."

The sensation of being the older, responsible sister in these ancient times was strange, because the older Coco in Florida had all the answers. She worked hard to give them both stability.

"Are you really going to marry him?" Coco asked, clearly distressed. "I heard mother and father speaking about it last night. They said with the rebellion, you'd be staying in his castle right away."

Adrielle nodded.

"But what about Angelo? How can you do this to him?"

Adrielle cringed. Angelo was still within earshot. Of course she'd ask, Coco always considered other people's feelings.

"I have responsibilities," she said.

"He can protect you. Angelo is the army's leading soldier."

Adrielle felt ambushed. She reminded herself not to be overly sensitive.

Coco took hold of Adrielle's hand. "Make sure you know what you are doing before you make a mistake you can't undo."

Adrielle nodded. She took one last glance at her old house to collect memories.

"Dom is around here somewhere. He'll protect me," Coco said. Her expression said they both knew Domenikos only thought of himself.

Dom—Domenikos. Murderer. She needed to remedy that she hadn't told future-Coco he was their brother, before she found out from some other source. Soon, here too, Coco would discover what atrocities Domenikos was capable of. He would slaughter their father and other Achaean leaders in the town square. And she wouldn't be around to stop it.

"I really have to go. Be safe," Adrielle said, hugging Coco tightly.

Coco would be safely tucked away in Florida. A younger version of herself with no memory of these troubled times. Perhaps it was better this way. Coco would have a greater chance at a normal life.

Outside her family home, it was easier for Adrielle to stay on task. She'd only just discovered she didn't have the ability to fly in this memory tunnel. Angelo thought it was because in linear time, she hadn't earned the traveler's crest yet. Maybe he was right.

Adrielle touched the space between her shoulder blades with her fingertips. The crest was gone. And to her surprise, disappointment flooded through her.

Chapter 23

Liz, Dave, Coco and Astraia
–Inside the Memory Tunnel–Back in Time–
Florence 1504

"ISN'T ANYONE MANNING the Diamond center?" Dave said, as casually as if it was a retail store. "Domenikos could be back there, up to no good."

"Oh, we *know* he's up to no good," Astraia said, absorbing their surroundings. She didn't look pleased. "What we don't know is—what are we doing *here?*"

"Chasing Liz," Dave said.

"We shouldn't be tampering with the timeline," Coco said, clearly irritated.

Dave winced. "I know, I know. But Astraia said to get Liz back. I was trying to figure out where she could've gone, when someone pushed me through." He gave Astraia a stern look.

"Well, I didn't push you," Coco said.

"Someone did." Dave gave Astraia the side-eye.

Astraia sneered and narrowed her eyes at Dave. "Why *here* of all places?"

Dave tugged at his polo shirt and averted his gaze. "I told you—Francesco. Liz was missing Francesco while she was twirling. And *poof.* She was gone. Right through the diamond's edge."

Astraia's face remained blank.

"Dah, she was in love—"

Astraia sighed with obvious distaste.

A crowd gathered and began to get hostile. Someone threw a pepper and yelled angrily at them.

"We need to get moving," Dave said, meeting Coco's eyes. "We're easy targets with these clothes. Let's get to the studio."

Coco agreed.

Dave led them down a narrow street away from the main square, a shortcut route to Michelangelo's he'd taken a hundred times. Although not convinced Liz would be there, at least they'd find a friendly face.

As they wound around and around the Florentine back streets, familiar smells bombarded Dave's sensory glands. The sweet aroma of baking bread. Soups. Spicy tomato-based sauces. Even the acrid smell of garbage was a welcomed smell.

Dave was surprised that despite the dangers involved, being back in these times was like coming home. He navigated the narrow streets for longer than he remembered and was relieved when they finally arrived at Michelangelo's front door.

Dave tapped the heavy iron knocker on the aged and gnarled wood and waited. He couldn't wait to see Michelangelo's surprised reaction. When no one came to the door after a respectable amount of time, he banged vigorously on the knocker. The sound echoed throughout the street.

"Buongiorno," Dave hollered.

Still nothing.

"Maybe he's in the studio and can't hear. I'll check around back," Dave said, anxious to get away from Astraia's glaring stare and headed for the side of the house.

"Doubtful," Coco shouted. "Remember how the knocker boomed throughout the house?"

Around back, Italian cedars soared like tall fingers. Dave tried the studio door, but it was locked. For some reason, the windows were boarded up. A shiver of nerves worked its way down his back. What if he'd moved away? Or was on a trip? He scrambled to remember Francesco's surname; sorry he'd never paid much attention.

How else would he find Liz? He thought about Leonardo. Florence wasn't his permanent home. Would he still be in town on business?

Dave skulked back to the front, hesitant to deliver bad news. A neighbor was in a heated discussion with Coco.

Dave picked up enough Italian to make out Michelangelo was out of town. *Damn.* It seemed he wouldn't be back for some time.

He glanced at Astraia, who stood menacingly watching the debate. He had no idea how to get Liz back. How to contact Adrielle. Visions of them sleeping on the streets like beggars brought terror. Should he try to talk to the neighbor?

After some deliberation, Dave stepped in. In broken Italian, he explained Michelangelo had offered their use of his home.

"Surprising, because the artist values his privacy almost as much as the arts," the neighbor said. He stared at Dave suspiciously. "Do you have a key?"

"Of course," Dave lied.

The neighbor hesitated, before turning away. The three of them watched as he retreated to his house across the street.

"Now what?" Astraia said, temper flaring in her eyes. "Where's that supposed key of yours?"

"Um. Guess we pretend we have it. And break in around back, where we can't be seen," Dave offered.

"Are you nuts?" Coco squealed. "If we get caught, we could go to jail. I'm seeing stone prisons. With medieval tortures." She stroked the nape of her velvet choker. "We could get the guillotine."

"Not likely. That contraption won't be invented for another three hundred years. Let's be real. It's France, not Italy," Dave said, pulling on his collar. He chuckled nervously.

"You've lost your mind." Coco stole a look around. She glanced at Astraia and lowered her voice. "Does anyone else know how to get a hold of Adrielle?"

Stone-faced Astraia shook her head.

"How about getting back to the diamond?" Coco asked, panic in her voice.

"We're not going back without Liz," Dave said flatly.

Across the street, the neighbor had stopped at his doorstep. He appeared to be waiting for them to go inside.

"Better hurry," Coco said.

Dave went around back again, circling the other way. He scanned the façade and noticed the second story bedrooms had windows. They were too high. Doubtful he could reach them. Not unless he could scale up the wall like Spiderman.

Astraia. For a moment, he wrestled with asking her for help. Then thought better of it. She wasn't in a good mood. And he didn't want to be indebted to her.

He couldn't stop thinking about Astraia's sister. A full-fledged bird doomed to spend her remaining days perched on Monika's shoulder. He shuddered. Imagine . . . doing that to her own sister.

He jiggled the studio door. It appeared to be bolted from the inside. He stood in front of it, wringing his hands until his fingers ached. Then he remembered the kitchen window over the sink. It might just be low enough for him to climb in. He marched over to it.

On closer inspection, the boards attached on the window's exterior could be easily removed. He used a stick he found in the yard and pried the boards off, one by one. He then jiggled the window frame. The damned thing was jammed.

He slid his hand into his jacket to punch through the glass, when a pang of guilt hit him: this colorless renaissance glass was worth a fortune. The glass was historic. Irreplaceable. Well, maybe not in these times.

If he didn't get in soon, the neighbor would come by. Maybe call the police. And they needed time to find clues to locate Francesco. *Forget it.* Dave punched the glass hard. Shards sprayed into the room and pinged on the stone floor. He winced, not entirely convinced he should have done that.

Careful not to get cut, Dave squeezed through the opening and rotated his body to land feet first. He lowered his right foot and was about to put all his weight down, when something rolled under his foot. He spiraled down, crashing hard on his buttocks.

"Xixo#@%b9)/--son of a—g—sh—"

A sharp pain shot from his backside to the tips of his limbs. He lay sprawled on his back and stared up the ceiling, waiting for the pain to subside. Then he got on four knees and searched through the broken glass for the source that caused his fall.

There it was, still rolling under the table beyond his reach. His heart fluttered. Liz's *Burt's Bees* Chapstick.

WITH LESS THAN one mile to go to reach Francesco's home, Liz skipped rather than walked. She couldn't believe her luck. She was in Florence, on her way to see Francesco.

It had been months since she'd felt so free. So happy. *Months.* If she had to pinpoint it, it was the last time she saw Francesco.

The grounds of Francesco's estate came into view, and Liz glimpsed the stately manor between the trees.

What would she say? He'd see the change in her appearance. She was thin and toned now, thanks to her daily workout. She wondered if he'd like it. Excited and nervous all at once, Liz ran.

Golden pecan pie, Liz muttered—this grand house was friggin' huge. Oodles larger than she'd remembered. A palace.

She paused mid-step, her breath jagged as she took in the view. The building's façade was a vision of windows and stone columns. A small waterless moat surrounded the estate, she guessed for fortification against thieves.

Dotting the grounds were cows, sheep, pigs, and the outbuildings that housed them. *Imagine, farm animals,* she giggled. Francesco had quite the collection.

As she ran, she reviewed his staff in her head, struggling to match faces with names. His main steward lived in the apartments next to the main hall and took care of this home along with Francesco's other manors. She scrambled to remember his name. There was a bailiff, entrusted with the day-to-day administration.

The maids and other help came and went, so she couldn't remember them very well.

Antonio. That was it. Francesco's main Steward. Pudgy face with burly eyebrows and a red nose. Piero was the bailiff—long face with sunken eyes and wrinkled skin. Lorenzo was the head cook. He made the most delicious scones that melted in your mouth. *Mmmm.* His apron was always streaked with flour and food and wrapped so tightly around his body it accentuated his round belly. He had a good sense of humor though, laughing at a moment's notice. Liz decided she liked him best of all.

Liz could barely contain her excitement now. She felt like a queen coming home. She sprinted. Then she heard a loud squeal. Something was underfoot. A piglet. In trying to dodge him, she twisted her ankle sideways.

Before she could brace for the fall, her nose and mouth were inches deep in—*gross, what?* Liz brushed the moist paste off her face.

Little piglet ran off at a surprising speed, oinking and squealing, and not stopping until he was safely tucked under his mother's legs. Mother pig gave a loud grunt. She nudged him with her snout, which seemed to calm him, and both waddled off toward the outhouse, leaving Liz to fend for herself.

Spitting out as much debris as she could, and trying her best not to taste it, she swept gobs of it off her face and eyes.

Oh no. No! Her clothes were covered in it. Tears welled before she could stop them. She was shaking so hard she couldn't catch her breath. Then the hiccups came, as they usually did, when she got this upset.

She concentrated on her breathing and tried to stand. Shooting pain exploded up her ankle. She rotated it, rolling her foot side to side, but that only made things worse. The house was still a ways off.

There went her surprise appearance. She began to hobble. She yelped. The pain was excruciating. And then her ankle started to swell.

The manor that only seconds before looked close enough to smell Lorenzo's baking, was now unreachable. Did they have crutches in the fifteen hundreds? She got on all fours and crawled through the field toward the main doors.

Chapter 24

Adrielle and Angelo—
Inside the Memory Tunnel—
Back in Time to Ancient Achaea

ADRIELLE CLUNG TO Angelo's back and braced against the sudden wind velocity. They sped upward, the wispy clouds dissolving into nothingness. The city of Achaea vanished below them.

Adrielle could barely keep her eyes open to search the azure sky. At this speed, it didn't take long to reach the jagged line resembling a scar. The tear was so out of place, it jumped out at them like a bold brushstroke on a canvas.

Angelo secured his arms around Adrielle's torso. "Hang on." He came to a stop and hovered over the tear.

"I should go first, in case it's a trap," Angelo said.

"If it is a trap, we're both screwed," Adrielle said, inspecting the tear. "I'd lead but, I've lost my wings."

Angelo glanced over his shoulder and gave her a worried look.

"I know, let's hope it's not permanent," she said. She missed her feathered crest. It made her feel empowered. She was only just beginning to understand what it enabled her to do. "Let's go in together."

Angelo clasped her hand. Adrielle glanced down at their interlocked fingers. They fit so well. She looked back at the tear.

With Angelo in the lead, they approached the opening with caution. When they were right up to it, Adrielle rammed her hand through the rip. A shock-like current zapped her, and she pulled back her hand.

"There's a current. I'm not sure we can cross it without armor."

"I have armor," Angelo said and enveloped her with his wings. "Close your eyes until we're through. I suspect the current may only be active on the periphery."

Angelo kept his third eyelid sealed, and she suspected he was able to see clearly through it. Adrielle closed her eyes. The current buzzed and zapped as they crossed, then everything went quiet.

They were hovering above a vast space so dark, Adrielle couldn't see the dimensions. It reminded her of the undefined space where Domenikos had kept her mother and others as prisoners.

"Do you see that down there?" Adrielle whispered.

Angelo cupped his hand over her mouth and gestured for her not to speak. Below them, two sentinels flanked a gigantic metal door. Angelo angled his head and rested it on Adrielle's. Her head whirled with Angelo's thoughts.

"This could be dangerous. She smells of jasmine and tuberose. Mmmm . . . Both guards look like Brix—strange."

Despite the seriousness of their situation, Adrielle suppressed a giggle. *"I'm hearing your thoughts. Can you hear mine?"*

"Yes. It's one of the perks of being an Achaean soldier. Technically, I guess that's why you're able to reciprocate. Touching our heads makes communication easier."

"Of course, less interference," Adrielle said, then concentrated on curbing her thoughts. She turned her attention back to the guards.

"Why do you think they look like Brix? Is it possible they're twins?"

Angelo didn't answer right away, and a dark sensation overcame her. One of the guards looked up, and Adrielle ducked into the safety of Angelo's wings. *"Oh, oh. Can they see us?"*

"Relax. Not while my wings are binding us."

She exhaled. *"Why do you think they look like Brix? Give it your best shot."*

"I believe we have reached the opening of the Time Vault. And, no, I don't think they're twins. Brix is a full-blown Achaean, so it would be impossible for him to be a twin. You're a twin because you're half mortal. The answer here is far more disturbing. I believe your brother has travelled to the future and cloned him."

"No . . ."

Adrielle heard metal scrape against metal; the clanging of giant wheels, turning and grinding. Then came the sound of a thousand locks unlatching, reminding her of a clip of ammunition.

They clung to one another as they looked at the door in time to see it open. The drum of marching soldiers began.

"What's happening? What are they doing inside the vault?"

"Not sure. They all look the same."

"I know. More clones? They don't look like the Brix guards."

"The others . . . the soldiers, all look like Vladik."

"Vladik? As in Domenikos' gnome?" Adrielle had a terrible feeling about this.

"That's the one."

They watched in silence, unease stirring through Adrielle. The soldiers were identical. Rows and rows, three men deep, marched out of the vault and turned, before disappearing into an adjoining room.

"We should follow, but I want to explore the inside of the vault first, before the door shuts."

Angelo agreed. The door was so thick it would be impossible to break in. It was at least twelve inches thick and appeared to be made of solid steel. *"Keep close,"* he said, his arms tightening around her. With one smooth swoop, they soared through the massive door at a fantastic speed.

Damp stale air filled their nostrils. Tucked safely in Angelo's grip, Adrielle kept her eyes locked on the action. The army seemed oblivious to them. They marched onward, seeping out of the Time Vault like an ant colony.

Adrielle and Angelo hovered over the rows. They followed the serpent trail inside the vault to where the soldier parade began, deep in the guts of the Time Vault.

There they hung mid-flight, in a high spot so not to be seen. When the last of the soldiers disappeared, Adrielle whispered, "Are we alone?"

Angelo shrugged, she saw his raptor vision scaling the walls and ceiling for surveillance.

In the middle of the room, a diamond glowed inside the beak of a golden metal bird. It was on display, showcased like in an art gallery.

The statue was two feet high and seemed to be made of solid gold. Its ominous beak opened just enough to grasp the brilliant diamond, as if in offering to a sky god.

Adrielle inspected the icon closely. This diamond was much smaller than the one in the scepter staff and was not expertly cut. This diamond had rough edges, as though a wild animal had ripped it from the body of a larger stone. Adrielle shuddered. It reminded her of a hunt, a predator ripping out the heart of its prey.

As they neared the golden icon, a single beam of light escaped from the heart of the diamond and led into another room. They followed the light.

Identical soldiers were gathering around a central stage, and in the middle of the stage, wearing a long silky red gown, was Scarlett.

Adrielle gasped. *Scarlett?* Like the others, she was mesmerized as Scarlett held up a giant gilded mirror. Instead of Scarlett's reflection on the surface of the mirror, Arielle saw through the mirror. Deep inside it, a multitude of people gathered. They looked ordinary. They could be her neighbors in Palm Coast. Teachers. Friends. Individuals of all ages, both young and old.

Adrielle sought out Angelo's gaze. He was seeing it too. She motioned for him to take her to the backside of the mirror, to confirm it was a mirror and not a parlor trick. On the backside, none of the people she'd seen through the mirror were there.

Adrielle turned her attention back to the rows of the identical soldiers that had marched from inside the vault. They sat spellbound, transfixed by Scarlett.

She followed the beam of light from the diamond into this room. It was aimed to hit the mirror's surface and pierced the glass. It bore deep inside it, and Scarlett, like an expert sniper, angled the mirror to direct the light beam so it would strike one of the many people gathered, squarely in the forehead.

Adrielle watched the light hit one of the people inside the mirror. On contact, they thrashed about, raised their hands to their head, and pressed their palms to their temples as though they were in agonizing pain. The light bounced off them and back through the mirror, onto one of the Vladik soldiers. Once the light reflected onto the soldier's forehead, a plume of intense light shrank the soldier in size, and the soldier popped like a soap bubble and vanished.

Adrielle was stunned. She exchanged a look with Angelo. He appeared as mystified as she was.

She turned hungrily back to the mirror. Scarlett's hands looked like an advertisement for Cartier. Diamonds poured off her fingers as she maneuvered the light beam, aiming at the unsuspecting humans on the other side of the mirror. Who were they?

Why would Scarlett be here? Domenikos must have recruited her for his dark acts the night he killed Josh and took Scarlett captive. It made sense, Scarlett thrived on another's misfortune. She would do anything to save herself.

But why would Domenikos do this? If the beam was a conduit zapping memories from people and placing them into the new soldiers, it would explain the memory-failure epidemic in Florida.

By extracting people's memories, Domenikos would have access to their deepest thoughts. Their weaknesses. This master plan could only have come from the depths of Domenikos' twisted mind.

Something was still troubling her. Why did the light beam shrink the soldiers until they popped like a soap bubble? Where did they go? Laws of physics dictate energy is neither created nor destroyed. Energy is transformed from one form to another. So, what happened to the clones? And were they clones?

This was a massively engineered operation. How long had it gone on? Had Domenikos known there was a backdoor to time travel before she banished him into the Diamond scepter?

She had to stop to it, before history was altered to Domenikos' version of the truth.

Chapter 25

Liz–Inside the Memory Tunnel–
Back in Time–Florence 1504

THE STRETCH OF pasture from the moat to the main house that first appeared to be a meadow of luscious beauty, became a field of insurmountable dread. A minefield to negotiate with utmost caution.

Anchored on all fours, Liz felt like one of Francesco's animals, rivaling desperately with nature to reach the main house.

Sections of the landscape were so steep and demanding, Liz found herself clawing viciously at the soil to make the tiniest headway. She was reduced to panting like a canine, her tongue wagging out of her mouth, dry and cracked like dessert sand. Her swollen hands resembled raw meat. Her chafed knees ached at her joints. The field was taking so long to cross, the golden sun that made everything appear magical dropped from the sky and was replaced by looming black clouds. Only a shriveled colored line of orange remained.

An angry clap of thunder followed by a flash of lightning unleashed the fury of a thousand rain pellets. The tiny drops froze midair and turned to hail, each one pounding hard against her skin. Liz raised her hands to shield her face, but she needed her hands to scale the terrain.

Icy wind gusts swept through the fields and cut through her skin, burrowing deep into her bones. She couldn't remember ever being this cold; her teeth chattered and rocked her entire body.

The hail only lasted several minutes but left its mark on the landscape.

Gone were the crisp clean lines and bright peaks of color. Long shadows extended along the vast meadowlands like bent fingers. Thin wisping fog leached out of the ground, so dense, when the remaining light passed through gaps in the trees, it illuminated and accentuated opaque objects.

Before her eyes the scenery blackened and changed into a moody sfumato. Obscured shadows appeared as ghosts, floating aimlessly. Her surroundings had transformed into a ghostly graveyard. Liz shivered.

Liz wasn't the type to lose her zest for anything she'd set her mind on, but her spirit was deflated.

When finally, the door loomed over her, she pulled herself to her feet and brazenly grabbed the knocker. She gave it one loud rap. Then another whack. It was the last barrier between her and Francesco.

Boom. Boom. The sound of metal clanging against wood echoed. Despite her crummy mood, Liz couldn't help but smile when low resounding footsteps approached and stopped on the other side of the massive door. It screeched open, and Liz bit her inner lip, so not to appear too eager.

A long narrow face with wrinkly skin and a wiry white beard appeared. She blinked, feeling a pang of relief as she registered his features. *Piero.* She almost threw her arms around him, but refrained, when he showed no sign of recognition.

"Buona sera," she said, in her best Italian.

He stared back with bright green eyes.

"Hola. "Oops." She giggled nervously and slapped her soiled hand to her mouth. *Hola* was hello in Spanish.

Piero swept his gaze over her, registering her soiled appearance. Her wet mop of hair dripping onto the stone floor. Her strange camo cargo pants and pierced navel exposed under her dryer-shrunk T-shirt. The man stood stone-faced.

"Me Liz," she said, raising her voice and heels in tandem. "Where's Francesco?" She rose on her tiptoes and stretched to see past him.

Piero's face was a granite bust, his distaste of her appearance apparent, by the narrowing of the open door.

"Holy fudge sticks!" Liz squealed. She blocked the door with her shoes and elbowed past him, hobbling on one foot into the main hall.

A sequence of his fast—very fast and loud Italian discourse—ensued. Unscathed, Liz forged on, leaving a wet trail behind her.

In the large living area adjacent to the foyer, a fire roared in the stone fireplace. Liz was so cold, nothing would feel better than a toasty fire. She headed there and paused. Someone was in the oversized tapestried chair warming their feet.

Flickers of light illuminated the rich Florentine silk of the sleeves on the cloak. Smoke rings floated up from a long-necked pipe. The aroma, thick and sweet like a flower on fire, mingled with the wood smoke and tickled Liz's nose.

On the third finger was a magnificent gold ring, encrusted with a large red stone. The light of the fire danced within the gem's many facets.

Liz froze, unable to move.

Piero burst into the room; his diatribe of Italian pinged off the walls.

As though in slow motion, the man in the chair turned toward her, the firelight silhouetting his strong profile.

"What is the reason for this intrusion? At this ungodly time of night?"

Tears pricked at Liz's eyes. "Francesco. Francesco my love." She hopped on one foot toward him.

In one swift move, Francesco's eyes met hers. All warmth drained from him.

What's happening? "It's me, Lisa. Mona Lisa."

"My Lisa? No." He shook his head and took a step back. His gaze swept over her with obvious distaste. He absorbed her mud-splattered appearance, her frizzy-hair. Her camo cargo-pants and pierced navel. He blinked hard and gasped, his mouth dropping open. Hot embers flew out of the pipe's chamber as it hit the ground.

Chapter 26

Inside the Memory Tunnel

DOMENIKOS STARED THROUGH the mirror, his mind racing. The wheels were in motion. He wasn't surprised Adrielle had taken the bait. He knew Adrielle better than anyone. It was in her nature to put others before her. He'd find out how far she was willing to break the rules, as his plan unfolded.

"She's inside," he said. His soldier gave a salute and exited the room.

Chapter 27

DAVE, COCO, AND ASTRAIA—
INSIDE THE MEMORY TUNNEL—
BACK IN TIME—FLORENCE 1504

DAVE DIDN'T BELIEVE he'd ever see Michelangelo's house again. But here he was, in the home of one of history's most influential artists. For months after they'd returned to Florida, he'd lain awake, mentally savoring their adventures in Florence. And now he was back.

He felt a rush of excitement as he slipped Liz's Burt Bees Chapstick into his pocket. He rubbed his tailbone and turned his attention to the broken window.

Despite reasoning that breaking the glass was the only way to get in, he felt a pang of regret. He'd tweaked history. He'd have to fix the panes, or they'd never hear the end of it from Michelangelo. And what kind of guests would they be if they didn't respect his home?

He stood up and brushed himself off, then quickly made his way to the front door. When he unlatched it, Astraia didn't look happy.

"Sorry, had to break a window. Could've used some of your magic."

"It's not magic. Move aside," Astraia said, brushing past him into the small kitchen. Coco followed her in and latched the door behind them.

"I'll see about getting the glass replaced tomorrow," Dave said, heading for the back room.

"We won't be here long enough," Astraia said.

Dave found a broom in the back and returned to the kitchen. He began sweeping up the glass into a bucket by the door.

"No one is here. And you're wasting time," Astraia said.

"We can't leave this mess. Not after he helped us with the forgery."

"In case you're confused, we're here to find Liz and get back to the diamond before Angelo and Adrielle return. Now where is she?"

Dave pulled out the Chapstick and held it up triumphantly.

Coco was watching him closely.

"That's supposed to be Liz?" Astraia sneered.

"No, but it's hers. Which means she was here. So, we're on track."

"How do you know it's not left over from before?" Coco said, taking the Chapstick and inspecting it. She handed it back. "She has dozens of them. I'm starting to feel like this is one big mistake."

"It's not," Dave said. "It's their new flavor—watermelon. Just came out this week. Liz and I went to Sephora to pick it up."

"Watermelon Chapstick doesn't amount to much. What we need is to find Liz," Astraia said.

"Did you check the house?" Coco said.

"No, not—"

Astraia went upstairs and returned too quickly.

"Like I said, no one is here. So, what's the big plan?" She shot Dave a look and rested her fists on her hips.

Dave shifted and averted his eyes.

A crack of thunder split the silence. Then rain pattered down.

"Looks like we got in just in time." Coco walked over to the window and sighed. "We'll have to block the rain somehow."

"The plan is to find Francesco, right after I block the window," Dave said, gesturing to the rain pouring in the house. "I'm sure Liz is there."

Astraia cocked an eyebrow. "So, let's go." Her voice was tight and stern.

Dave exchanged a look with Coco. He hated to admit he didn't know where Francesco lived.

"Oh, you don't know how to find him? Is that it?" Coco said.

Dave nodded. "I'll think of something while I go out and see if I can block the rain." He couldn't wait to get out of there. He avoided Astraia's glare as he stepped outside.

The rain was coming down in torrents. Dave rounded the house to the window and saw the window had hinged shutters. He closed them and it seemed to block most of the rain. *Now what?* He hated to go back in and be interrogated by Astraia.

If Liz had ever told him where Francesco lived, he was drawing a blank. He stood there, outside, fretting over what to do.

The storm and late hour darkened the sky. By the time Dave went back inside, the lanterns were lit, and Coco had prepared a pot of hot tea.

Dave was stunned by the cozy homey feeling. They'd spent so much time in Michelangelo's house, they'd all become familiar with the layout and knew exactly where Michelangelo kept clean linens, where the oil for the lanterns was, and how to use the wood burning stove. It felt like home. He was surprised how easily Coco had made herself at home, despite the stressful, dire situation.

"You're soaked," Coco said, handing him a towel. She looked up at Dave expectantly. "Let's uh, change out of our clothes. Then we'll figure out how to find Liz."

Dave was relieved her tone wasn't accusatory. No matter how disappointed or worried she might be, Coco had a way of relieving the pressure and making you feel nurtured.

He searched the room for Astraia. "Where is she?"

"Having a look upstairs. She'll be back," Coco said.

"Fantastic." A part of him hoped she'd left. He was still unsure if she was on their team. "I'm going to ask around to see if anyone knows where Francesco lives. Someone must, Liz's portrait was the talk of the town."

"What portrait?" Astraia said, appearing back in the kitchen.

"The engagement portrait. Francesco commissioned a painting when he asked Lizzie to marry him and—"

"Stop." She held out her hand. "Not interested. You mortals are so sentimental." She pulled out a chair and took a seat at the table. "Guess we're stuck here till morning."

"I'll start on the stew," Coco said, and began lighting the wood-burning stove. "There's cured ham and potatoes in the pantry."

"Great, I'm starved." Dave went to fetch the ingredients. He cut shavings off the ham and put them into a pot. "You do eat, don't you?" he asked Astraia.

Astraia's eyes blazed. "Of course I eat." Her expression said this was the stupidest question she'd ever heard. "I do regular things."

Dave shrugged. Who knew? Though Angelo was Achaean like her, Astraia seemed much different from him.

ONCE THEY'D EATEN and cleared the table, they headed upstairs. "Where are we sleeping?" Dave whispered to Coco as they reached the guest room.

"In here." Coco opened the armoire and tossed him Michelangelo's nightgown.

"I'm taking the master," Astraia announced. She disappeared down the hall.

Dave was relieved. He slipped on his pajamas and waited for Coco by the bed.

"Wipe that pathetic smile off your face and get some sleep," Coco said, pulling back the covers and hopping into bed.

Dave fluffed his pillow and got in on the other side. "It's just that . . . I'm so happy to be here. After we left, I felt badly we'd been so rushed to make the forgery, I didn't get to savor this time period." He searched Coco's eyes, and she appeared sympathetic. "You know what I mean?"

"I do."

Dave folded his hands behind his head and stared up at the beams on the ceiling. "Look how thick the beams are. They're probably hundreds of years old." He sighed. "The architecture is amazing. Everything about this place is amazing." His eyes felt heavy. He sucked in a long breath and released a slow shuddery breath. This was the first time he'd relaxed in a long while.

"Night, night, Coco," he said, drifting off to sleep. "Don't worry, we'll find her tomorrow."

"Night," Coco said, stretching her legs as a long yawn overcame her. "Didn't know Michelangelo got himself a hot-water bottle. He didn't used to have one."

"Modern hot water bottles weren't patented till 1903. I don't think they had them in these times," Dave said.

"Then what's warm and fuzzy at the end of the bed?"

Dave cracked his eyes open. Coco pulled her feet in and something large and black sprung from under the covers.

"Aaargggg," Dave squealed. He jumped onto Coco's side of the bed and hopped from one foot to the other. "What was that? Hurry, bring the lantern."

Astraia appeared in the doorway. "What's happened?" A large looming shadow scurried along the wall.

"EEEEK!" Dave scrunched his eyes shut. His knees felt like jelly. "I think it's—"

"A rat." Astraia swatted at it, then grabbed its tail, and dangled it back and forth, menacingly close to Dave's face.

Dave squealed louder, and Coco laughed. "Still glad we're here experiencing these times?"

Astraia tossed the rat out the window. "Get some sleep. We've got a long day ahead of us."

Chapter 28

Liz—Inside the Memory Tunnel—
Back in Time—Florence 1504

OPEN-JAWED FRANCESCO froze mid-step, the look of disbelief sealed in his eyes. His reaction to Liz was like a jackhammer through her heart.

"You are not my Lisa," Francesco said, and with the jerk of his chin, directed Piero to drag her out.

Piero clenched his hands around her, and Liz didn't resist. She was emotionally traumatized. Despite his elderly appearance, Piero plucked her easily from Francesco's study. She felt her tiny body flail upward and outward in the direction of the door.

She clung onto the doorframe. "Francesco, please." She wriggled from Piero's grasp in one desperate attempt. "I can explain."

Francesco placed his hand on his chest and their gazes collided. "I gave you my heart," he said coolly, any trace of warmth gone. "When you left, you took my future, Lisa. You made a joke of me, in my own town." He turned his back to her.

Liz felt a sharp pain in her gut. Her body became limp. Piero tightened his grip and pried her from the front door. A succession of quiet whimpers escaped her.

"You look like a drowned rat, Lisa. Madre mia . . ." Francesco slapped his hand to his forehead. "What has happened to you?" He glanced over his shoulder. "Piero, take her to the kitchen for something to eat. You'd think she hasn't eaten since she left." He walked back to his study. "And while you are at it, get her some dry clothes. Something that covers that skinny waist."

Piero loosened his grip, a scowl overtaking his face.

With a steaming bowl of tomato soup cupped in her hands and a warm blanket around her shoulders, Liz finally stopped shaking. Francesco was livid. She'd never seen him like that.

Who wouldn't be? She'd vanished after promising to marry him. He was right. She'd ruined his reputation and made him the laughingstock of the city—especially after all the portrait gossip. He felt abandoned. She'd blown it. The only man who'd accepted her for her.

She sipped more soup, the liquid warming her mouth. As it heated her insides, she felt herself relaxing. It was a wonder what food could do, she thought, sipping mouthfuls of the creamy broth.

Piero knocked on the kitchen doorframe and entered without reservation. Liz looked over the rim of her bowl. He was holding a clean linen nightgown in his arms. Excitement flooded through her. Was she invited to spend the night? This felt like the beginnings of something good. Something real.

She thanked Piero for the nightgown and trailed closely behind him down the hall. Luckily, he didn't move fast. Her ankle throbbed, and she was able to baby it. They passed room after room and finally stopped at the last door.

Before opening the door, Piero met her gaze and said, "I've prepared a room for you to stay the night. You can leave in the morning."

The door squeaked open to the musky smell of an unused room and burning firewood.

There was a large canopy bed lined with heavy red velvet curtains, and a matching bedspread. Gilded paintings of religious scenes lined the walls with a grand fireplace in the corner. Liz hopped toward it. She stretched her hands to bask in the warmth of the fire, and before she could thank Piero, the door latched. He was gone.

Liz stood by the fire for a long moment. The room was larger than any she'd ever stayed in and more beautiful.

The warmth from the fire was heating the room, but she felt cold again. Francesco looked like he hated her. She felt lonely. Dave wasn't there to soften the blow.

It was okay. She'd felt lonely before.

Liz stripped off her wet clothes and spread them on the chair by the fire. She'd need them in the morning.

Tired and exhausted, she changed into the nightgown and crept into bed. She shivered. The sheets were freezing. She pulled her knees up and turned onto her side. A sliver of moonlight shone in between the window curtains, the curl of the moon peeking in.

Liz tugged at the blankets and pulled them up to her chin. She wondered if Adrielle and Angelo had made any headway. Or if things got as convoluted for them, as they had for her. The day's problems began weighing her down. She breathed deeply in and let it out, promising to take things one day at a time.

Things hadn't turned out the way she predicted, she admitted, they seldom did. And sure, this wasn't the best start. But it was a start.

Chapter 29

Adrielle and Angelo—
Inside the Memory Tunnel

"WE'VE GOTTA keep moving," Angelo whispered. They were following the trail of soldiers back to the main room. He stayed far enough behind to keep out of sight, while simultaneously scouring the walls for anomalies.

Adrielle struggled to keep up. With the exception of the glow coming from the diamond gem, the circular room was dimly lit.

"Forget about the main beam for now, look closely at the Time Vault walls. If you avoid those glimmering reflections from the diamond, you can see slight imperfections, exactly where the refractions from the light shine. The light is bending. It could be revealing openings to different pathways inside the walls," Angelo said.

Adrielle turned to inspect the wall's surface closer, trying not to get lost in the refraction of the light from the diamond, even in the Time Vault. The stone's facets acted like a prism creating a spectrum of different colors. Adrielle struggled to concentrate.

She narrowed her eyes and saw the slight alterations in the wall's surface. "You're right. Something's definitely happening there."

They neared the spot where the surface appeared as though it were shifting with their slightest movement. Adrielle touched the wall. Her hand went through it, much like it had in the diamond center. She pulled her hand back and pressed her face as close to it as she could, without crossing the barrier.

She held her breath and remained still, then moved slightly to one side. It was like a hall of mirrors. Hundreds of pathways converged to this central atrium.

Adrielle felt a rush of excitement. "You're right. I see tunnels. But I don't know where they lead."

Angelo came to her side. "I'm not sure either."

Adrielle closed her eyes to concentrate. Had she missed one of Monika's clues? They had to focus on Angelo, to restore his memory.

Adrielle felt a pang of urgency and turned to him. "Angelo, do you remember why we didn't get married? Why I married Haden instead?"

He met her gaze and, for a moment, saw the pain reflected there.

He shielded his eyes from her. "No. I never understood that. We *are*—were—in love, I thought. Then everything changed."

Adrielle felt the sting of betrayal she had caused him. She took his hands and pulled them to her chest.

"Angelo, this is really, really, important. Do you seriously not remember?" The pain in his eyes left her breathless.

Angelo shook his head.

"That's what I thought."

Adrielle turned back to inspect the wall. "Your memory isn't fully restored. I have a hunch this room is a conduit, much like the diamond in the scepter. We entered a joint memory tunnel and accessed some of your memories from there, by reliving some of our joint past. But there are pieces missing. One of these pathways must lead to your life's memories. I believe we can access the rest of them, if we find the right access point and follow it to the core."

Angelo turned to wall and stared at it a long time. "How do we know which pathway? With so many choices, we could easily get lost."

Even before earning the Traveler's Crest, Adrielle had followed her intuition. She felt that if her heart directed her, she'd locate the right opening.

She closed her eyes to absorb the energy from the diamond. A low hum, a force, was coming from it. She concentrated on it, and on Angelo's many attributes.

Soon a strange sensation overcame her—a force, an attraction pulling her. With her eyes shut, she took hesitant steps in the direction of the pull until she reached the point where the draw was the strongest.

"Angelo, I think it's here. Come see if you feel differently, once you put your hand through the barrier."

Angelo rushed over and stood very still. "You're right." He pressed his hands to his head. "Flashes of my past are passing through my mind by just standing close to the opening." He neared his hand to the wall.

"Stop." Adrielle grasped his wrist. "I'm not sure why, but my heart is pounding."

"Mine too." He turned to her. They held their gaze for a long moment.

"I think you need to go alone."

Angelo studied her expression. "Are you scared?"

"No. A little, maybe."

"Of being here alone?"

"No. Of what you may find. What you'll think of me afterward," Adrielle said.

He lifted her chin. "Adrielle, nothing will make me think differently of you. This is where you have to believe in yourself. Finding your voice as a leader is never easy. You've had some hard choices to make, but you shouldn't have to justify them to anyone. Least of all to me."

She swallowed around a lump in her throat. She couldn't be certain why she had the feeling they wouldn't see each another for a long while. The thought was irrational because they needed to get their answers and get out of the Time Vault. But she couldn't shake the feeling she was losing her best friend.

Angelo winked at her and before she could stop him, pushed his hand through the opening, and disappeared. The smell of earth and musk filled her lungs.

Chapter 30

Liz—Inside the Memory Tunnel—
Back in Time—Florence 1504

THE DREAM FELT so tangible. Francesco snuggled in beside her, his burly arms encircling her waist. He smelled like wine and sweat. He nibbled at her ear lobe and trailed soft kisses down her neck. Liz moaned, the warmth of his lips sending chills on her skin. *If only this were real.* I blew it. I really blew it.

Her heart felt heavy. At least she had this—memories of their love. Resigned to enjoy the thin remnants of sleep before tackling the problem of how to get back to the diamond, Liz willed her dream to continue.

Francesco's hands caressed her. He stroked her arms and traced small circles on her back.

"I've missed you so much," she murmured.

His body crushed down onto her torso. He pressed his lips to hers and slid his tongue hungrily into her mouth.

"Ooof. I can't breathe." She inhaled a strong combination of Jasmine and Rose water, Francesco's favorite perfume and cracked her eyes open.

"Francesco?" She squinted. His almond chocolate eyes stared back at her. She struggled to push him off her chest, but he was at least twice her size.

Francesco slid off her grudgingly but remained close.

Liz rubbed her eyes with the heels of her hand. "I thought I was dreaming." She took a long look at him. "You've grown a beard." She touched his face lightly. It was prickly. Tears flooded onto her cheeks. Embarrassed, she swiped them away.

Francesco laughed a throaty laugh. "Si bella, I am here." He turned onto one side. "Do not be shy with me." He smiled and stroked his beard with one hand. He was studying her closely.

Liz reached for her glasses and slipped them on.

Francesco pulled the covers away and slid his eyes down her body. It made her feel uncomfortable. She wasn't used to being ogled. She scrunched her knees up.

Francesco shook his head. "Bella mia . . . you are too skinny. You must eat."

"Eat? How can I, when you were so angry? You told me to leave."

What was happening? Did he want her to stay?

He turned away. "You were quite a sight yesterday." Liz could see he was wrestling with his emotions. "I was surprised to see you, that is all. You deserted me."

"I didn't. I tried to explain—"

"You abandoned me." His eyes flashed with emotion. "I looked everywhere for you, but you vanished. I had resolved to live alone. Like a monk, Lisa."

Liz didn't know what to say.

"And then you come back . . . and I have to ask what I have been asking myself since you left." He leaned in to her and whispered, "*Why* Lisa? Why did you leave me?"

Liz was relieved he wasn't angry anymore, just hurt. Deeply hurt. She swallowed hard. "I live in a faraway place. Years from now. I . . . I live in the future—"

"Nonsense," he said, raising his voice.

She couldn't blame him for getting agitated.

He seemed to be mulling something over. Liz wasn't sure if she should get out of bed and get dressed or stay. She liked having him close, Feeling the warmth of his body. His large kind eyes never left hers as he took her hand in his and kissed it softly.

"This can be your home too. I've missed you." His eyes bore deeply into hers.

"Me too," she whispered. "That's why I came back."

Francesco enveloped her in his arms. He crushed his lips to hers, and Liz lost herself in that kiss.

"Ahem."

Startled, Liz opened her eyes. Piero stood at the side of the bed. Liz felt her skin reddening. She pulled on her nightgown to cover her chest.

Keeping his eyes averted from her, he said, "Master, I have the ladies waiting."

"Good, good," Francesco said, a thrill of excitement laced in his voice. He turned to Liz and gave her an assessing gaze. "Give us a minute and send them in."

Piero nodded and bowed his way out of the room.

Liz gave Francesco a questioning look.

"Lisa, I love you. And you say you love me. There is no reason for us to be apart. Will you marry me, Bella?"

"Yes." Liz wasn't sure how she was going to swing it, but she was going to try.

She looked up at a timid knock on the door.

A corner of Francesco's mouth quirked into a smirk. He squeezed her hands in his. "I present you, your wedding gift."

On cue, two young girls with long braided hair waltzed in, carrying two gilded boxes. They approached Liz's side of the bed.

The first girl laid a box down on her lap.

The box was light, covered in hand-tooled leather with golden daisies inlaid along the edges. A decorative gold plate had her name engraved. *"Lisa."* She glanced at Francesco. He smiled and urged her to open it. Liz lifted the lid.

She inhaled a quick breath and clasped her hand to her mouth.

Inside, an exquisite diamond-encrusted necklace lay on a bed of deep blue velvet. She turned to Francesco. "It's the most beautiful thing I've ever seen."

He lifted it out of the box and moved her long mane of hair to one side, then clasped the necklace around her neck.

Liz felt the coolness of the smooth diamonds. The girl who'd brought it, seemed to be struggling to remain calm and a faint moan escaped her as she pulled out a small silver mirror from her pocket and held it up for Liz to see. Liz exchanged a look with her and peered in the mirror.

Liz gasped. She'd never seen anything as lovely. She was struck by how the diamonds sparkled in the dawn light.

The second girl approached and laid the second box down on her lap. This box seemed to be made of white gold, with yellow golden leaves enhancing the edges.

Liz was afraid to open it. She turned to Francesco and searched his eyes. He looked like he was going to burst. He nudged her on.

She lifted the lid with shaking fingers. Inside was a braided diamond bracelet matching the choker. She couldn't speak through sudden tears. She was mesmerized by the sparkle of the diamonds. "It is too beautiful."

"Nothing is too beautiful for you," he said, clasping it onto her wrist. He broke into a wide grin and appeared extremely pleased she liked her gift. He clapped his hands loudly.

The door swung open, and Liz realized it was a signal for a third girl to enter the room. A white silk dress with an ornate brocade skirt was draped in her arms.

Liz turned to him in surprise.

"Your wedding dress," he said.

The girl laid it on Liz's lap. From the corner of her eyes Liz saw the girls clasp their hands and watch her closely for a reaction.

Liz ran her fingers on the smooth flowy fabric. It was beautiful, but . . . it looked five sizes too large. She raised her eyes to Francesco and before she had a chance to thank him, he jumped off the bed.

"We must hurry, Lisa, our coach leaves soon."

"Uh . . . where are we going?"

"To Roma. To get married."

"Now?" Liz turned to see the girls' reactions. They squealed with excitement.

A wedding. She said yes.

"Yes, my Bella Lisa. The pope awaits."

Pope? Married? This was happening so fast. How could she get married without Dave?

Chapter 31

Dave, Coco, and Astraia—
Inside the Memory Tunnel—
Back in Time—Florence 1504

MORNING COULDN'T COME soon enough for Dave. He tossed from side to side and punched his pillow. He could hear Coco's rhythmic breaths beside him and felt a stab of jealousy. He'd kept his knees pulled tight against his chest to avoid the bottom of the bed. Every little noise woke him up. And being that the house was old, the walls creaked every time the wind blew.

The instant a small triangle of light shone through the window onto his face, he opened his eyes.

He massaged the lower part of his back with his knuckles and stretched his body from the waist up. He gently nudged Coco. "It's morning."

Coco didn't respond. She slept sounder than anyone he'd ever known.

"Get up. We need to find Liz today. Let's find something to eat and get going."

"Five minutes," she groaned, pulling the covers over her face.

Dave rolled off the bed, the wood creaking and clattering. Before setting his feet down, he checked the floor for pests. Rats, mice, bats—anything that was squirmy. He detested them.

He ticked off lists to leave as little a footprint in this timeline as possible. *How to find Francesco's house*—ask around town. *How not to get noticed . . .*

His looked at his clothes. Jeans and a pink shirt were too modern. Besides, jeans weren't invented until 1873 when Levis Strauss—

"We need clothes," he blurted. "To blend in."

Coco moaned. "Michelangelo had a slight build, not too tall."

"Ok. I'm going upstairs to check."

He went up to Michelangelo's room. A wave of melancholy hit him. They'd spent so much time in this home. He missed the others. He felt a jolt of relief Astraia was nowhere in sight and opened the heavy wooden doors to the large armoire.

Amazingly, for such an important artist, Michelangelo didn't own many clothes. The armoire was full of sketches and paints and other art related items. What little clothes he did find were more along the lines of work attire. He rifled through them, feeling a little obtrusive. Paint splattered linen pants and shirts. Everything looked very used except for one linen shirt—more of a sack really—and a pair of dark linen pants with a cinch waist.

Maybe it was silly, but he didn't want to help himself to any of Michelangelo's clothes. He slipped on the dark linen pants and cinched in the waist, then folded his jeans and shirt and laid them on the bottom of the armoire where they could be seen. If he didn't get back after finding Liz, Michelangelo would know they'd come back from the future.

He checked the two bottom drawers and found a linen nightgown for Coco. It was just long enough to be considered a dress, if she belted it in. There had to have something. Anything. *The leather cord binding a stack of sketches.*

He untied the leather cord, re-stacked the sketches neatly, and laid them back where he'd found them. Coco could use the cord for her belt.

Astraia would have to fend for herself. Maybe she'd turned herself into a bird. He didn't want to admit he really didn't like her. And now they were stuck in the past without Adrielle to mediate.

Holy—what if she'd left them? Where *was* Astraia? He hadn't exactly been trying to be quiet, and he hadn't seen her since the night before. Hadn't she said she was sleeping in the main bedroom? The bed was made up. He grabbed the nightgown and cord and closed the armoire.

By the time he reached the guest room, Coco was already downstairs. He could hear her clanging dishes in the kitchen. Dave straightened the linens on the bed and hurried down.

Coco was in the pantry, slicing pieces of pancetta from a dangling salt-cured ham and placing them onto a plate. "Have you seen Astraia?"

"She's out back. Something about checking the area," Coco said.

"I really hope she's not a problem." Dave wrung his hands. "I don't trust her."

Coco wiped her hands on her apron and sighed. She gave him a stern look. "It's not like we have a choice. Give her a chance, Dave. We have the same goal. To find Liz and get outta here."

He glanced down at the plate of heaping food. "Don't forget we need to leave as little a footprint as possible." He held up a finger and wagged it. "And . . . and I still worry about—"

"What?" Astraia stood watching them. She had an armful of oranges from the garden in an apron.

Coco glanced up. "Oh, good. You found the orange tree. At least we'll have something more than cured ham for breakfast."

Dave cringed. He hoped Astraia hadn't heard everything. "Here. I got you some clothes." He tossed the nightgown and the leather cord to Coco. "We'll blend in better." He turned to see what Astraia was wearing. She had some of Michelangelo's paint-splattered clothes on. "Good, you found something to wear too."

"They were outside on the clothesline. Good thing it stopped raining," she said and handed Dave an orange. "Thought you might like one."

"Thanks." Dave took the orange and peeled it. "Look, I don't mean to be—"

"A pain in the ass?" Astraia chuckled. "Sure you do. You can't help yourself, can you."

Dave decided to ignore her. It wasn't the first time someone thought he was obsessive compulsive. And it wouldn't be the last.

They finished breakfast, and Coco washed the dishes and stacked them on the shelf where she'd found them. They pushed the chairs in under the table and cast a quick look around. Everything looked like they'd found it.

"What are we doing about the window?" Coco asked.

Dave had been thinking about that too. "It'll have to stay that way, for now. I'm sure Michelangelo will have it replaced. At least the rain won't get in."

Astraia gave Dave the hard stare. "So, what is the plan?"

"Let's go into town and ask if anyone's seen Liz. Or if they know where Francesco lives. I'll check upstairs one more time, then we'll go. Everything has to be exactly the way we found it."

Astraia turned to Coco. "He's a little compulsive, isn't he."

Coco winked at Dave. "Yes. I'd say quirky. But quirky is good."

WHEN DAVE WAS satisfied everything was tidy in the guest room, he went back into Michelangelo's room for one last look. At first glance everything looked right. There were stacks of drawings on a small round table at the side of his bed. Dave walked to it and leafed through the top few. He paused and studied the sketch of a man's torso. Excitement rifled through him. Michelangelo was truly a masterful artist.

He wondered if any of these drawings had survived the centuries. One of these sketches alone could bring him a large fortune. As tempted as he was, he left them the way he found them and paced back to the armoire. He peered inside.

Everything's good. Except the drawer he'd found Coco's dress in wasn't properly closed. He tried pushing it in, but it was wedged. Painting supplies were crammed in so tightly, the drawer wasn't sliding properly. Had he done it when he'd shuffled through? Dave shifted the paints. *Still jammed.* If he could open it all the way, he might be able to align the drawer back into the track.

Dave pulled and yanked until finally the drawer slid open. Drawings were scrunched and crinkled at the back of the drawer. *Jeez.* Had he done that rifling for Coco's outfit? He took the sketches out carefully and assessed the damage.

My god, they were masterpieces, all of them.

Wrinkled, but not torn. He smoothed them out and tapped them like a ream of paper.

"Ahrgggg." Dave let out a high-pitched scream. There it was. The thing jamming the drawer.

Astraia arrived first. Then Coco, clipping at her heels.

"What is *that* doing here?" Astraia screeched, rushing to his side.

"Oh my God." Coco clasped her hands to her mouth.

Dave couldn't breathe. He crouched onto his knees as he held the *Book of Feathers*.

"It was here when I pulled out the drawer."

"Is that real?" Coco said.

Dave exchanged a look with her. Of course it was. The better question was: What was it doing here? Hidden in Michelangelo's armoire?

Chapter 32

Dave, Coco, and Astraia–
Inside the Memory Tunnel–
Back in Time–Florence 1504

"IS IT?" ASTRAIA'S voice had that *"don't give me any bullshit"* tone with an attached warning.

Dave cringed. He dropped his gaze to break eye contact from Astraia's hard stare. What horrific tortures was Astraia was capable of? Especially if she had something to do with Arnadella being perpetually perched on Monika's shoulder.

Dave rubbed the book's hand-tooled binding. He really didn't want her to see the book. Adrielle warned them all: in the wrong hands, it could endanger everyone. And Adrielle wasn't here to protect them.

His gaze drifted to his torso. His scrawny one-hundred-and-forty-five-pound frame was no match for Astraia's superhuman powers. If she wanted to take it, she'd flatten him like a fly.

"What. Is. It. Doing. Here?" Astraia said, her voice low, her gaze intense. "If it's the real deal, the *Book of Feathers,* which I can tell by your pathetic response it is, why is it here? Unguarded? I don't have to tell you if it gets in the wrong hands, we're screwed!"

"Really?" Dave was surprised his voice came out a squeak.

Astraia narrowed her eyes. "What do you mean—*really?"* She mimicked Dave's high-pitched tone.

"We—on the same side," she said, Queen Latifa-ish-ly. She planted her hands on her hips. "Remember?"

Dave swallowed. "Yep. That's the plan." He flinched at a cold hand clamped down on the scruff of his neck. He scrunched his eyes and squealed like a pig.

"Put it back where you found it and let's go," Coco said.

"Oh it's—you," he exhaled. He twisted his neck to relieve tension.

Coco snickered. "Really, Dave. You're such a scaredy-cat."

Dave brushed himself off. He felt stupid. "It's this place. The rat."

"Uh-huh," Astraia said, a wry look of satisfaction on her face.

"If Michelangelo has the book stashed here, Adrielle must have brought it to him," Coco said. "She must have thought it was safer here. We'll ask her when we get back. *If* we ever get back."

"There's that," Dave said, placing the book carefully into the drawer. They still hadn't figured out how they were getting back to the diamond center. He tried to close the drawer, but it was jammed again.

"Let me," Astraia said, shoving Dave to one side. She jiggled the drawer, and it glided smoothly in.

Dave felt his face burn red.

"C'mon." Coco led the way out. "we'd better get a move on it."

They left Michelangelo's house secured and walked the half mile to the market district. Things were bustling in town, and thanks to Michelangelo's clothes, they blended in with the locals.

ASTRAIA TRANSFORMED INTO her natural bird form and soared into the sky. She preferred her bird body to the adapted human shape. As a bird, she felt lithe and free and could travel at great speeds. She could also cover more area and detect oncoming danger.

Far below, the city of Florence stretched for miles. Astraia's raptor vision scrutinized anything that might be out of place. It worried her the *Book of Feathers* was unguarded, but she saw nothing to indicate a red flag. To her, Florence appeared to be business as usual.

DAVE AND COCO wove through the narrow, cobbled streets to the market area.

Dave marveled at the hub of activity. A visual and olfactory feast, dozens of carts were loaded with silks and other goods for sale. Spices and vegetables of every kind were being traded. The smell of cooking permeated everything. Merchants peddled their goods, customers purchased them, and everyday life continued. All, with no sign of Liz. He glanced at Coco, who was scrutinizing countless faces, and wondered if Liz was okay.

After what felt like hours, they stopped in front of a bakery store. Dave gazed longingly in the window. "Italian pastries are the best. My stomach's growling just looking at them."

"Let's treat ourselves," Coco said, one foot already in the door.

Dave tugged at her linen dress. "We don't have any money. Remember? At least in a currency they'd accept."

Coco held out a little cloth sac and shook it. A look a satisfaction gleamed in her eyes.

"Where did you get that?"

She laughed. "Michelangelo's. Salai showed me where he keeps spare change in the pantry. I thought it might come in handy."

Dave hesitated. Would this alter the past?

"I know what you're thinking. But this won't change anything more than breaking into his house."

Dave nodded in approval, and they walked into the bakery.

The line inside wasn't very long. Two women ahead of them chatted up a storm. And another at the counter couldn't decide what she wanted.

Aside from the prosciutto hanging in Michelangelo's storeroom and the oranges, they hadn't eaten much, so the smell of freshly baked goods was making Dave ravenous. They settled in line to the cadence of the foreign language behind the two gossipy women, while the front customer placed her order.

Coco pointed, "Oooh, look at those lemon tarts." She was already pulling out coins. She beamed radiantly at him. "Should we get some for Astraia?"

"That would be a firm no. By now, I'm sure she's had her fill of worms and birdseed."

Coco giggled.

Somewhere between lemon tarts and the women's idle chit-chat, Dave heard the name Francesco del Giocondo.

He jabbed Coco. "Listen." There it was again—Francesco del Giocondo. And then came Lisa. He felt a crazed kind of happiness.

Apparently, there was a buzz around town: Lisa, the woman who'd vanished, who'd left Francesco del Giocondo shattered with nothing but an unfinished portrait, reappeared suddenly. The city was ablaze with plans of a wedding and divided into two camps. Those crushed that Francesco was off the market and those relieved.

"Jackpot!" Dave cried. He gave Coco a hard squeeze and sent her coins flying. All they needed now were directions and a ride.

Chapter 33

Adrielle–Inside the Time Vault

ANGELO'S LEAP INTO the memory tunnel siphoned off all sound out along with a surprising ache of loneliness. Adrielle grabbed at her stomach. This was insane. Why was she so distraught? She hadn't realized having Angelo around had become such a great source of comfort.

She braced her hands on her knees. It was all her fault. Her duty was to stop time travel and here she was. Complicating everything.

She shook her head. It was futile to think about the unexpected feelings revisiting Achaea had re-awakened. Her role as the head traveler came first. The future of the world depended on it. On her.

If her father hadn't been so blinded by his love for her mother, perhaps he'd still be alive. Maybe he would have seen the anarchy under his own roof.

So here she was, in a place she didn't know existed, needing to conjure up a plan and to unlock the mystery of the soldier clones.

Why Scarlett? Why would Domenikos bring her, of all people, inside the Time Vault? And how did he do it while imprisoned?

Obviously, but not surprisingly, he'd found a way around his bondage. It was what he did best—bend the rules to benefit himself. *But how?*

The darkness was stifling along with a dank and musty smell. She swept her hair off her forehead and thought of Liz. Liz always said there were clues. She felt an ache of homesickness and a wave of strength from her friends.

Adrielle turned away from the wall, determined to find clues. She glanced at the creepy, golden bird. The beak savagely clutched onto the only glimmer of light in the room.

Adrielle stepped cautiously toward it, to study the diamond.

The light within the gem's core seemed to have gone dormant, leaving the room bleaker. She shuddered. Musky smells were amplified in the grim surroundings. It reminded her of the forbidden caves of her youth. In Achaea.

She'd always been drawn to the north end of the shoreline. Rugged and steep, the cliff soared skyward like an appendage taunting to be mastered. When she'd mentioned she was drawn to it, a darkness crossed over her father's eyes. He'd forbidden her to go there. But she'd disobeyed.

One night when the moon was large and low to the ground, and its rays so bright she couldn't sleep, she crept out of her room. Somehow, she managed to leave the house complex without anyone noticing. She ran the entire way to the beach, a cool breeze slapping her cheeks. Her feet pounded the ground, moist sand squished between her toes. The tall pillar rocks of the forbidden cliffs beckoned to her, the sound of the tide ebbing out to sea enticed her.

She stopped at the foot of the bedrock, salt spray covering her skin. She climbed the sheer, vertical rock face. Her fingers and toes sought crevices to provide secure footing. She thrust herself upward, not daring to look down or stop until she reached a landing.

At the top she hauled herself over the edge. She lay on the cold flat stone heaving for breath.

She stood up and looked onto the ocean as it blended with the sky into a seamless canvas. The moon shimmered onto rippling wave caps. She'd never seen anything so beautiful. Behind her, musky cool air seeped out of a deep cavity. Perhaps to another this cave would be frightening, but to Adrielle it offered refuge. A sanctuary from the chaotic world.

Adrielle lay back down and listened to the sounds of the ocean until the first streak of sunlight exploded across the horizon. Out of nowhere a murmuration burst over the low-hanging moon. The birds swept in a tide over Adrielle, their deafening shrieks assaulting her. They disappeared into the depths deep within the rock, pulling at something inside her.

Adrielle opened her eyes. She pressed her hands to her head. The stillness inside the time vault was playing with her mind. The memory seemed so real it almost fooled her.

The room was silent, but she knew it wouldn't stay that way for long. She had learned from that day long ago, in the forbidden cave, about the stillness before a storm. She expected a lone squeak to explode into a chorus of shrill screams.

She couldn't confer with Coco and her friends. She was on her own She crept toward the chamber to see what, if anything, was going on. The room was empty now. Only an empty stage remained. No mirror. No Scarlett. No clones. Nothing.

Where had they gone?

She didn't see any exits or entry points except for the one leading to the inner chamber with the golden bird. And yet, the room had been full of soldier clones.

When they'd pushed through the electric field from the rip, there had been an opening flanked with two of Brix's clones. Where was that door now? How could it have disappeared when it was thick and solid and real? Was the door only visible when it was open? Is that why Monika warned they could get trapped inside?

Imagining a rolling boulder and encroaching walls like an *Indiana Jones* movie, Adrielle hurried back to the central alcove.

The diamond was perched like a cut of ice, dormant and harmless. But ice wasn't harmless. Sharp shards could make it a weapon. DNA millions of years old was stored in blocks of ice. The most dangerous part of a glacier was the unseen part and could become deadly without notice.

Adrielle moved closer. The cuts were crude. Raw. What if this diamond possessed unimaginable powers—a heart waiting to beat? How far could its tentacles reach?

Why was it encased here? In the most secretive of prisons? Locked away in a vault with a door so thick it was impenetrable?

Adrielle studied the wall, which was disguised as a solid surface, but held folds of memory within its skin.

The scepter diamond was a prison and a conduit with millions of memory tunnels hidden within its walls. So . . . it had escape and access tunnels. Somewhere, there had to be a map of the millions, perhaps billions, of circuits.

If only Monika's speech wasn't laced with so much drama. It was exhausting deciphering everything she said. Every word in code.

She had a hunch the diamond clutched in the bird's beak was working like a mini-scepter. *Was this possible?* Could this raw gem have been part of the scepter diamond? Clawed from the mother diamond by a savage such as Domenikos?

If so, it could possess the same properties.

Domenikos had cloned his best soldiers, Vladik and Brix. Maybe even tried to implant the stolen memories into them to make the clones superior to the original. With this capability, Domenikos could create an army to subjugate mortals and enforce his rules. But why use stolen memories when memories were the very component that made up an identity? That gave mortals their humanity?

If the clone minds were blank when Domenikos had created them, he'd need to implant or program a base of knowledge deep enough for them to become functional. And who better to use than humans. Modern day humans, with an entire knowledge of history.

Given the news reports on the mass memory lapses, he'd targeted Floridians. He could have accessed their memory banks within the walls of the Time Vault.

This was starting to make sense. She touched her crest on her back. If only she had her powers back, she'd know the truth. The black feather would confirm. She sighed.

Monika said *all* memories were stored *here*, inside the Time Vault. So, everything was accessible from here, the core memory data location. She'd warned if memories were destroyed, or altered, or not processed correctly, it would be as though they'd never existed.

Adrielle was horrified at the implications. History would be changed forever. The fallout was cataclysmic.

Somewhere within this Time Vault was the key to where Domenikos was hiding. She needed to find out if this was his master scheme to conquer the world.

Adrielle approached the wall. She pressed her face to the surface and studied every detail. These memory tunnels shifted exactly like the tunnels lining the walls inside the scepter diamond.

Adrielle backed away from the wall. She retraced her steps to the memory tunnel Angelo disappeared through and placed both hands on the surface opening. She shifted her perspective a few degrees, enough to create a slight deviation from where Angelo had gone. She concentrated on where his path led.

Murky bits of information sprang and swam inside her head. She focused on them until they became organized. And finally, she saw him. Angelo. The same majestic supreme Achaean specimen he once was.

But was this her Angelo? He looked older. Much older. He had greying on his temples and crinkles at the corners of his eyes. If she had to guess, she'd say he was about her father's age. Forty-five? That meant this must be hundreds of years into the future, because Achaeans lived thousands of years and aged extremely slowly.

What was going on? What in the frigging world was happening?

Adrielle concentrated on blocking out everything but this answer. She singled out an Instagram feed on an electronic device. A scandalous post, about the famous movie actress, Scarlett, and her new beau, Angelo.

What?

Social media was filled with images of Scarlett and Angelo. Adrielle snapped her hands away from the wall. She felt sick.

Was this the future? Or a possible pathway?

An electric current buzzed through her veins and sent her flying several feet back. A sharp pain shot through her left hip as she hit the ground. Someone grabbed her hair, yanked it back, and slammed her head against the cold hard floor.

Chapter 34

Liz–Inside the Memory Tunnel– Back in Time–Florence 1504

THE CARRIAGE WAS waiting downstairs. Dazed, Liz handed the wedding dress to the third maiden, fully expecting her to leave, but the girl remained, watching her.

Liz straightened the bed, her hands trembling. The morning's turn of events was surprising, and she couldn't stop thinking of Francesco's rejection. She'd hated seeing him so upset.

She tucked the velvet bedspread and fluffed the pillows, peeking at her wrist every few seconds. Jewels? A princess bed? *Jeez, was this for real?* She felt like a Kardashian.

She placed the two gift boxes on the night table and studied the bracelet on her wrist. The slightest movement caught light in the diamond facets. Dave and Coco would flip when they saw it.

It struck her how opulent Francesco was. She'd often wondered what it would feel like, not to worry about gas money.

Liz rubbed her still sore ankle, then hobbled to her clothes on the chair by the fireplace and picked up her top and pants. The fire had dried them nicely.

She glanced at the fireplace. With its gigantic firebox and ornate stone surround, it looked like something out of an old castle. All that remained of the fire was a pile of ashes and the smell of wood smoke.

She thought about Kate and Veda. Adrielle said Domenikos showed her and Coco a box of ashes, and said it was them. Imagine . . . burned to ashes. Could it be true? Could you trust anything a monster said?

She missed having them around. Veda, with her constant flow of gossip. And Kate—funny and for lack of a better word, ditzy. She was the froth in a Cappuccino. The giggle at the end of a cry. Liz fought back a surge of tears. How could they be gone?

Kate's grandma had told her once, you only live as long as the last person who remembers you. Liz placed her hand on her chest and inhaled a quick breath. There was a hollow ache inside her. She was the keeper of their memories now. Imagine . . . two lives erased in a blink.

The stories Kate told her about her grandmother were so detailed and engaging, she'd adopted the woman as her own grandma. She'd never known her own grandmother. Only now, after seeing what the loss of a memory had done to Angelo, did she truly understand the importance of safeguarding recollections.

Losing his memory had erased who Angelo was. Jumping jelly beans. He didn't even know what he liked. Or who he knew. It deleted his entire history and turned him into a shell.

Liz caught a reflection of the morning sun on her bracelet. It was beautiful, but in light of all this, all the diamonds in the world didn't mean much. They were glitzy, sure, but distractions from what really mattered.

She glanced around the room. What was all this opulence worth without friends? Without loved ones to share a life with?

She brushed her fingers over the bezel set stones on the diamond choker. Francesco had been more than generous. But she loved Francesco for more than his money. He was sensitive and fun. She'd missed him so much, in modern day Florida. She was lucky to have someone love her for who she truly was.

But was she ready to get married? Truth was no. Obviously, Francesco was. Could she postpone the wedding? Not likely. He'd think she was doing the same thing as the last time she promised to marry him.

They'd never discussed living arrangements. How would they compromise when she lived in Florida, and he lived here?

When she'd confided to Dave how much she missed Francesco, he'd been adamant it wasn't meant to be. That if life were different, which it wasn't, she'd be living in the Renaissance times with Francesco. But things didn't turn out that way. She had to squelch the idea pronto. Her life was in modern day Florida.

But here she was. When all she'd been doing to change her life was twirl and dream. Twirl . . . and dream. Poof! She was with Francesco. Maybe the universe had other plans. Maybe this was her destiny.

Her gaze drifted to her exquisite bracelet. She'd never imagined owning anything this ritzy. She sighed a long heavy sigh. She didn't want to ever take the jewelry off. She was meant to wear it. It made her feel pretty. And it commemorated the moment, a chance to live her life with Francesco. Well . . . that was thrilling. The stuff of dreams.

She glanced at the girl in the room, still holding the wedding dress in her arms and watching her thoughtfully. Why didn't she leave?

"Are you okay?" Liz asked. The girl smiled shyly. She showed no sign of leaving anytime soon. So, Liz yanked her nightgown over her head to get dressed.

The girl rushed to her side. "Let me help."

"No."

"But I'm your handmaiden. Your dresser."

"Dresser?" Liz giggled. She tossed her nighty onto the chair and pulled on her shrunken t-shirt. "That's ridiculous. I've been dressing myself since I was three."

"But you are the new Donna." The girl unfolded the wedding dress. "Dressing you is part of my job. To make you look presentable at all times. You are going to be Francesco Del Giocondo's wife. The position has to be upheld at all costs."

Wowsers. Was this girl for real?

"That shirt—it's not—" She pressed her lips primly together, and her gaze drifted to Liz's pierced navel. A sour-faced-pucker replaced her smile.

Liz covered her belly. If she'd known she was coming here, she would have dressed appropriately.

The girls held the dress for Liz to step into. As expected, it was huge. The waist twice her size.

"I'll look ridiculous in this," Liz said, looking up at the girl. She pinched in the sides. There were at least six inches to be taken in.

"We'll use this silk sash until we can take it in," the girl said, wrapping it around Liz's waist. She handed Liz the mirror.

Liz stared at her reflection. She clasped her hands to her mouth. She looked like a bride. Her rush of tears surprised her. Maybe she was destined to be Francesco's wife, though she wasn't sure how it would work.

She glanced at the girl. "Uh . . . shouldn't I wear something else for the ride? It must be a long way to Rome without a car."

"Car?"

"Never mind. Do you have anything else I can wear? I don't want to dirty the dress."

The girl shook her head.

"I'll wear my own clothes." Without waiting for an answer, Liz slipped the dress off and put on her cargo pants and t-shirt. She thought about what everyone would say, if she was already married when she got back to the diamond center. If she figured out how to get back there, that was.

She hoped Adrielle was successful in restoring Angelo's memory and in protecting the Time Vault.

A heavy knock sounded on the door. It swung open without a pause. Piero stood very erect in the doorway, stone-faced. Liz hadn't remembered him so somber. Perhaps something had happened since she'd left.

"The master is waiting," he said.

"I'm coming," Liz grumbled. She leaned onto the young girl for support and wobbled out of the room on her twisted ankle.

Chapter 35

Dave, Coco, and Astraia—
Inside the Memory Tunnel—
Back to Florence 1504

"SCUSI. COULD I trouble you for directions to Francesco Del Giocondo's home?" Dave said, in choppy Italian.

"Home?" The women laughed and proceeded to give him directions.

Coco returned from paying for the pastries and handed Dave his pastry.

"It's not too far, Coco," Dave said.

"Great. Let's go." They headed for the door.

The road to Francesco's house was easy to follow, but there were disjointed turns that came up abruptly. They kept an eye out for the twists in the road and trudged along.

The women said Francesco lived not too far away, but they'd laughed when Dave called it a home, and this detail was weighing heavily on his mind.

"Casa? Casita? I don't get it. I'm sure that's how you say home in Italian."

Coco grabbed his arm and shot him a look. "Stop."

He turned to Coco, confused.

"You're doing it again," she said.

Dave raised his eyebrows. "It?"

"Over analyzing. And it's driving me craaaaazzzzzy. So, stop."

Dave cleared his throat. "Sorry. Don't mean to be rude."

"It's not that," Coco said, looking annoyed.

Dave stuffed the last bit of pastry into his mouth and coughed a couple of times. He held up his forefinger. "Stuck. A piece of almond is . . ." He couldn't stop the coughing fit.

Coco wrapped her arms around his chest and pounded hard under his sternum. After coughing a few more times, Dave wriggled out of her grasp.

"What are you doing?" he said.

"Saving you."

"I wasn't choking, just kinda—" He gestured to his throat. "It was in my larynx. I'm fine now. For the record, I don't need saving."

"You sure about that?" Coco held her arms up in surrender, but her eyes were pinned on something in the distance.

Dave raised his chin to protest and saw the barrel of a shotgun aimed straight at them, a farmer wearing overalls and gumboots at the end of it. The farmer cocked the gun.

Chapter 36

Adrielle—Inside the Time Vault

ADRIELLE SAW PINPOINTS of light before her vision cleared. She ran her tongue over her teeth and tasted the salty metallic taste of blood. She was relieved her teeth were all there. Under the circumstances, a dentist would be hard to come by.

The inside of her cheek hurt. She'd bitten it when the assailant hit her face. She rubbed the inside of her cheek with her tongue and rolled onto her back to assess the damage. Her tailbone hurt, but her limbs felt okay. Overall, she felt like she'd been run over by a Mac truck.

As her vision cleared, she saw a face staring back at her. She blinked. Brix. He was inches away. She couldn't tell if he was the real deal, or a clone.

"What are you doing here?" he asked.

Adrielle struggled to sit up. A sharp pain bit her side. She winced and placed her hand on it. "I could ask you the same thing."

She glanced down. No blood, but he'd jabbed her with something. *A club?* Hopefully her ribs weren't broken.

"Aren't you supposed to be dead?" she asked, scrambling for her next move.

"You wish. How did you get in here?" he barked. An angry scowl was fixed on his face.

"Guess the same way you did." She avoided his eyes. If she could stall him, she might be able to see where she was and make a run for it.

The golden bird and diamond were in the center of the room. *Good.* She was still in the Time Vault.

Brix, Brix's clone—or whatever he was—reached out to grab her. She swiped away his arm, rolled away from him, and spun to her feet. He hissed.

"Thank you, Lizzie bear," she mumbled, pleased with herself. Liz's daily wrestling training sessions were paying off.

Adrielle backed away from Brix. She shifted her weight from foot to foot and spread her arms for additional balance. If he came at her again, she'd be ready.

A blinking red light flashed on his wrist. Brix's attention went to it. *An alarm?* It looked like a Fitbit flex band. He started fiddling with it. *Was he calling for reinforcements? Summoning soldier clones? Or worse, Domenikos?*

She couldn't face him yet. Not in her condition. She moved a fraction to her right.

Brix raised his eyes. He seemed appeased she was still there and dropped his gaze.

She slid to her right a bit more. By her estimation, the tunnel Angelo went through should be right behind her. If Brix lunged at her, she'd spin around and dive into the wall. Zip down the tunnel and find Angelo.

A quiet rumble started in the distance. A drum? No. A hundred soldiers heading her way. *Damn.* She was out of time. Her heart pounded in her chest.

She saw the soldiers' shiny boots. They were coming out of the wall!

In seconds there were at least fifty of them. More kept coming. Terror clogged her throat. She spun and leapt into the tunnel.

She tumbled into the dark. Tumbling. Tumbling downward.

Chapter 37

Liz–Inside the Memory Tunnel– Back in Time–Florence 1504

THE HANDMAIDEN LED Liz outside through the side entry. Three handsome horses with gleaming coats were harnessed and ready to pull an elaborate wood carriage with a private box seat.

The carriage was something out a Jane Austen movie, with a high bench in the front for a coachman. The seat was currently empty, with packages neatly fastened on, in preparation for their journey.

Liz recognized the box containing her wedding dress. The box had a tiny silver leaf design around all the edges.

She was Cinderella, traipsing off to marry the prince. She giggled at the thought, until she saw Antonio, Francesco's main steward approaching from the yard. He appeared to be in a sour mood. Or maybe he was just surly, she couldn't remember which. He reminded her of the Tasmanian devil. She squelched the impulse to giggle by sucking in her cheeks and waited as he neared. Would he remember her?

The day before, as she was crossing the green fields, she'd tried to envision what each of Francesco's staff looked like. And in anticipation of seeing Francesco, she'd wondered if more time had passed in Florence than it had in future Florida.

Seeing Francesco in person reminded her what damage an elusive memory could do when identifying a suspect. Or when prompted to describe someone strictly from memory. Francesco was much more handsome than she'd remembered. His eyes were more vibrant. His smile warmer. Granted, not at first . . . but once he'd calmed down.

Antonio's pudgy face and burly eyebrows were a sharp contradiction to Piero's sunken features and wrinkled skin. With nothing more than the vaguest tip of his head to acknowledge her, he headed straight for the horses without pausing.

Like everything else he owned, Francesco's horses were exquisite long-legged animals, large and strong, deep brown in color, with dark legs, mane, and tail.

Until the moment Antonio approached them with a leather whip in his hand, all three appeared to be asleep. His short, clipped steps alerted them, and their ears pricked back.

Fearing the horses might bear the brunt of his mood, Liz's stomach tightened as he neared the high seat of the carriage. Unsure what constituted animal cruelty in these backward times, she hoped he wasn't going to use the whip. She couldn't bear it. But the whip remained loosely held in his hand. The horses shifted slightly, steadying themselves against the movement of the carriage as he mounted the high seat.

Antonio was a heavy man with an ample belly. He shifted his weight uneasily, the carriage rocking as he pulled his coat tails out from under his bottom.

Once he was settled, he turned to the young girl at Liz's side and gave her a quick nod, motioning for them to enter the private box.

"Let's go," the girl said, gesturing for Liz to enter first.

"Isn't Francesco coming?" Liz said.

"He is already on his way. It is bad luck for the groom and the bride to travel together before they are married."

"Bad luck? Isn't this going to be a long trip?"

"Maybe. I'm not sure. It's my first journey to Rome." She placed her hand on Liz's back and waited for her to enter the carriage.

"Mine too . . . but . . . is it safe to go without Francesco? I mean, how fast does this thing go?"

The young girl shrugged. "I'm not sure."

"How many days travel?" Liz asked Antonio.

"The master said he'd see us in three days," he answered gruffly.

"Three days? On that?" Liz pointed.

"Yes. It is the best coach available. The latest model, the Hungarian coach. Master just bought it." The girl smiled.

Having excelled at math, Liz calculated that Rome was at least one hundred fifty miles away. Barring unforeseeable delays, covering say . . . thirty miles each day—if they travelled only daylight hours—meant at a three-day journey at best, a sizeable distance to cover by coach.

Liz was starting to feel panicky. Was it a good omen for Francesco to have left without saying goodbye? Her temper flared. Maybe this was the way they did things when women didn't amount to much, but this was certainly not the way she'd expected him to treat her.

"If we are going to make any distance at all, before the horses are thirsty, we must hurry," Antonio said over his shoulder.

"You first," the girl urged again, opening the door to the private box.

Liz sighed. "Here goes." Liz used the door handle to yank herself up. She caught the glimmer of the sun on her bracelet and paused mid-step. The sparkles were blinding.

The girl pressed a hand on the small of her back, and Liz eased onto the carriage step, left foot—the good one—first, then raised her right foot over the threshold without putting much weight on it.

Once inside, Liz rotated her body until she was close enough to the seat. She settled back and released a long exhale. She hadn't been sure if she'd be able to hoist herself up that distance, with her sore ankle.

The young girl followed her in, closed the door, and settled in beside her, their shoulders touching.

Through the front window, Liz saw Antonio pick up the reins. The horses' ears pricked forward. Antonio flicked the reins with his gloved hand, and all three horses leaned into the harness. They took the weight of the coach and eased into a rhythmic trot.

The constant movement of the box made Liz's body vibrate up and down, and caused her glasses to slide down her nose, making it hard to see. She pushed her glasses up.

"Comfortable," the girl said, smiling.

Obviously, the girl had never been in a Caddy. "What is your name?" Liz asked.

"Isabel."

"Isabel. How pretty," Liz said, making an effort to commit it to memory. *Convenient,* she thought. Isabel wasn't that different from her name. Elizabeth. Lisa. Isabel. She placed an arm around the girl and gave her a friendly squeeze.

Isabel a classic beauty, with large almond eyes, a full curvaceous mouth, and bronzed olive skin. "Isabel, how old are you?"

"Fifteen," Isabel said.

"Fifteen? So young to be traveling without your family."

Isabel flinched.

"Do you have a family?" Liz asked.

"My parents died of influenza. My sister too. I was the only survivor." Isabel's expression was filled with melancholy.

"How did you come to work at Francesco's home?"

"The master saw me at the mortuary, when I was making arrangements for the bodies. I had little means to support myself. He hired me soon after that." She placed her hands primly on her lap.

"How nice." Liz gave Isabel another squeeze. "Isabel, you and I are going to be great friends."

The young girl nodded, looking uncertain, and remained stiff. Liz removed her arm from the girl's shoulders and wondered if the girl was impassive because it was hard to get close after such a great loss. Or if it was because the help wasn't supposed to mingle with the boss' wife.

After what seemed like hours, with very little conversation, they stopped to water the horses at a small pond in the center of a clearing with a spectacular view. Wildflowers dotted the green field making it the loveliest scenery.

Isabel and Liz got off the coach box to stretch their limbs.

"I, uh, have to pee," Liz said shyly. Isabel helped Liz navigate to a private spot where she could relieve herself. She excused herself and waited a few steps away to help Liz get back inside the coach.

Liz wasn't the only one who'd needed to take a personal moment. Antonio was approaching them from behind a clump of shrubs.

"You should go too. It'll be a long while until we stop again," Liz told the girl and then hobbled to the horses to pet them.

Having been watered, the horses were calm. With their heads bent down, they were seemingly disinterested in their surroundings. Liz raised her hand slowly and waited for them to lift their heads, before petting their noses. Their skin was soft. She'd only gone horseback riding once, while on a vacation with her parents, and she'd been quite young, so she didn't remember much. Only that slow movements were the only way to go, or else they'd get spooked.

Antonio grunted it was time to go and checked the leather ties on the bags. When he was satisfied everything was secured, he climbed onto the high seat of the carriage and signaled for the horses to go.

The sun was high in the sky as they continued on their journey. Liz couldn't relax with the constant trot of the horses. She wished she had her handbag to pass the time. More specifically, Adrielle's journal. It was a good read and crammed with information. Every time she picked it up, she learned something new.

"Isabel, have you ever been in love?" Liz asked, hoping to make the dreaded trip pass more quickly.

Isabel shook her head no.

"Let me tell you of a great love story. One that spans hundreds and hundreds of years."

Isabel smiled. "Hundreds of years? Impossible."

"Is it?" Liz raised one eyebrow. She shifted in her seat and rubbed her sore tailbone. She was amazed Isabel could keep still for so long without complaining.

"I'm going to tell you the story, and you're not going to believe me. Not at first. But one day, maybe you'll get to meet them," Liz said.

Isabel looked at Liz with renewed interest.

"Once upon a time, there was a beautiful girl named Adrielle, who had hair as white as snow. And eyes the color of ice."

"Ice?" Isabel laughed. This is make believe?"

Liz shook her head. "No. They are very pale and beautiful. Her father, Aaron, was the leader of a great ancient society, the Achaeans. He betrothed his heir, Adrielle, to marry Haden, the head of his powerful army. Haden loved Adrielle with all his heart. But Adrielle, the beautiful maiden, had already fallen in love with another warrior named Angelo. Haden's brother."

"Don't tell me," Isabel said, excitement building in her voice. "She decides she loves Haden and marries him."

Liz frowned. "Why would you say that? It could go either way."

"No. When your father tells you to do something, you do it. Women don't have a choice."

"Is that so?" Liz frowned. "If that's what you believe, then I think you may be more than a little surprised. This story is about making your own choices. Life doesn't always turn out the way you believe it will. Thankfully, there are some exciting turns of events." Liz patted Isabel's knee.

"Ok, now listen closely. It doesn't get any better than this. A fair maiden. Two brothers in love with the same girl. An evil nemesis ready to destroy everything and everyone. This story will sweep you away into a world you never imagined."

Chapter 38

Adrielle–Inside the Time Vault

ADRIELLE LANDED AT the end of the memory tunnel in the dark on a deserted beach. The only light came from the bright moon high in the sky.

She stood up and rubbed her side. Brix, or the Brix clone had done a number on her. She worked through the pain that still throbbed, as she walked along the shoreline. She sank her toes into the wet sand and let her mind roam.

Monika had a power Adrielle didn't like. These tunnels, accessed through the scepter, could alter history.

Adrielle pressed her hand to her chest and felt the long chain. She cradled her chronometer in her palm and read the dials. They said she was two years into the future.

How was this even possible in a memory tunnel?

Adrielle angled her watch until the moonlight lit up the face dial. For a moment she believed the watch was malfunctioning. But the second hand clearly moved.

She studied the houses peeking over the dunes. They had bright tiled roofs, like the ones in Florida. Modern day Florida, not the homes in ancient Achaea, where Angelo had gone to restore his memory.

She raised her hand and felt between her shoulder blades. *The crest was back.* A flutter in her stomach surprised her.

She clutched the chronometer in one hand and concentrated, until the outside world disappeared, and her inner eye took over. She went to the inner space within her mind, where the black feather on her crest would always confirm the truth.

Am I really in modern day Florida, two years ahead in time from when I left the diamond center, to go down the memory tunnel with Angelo?

A strong impression burned in her chest. She was.

Is Angelo safe? Did he regain all of his memory?

Yes, on both counts.

Are Coco and my friends safe? Are they ok inside the diamond center?

A pang of unease spiked, but she found comfort knowing the powers in her crest were in full force.

What should I do? What can I do? Adrielle asked, over and over. But no answer came. She decided to go to her house, to see if everything was normal. She closed her eyes and visualized her bedroom—all she needed to be transported there.

She opened her eyes and was in her room. At least the future version of it.

Her bed and personal items were in place. Her guitar was in the corner on a stand, by her dresser. She wandered over to her bookshelves. Strangely, all her ancient Greek history books were gone. So were her books on the Holocaust. More alarming was the set of six books that replaced them.

The volumes were covered in red tooled leather of a high quality. She slid a volume off the shelf and inspected it.

"The Domenikos Chronicles."

She flipped through the pages, skimming over the contents. *He couldn't have . . .*

The foreword was written by Domenikos. A history of when he came into power, dating approximately back to the same time Scarlett was in the room adjacent to the diamond room, inside the Time Vault. This was not a good sign.

Adrielle turned page after page. This was a history book. More precisely, the altered version of the world's history—a la Domenikos.

Adrielle pulled out the next volume. It had the same forward. She turned to chapter one and skimmed it. This book went further back in history, to where the other one left off. There was no WWII. No WWI. Those wars never existed. According to this, the Earth's history of how humankind had evolved through the ages, was a different account altogether.

She'd failed.

Adrielle dropped onto the bed, the weight of the situation crushing. Her ribs ached. She pressed her hand into her side and massaged her muscles in small circles. Her head swirled. This was a serious offence. This could not go unpunished.

She had no one to turn to. She was the enforcer, as her father had once been. But he'd had Haden to help. He'd designated him as the head of the Achaean army. Where was Haden now? She needed him.

Her heart ached for the past, the real past. The way it was meant to have evolved naturally.

Angry and confused, she searched out the other items in her room. She realized it wasn't her room at all. The folder of her guitar music—her original songs—was gone. In its place was a folder with published sheet music, with an anthem: *Ode to Domenikos, our leader.*

No, no, no. She tossed it down, feeling sick. Everything in here was a prop. She rushed down the hall to Coco's room, her footsteps clipping on the wood floors.

"Coco? Anyone here?"

The house was empty. Coco's jewelry cases were gone. No makeup or scattered dresses. Not much in her closet either—only a few identical uniforms, which was very unlike Coco, who preferred one-of-a-kind finds.

Shiny black combat boots—which Coco refused to acknowledge as fashion—replaced her leather pumps and wedgies. Adrielle swallowed hard. She pulled out one of the uniforms and recognized it and the boots were exactly the same as the ones the Brix clones wore.

She walked out of Coco's closet. Thankfully the large screen television was still in the room. She clicked on the remote and waited anxiously for it to boot up.

Two anchors were seated behind a news desk. The chatter sounded normal, but the news was a summary report on the monthly consensus.

Everyone was in agreement that the country was in tip-top shape. Zero crimes to report. Zero famine. Fifty thousand new soldiers had joined the world army this week alone. And training sessions were being conducted in the central arenas at daybreak. Every day. All were welcome.

Her mouth went dry.

If there was no crime, why did they need an army? Who was Domenikos afraid of?

And then it hit her. She was his nemesis. And as long as she kept trying to stop him, there was still hope for the world.

Chapter 39

DAVE, COCO, AND ASTRAIA—
INSIDE THE MEMORY TUNNEL—
BACK TO FLORENCE 1504

DAVE'S GAZE WENT from the scared-looking farmer to Coco, to the shotgun's trigger, and then to the sky.

"What would a farmer holding a shotgun and wearing Levis, be doing in Italy in 1504?" Dave whispered, as he focused on the rectangular orange tag sewn into the seam of the man's bib overalls.

"Huh?" Coco whimpered.

"It doesn't make sense. LeFever wasn't born yet."

Coco gave him an exasperated look. "He's pointing a shotgun at us and you're quibbling about dates?"

"Daniel Myron LeFever introduced the first hammerless shotgun in Syracuse NY in 1878. And Levis Strauss didn't get their patent for the process of riveting pants until May twentieth 1873."

"Really?"

"Yeah really. How is this possible?" Dave pointed at the man and shook his finger. "Both the jeans and the gun. And why would he appear here? In the middle of nowhere?" He ignored the man and twirled a full three-hundred-sixty degrees, taking in the Italian farmland landscape surrounding them. "There's no one around for miles."

"Not exactly what I was going for," Coco said.

The wide-eyed man examined their surroundings with a frightened expression and shook his gun.

"Careful there. Those things have a history of going off," Dave said, raising his hands up in the air.

"It's okay," Coco said.

She flashed the man a smile and approached him slowly with her hand out. She stopped at arms-length and pressed down on the barrel of the gun until it was pointing to the ground.

"Where did you come from?" she asked, in a calming, soothing tone.

The man, who looked about forty-five with a short-cropped peppered beard, shrugged. "Dunno." He swiped his brow with the back of a hand. He clutched his gun tighter and shook his head. "I just dunno."

"You speak English. Wonderful." Coco jumped happily up and down. She turned to Dave, beaming. "Isn't this great? We don't have to translate."

"The coolest," Dave said dryly. Did Coco not get it? This man had apparently popped out of thin air. This was bad. Very, very bad.

Chapter 40

Liz—In the memory tunnel—
Back in time—Florence Italy 1504

LIZ FELT A sharp jab in her ribs. She opened her eyes with a start and realized she'd dozed off with the cadence of the trotting horses. Through the small carriage window, she saw Antonio take a firm hold of the reins and tug. The horses pulled back and came to a stop.

Liz fell forward, slipped off the bench, and smacked her head against the front of the carriage box. "Ouch!" She rubbed her forehead. "What's going on?"

"Bandits." Isabel, pale with frightened eyes, squatted low on the floor.

"Are you kidding me? Bandits?" Liz poked her head out of the carriage. Isabel tugged at her clothes, but Liz was determined to see. "Fried lizard guts. Two men on horses are blocking the trail ahead." She looked behind. "There's only two. Wait . . . there's a third in the bushes. His hat is sticking out of the greenery."

Liz ducked back in the carriage and crouched low. "Listen, Isabel . . . we can't just pull over and give them whatever they want."

Isabel's eyes widened, terrified. Antonio's weight shifted in the footman's seat, and the carriage rocked. He was getting down.

Yikes. Liz glanced down at her sparkly new bracelet. No way was she letting them have it. She slipped it off her wrist and stuffed it into her bra. Then unclasped her necklace and did the same.

She glanced at Isabel, who was watching her closely. She was shaking and cowering in her clunky long dress. Liz gazed down at her own clothes. Luckily, she'd insisted on changing into her cargo pants and tank. More mobility this way. She crouched deeper onto the carriage floor. "Don't leave this box. Understand?"

Isabel nodded. Liz poked her head out the window trying not to be seen. The men ahead were younger than she'd first thought. Boys. Maybe only thirteen- or fourteen-years old. One of them was pointing a knife at Antonio and shaking it. *Thugs.* She shook her head. The other got off his horse and started ranting something in Italian as he approached.

Liz didn't understand what was being said, but Antonio's hands were raised high in surrender. *Spineless old coot.*

The punks didn't deserve her jewels. What they deserved was a swift kick in the butt.

The one nearing the coach hadn't seen Liz. He was busy eyeing Antonio. He barked something at the second boy.

"Isabel, quick. Get out and distract them," Liz ordered.

"No. They could hurt me." Isabel's hands were shaking.

Liz felt badly for her, she was so young. She pulled Isabel close. "Trust me—they're all show. Tell them you're the only one in here. And when they start to unload the luggage, I'll jump them."

"You'll what?" Isabel's expression was incredulous.

"Never mind." Liz opened the carriage door and pushed Isabel out. She toppled out of the carriage and startled the two boys. The third boy jumped out of the bushes and came running up the lane. He had a victoriously smug expression, which infuriated Liz even more.

Liz waited inside the box. She watched Isabel sidle next to Antonio. While one boy held the knife to them, the two others ran up to the carriage and began cutting the ropes to loosen the luggage. But the ropes were thick leather straps and wrapped many times over to hold the luggage securely in place. Liz's heart raced.

While they were focused on their task, Liz sprang out of the carriage and jumped them. She yelled a ninja shout that spooked the horses. They bucked the boys off the carriage and Liz scrambled to Antonio's place at the footman's seat.

She grasped the reins and snapped them hard. The horses leaned into the harness and leapt ahead, taking the carriage into a fast gallop.

Liz looked behind and saw the boy's horses scattering away to the fields. Antonio used the distraction to clobber one of the boys over the head with a rock. Isabel kicked the other boy hard in the shins. The third boy turned around and dashed after the horses.

Liz laughed. When she was up a ways and out of harm's way, she yanked on the reins and the horses came to a stop. She got off the coach and ran back to the others.

A piece of rope had fallen along the road. She picked it up and wound it tightly around her hands, then pulled the center of the rope taut.

Antonio was struggling with one of the boys. But he could hold his own. Isabel didn't know what to do with the other boy. She was standing in front of him with wide arms. Waiting for his move.

Liz snuck up and swung the rope around his neck. She pulled tight. The boy screamed, his hand grasping for the rope as it tightened.

Isabel's eyes were wide.

"Put your hands behind your back," Liz ordered.

Once he did, she fastened the boy's hands and feet together with the leather cord. She looked back at Antonio. He was holding the other boy against the ground, saw what Liz did, and bound his hands and feet together.

They left then tied back-to-back under a large tree at the side of the road. Liz figured by the time the third boy got help, they'd be far on their way.

Liz gathered the boys' knives and slid them into her belt. It was almost like the wild west, and she loved the adventure.

"Antonio, get into the carriage with Isabel," she said, as she stepped onto the footman's stool and grab the reins.

"What do you think you're doing?" Antonio yelled.

Liz narrowed her eyes. "I'm driving. Or else I'll tell Francesco how quickly you surrendered to the two underage boys."

Antonio shrugged and climbed into the box.

They reached the city at nearly nightfall. Candlelit windows lined the main cobbled street, and Liz was grateful people were still up. It had been a long day, and she was ready for a break.

A group of men were huddled in conversation at the side of the road. Antonio got out of the carriage and asked them where to park for the night. They pointed to a narrow side road. Liz gave Antonio the reins and got in the box, so he could maneuver the coach through the tiny street. They finally stopped.

Liz shivered as she got out of the carriage with Isabel. The temperature had dropped with the sun, making it too cool for a bare midriff. She stepped onto the mounting step and reached up to undo one of the ties on her luggage.

Antonio had secured them so tightly, to keep them from jostling on the trails and uneven cobblestones, that she couldn't get the leather binding all the way off. But she was able to loosen it enough to access her clothes.

Liz reached in the case and slipped out a long deep purple velvet cape with gold trim accents along the front, Francesco had given her as part of her trousseau. More ornate than she would have liked, especially for cross-country travelling, but it would have to do. She slipped it over her shoulders and buttoned it up, feeling immediate relief from the cold. The cape was dually useful—she should blend right in with the locals and not attract anyone's attention.

Liz waited at the side of the road while Isabel helped Antonio relieve the horses of their harness. They watered and fed them and tied them to a nearby stall. Then Antonio beckoned some boys over. He gave them a few coins to watch over the carriage and horses, and they set out to find a place to eat.

The street had plenty of eateries to choose from. It didn't take them long to settle on a place in the next block, with a lively atmosphere and music spilling out onto the street.

The smell of home-styled food made Liz ravenous, and the place was crowded—a good sign. They sat at a table near the front and ordered the special of the day.

Liz sat back in her chair and exhaled a long breath. After being on the road for so long, she felt like she was still in motion. She had gotten used to the trotting of the horses but not the hard bench. She rubbed her tailbone discretely and noted neither Isabel, nor Antonio, were complaining. She guessed the bumpy ride was about as luxurious a trip as one could get, in these past times.

Liz listened to the entertainment, a trio with two rebecs and a vocalist. They were talented. The music was a much-needed dose of culture, and Liz finally started to relax.

The meal came quickly enough. A Rubenesque girl with long curly hair and an easy smile placed a large bowl of food in front of them, along with a pitcher of red wine.

At this point, Liz would have eaten anything. Well, almost anything. She twirled a forkful of cheese-covered noodles and stuffed them in her mouth. The meatballs and sausage were to die for.

Liz polished off her serving with little conversation, for which she was grateful. She'd run out of things to say to Isabel.

Liz thought about Dave and the group, and how she didn't have to try to make conversation with them; it was fine to just be. She guessed that's how it was with family, or good friends. You didn't need to fill the void.

The server returned to clear their plates. Dave would have loved this meal. He'd taken to cooking since their last adventure in Florence where he'd picked up countless pointers from Salai.

Liz felt a pang of loneliness. Those had been good times. A warm house to stay in. The company of the most historically known artists, Leonardo DaVinci and Michelangelo. It had been an unexpected adventure. While they were racing time to finish the forgery of the *Book of Feathers*, their group had really bonded.

People didn't bond over small talk. They bonded over big things. It had been thrilling and dangerous and magnificent.

She glanced around the inn. Here she was. Eating at a fine establishment like a local. She felt a tinge of guilt. *What the heck was she doing here?* In a nameless city chasing Francesco to the altar? She felt terrible deserting Coco and Dave. Left them to fend for themselves with that bird-woman, Astraia, while knowing Dave was leery of her. It had been an accident, sure. But an accident she'd secretly wanted.

Truth was . . . they'd made quite the team together, Adrielle, Coco, Dave, and her. Their success over Domenikos last time they were in Florence, proved it. And Adrielle could use all of their help now.

She squirmed in her chair. What would they think when they found out she'd married? That this was a cop-out? The easy way to settle for the domestic life she'd never believed would be in her future? God, she'd hate them to think that. She felt hot and unbuttoned the top button of her cloak.

She really did love Francesco—didn't she?

She remembered she'd tucked her jewels into her bra. She slid her hand inside her cape, fingered through her shirt, and felt the pointy edges of the jewelry safely cupped in her bra. At least she'd have something to show her friends, when they reminded her what she was giving up. Namely, the journalism career she'd always aspired to. Perhaps the beauty of these jewels would change their minds?

Liz patted her bra and closed up her cape. This was probably the best way to carry them, until she rejoined Francesco.

"Ahhhh . . ." Liz placed her hands on her stomach. She was stuffed and satiated from rich food and wine. The carafe of wine was empty. Too much made her sleepy, so she'd stopped at one glass and let the others drink.

She couldn't remember the last time she'd eaten without counting carbs. How long had it been since she'd actually worked out? Too long.

Aside from the wrestling lessons she'd given Adrielle while they were sequestered in their Florida house during the hurricane, the most exercise she'd gotten was the trek crossing Francesco's estate. She'd have to remedy that. She rubbed her ankle, which was feeling much better.

What she needed now was a soft comfy bed, and hours and hours of sleep.

Antonio paid the tab, and they strolled back to check on the horses and the carriage, before finding a place to rest for the night.

Antonio, who had walked ahead of them, stopped and let loose a string of angry words.

"What's going on?" Liz asked Isabel.

For the second time today, Isabel was wide-eyed and speechless.

"What now?" Liz asked.

Antonio was yelling so fast and furious she couldn't make anything out.

"The horses, they're gone," Isabel said.

"What? Are you sure this is where we left them?" Liz asked, looking around. The street was so dimly lit she couldn't be sure. The candlelit windows were dark, making everything appear more sinister.

If this was where they'd tied the horses, they were definitely gone. So were the boys Antonio paid to keep an eye on them.

Liz wandered to the end of the street and looked both ways. Most of the lights were out now. The only light was from the moon high in the sky.

Liz remembered seeing a doorway with a weathered door, and an iron knocker that reminded her of Michelangelo's place. It was close to where they'd left the carriage. There it was. *Ugh.* She felt a sick feeling at the pit of her stomach.

Liz walked over to the doorway and studied the uneven cobbled stones. On the ground was the piece of the leather binding she'd loosened, to take her cape out.

They weren't only robbed, they were homeless.

Chapter 41

Adrielle—Two years into the future, Florida

WHY HAD SHE ended up her house, in the future? Before she headed back to the Time Vault, she wanted to know if this was a true future, or a probable one. Adrielle set her chronometer to alert her in twenty-four hours, in case she lost track of time.

No one was home. Nor was there a car in the driveway. She walked to the corner of the block to see if any of the neighbors were milling around in their yards. Strangely, no one was around at all.

She thought about knocking on a few doors, but if her hunch was right, and they proved to be brainwashed versions of their former selves, what would be the point? Perhaps by now, they'd even been replaced with the clones.

If Domenikos had the capability of cloning Brix, perhaps he'd cloned everyone else too. Maybe that was why there was no rebellion. But where had her friends gone? Were they missing from this future version because they were trapped inside the scepter diamond?

Adrielle wandered back indoors and headed to her room. Too worried to eat, she pulled the red leather history volumes from the bookshelves and tossed them onto her bed. Somewhere between the hand-tooled covers there had to be a glitch. She had to find the clues without Liz's help. There had to be something indicating when Domenikos took over the world. And how he'd done it.

HALFWAY THROUGH THE books, Adrielle had a thought. In the books revamped history lessons, Scarlett was dubbed as *the queen of America*. The idea made her sick. The constitution and everything America's forefathers worked for—gone at Domenikos' whim. No democracy, only a twisted version of a dictatorship, mingled with a monarchy. Domenikos was at the head, the reigning king, and Scarlett was his vampy queen.

She was furious. Her one consolation was knowing Domenikos had been careless and hasty. Because *she* was still here. And she remembered how it was. How it had been.

She wore the *mark of the traveler*. She touched the crest and felt some comfort. *That* was the glitch she'd been looking for. If someone remembered the past in a different version than the current one, then this could only be a probable future.

She had to return to the Time Vault right away and make sure her memories remained intact and were not altered.

She wondered if memories could be erased if a person wasn't actually inside the Time Vault. Angelo's had been. But if they were physically inside, was it possible they couldn't be?

It was a guess and all she had to go by. She wished she could run this theory by Dave and Liz. They were so intuitive. And they, along with Coco, were her army.

Adrielle closed her eyes and concentrated very, very, hard on getting back to the Time Vault. *Nothing*. She cupped her chronometer to try again.

Still nothing.

It was as though she hit an invisible wall, a firewall. She gave it one more shot, but she was still in her room.

What if she couldn't get back there?

The chronometer said it was well after three in the morning. She sighed heavily as she sat in the darkened room. She was exhausted.

She went to her bathroom and stared at her face. Dark purple shadows clung under her eyes. She pulled off her t-shirt and inspected her bruises in the mirror. They were bad. If Brix saw them, he'd know he had the upper hand.

Adrielle pulled her t-shirt on and splashed cold water on her face. If she was going to face her twin, *she* would have the upper hand.

She pulled out her exercise mat and unrolled it. Then opened her top dresser drawer and rifled through it. The instructions for the wrestling moves Liz had taught her were still there, along with other moves she hadn't yet learned.

Adrielle studied the diagrams until early morning. She practiced the moves and read the appendix on when and how to use them. As the sun rose, Adrielle collapsed onto the bed.

As she dozed off, the sting of her crest startled her. A gloved hand clamped over her mouth and muffled her screams.

Chapter 42

Dave, Coco, and Astraia—
In the memory tunnel—Back in time—
Florence Italy 1504

"EUGENE, LET'S GO over this again. You're from California. The year is 1905. You pointed your shotgun at your daughter's boyfriend, after she told you she was pregnant, and suddenly you're here. Anything else?" Dave said.

The man shrugged. "Dunno." He was highly agitated. He kept squeezing his eyes and reopening them.

Dave clapped Eugene on the shoulder and tipped his head for Coco to follow. "We'll be right back."

Coco followed Dave to where Eugene wouldn't hear them.

"This isn't good. I fear our entry into the scepter diamond triggered a response. The entire timeline might be screwed up," Dave said.

Coco watched Eugene with a worried expression.

"He doesn't know how he got here," Dave said. "After half an hour of grilling, aside from his name and that he lives in California in 1905, we know he owns a chocolate and mustard business with his two brothers."

"I think we should ease up on him. He's terrified," Coco said.

Dave side-eyed Eugene. He was sitting on a log from a fallen tree with the shotgun propped up beside him, giving himself a hug. "You have a point. He's safer with us, for now. We'll take him with us to find Francesco. Once Adrielle shows up, she'll know what to do."

They followed the road, and after a while, Coco stopped to catch her breath. "You sure we're going the right way? I could swear we've passed that tree before."

"You mean that cork oak with the bent branch that kinda hangs down?" Dave pointed.

Coco nodded.

Dave studied the large tree. It was on the periphery of the grove, but so were a lot of others. "I don't know. It has a low hanging branch, but I can't be sure it's the same one."

"The women said Francesco's place was only a couple of miles out of town. I'm convinced we've covered more ground than that," Coco said, studying their surroundings. "I need to sit. I have a rock in my shoe." She sat on a tree stump and unlaced her running shoes. She glanced briefly up at Eugene who seemed to have calmed down some.

"I'm going to relieve myself," Eugene said, tipping his head and disappearing over a small hill.

Once he was out of earshot, Dave asked, "What are we going to do with him once we find Liz, if Adrielle doesn't show up? Take him back to the diamond center with us?"

Coco raised her eyebrows. "I'm not sure. Maybe Astraia has some ideas. I'm still wondering how we're going to get back there."

"Me too. Let's take it one step at a time." Dave raised his hand to his brow and searched the sky. "Where is that black winged creature anyways? I thought, she was going to keep an eye on us from overhead. We haven't seen her in hours—not that I'm complaining."

"I know." Coco shook her sneaker and tapped it on the stump. Then slipped it back on and tied the laces. "She creeps me out too. It's weird she took off like that." She stood up. "I'm sure she'll turn up when she wants too. She knows how to find us."

"Let's hope. Our caravan's getting a little extended." Dave gestured in the direction where Eugene had disappeared. "Once we find Liz, we'll need help figuring out how to get back."

A shotgun went off in the distance.

"It's coming from over there," Coco pointed. "Dammit. I believed him when he said he had to pee."

"You're too trusting. With Astraia too. We have no idea what she's capable of. Or whose side she's really on," Dave said over his shoulder. He sprinted over the hill in the direction of the gunshot with Coco following.

They found Eugene in the middle of an expansive field, shotgun in one hand, dead chicken in the other. Several outbuildings spotted the grounds. In the far distance, a large estate house loomed.

Dave let out a long slow whistle. "I think we found Francesco's house."

"You think?" Coco said, smiling broadly.

"This explains why the women laughed when I asked where Francesco's *casita* was. Looks like a hacienda."

"Or castle."

A man wearing tights and a linen shirt buttoned at the neck, appeared from one of the buildings. He saw Eugene holding the dead chicken and raced toward him, shaking his fists and yelling.

Dave and Coco exchanged a look. "If we were smart, we'd run. But he's our best bet at finding Liz."

By the time the man reached them, they'd eliminated him as a viable threat. He was slender and aging with a wrinkled face and long white beard. He'd run out of steam halfway across the field. All he could do was puff and mutter what sounded like a string of obscenities, while half-heartedly shaking his fists and head.

In his best Italian, Dave asked for Francesco, and then Liz. And at the mention of Liz, the man brought both hands to his forehead and said, *"Mio dio,"* closely translating to "oh my god."

They followed him to the main house. He led them into the kitchen, then snatched the chicken out of Eugene's hand and tossed it on the table. He dug in a basket and pulled out a sack of carrots and potatoes and handed them each a knife.

"Is this in exchange for room and board?" Dave asked.

The man growled something incomprehensible.

They spent a large part of the afternoon chopping and peeling vegetables and plucking chicken feathers. When the work was done, a stout woman entered through the back entrance. She glanced at them, wiped her hands on her apron, and put on a cauldron of water to boil.

Coco was making Dave nervous, glancing at him as he worked up his courage.

"Ahem. We're looking for our friend Liz—Lisa," Dave mumbled in muddled Italian. "She's about this tall." He raised his hand to his eyebrows. "Too thin. Long curly hair down to here." He pointed to his waist.

"La sposa Lisa?"

"Sposa?" Coco repeated.

Dave was fairly certain that meant bride.

The woman nodded. "Si, il matrimonio e a Roma."

Coco's eyes widened. "I think she said Liz is getting married in Rome."

"What the—?" Dave ran his palms down his face. When? Please don't say it's already happened. That would be a catastrophe."

"Quando?" Coco said, looking worried too.

"Tra tre giorni."

"Three days," Coco translated.

"Can we make it to Rome in time? Without a car?"

"By horse," Eugene muttered. It was the first thing he'd said that made any sense.

Chapter 43

Liz—In the memory tunnel—
Back in time—Italy 1504

LIZ BENT AT the waist and heaved. Before she had a chance to stand, a second wave of nausea built up and projected out onto the battered cobbled stone road. She moaned and swiped at her mouth with the back of her hand and rested her hands on her knees. She looked over her shoulder at Isabel, who was pulling her cape back so it wouldn't get dirty. Liz unbuttoned the collar and handed it to her.

"Was the meat rotten?"

Isabel shrugged.

"Well, are you feeling sick? We both had the same thing."

"I feel full. That's all," Isabel said. She glanced to the place their carriage should have been. "Only sick we have no ride."

Yep. There was that. Liz rotated her foot to get the circulation going and rubbed her ankle. It was better, but still achy. She wouldn't get far on it.

Antonio returned with two men wearing navy jackets with silver cording. They were engrossed in deep conversation. Local authorities, Liz thought. Antonio took out a leather pouch and held it upside down. One of the men shook his head.

A knot clenched in Liz's stomach. Could he have spent all their money? She'd seen him take coins from the pouch to pay the boys to watch the horses and carriage. He'd pulled more out, to pay for their meals.

Liz jabbed her Isabel. "What's going on? Is Antonio out of money?"

Isabel nodded. "He wasn't sure if this city was safe, so he left the money in his luggage."

Liz slapped her hand to her forehead. "You've got to be kidding. It's common sense 101. You don't leave money in a car or carriage. Or on a dark deserted street."

"What is 101?"

"Never mind," Liz grumbled. Could things get any worse? They were homeless. Broke. And in the middle of nowhere.

The authorities extended their arms and shook their heads. Liz went to stand closer to them. They said there was nothing they could do. There were no witnesses, and Antonio's description of the boys amounted to nothing. *Dark hair and eyes, skinny. Came up to chin level.* Liz harrumphed. He'd just described every Italian boy in the city.

She walked back to Isabel and saw Antonio shake the policemen's hands. *Let's just thank them for nothing.*

The policemen waved at her and Isabel. Then their expression turned from sympathetic to hardened grimaces, followed by a flurry of fast Italian and flailing hand gestures. Antonio looked horrified as they headed toward Liz.

"Hurry put this on." Isabel said, with an urgency in her voice. She tossed Liz the robe.

Liz remembered Dave mentioning the strict sumptuary laws enforcing women's dress code in the fifteen hundreds. She slipped on the robe, terrified a bare midriff could send her behind bars.

The men approached with obvious distaste. Liz apologized profusely, but despite her objections, one of them clamped her wrists with iron-tight hands. They dragged her from the two people in the world who knew she was in Italy and might actually miss her. Except for Francesco, that was.

"She's Francesco Giocondo's fiancée," Antonio blurted. "We are enroute to Rome, for their wedding before the Pope."

The man loosened his grip.

Liz stepped away from him rubbing her wrists. She was both relieved and pissed off at her lack of rights.

Not for the first time, Liz began to rethink living here permanently with Francesco. This wasn't the love-laced paradise she'd daydreamed about. Oppression and drudgery were more fitting.

The officials prepared a horse for Liz to ride to their hotel. Antonio guided the horse, and Isabel followed, both on foot. They turned the corner, and Liz saw the ornate façade of the building's exterior. Her spirits brightened.

Apparently, Francesco's name came with perks. It did wonders for securing accommodations. Liz dismounted and thanked the officers.

She'd always been a fan of Renaissance architecture. The entry had a tall hand-carved door with pilasters flanking it. She felt herself floating along the length of the interior hall, elated at the luxury they were being offered. The inn keeper took her and Isabel to the last room on the left.

Liz gasped. Soft bed linens were draped back on the large canopy bed. Two crisp white nightgowns were laid out, flowy, and long, and romantic. The kind she'd see in old movies like *Scrooge* or *Pride and Prejudice.*

The inn keeper seemed pleased at their reaction. After he left, Liz changed into one of the nightgowns and spared no time climbing into bed. Pure exhaustion from the day's events was the best sleep aid a girl could have.

Halfway through the night, Liz awakened with a full bladder. For a moment, she was confused about her whereabouts; the glorious room with gilded paintings and the ornate fireplace. *Was she dreaming?* And then she saw Isabel, splayed under the heap of blankets with her mouth open.

The poor girl had probably never slept in such comfort. Francesco's maids' quarters were paltry, a small undecorated room with a single cot.

Where was the five-piece ensuite to go with the elaborate decorations of this room? Liz grudgingly pulled out the rusty bedpan tucked into her night table and hiked up her nightgown. *Yuk.*

She squatted and stared at the bedpan. Was she was supposed to slip it back in the night table or leave it out? Out of sight sounded best, so that's what she did.

A LOUD TAP and soft voice announced it was morning, and breakfast was being served downstairs. Liz cracked an eyelid. Had she even slept? Last night's dinner felt like daggers cutting into her. She clutched at her tummy and groaned. With little time to spare, she opened the hinged door and pulled the bedpan out. Half of it spilled onto her hands.

"You're still sick? Should I stay?" Isabel asked.

"Get out. I need privacy," Liz yelled.

Breakfast came and went. So did lunch. Liz climbed in and out of bed. The bedpan went in and out of the night table. Her head swirled with all the reasons she should have stayed in the scepter's diamond.

And then as she laid her head on her pillow, she slipped her hand underneath and felt the jewelry Francesco had given her. She pulled it out and was mesmerized by the dazzling sparkle. She thought about Francesco, and the look on his face when he'd given it to her. She loved him. She still felt the same rush of emotion she'd had the first time she met him. But how could she live in a place without iPhones, and internet, and toilets?

Without her friends?

Chapter 44

Adrielle–Two years into the future, Florida

A GLOVED HAND clamped over Adrielle's mouth. She'd expected the attack. She twisted around and trapped the Brix clone in a side headlock, rotated her body until she was horizontal with him, flipped him over her back, and threw him onto the other Brix soldiers. The maneuver was so quick, the clone offered little resistance.

Pain cut through her torso. She resisted the urge to clamp her hand to her side. "What do you want?" she screamed. There were too many of them.

She glanced at the opened window. Would her winged feathers spring out of her back, like when she'd confronted Domenikos on the cliff?

She jumped on the windowsill as the soldier clones reached for her and flung herself outside.

The ground raced toward her. Adrielle braced for impact, then she felt her wings pop out. She exhaled with relief and slowly flapped. She caught a wind current and glided upward.

It surprised her, Flying felt as natural as walking. Breathing. She headed for the beach.

A new building stood on the corner by the gas station. A large high-rise complex sprawled where there'd been a small community center.

She landed on the strip of sand with a thud and caught her balance at the water's edge. Her heart was pounding. She pressed one hand on her chest to slow it.

Wow, she'd flown. She couldn't remember feeling this euphoria. She surveyed her surroundings. She was alone. *Good.* The tide was ebbing in.

She bent over and braced her hands on her thighs to catch her breath. The cool water rolled onto her toes and disappeared into the wet sand, soothing her. Reminded her of home.

She watched an osprey carried a fish in its beak overhead and disappear into the distance and thought of Achaean freedoms compromised by her father. Once, they'd been able to travel through time. Fly whenever they wanted.

Domenikos said the Achaean Act was unfair to their kind. Said it bound them. *Bound.* That was the word he'd used. Powerful. A feeling of unease stirred inside her. She could see that now. It was like never running again. Or being confined to a wheelchair.

He was right, partially. The Achaean Act clipped their wings. She could see why Domenikos had rebelled. Why he started the revolution. It must have been a hard decision for her father.

Hmmm. Hard choices were never easy.

A leader had to make hard choices. Freedoms of the few were sacrificed for freedoms of the greater— a compromise, so each could have a life.

She felt crushing sadness.

For the first time in her life, Adrielle Maddox understood what the war was about.

Chapter 45

Liz—In the memory tunnel— Back in time—Italy 1504

OVERCOME WITH EXHAUSTION, Liz spent most of the day in bed. Isabel stood by, waiting for her to feel better.

There was a knock on the door. Without waiting for a response, Antonio barged in. "The carriage has been located."

Liz sat up. "Where was it?"

"At the edge of town, deserted. With one broken spoke on the large wheels. We've taken it to the nearest blacksmith. He is going to whittle a spoke."

There was another knock on the door. The inn keeper. He smiled at Liz. "Can I get you something?"

Antonio began to object but the inn keeper said, "Everything is on the house."

Antonio nodded in relief.

Liz could barely believe it. It seemed no matter how far from home they ventured, Francesco's name carried heavy weight. Serious weight. She guessed it was because he was the largest silk provider in Italy.

Liz lay back down to doze, and after a while, there was another knock. Isabel went to the door and returned with an envelope.

"Who was it?" Liz asked.

"A young maiden delivering a note," Isabel said, and handed it to her.

It had a crested red wax seal and was addressed to *"Signorina Lisa,"* in beautifully handwritten ink script.

Liz stared at the meticulous handwriting. There were only three people in the world who called her Lisa. Francesco, Leonardo, or Michelangelo.

Isabel stood by the bed. "Is it Francesco? News of our mishap has carried far and fast."

Liz ripped the seal, anticipation mounting. She recognized the flourishing script and skimmed the note. "No, it's from Leonardo Da Vinci. He's been traveling nearby and heard talk of a young lady promised in marriage to Francesco Del Giocondo. He knew it could only be me." She pressed the note to her chest, feeling elated. "It's an invitation for dinner at the local inn."

Isabel clapped her hands together. "You look better already. Shall I pick you out something to wear?"

Liz waved her hand and chuckled as she reread the note. "He must have heard about my clash with the authorities. He said not to worry about my attire. He's well known in these parts, so anything I wear will be respected."

Isabel smiled.

Liz traced over his flamboyant script and re-read the note two more times. This was exactly what her heart ordered. She'd grown quite fond of Leonardo. *Leo,* as Dave would say.

She folded the note and tucked it into her cargo pants pocket for safekeeping.

Dinner couldn't come fast enough. Isabel put lavender into her bathwater, and after a long soak in a hot bath, most of Liz's nausea was gone.

Isabel braided her long woolly hair and secured the end of the braid into a low bun. She handed Liz the mirror. "I'll get your silk dress."

"I'd rather wear my cargo pants and top," Liz said.

"I washed them. They're hanging in the patio to dry."

"Oh no, I'd put Leonardo's note—"

"On the night table." Isabel pointed, smiling.

Liz looked at Isabel's red and chafed hands. Another reminder that even the simplest tasks back home were tiresome chores here.

ANTICIPATION AT SEEING her old friend lifted Liz's spirits, and doubly so, when they entered the inn. The smell of roast duck and onions, bubbly chatter, and lively music, was a feast for the senses. Liz gave a fast glance and saw two musicians playing a tune on the rebec and lute. Though the place was crowded, she spotted the long graying beard right away as Leonardo stood.

He appeared genuinely happy to see her. Overjoyed to see a friendly face, Liz weaved her way to his table, where a lit candle illuminated Leonardo's notebook. It lay open with a handsome quill beside it. Liz caught her breath. A silver feather. *Angelo's.*

A strong wave of homesickness flowed over her.

Leonardo followed her gaze. "Yes, it is Angelo's. I remember well how you too, like to write down your thoughts." He lifted his crinkly eyes to her right shoulder where her purse usually hung.

Liz shrugged. "Temporarily misplaced, I'm afraid."

He gave her a bear hug and attempted to pull out her chair.

"I've got this," Liz said, sidestepping his chivalry.

Leonardo nodded, his expression saying he remembered she didn't like anyone doting over her.

Liz pulled out and sat in the chair across from him and settled into the seat across from him.

Leonardo Da Vinci reminded her of herself. Not because he was the genius inventor of so many creations, which she wasn't, but because of his inquisitive mind. His notebook was a testament to passing thoughts and ideas.

Liz regretted not having her purse with her trusty notebook and pencil inside. Jotting down random thoughts had become second nature to her. Reading these entries took her back to that time and place and brought her great joy.

"I was surprised to hear Francesco was getting married. I knew at once it could only be you," Leonardo said. He shook an aged finger. "You've come back for him, Lisa."

"It was a sort of an accidental longing." She laughed. "And then poof, I was in Florence."

"Accidental?" He searched her eyes. "Ah, Adrielle's feather." He lowered his gaze to the silver feather glimmering in the candlelight and looked pensive, his face giving off secrets his lips didn't share.

Liz leaned into the flame. She suspected he was thinking of Angelo and the others, but she couldn't be sure. "Leonardo, what is it?"

He raised his eyes to hers and held them. Reflected in them were wisdom and loyalty, two of his outstanding attributes.

"Lisa . . . you are one of my most treasured friends. We have been through trying times together. I would hate for you to get hurt."

"Hurt?" Liz leaned back. She looked at her ankle sticking out from under the table. She chuckled. "Nothing gets past you, does it. You must have noticed I was favoring my other foot." She tucked it under the table. "It's healing slowly."

Leonardo shook his head. "No, Lisa. That is not what I mean." His gaze searched hers and held. His expression grew serious. "You remember our talks about Francesco? How I said he is extravagant and likes to show his affection?" He looked at her twinkling bracelet, and then the gem-studded necklace.

Liz brushed her fingers over the diamonds and felt embarrassed at the luxury.

"Material things do not fulfill, they do not sustain happiness."

"It's a gift from Francesco. For our wedding." She slid her hand onto her lap.

He raised his eyes to hers. His expression remained somber, and Liz squirmed.

"Liz, he is not . . ." Leonardo shook his head. "Forgive me for what I am about to say. Francesco is not the kind of man who will be faithful. Marriage? Yes, he will honor the contract. He will love you as his wife. But he will expect you to stay home and be satisfied there. Waiting for him, for the days when he decides to return home."

Liz picked up her napkin and dabbed at her forehead.

"He will want children."

"Children?"

"Yes. Will this be enough for you?" His gaze held hers.

After a pause, he leaned in and lowered his voice. "There is no good way to say this, so I will be direct. Michelangelo is in Rome for a new commission. I'm sorry to relay, he has seen Francesco with women dangling at his side." He lowered his gaze and twisted his wine glass, then raised his eyes to hers.

"As his wife, Francesco will pamper you. You will have trunks overflowing with silks, and enough jewels to flit around Florence with the best of them. But I remember you once told me of your dreams. You are as innocent as a freshly sprouted flower shooting up to the sun." He leaned back into his chair and shook his head. "I could not bear to see you wilt, because you got too close to the fire."

Liz was stunned. She dropped her gaze to the candle.

Could Leonardo be right?

As the flame burned up oxygen, it emitted poisonous carbon dioxide. Liz slipped her fingers between the necklace and her throat. It felt tighter now. This trip to the past was starting to feel like one big mistake.

He wagged his finger. "Do not be in a rush. Young people seek love. They believe there is only one person who can complete them." He gave a slight nod. "You will learn with age you are the only one who can do that. Believe me, Lisa, if you give up your dreams for someone else, you will never be complete. You will become a sliver of what you could have been. And one day, you will resent him for this."

Leonardo pushed away from table and stood up. "Come with me." He walked around to her and held out his arm.

His beard almost reached the crook of his arm. Liz looped one hand through it and followed him through the inn to a rear open-air courtyard.

It was quieter here, only the faintest sound of the rebec reached this hidden oasis. The sweet smell of wisteria made Liz feel woozy, and she leaned into Leonardo for support.

Leonardo raised his hand to the sky and pointed. "See the myriads of stars?"

Liz nodded. The shape of his arm extending to the sky with his pointing index finger reminded her of Michelangelo's Sistine chapel fresco, the Creation of Adam.

"Francesco is but one of the many." He looked at her, the corners of his lips curling up. "This is a magnificent world. You have much to learn. Your lifetime exists hundreds of years from now. I cannot imagine the unfolding of discoveries you have seen, though I do try."

Perhaps he was right. Michelangelo wouldn't even start working on his masterpiece, on the Sistine chapel, for another seven years.

They stood stargazing until the server came to announce their meal was ready. Leonardo wrapped one arm around her shoulders and pulled her into his side. "I have grown quite fond of you, my Lisa. Francesco, with his concubines of women, will only snuff out the light that burns inside you. I thought you realized this when you broke off the engagement."

Leonardo's words held a hefty weight. He was a leader in thought and speculation, and probably right in his assumption.

They weaved into the inn and sat down to two large portions of the house specialty—roast duck with grilled onions, potatoes, and carrots. And a decanter of the house wine.

The candle in the center of the table had burned out.

Chapter 46

Adrielle—Two years into the future, Florida

ADRIELLE TROLLED THE grounds of the new building—more like a fortress. There were no windows on the front side, only doors flanked by two Brix clones. It reminded her of the Time Vault.

To avoid being recognized, Adrielle tucked her long platinum hair into a cap and pulled down the visor. If the Brix clones spotted her, she might not make it out alive. It had taken every bit of strength to wrestle out from underneath the clone during their attack. She pressed her hand to her side. The pain from the beating had dulled but still ached.

Adrielle started toward the entry. A group of young boys lingered a few feet away, jostling with one another, daring each other to go in.

New recruits.

According to the news report, training sessions were held daily at the facilities. Five hundred new recruits each week. With numbers like that, it made sense there were other recruiting centers. Perhaps all over the state. Or even the country.

They said everyone was welcome. Everyone but her, she imagined.

Thoughts of multiple clone-churning arenas were frightening. Brainwashing multitudes into following him did not make Domenikos a leader. Leaders were trained to care about the people they led, and all Domenikos cared about was himself.

She checked her chronometer; Three hours before her self-imposed twenty-four-hour deadline to get the hell outta there. It had taken her longer than she'd anticipated to sort through her plan. But she'd come up with something solid, barring any hiccups.

For a fleeting moment, Adrielle considered running down to the Goodwill store and picking up a pair of cargo pants, to look more like a recruitee. But the boys were headed toward the main entrance, and she needed reinforcements. Her shorts and tank would have to do.

As much as Adrielle hated the idea of entering the training facility, she couldn't afford not to check it out. What could be worse than what she'd already faced? She decided her best bet was to attach herself to a group. That way no one would single her out.

She scoped out the boys hanging around the entry. They were young, fifteen maybe. She walked up to them and to her relief, she was about their same height. Maybe even their weight. Without makeup, she might pass for one of them. Granted, a paler version, much paler.

Adrielle lowered her voice, in hopes of sounding masculine. "You guys check this place out yet?"

"Not yet," one of them said, eyeing her. "You?"

Adrielle shook her head.

"Sounds awesome," he said. One of the others punched his shoulder and gave her a quick side-eye, his expression warning he shouldn't be talking to her. She was a stranger.

"How long does it take?" Adrielle asked.

"Who knows," one of them grunted.

As they entered the big double doors, Adrielle inched closer to them. To her relief, the guards nodded as they passed. No one singled her out.

THE RECEPTION ROOM smelled of strong antiseptic and was sparsely decorated, devoid of fancy décor. It could have been a doctor or dentist office. Gray chairs lined the walls, and end tables were in the corners. The walls were painted a soft gray. On the feature wall hung a large portrait of Domenikos dressed in a dark grey military uniform with clunky black combat boots.

The boys scribbled their names on the sign-in sheet and took a seat. Adrielle waited until last, and did the same, using *Riley Raven* as her alias. It seemed fitting. Raven, like Edgar Allen Poe. Riley was a unisex name, in case she got busted for being a girl.

Adrielle sat on the far end of the room and picked at the gray upholstery as she leafed through a magazine. It was all about hunting, the kind selling guns and bird whistles. She feigned interest until a man in a white jacket entered the room. She set the magazine down and sat upright.

The man scanned the sign-in clipboard and began calling out names. Bob, Doug, Tom, Joey . . . they stood up one by one and walked toward him. Finally, he called out Riley.

They gathered in the center of the room and stood in a semi-circle around him. He explained they'd be going into a training room to watch a video that would introduce them to the program. He said it would change their lives. The boys already looked bored, their gazes searching out the nearest exit. Wanting to blend in, Adrielle mimicked them and yawned.

When he was done his spiel, he led them out of the room into a long hallway with glaring fluorescent lights. A couple of turns later, they entered a large auditorium with stadium seating. While the boys headed up front, Adrielle aimed for the top row. From here, she had perfect view of the stage and could evaluate the kids who'd turned up, without being watched. Not surprisingly, they were mostly guys, but surprisingly, there were also some girls.

The excitement level was through the roof. It amplified when loud music blasted from center stage, demanding everyone's attention. An unseen voice introduced the guest of honor. "Angelo, the mighty warrior."

The audience roared.

What? Adrielle felt a hard punch to her heart and jumped out of her seat. From where she was, it looked like Angelo. But how could it be? He'd never go along with anything Domenikos was involved in.

The Angelo on stage stepped up to the podium and held up both hands. "Thank-you for coming," like a politician, as though this was the most natural thing in the world. The audience roared.

Adrielle's heart dropped. *The voice*—she closed her eyes and let the rhythm of his speech sink in. *Definitely the same. Identical even.*

Adrielle got angrier with every word he spoke. At the end of his speech, he snapped a salute and gave allegiance to Domenikos. Touted him as a great leader.

And then the stage floor opened up like in a Super Bowl half-time show. A bright spotlight shone on a figure rising up on a platform. A blonde in a red satin dress. Adrielle couldn't breathe. It was Scarlett.

Scarlett stepped off her rising platform and took Angelo's hand. She leaned into him and whispered something in his ear, and they smiled, then she gave him a full-mouthed kiss that seemed to last forever.

"No!" Adrielle shouted, unable to control herself.

Chatter in the auditorium buzzed.

Adrielle clenched her fists as her anger flamed to full-blown rage. This was a charade. Her mind filled with horrible ways to torture Scarlett. Torturous ways, even Domenikos would relish. Especially Domenikos.

Angelo and Scarlett's loosened their embrace. Scarlett bowed, then gave a pathetic royal wave.

Kids all around turned and were gaping at her. They pointed and jabbed one another to turn and look at her.

They were staring like she was a freak. This is what she hated most about growing up in Florida. Taunting rants burned into her like a branding.

It was unnatural to be so white. To be Albino. The painful words sliced into her core.

Her traveler's crest burned the skin between her shoulder blades, and she let out an involuntary scream.

All her muscles contracted, then released, as if she was shedding of everything physical.

Where did he go? Or she? Someone was right there, they pointed. *They've vanished.*

The ruckus came from all directions. Angelo left the stage and started toward her, fury in his eyes.

Adrielle was stunned. Wasn't she the one who should be angry? He was the one who'd kissed Scarlett. Who'd sided with the enemy.

Angelo barreled up the steps and stopped in front of her. Adrielle stood up and braced for the worst. But Angelo looked straight through her.

She looked down at her hands and saw she was invisible.

Chapter 47

Dave, Coco, and Eugene–
In the memory tunnel–
Back in time–Florence Italy 1504

FRANCESCO'S STAFF TALKED of an extensive honeymoon to Venice, and it became clear to Dave they needed to find Liz before they lost her trail. But they had no way to get there.

Asking Piero for horses was out of the question, since he took a special satisfaction in making them work for their supper. Instead of offering them lodging in the big house that first night, he tossed them horse blankets and pointed to the stables.

After much thought and a restless night, Dave came up with a plan. "Eugene, your gun is the only valuable thing we have. If we could barter and trade your gun for horses—"

"My gun? No way."

"The only way to get you home is to find Liz. And for that we need horses. We need to get to Rome."

As much as Eugene hated to part with his shotgun, Dave was convinced he wanted to get home more. Over breakfast, Eugene haggled with Piero and traded his hammerless shotgun for the use of three horses and supplies for the journey to Rome. He even negotiated one bottle of wine.

Piero loaded the horses with blankets and enough food and water for three days' travel. Then he pointed in the direction of a dusty dirt trail.

"IT MAY AS well be the Trojan horse. It's huge. I am never going to get on," Dave said.

"Nonsense. Haven't you ever been on a horse?" Eugene said.

Dave shook his head.

Eugene sighed. He got off his horse and guided Dave's foot into the stirrup. "Hang on."

Coco climbed on her horse, and the three went on their way. Eugene was at the front, and Coco behind Dave. She stayed close by until Dave got the hang of it, then she fell behind.

They'd been riding for several hours when Coco spotted a clump of trees ahead. She'd been noticing Dave kept his head down and didn't keep an eye on the road ahead.

"Watch out. Look up ahead," she said, trying to catch up.

Dave turned to look back at her, ran into a canopy of trees overhead, and toppled to the ground.

"Are you ok," Coco said, catching up.

Dave stood up and rubbed his head. "I think so. I've got a large bump, but I feel ok."

"Enough excitement for one day. We're in between cities and it's getting late. We should make camp," Coco said.

Dave agreed.

They collected dry wood for a fire and set up blankets close to it.

Dinner consisted of bread, Italian sausage, and wine.

"I've got a headache. I'm going to lay down," Dave said.

Coco stayed up with Eugene. After his second glass of wine, he started to open up.

"How did your family end up in California, when they were from Italy?" Coco asked. She was thirsty for conversation.

"As a child, my father apprenticed in a candy maker's shop in Rapallo. By the time he was twenty, he'd sailed to Uruguay and worked in the chocolate and coffee business."

"Ahh . . . so he got around," Coco said, enjoying the conversation.

"He moved to Peru a year later and opened a confectionary store. Nine years after that, he exported six hundred pounds of chocolate to California.

"No. Six hundred pounds? Jeez. I can't even imagine. Sounds like he was very successful."

"He was," Eugene said, a melancholy seemingly overtaking him. "My brothers and I miss him very much. He passed some years ago."

"Sorry to hear that," Coco said. "My mother passed away too. And I never knew my father. I would have liked to. Family is all that ever mattered to me and my sister. And of course, my friends." She glanced at Dave who appeared to be asleep. "They're our chosen family." She smiled.

They stared into the fire and listened to the crackling flames.

"That doesn't explain how he got to California," Coco said, after a bit. "You only said he exported the chocolate."

Eugene smiled. He refilled his glass of wine and held it up in toast.

"To my father, Domenico. If it wasn't for him hearing of the gold strike at Sutter's Mill, I wouldn't have a business. He wouldn't have sailed to California."

"Ah, the gold rush. To Domenico." Coco raised her glass and joined him in the toast. "Funny, I know someone whose name is close to that. Domenikos." She shivered.

"Sounds like you don't like him," Eugene said.

"I don't. He's not a good guy. I don't know what I'd do if he was related to me."

Eugene pondered this for a long moment. "My father was brilliant."

"I'm sure. Speaking of chocolate, I've been saving this." Coco slipped her hand in her pocket and pulled out a chocolate bar. She broke off one square and handed it to Eugene.

"It's better if you let it melt," she said, breaking off a piece for herself. She glanced at Dave, who still appeared to be sleeping, and folded the wrapper.

"Can I see that?" Eugene said. "It's delicious."

"Yeah." Coco handed him the chocolate bar. Eugene studied it for a minute. A puzzled expression appeared on his face. "How can this be? I've never seen wrapping like this."

Dave bolted up. "Oh my god. Oh my god."

Coco scurried to Dave's side. "Are you okay? Is it your head?"

"Yes. No. A slight headache." He cradled his head in his hands, then pointed to Eugene. "Did I hear you right? Peru? Your dad is a major exporter of chocolate and sailed to California after hearing about the gold strike at Sutter's Mill?"

"Yes. He opened a general store in Stockton California for miners."

"Eugene, please tell me your father isn't Domenico Ghirardelli."

"The one and only." Eugene smiled and handed him the foil wrapped chocolate bar. Dave stared at the candy bar.

"My father retired in 1892, and my brothers and I took over the business. We've sold the coffee and spices division and are thinking of selling the chocolate and mustard business too."

"So, your last name is Ghirardelli?" Dave asked, wild excitement in his eyes. "You own Ghirardelli chocolate?"

Eugene nodded.

Dave looked pointedly at Eugene. "Drop the mustard, but stick to the chocolate."

Dave exchanged a look with Coco. He didn't have to explain if they didn't get Eugene back soon, they'd be altering history big-time.

Chapter 48

Liz–in the memory tunnel–
Back in time–Florence Italy 1504

LIZ COULDN'T SLEEP. The talk about children was unsettling, to say the least. She and Francesco hadn't used protection.

"Children? Not for a long time," Liz had said to Dave, after she told him she was engaged to Francesco.

It didn't take long for Dave to point out all the reasons why it would be insane for her to have children with Francesco. Starting with the obvious: How could they raise a child when the parents lived hundreds of years apart?

A discussion about childbirth death rates eased into "C-sections." It was enough to scare the bejeebies out of her.

Argh. She wasn't ready to settle down, only to die with her first child. No wonder Dave had been adamant against her marriage. He'd gone as far as to say there was nothing they could do for infection either—because penicillin wasn't discovered until 1928. She remembered this because Kate's great-grandmother was born in 1928.

If Francesco was sleeping with other women, had he contracted a venereal disease and passed it on to her? She had to pee more often these days, and she wasn't sure if this was a symptom. No technology to look up WebMD. Nope. But Dave would know.

She felt sick. Was she being overly dramatic?

Argggh, she pressed her hand to her stomach. She missed Dave and his idiosyncrasies. How would she survive without him? A girl needed someone to run things by.

The more she thought about it, Leonardo would never have brought up these indiscretions unless he believed them. Leonardo dealt with facts. And he calculated potential outcomes. But she had to find out for herself.

First, she had to survive the long trip ahead. She pulled the linen sheet up to her chin and closed her eyes. With the carriage wheel repaired and financial things sorted out, their trek to Rome would continue. Barring more adventures, in the next twenty-four hours, she'd learn the truth.

THE NEXT MORNING, Isabel held up Liz's cargo pants and cropped tee. "They are clean, dry, and ready to wear."

Liz thanked her, then reminded Isabel she could dress herself. Isabel pouted in the corner while Liz dressed.

Surprisingly, she had a difficult time stuffing all her jewels inside the bra cup. It seemed to have shrunk. She wondered if Isabel had used too hot of water. Her breasts were bulging over the top. Not that she was complaining, but they felt tender.

Perhaps it wasn't the bra at all, but an after-effect from last night's wine. Sulfites? Could that cause swelling? Between the two of them, they'd consumed the large decanter of wine. She slipped her t-shirt on and glanced around the room one last time.

Since their luggage hadn't been recovered, leaving wouldn't take long. Liz picked up Leonardo's note and stuffed it into her pocket as a memento. Then she folded her new silk dress and cape and draped it over one arm. "Let's go."

Isabel objected, but Liz held her ground. Why should the girl dote on her? She wasn't even sure she'd remain Francesco's fiancée. And if she didn't, there was absolutely no reason to carry on the charade.

Liz and Isabel waited on the front porch for Antonio to ride up with the carriage. This was the final leg of her adventure, and she wanted to freeze this memory.

The sky was gray and overcast, with a distant storm brewing. A strong breeze blew her hair as she studied the cobbled street. She took in the weathered wood doors in the coved doorways. The smell of baking from the bakery down the street.

Her conversation with Leonardo circled in her mind like a dog chasing its tail. It left the sting of betrayal. Perhaps Leonardo was right. There *were* a zillion stars in the sky. So why would she settle for something less than what she'd dreamed of?

Truth was, she'd saved herself for love. And love did what it usually did. Love brought pain.

She'd go to Rome to see what was going on. If Leonardo was right about Francesco, she'd be bleeding tears.

Antonio pulled up with the coach. These horses were a deep chestnut and every bit as handsome as the others. They appeared well rested and fed. Aside from the occasional flick of the tail for a pesky fly, they waited patiently for their master's command.

Liz scrutinized the spoked wheels. The blacksmith had done a first-rate job of reinforcing the broken spoke with steel. She hoped it would last this final leg of the trip.

Antonio signaled for them to board. Liz stepped onto the folding step and hoisted herself into the box. Isabel followed and settled on the bench beside her.

Through the front window, they could see Antonio pick up the reins. A subtle movement alerted the horses it was time to go, and they leaned into the harness.

Liz was sad to leave Leonardo. He'd become a good friend. In some ways, he was more of a father than her own dad, who'd constantly dodged visits after the divorce.

Liz had caught Leonardo up on Adrielle and the others, and they'd discussed recent findings about Domenikos, and what was happening inside the diamond scepter.

She thought about when she'd told him Angelo's memory had been stolen, and he was trying to find it. Leonardo had been amazed. He'd said, "Never could I have imagined memories are in danger of being stolen."

"Welcome to the future," she'd said, knowing too well that life was unpredictable and full of surprises.

Chapter 49

Adrielle—Two years into the future, Florida

YOU'VE GOT TO be kidding!

Adrielle dropped into her seat, overcome with a whirl of emotions cycling inside her. Emotions she needed time to process.

She was confused by her response to the kiss. Why was she so angry, so hurt? She liked Angelo, but she'd chosen not to get romantically involved with him. Could she really blame him for going elsewhere?

If only it wasn't her.

Angelo acted as though she wasn't there. He stretched his hand out and it went right through her.

Adrielle's chest tightened. How could this be? She lifted her arm and touched Angelo's arm. It felt solid, flesh and bones. She felt better, but Angelo swiped his arm through her body as though she were a hologram. He did it again and again and again.

Everyone started laughing.

"Can someone turn up the air? We need a little air up here," Angelo said to the stagehands. "These guys are seeing things."

Someone in the back gave him the thumbs up and walked away.

Adrielle leaned into Angelo. "Can't you see me?"

He didn't respond. Sounds from the roaring crowd thundered so she was unsure if he'd hear her. She stared into his eyes. They were dim; the vibrant green flecks of his irises reduced to a muddy grey.

Scarlett's annoying voice blasted over the speakers. Adrielle cringed. Even after years of bullying, Scarlett summoned that kind of response. And yet, Adrielle often prided herself that Scarlett didn't matter. That she was immune to her tirades.

Scarlett spoke in a beguiling voice, and the audience closest to the stage quieted.

Adrielle ripped her attention away from Angelo.

A giant, gilded, mirror rose up from the floor. Words of praise seeped out of Scarlett's mouth. Nurturing, encouraging words. "Come down . . . everyone.

Look how handsome you'll be, as part of the royal army. *You* are the chosen ones. Hand-picked to be the most revered."

Scarlett's voice was a magic potion. People stood up in waves and filed down the stairs to the stage. Young men swooned like cattle to a salt lick.

Adrielle was terrified for them. There'd be no turning back once they looked in the mirror.

Adrielle found herself standing in front of Scarlett on center stage. She feared Scarlett would say something, challenge her, or expose her. But Scarlett didn't seem to see her.

Adrielle thought about Veda and Kate. Veda loved gossip, but she'd always been perceptive when it came to people. Veda had called Scarlett a tyrant. A mini-Hitler.

And here she was.

Kate, the eternal optimist, hadn't liked Scarlett either, which, in itself, said something. Because Kate liked everyone.

A deep pang of melancholy ached inside Adrielle. She missed them.

And now Angelo was the target. Doomed by the sting of a black widow.

Domenikos had done this to throw her off her game.

Adrielle summoned her self-control. She wanted to yank Scarlett's hair. Instead, she turned to the mirror to see what the others were seeing in it—if she'd see herself decked out in a Royal army uniform with golden medallions dangling at the shoulders.

Adrielle froze. She didn't see her reflection at all. She saw rows of boys in line behind her—a trail of ants leading up to the bleachers.

She had a terrible feeling. What if this ceremony was the reverse of what she'd seen inside the Time Vault? Could this mirror be a conduit leading to and from the Time Vault?

The mirror seemed to come alive. Iridescent bubbles burst from the glass surface and grew until a thin organic membrane matched the approximate mass of the first kid in the lineup and enveloped him like cellophane.

The boy seemed oblivious to what had happened to him. One by one the boys were wrapped in this membrane.

What if the bubbles were cocoons? Organic biospheres hatching thin and fragile pods. A parasite attaching to the host until the metamorphosis process was complete?

Adrielle shuddered.

Domenikos was gaining power. He was accessing the boy's mortal memories. Stealing them. Manipulating them. Then re-depositing them into his clone bodies, which would become his devout soldiers. An army of fully homogenized soldiers groomed into Domenikos' version of the perfect warrior.

Angelo, or more precisely—Domenikos' Angelo-clone—was the perfect protégé. His prized warrior.

Chapter 50

Dave, Coco, and Eugene—
In the memory tunnel—
Back in time—Florence Italy 1504

THE RED AND purple sunset had warned of a hot day ahead. At the first rays of sunrise, Dave gathered his sparse belongings and loaded them onto his horse.

He massaged his lower back and watched Coco and Eugene mount their horses effortlessly. He was sore. Why did people assume this was enjoyable? Next time someone told him horseback riding was fun, he'd tell them the truth. It was hard work.

He stood staring at the large chestnut animal that would become his ride for the next two days. The last thing he wanted to do was mount.

"What's wrong?" Coco asked.

"Nothing." Dave put his reservations aside and slipped his foot into the stirrup. They needed to find Liz before she made the biggest mistake of her life. After a few tries, he hauled himself up, took the reins, and waited for Coco's lead.

"Keep your body straight and move to the rhythm of the horse. Stay calm. Eyes on the path ahead," Eugene coached.

Easier said than done. Dave exchanged a look with Coco. The expression on her face said this was exciting. Of course it was, she was a natural.

Coco shook the reins, and her horse broke into a trot. Dave and Eugene followed.

They rode for several hours until the sun was high in the sky.

Dave wiped the sweat from his forehead. "Let's water the horses. It must be noon," he said, dying to get off his horse.

"No, let's ride on," Coco said. "We have a lot of ground to cover."

Mid-afternoon, they ran into a small creek. Before Dave could slow his horse down, Eugene was off his horse and at the water's edge. Dave pulled on the reins and pressed his heels into the horse's side. By the time he dismounted, Coco and Eugene were studying a couple of deserted canvas bags they'd found by the riverbank.

"Beautiful workmanship," Eugene commented. "Too bad someone ripped the leather trying to get at the inside."

"Do you see anyone? The rider could have been thrown of a horse and badly hurt," Coco said.

"No. The bags look rifled through but not thrown. Maybe they were stolen. I'll have a look around," Eugene said. He wandered around the clearing and picked something up next to a bush. "Found this." He held up a wad of scrunched paper.

"What is it?" Coco asked.

"Not sure." Eugene smoothed it out and studied it closely. It was brown and white with gold foil. "I've never seen anything like it. It says Caramilk."

"Caramilk? Liz's favorite candy bar." Dave snatched it out of Eugene's hand.

Dave rushed to the bush and looked around. "Someone's been here." He picked up a piece of leather strap by a tree. "They must have made camp. Anything else in the bag?"

Coco held up a white pointy-toed silk shoe with an elaborate jeweled broach adorning the front. "Kitten heels. They look expensive." She turned the bag over and studied the tooled leather. "It's embossed with an LG for initials."

Dave dragged his palms down his face. "Oh no."

"What?" Coco said. "You look like you're going to pass out."

"LG. As in—Lisa De Giocondo. Aka, Lizzie."

"You think?"

"Yes. Definitely yes. The Caramilk and now this." Dave squatted next to Coco and inspected the bag. "Here's a piece of torn white silk."

He carried it to the water's edge and followed the riverbank to look for clues. A ways up along the shore was a flowy white dress, sunk halfway in the water. He raced over and fished it out.

"Wedding dress," he shouted over his shoulder. "There's a dark red stain." He inspected it closer.

"Blood. There's blood!" Dave screamed.

Chapter 51

Liz—In the memory tunnel—
Back in time—Italy 1504

AS THE CARRIAGE rolled into Rome, Liz felt as though she was headed for the guillotine.

Holy caramels, this is a nightmare. Was this the kind of thing she'd have to look forward to on an ongoing basis? As a silk merchant, Francesco travelled extensively. She wondered if his travel included her. If Leonardo was right, she'd have to wonder what he was up to every single time he left.

She'd always believed work travel in a marriage was justified. But not if the spouse was required to stay home and perform domestic duties strictly because of their gender. Francesco did seem the chauvinist type. He opened doors, chose what she ate and wore, and even picked out her jewelry.

Liz dropped her gaze to her gem-studded bracelet. She'd slipped it on once they reached the city limits. What wasn't there to like? When the sunlight hit the diamonds just right, hundreds of tiny reflections danced off them. They were magical. At least they appeared so. But now . . . with her newly thought-out perspective, they looked more and more like a dowry paid in exchange for a lifetime of slavery.

Was she really considering being the little wifey that stayed home, while the fat mouse ran off to play? Didn't sound like a good exchange. Or life plan, any way she looked at it.

Settling for homemaker didn't cut it for an aspiring journalist. Living in an age without modern conveniences wasn't cutting it either.

Noontime bells clanged as the carriage clicked through a central street. Liz poked her head out the window and studied the intricate church facade as they passed. By midday tomorrow, she'd be climbing up those steps to take her sacred vows. Her stomach clenched.

Leonardo said a powerful papacy sponsored many artistic projects. Masterful artists from all over the country were flocking here. There was talk of a large upcoming commission. A contract to paint the ceiling of the chapel in the Vatican. Liz smiled, knowing this would become one of Michelangelo's masterpieces, enjoyed for centuries to come. The painting of the Sistine chapel would be awarded to him from Pope Julius the II, one of Michelangelo's biggest patrons. Of course she hadn't said anything.

It was exciting to know the future before it happened. Michelangelo had completed the Pieta, another important commission from cardinal Jean De Billheres. A sculpture inside a side chapel of St Peter's Basilica. It was so successful it launched Michelangelo's career like no other.

Dave often said history was defined by moments that shaped society and the world. Liz thought about Dave and his love of history. She knew this was an exciting era to be in Rome.

Along with being the hub of learning and the arts, Rome was exploding with expansion and innovations. But even without the luxury of hindsight, Liz could already feel the synergy from the residents. This was, after all, the Renaissance.

She ducked back into the box and slouched on the bench. *Ughh.* Her stomach churned and twisted. Was this how a bride was supposed to feel? Dreadful?

The bumpy ride caused by uneven cobblestones hadn't helped. She'd been nauseous since leaving Florence, and it was starting to worry her. She pressed her hands into her stomach and leaned forward. God, she hoped she didn't retch until she got out.

They pulled up under a large portico and Antonio hauled the horses to a stop. The carriage bopped up and down as he climbed from the coachmen's step onto the street, making Liz feel even more woozy. He tied the horses to a side rail and instructed Liz and Isabel to wait until he returned.

Antonio disappeared behind a large carved wood door, and she wondered if she should get out now. Find a nearby tree to throw up on.

"Still feeling sick?" Isabel asked, searching her face.

Liz nodded.

"It is the trip," Isabel said. "And this coach. Not as comfortable as I thought."

Liz didn't respond. She was afraid if she moved, or talked, she'd be wearing her breakfast.

Antonio returned, accompanied by two older women, who helped them down from the carriage and led them inside while Antonio tended to the horses.

On the outside the house looked grand. The portico had large pillars and a decorative door.

Liz looked around as they stepped inside what appeared to be the servant's entry. The large room was stocked with supplies and barrels of provisions. They walked down a long hallway to the kitchen, which had a large table in the middle, a brick stove, a stone sink, and shelving.

Garlic and cooking smells permeated the kitchen where three women glanced at them and then continued chopping vegetables, stirring something in a large iron cauldron on the stove, and kneading a large ball of dough.

None of them seemed to be enjoying their tasks, just going through the motions with perfunctory movements, each lost in their own world.

They continued through room after elegant room, some large enough to house balls.

They finally stopped at a door upstairs and entered a ritzy and spacious suite, with tall windows that opened to a small balcony.

Liz stepped out to get air. Below was an intricate garden, a maze of hedges with pathways lined with manicured flower beds.

She glanced back at the sound of a maid carrying in Liz's cape and silk dress and laying it on the canopy bed. "Someone will be right up with your trunk."

"Trunk? Oh no. There's no trunk. We were robbed, so what little we had is long gone."

"There is a trunk, my lady. The master ordered some things he thought you might need. I'll send someone up with it right away." She curtsied and closed the door behind her.

Liz wandered back to the window to gaze onto the garden. She heard a loud scraping sound and went inside to peek out into the hallway.

Two male servants heaved the large trunk up the flight of stairs. She stepped aside as they entered the chamber. They put the trunk at the foot of the bed and bowed as they exited the room.

Liz approached the trunk and looked down at it, unsure whether to open it right away, or have the talk with Francesco first.

This trunk may very well prove her point. A trunk full of things Francesco thought she might need. If this contained anything near what was going through her mind, it would make it harder to keep a level head. She squeezed her hands into fists. If only Dave was there. He'd know what to do.

What to do. What to do . . .

Curiosity won over pragmatic thinking. In two minutes flat she had the trunk contents spread over the entire bed. Seven silk dresses—one for every day of the week. Seven matching silk mules—one with so much glitter it reminded her of Cinderella's glass slippers. A box of gold earrings encrusted with sapphires and a matching gold choker. *Oooh.* And a large box tied with a silk blue ribbon.

Hmmm. It wouldn't have helped to have Dave see this. He was a sucker for silk. His opinion would be deeply biased.

Not proud of her reputation for not being able to keep a secret, Liz did what she did best. Investigate. She couldn't help herself, it was part of her DNA. An unopened package may as well have screamed "OPEN ME NOW!"

Liz pulled on the ribbon and slid the lid off. She sucked in her breath. Inside was a white silk dress with layers and layers of fabric. Matching silk shoes with a gem detail on the front matching the sapphire earrings and choker.

Something blue . . .

She lifted the dress out of the box. This was the most beautiful dress she'd ever seen. A flood of tears welled and spilled.

It was a dress she would never wear.

Chapter 52

Adrielle–Two years into the future, Florida

WITH MORE INFORMATION on how Domenikos had tapped into people's memories, Adrielle was ready for step two of her plan: finding Haden.

Aside from her father, Haden was the only other Achaean who'd studied the *Book of Feathers* in detail. As head of the Achaean army, he'd been in sole charge of its protection. Of the sacred information contained within its covers.

The book was a powerful culmination of Achaean knowledge, and the only account of their history, going back thousands of years. It contained ancient mystical secrets, spells, and virtually anything pertaining to their species. It also cited atrocities against Achaean leaders and rules enacted by the leadership. Domenikos' name and actions were cited all over it.

After spending time with the book, Adrielle realized reading it was not enough. It was too deep, too interlaced with intricate information and hidden meanings. To truly understand it, she had to study and ponder the material it contained, perhaps for centuries.

She was overwhelmed with responsibility. There were so many missing pieces. Too many for one person to get a clear overview of everything involved. If anyone had insight to what was happening in the world currently, with the shifting of memories and Domenikos' sudden rule, despite being a prisoner inside the scepter diamond, it would be Haden. Haden had experience she didn't.

Domenikos was building his army at an alarming speed, so she needed Haden *now*.

She thought it inconceivable she hadn't heard from him since her confrontation with Domenikos at the cave. *No, infuriating.* She decided he was up to something. *But what?* No contact was out of character, given their history.

Haden had professed his love to her countless times. He'd also been the one to propel her forward into modern day Florida by using a spell. Afterward, because there had been no way of knowing where she'd propelled to, he told her he'd spent years searching for her. So, the lack of communication once he'd found her didn't add up.

Adrielle headed to the beach, the one place she could think. With Palm Coast's city lights behind her and the ebbing ocean tide lapping onto her bare feet, she felt more at ease.

The weight of responsibility was crushing. How could she lead the Achaeans? She wasn't thousands of years old like her father had been. Or like Haden and Angelo were. She wasn't even a full Achaean. She was just a girl.

Adrielle sucked in a long breath. She loved the smell of the ocean. The salty ocean mist felt cool on her skin. She reached around her back and touched her encrusted crest, intricately a part of her now. Like it or not, she'd been the one to earn this crest of the traveler. The fate of the world rested entirely in her hands. And she was determined to succeed.

The four interweaved feathers of her crest were the same ones embossed onto the cover of the *Book of Feathers*. The crest came with accountability. And powers.

The red feather stood for war—Haden's specialty.

The silver feather stood for conquest and military subjugation. Angelo's field.

The black feather stood for truth. Astraia was the only other Achaean who bore this power

The last feather mystified her the most. Green. Green stood for death. More precisely, overcoming death. For some reason, Domenikos held this power. Why? As the Achaean leader, so did she. She was determined to find out what this power could do.

She ran her fingers over her crest, and it tingled. It was time to learn how to use it.

Adrielle raised her face to the sky. Twilight, her favorite time of day. Despite it all, she felt happy. Stars appeared like diamonds in a net of periwinkle. The ocean breeze grazed her skin with a refreshing coolness. Since her youth, the smell of salt and seaweed and all things ocean brought her peace. She closed her eyes and remembered.

On the night before her wedding, in Achaea, she'd gone to her favorite spot, the ancient cave. It was her sanctuary from the chaotic world of Achaea. She'd been surprised to find Haden there, musing over recent events creating turmoil in their world.

The forbidden cave.

Thinking of it awakened Adrielle's crest. A burning sensation confirmed she'd find Haden there.

Adrielle evoked every detail of that memory, that dark cool cave hidden within the rocks. She clenched her hands into fists and ran across the sand, her arms thrashing. She sped toward the spot where she'd appeared in this future time and searched the darkening sky for the almost invisible tear in the fabric of blue.

The stars weren't bright enough and the sky was darkening at an alarming rate. She looked around her, searching. Searching . . .

There, an almost indiscernible scar. Adrielle mustered all her energy and jumped up into the gash. She closed her eyes as she pierced the veil.

The tingling coursed through her veins until her whole body prickled. She kept her eyes clamped shut, as her body travelled along the hidden time tunnel. Her heart felt like it would burst.

Her body stopped moving. The tingling subsided, and Adrielle sat still. The salty ocean breeze was replaced by the dank musky smell of the forbidden cave. Adrielle opened her eyes. She was there, sitting on the stone floor in the dark cavern.

Adrielle stood and walked toward a small opening on the edge of the cave, where a sliver of moonlight shone in.

Outside the cave, a large yellow moon illuminated both sky and ocean. Roaring waves crashed onto the rocks below, the sound travelling up the near vertical rock face. The drop at her feet was terrifying and breathtaking all at once.

She turned back to the cave and went deeper into the dark, one hand on the rock face.

A frenetic noise burst from deep in front of her. A fluttering. Thousands of bats rustled out of a small opening and brushed against her.

Adrielle screamed.

She lost her balance and fell back, hitting the rock hard. Pain from her tailbone shot up her vertebrae. She stayed down, crouching until the last bat was out of the cave. Then she crawled on her hands and knees, every cell in her body screaming this was the way.

But no sign of Haden.

Chapter 53

Liz—In the memory tunnel—
Back in time—Rome Italy 1504

THE HOUSE WAS bustling with commotion. Extra help had been hired for the preparations of the wedding reception party, and everyone but Liz had a list of chores to complete. Even Isabel, who was usually at Liz's side, was gone.

Liz toyed with the idea of finding her, but the house was maze. Besides, she'd been told to stay put and relax, relax being the last thing Liz wanted to do with the upcoming wedding.

At any moment she expected Francesco to walk into her room, and she'd been debating how to broach the situation. After some thought, she decided a confrontation with Francesco about his indiscretions was not only off the table, but ridiculous.

It was impossible to make someone see something deemed acceptable in their upbringing was wrong. That was like telling a hunter killing animals was wrong. Or telling Picasso his portrait of Dora Maar was not a portrait at all, because no one actually looked like that. Eyes were supposed to be somewhat symmetrical, weren't they?

According to millions of art lovers, they didn't have to be. It was all a matter of perception.

And so, with the confrontation off the table, what was she going to do about it?

She loved being in love. Wearing the perfect dress on a perfect wedding day. But this wasn't her reality. Perfect was a term that wasn't in her vocabulary.

If it was, it would have included Dave as her maid of honor. Adrielle and Coco as her bridesmaids—and Veda and Kate. Instead, she was spending the day before her wedding alone, nauseous, and intermittently heaving and peeing into the same bowl she stuffed into the night table cabinet beside her bed.

She glanced at the trunk with the seven dresses. She'd be returning all of it. However, her diamond necklace and bracelet, she'd keep.

As the light turned into the golden hour, there was a bold knock on the door.

"Come in," Liz said, believing Francesco had arrived.

The door opened brusquely, and a small slim man with a thin moustache, carrying a black leather doctor's bag entered the room, with the maid following behind. He stood at the foot of the bed and was watching her curiously.

"You're not hungry?" he said, seeing the untouched bowl of vegetable soup on her night table.

Liz shook her head. She was still nauseous and could barely keep anything down.

"I'm doctor Severino." He reached into his bag and pulled out what looked like a speculum. "I've come to do the pre-marital exam."

"The whaaat?" Liz hunched her knees to her chest and pulled the bedspread up around her chin.

"We need to make sure everything is intact. Lower the covers," he said dryly.

Could this day get any worse?

"No." Liz squeezed her thighs together.

"*Scusami?*"

"No," she said, her voice sounding a notch higher.

Dr Severino glanced at the maid, who shrugged. "This is tradition," he said, his face showing confusion and irritation. Then it changed to a look of understanding. "Oh, it is your time of the month. Do not worry, I have seen it all."

"Ewww, no," Liz squealed. *Oh-my-god!* She let out a ragged moan. Could she be pregnant? They hadn't used protection. The nausea. The swollen tender breasts. Having to pee all the time . . .

But what if she'd contracted syphilis? Dave said a baby could become blind at childbirth. God, she missed Dave.

If she was pregnant, did it change her decision not to marry? It wouldn't be fair to raise her baby in Florida, when the father lived hundreds of years in the past, before they were born.

A flash of heat overwhelmed her, and she swiped at her forehead. Holy pickles on chocolate ice cream—there was no good way to resolve this. And there was no easy pregnancy test to confirm or deny her suspicions.

The doctor was watching her closely. The maid took her soup and laid it on a tray outside the room, then returned to remove the basin inside her night table. She said a flurry of things to the doctor, too fast for Liz to catch any of it.

The doctor attempted to pry the bedspread off to examine her and finally left.

If only Dave was here. Or someone from her own time. She had no idea how to get back to the scepter diamond.

The last person she wanted to see was Francesco.

Chapter 54

Adrielle—Inside the forbidden cave

ADRIELLE LOST HER footing and tumbled into a chasm. She braced for the drop as her stomach lurched into her throat.

The rock walls scraped against her body as she fell in an out-of-control tumble and couldn't grab onto the wall. Shooting down. Down. Down.

No sounds came from the earth—only the sound of her heart thrummed in her ears. Terror paralyzed her as she fought to suck in thinning air.

If she could propel her wings outward to break the fall, she might avoid broken bones. But how?

She could die here in the dark. Alone. No one knew where she was. No one could help. No one could hear her screams.

A calming reassurance blanketed her. Defiantly, the pounding in her ears got louder. Was it her heart?

She was alive, for now.

Adrielle concentrated on breathing. She willed her ribcage to expand and contract. Her heart thundered. Boom. Boom. Boom.

Then—*poing!*

Something came at her like a spider's web and wrapped her snuggly in its sac, breaking her fall. For a moment, it was reassuring. Until the silk-like threads tightened around her torso.

"Help. *Help*!"

Adrielle screamed until she could no longer breathe.

Chapter 55

Liz—In the memory tunnel—
Back in time—Rome Italy 1504

LIZ SKIPPED THE pre-wedding ball held in her honor and stayed in her room to brood. If she was pregnant, she was caught in a difficult situation.

A timid knock woke her from her semi-dazed state. Liz sat up, fragments of questions filling her mind. *Francesco?* What would she say? That she was cancelling the wedding again?

"Go away, I'm sleeping."

"It's Isabel." She entered without hesitation and laid a crystal vase on the night table. "I picked some flowers from the garden." She glanced at Liz. "Everything all right? You are not at the party."

Liz rolled onto her side. "Too tired."

Isabel's worried expression turned to disappointment.

For a moment, Liz felt a tinge of guilt. But if Isabel wanted to hang out, she would have. Besides, Isabel could lend a listening ear, but she'd never be able to give adequate insight on her situation. No one from these times could. Only Dave, Coco, or Adrielle.

She realized if she were back home in Florida, she'd have options. Perhaps it was her Italian and Puerto Rican heritage, or years of hanging out with Kate and her catholic grandma, but not having the baby wasn't an option she'd consider, nor giving it up for adoption. So, after some thought, the decision was made, she was keeping the baby.

She'd raise it on her own, for lack of a partner in the same time epoch.

This brought a fleet of questions, and more decisions. Serious ones with consequences. A baby involved another human being and affected her entire life. Without her notebook, she made an imaginary list in her head.

Pros: She'd always wanted kids. She'd never feel lonely again. It would give her divorced parents one more thing to fight about. And maybe they'd squabble over how much time they could spend with it, which would cut down on daycare and babysitting expenses.

It?—what kind of mother was she, already calling her baby—an it?

Who was she kidding? Her parents never wanted to spend time with her. So why would they with their grandkid? If she hadn't found Dave, who was in the same predicament because his parents were the same, she'd probably be miserable. And in years of therapy.

Coco and Adrielle didn't have parents, so ditto. They were all drawn together.

How old until the baby had friends? How soon could she send it on play dates? No, no, no . . . this wasn't a good way to look at parenting. She felt pressures beyond her years.

Daycare and babysitting costs were a definite con. *Cha-ching!* Add the cost of a baby crib, swing, playpen, stroller—some were upward of a couple hundred dollars—*Cha-ching!* A car seat—she didn't even own a car. *Cha-ching! Cha-ching!* Add doctor bills, formula, diapers, clothes . . .

Goodbye college, she thought sullenly, a sinking feeling overtaking her. She'd have to get a job right away. Any job, to cover the mounting baby costs. It might even mean forgoing dreams of being a television anchor. Maybe prevent her from being a journalist. How much did they get paid? Would it cover the cost of diapers?

The slant of the sun streaming in the window announced the late hour. Liz was overwhelmed. She laid her head on the pillow and closed her eyes. Something sickly sweet churned her empty stomach.

What was that?

She followed her nose to her night table. The floral bouquet was making her sick. Liz moved the arrangement to a table at the other end of the room. She opened the window for some fresh air.

The garden below was beautiful. Someone had taken the time to design and plant flowers in circular beds and all along the walking pathways. She soaked in the beauty.

Life could be good here. Simple. But Dr Severino handling the pregnancy was frightening. So were complications. Breach baby. Or worse, a third trimester miscarriage? Thanks to the internet, all sorts of horrible possibilities were at her fingertips. Or not, she realized.

No internet. No information.

She'd have to find a good OBGYN right away—in Florida. She sighed. Another decision made.

There were a zillion pressing details to attend to. She went back to bed and curled onto the crumpled linen sheets. She drifted to sleep to be awakened by another rap on the door. This one was harsh and hurried.

At first the sound meshed with her dream—the baby cradle was tapping on the window. The sound grew more and more urgent. In her dream, it morphed into Monika's black bird, Arnadella, rapping its beak on her windowpane. She ignored it.

"Lisa? Lisa are you awake?" Francesco called out.

She snapped her eyes open, a tight knot forming in her chest.

Chapter 56

Domenikos–Inside the Time Vault

DOMENIKOS LAY ON his side clutching his torso. His chest was hurting. It hurt to breath.

"You all right, boss?" the Brix clone asked.

"Go away," Domenikos snapped and waited until the clone left the room. It took him a minute to catch his breath.

He was surprised to learn something serious had happened to her. And even more surprised that it affected him so profoundly. Though he'd never admit it to anyone, Domenikos felt a deep sense of loss. A sense of injustice shook him. And then resentment settled in his bones. He felt cheated, as though it had happened to him.

Chapter 57

Adrielle–Inside the forbidden cave

ADRIELLE HAD NO idea how long she'd been incubated inside the cocoon. Her body was stiff, and a gauzy membrane, thin enough to see light through it, covered her eyes. She struggled to remove the gauze, but her arms were wrapped so snuggly around her body she couldn't even wiggle them.

She rubbed her face against the side of the covering until the gauze lifted away from her eyes. She looked down and determined she was encased in intricate fine threads, thousands of them.

Instead of panicking, she took comfort in the fact she was still here. She sucked in a slow, painful, breath. The cadence of her expanding ribcage became slow and steady, and she relaxed.

She was alive, and that was something. She felt vindicated and excited. No bones were broken, as far as she could tell.

She struggled to touch the walls around her, but her hands were still constrained. She dropped her gaze to her sides and—

Whaaa? She had no arms, no hands. Only white feathered wings pressed tightly against her sides. The feathers were iridescent, lustrous, and shimmering. And beautiful.

But she already knew she had the capability to shift into her true Achaean bird form—an ability she'd earned with her traveler's crest. She didn't know how she'd shifted in the turmoil. Or why.

This phenomenon defied natural laws. And then it hit her: everything Achaean defied natural laws.

With her beak, she pecked at the fibers binding her in— a tedious task, taking an extraordinary amount of time. She considered trying to shift back into human form, if she could figure out how to do that, but something held her back.

Every slight movement caused the cocoon to sway. It was likely suspended by a thread or threads.

At least in bird form, she'd be able to fly and cover more ground than her human legs allowed.

The downside was her hands could rip at the sides of the cocoon at a swifter rate. She paused for a moment and determined that bird form was more fitting in this situation.

Adrielle continued to peck at the threads despite the stifling warmth inside the cocoon. The smell of sweat mingled with a foul decaying odor made her nauseous. Finally, her beak cut through the threads, and she poked her head through the cocoon into a chilling darkness.

The light was only inside. To leave this most undesirable shelter meant to face the unknown.

Adrielle wriggled in the cocoon until the fibers loosened, and she was able to move freely inside it. She inspected her wings. They appeared to be intact. Her natural Achaean form was empowering. In bird shape, she felt truly beautiful.

Adrielle ripped at the small hole she'd made in the wall of the bubble until it was large enough to squeeze through and made a bold and dashing leap out of the cocoon into the unknown.

Not knowing how to flap her wings, she spun into a tailspin, plummeting downward. Falling, falling . . .

Chapter 58

DAVE, COCO, AND EUGENE—
IN THE MEMORY TUNNEL—
BACK IN TIME—ROME ITALY 1504

DAVE, COCO, AND Eugene rode into Rome long after the sun had set. Heat radiated from the worn cobblestones and the stifling smell of humidity and sweat clung to them. The smell of manure to lead them to a local stable. After watering and feeding the horses, Coco exchanged a couple of coins for their shelter, and they left to explore the city.

Even at night, Rome was thriving. Inns and food establishments bustled with people and churches anchored every corner. But without modern day navigation, they had no idea where they were. Only that they'd arrived in one of the busiest cities in the world.

After rounding several blocks, Coco slipped her arm through Dave's. "You've been upset since we found the suitcase. That blood could have been anyone's. I know you're worried, but Liz is resourceful and can hold her own."

"I can't stop from going to the worst scenario," Dave said. "She's all alone, and so many things could have gone wrong."

"Or just as easily gone right."

Dave nodded. "I just want to find her. Get her home."

"We're close, I can feel it."

Dave looked up at Coco's angelic face. With her large almond eyes and wide smile, she was the epitome of optimism. "If anyone could right this by sheer will, it's you."

Coco tipped her head. "Thank you. I'll take that as a compliment."

"Let's eat there," Eugene said, pointing to an eatery, brimming with patrons, down one of the narrow side streets.

"Got more spare change?" Dave asked Coco.

Coco jiggled her pouch. "It's emptier than before but should be enough."

"Great, someone there may know of a place to crash tonight," Dave said.

"Why would we want to crash?" Eugene said, with a puzzled expression.

Coco giggled and exchanged a look with Dave.

They sat at a table in the back of the establishment, and ordered lamb stew, the house specialty.

"Do you know Francesco del Giocondo?" Dave asked the server.

"The silk merchant? Who doesn't? Everyone is wearing his silks."

"Where can we find him?" Dave asked, his mood hinging on her answer.

"He has a place on the edge of the city." She met his eyes. "Don't even try. It's a fortress. And he's getting married in the morning, so you'll never get close. They'll be lining the streets to see the carriage roll by."

"In the morning? You sure?"

"Yes. The bride broke it off once before—she's the one he commissioned her portrait for, from Da Vinci. Hear about that?"

Dave stole an exchange with Coco. "Sure."

"I'll be back with your food soon."

"What time?"

"Eh?"

"The wedding. What time?"

"Eleven." She tipped her head. "At the cathedral three blocks down."

"That narrows it down to about five churches," Dave said sardonically.

Chapter 59

Liz—In the memory tunnel—
Back in time—Rome Italy 1504

SOMETIME DURING THE night Francesco crawled into bed with Liz. The smell of wine tickled her nose, and she squirmed to fight off a sneeze. He laid his hand on her chest and scrunched in close, the smell of lamb stirring her recent nausea.

She'd planned to tell him marriage between their two timelines was impossible. But it would have to wait until morning. She rolled onto one side and remained still, pretending to be asleep. Francesco groaned, but soon his loud rhythmic snore told her he'd fallen asleep.

She lay awake, worry consuming her. She wished she could disappear to avoid the confrontation altogether, but it was impossible without Adrielle's feather snippet.

A clatter from voices and dishes and laughter announced it was morning. Liz opened her eyes and was relieved Francesco was gone.

Everything will be all right, she told herself, seeing the bright sunlight streaming from the balcony. She jumped out of bed determined to put a stop to her wedding and saw her wedding dress laid out on a chair.

She rummaged the room for her clothes as she made her plans. Could she get back to Florence and buy some time until she figured out how to get back to the diamond center? Would Michelangelo be home?

Her clothes were nowhere to be seen. Liz traipsed to the bedroom door and opened it a crack. The bustle of the wedding preparations was in full force.

"Isabel. Isabel?" Liz called from the door. "Where are my clothes?" She glanced back at her wedding dress. She was running out of time. She could go downstairs in her nightie to look for her clothes or wait for someone to show up. Either way, she wasn't putting the dress on.

Liz closed the door and waited. And waited. She scraped blue nail polish from her nails. Raked her fingers through her knotted hair. Why wasn't anyone coming? It seemed unnatural for the bride to be left alone on her wedding day.

Minutes stretched to hours, sparking a thrumming in her heart. Finally, Isabel appeared with towels and fresh lavender. "It's time for your bath."

"Where are my clothes?" Liz said, trying to make eye contact.

Without slowing, Isabel marched past her and opened the balcony doors. "Hanging on the patio to dry."

"They're wet?" Liz said, feeling a tightening in her chest. If she tried to leave in her nightgown, she'd get picked up by the police. "What am I going to wear?"

"Your dress." Isabel's expression was incredulous. She pointed to it, on the chair. "I'll help you put it on, after your bath."

Liz balled up her fists. "I want my clothes."

"Don't worry, they will be dry by tomorrow, if you still want them."

"Of course I do."

"Francesco has ordered more dresses."

"More dresses?"

"Yes. You will have a new wardrobe after the wedding. The trunk should be arriving soon."

Liz gnawed on her nails. This was both good and bad. It proved how controlling Francesco was. And how sweet, which was what attracted her to him in the first place.

"Hurry, your bath is ready." Isabel waited impatiently by the door with toiletries in hand. Her expression said she'd rather be downstairs where the celebratory activities were unfolding.

Complaining was pointless. She couldn't do anything about the wet clothes, and a long, drawn-out bath sounded good.

Liz followed Isabel down the hall to a small bathing chamber——smaller than expected, given the size of the house. There was a circular metal tub filled with water and a side table with a sponge, pitcher, and soap. Isabel hung her towel on a wooden rack and waited for Liz to get in.

The tub was too small to completely lie down in. Liz sighed. Luxuries were so much more luxurious at home. She slipped off her nightgown and let it drop to the floor.

"Yaousa!" she screeched, as she stepped into the tub. "The water is cold." Liz jumped out, water pooling onto the floor.

Isabel looked puzzled.

"It's too cold," Liz said.

Isabel rolled her eyes. "It was hot a while ago. I have to get back downstairs."

So much for a relaxing soak. Liz wiggled her toe in, then lowered it an inch at a time until she sat waist high in an upright position, her knees folded against her chest.

Isabel dunked the pitcher and Liz braced for shock. She shivered, holding her breath as Isabel poured cold water over her hair.

"I-I ca-an t-t-take it from here," Liz said.

Isabel looked relieved. She curtsied and latched the door behind her.

Liz lathered and rinsed her hair. She raked her fingers through her long coarse curls. Without a hair dryer and straightener, it would remain a wooly mess.

Once she got used to the water temperature, she decided a cool bath was better than no bath. She ran her hand over her stomach and closed her eyes to think.

A baby was unexpected, but what scared her the most was not the baby. It was having a baby in these backward times. The ratio of women dying during childbirth was high.

She rubbed her belly. Francesco needed to know. She wouldn't leave without telling him.

Chapter 60

Adrielle—Inside the forbidden cave

ADRIELLE SPIRALED INTO the narrow and confining abyss of the tunnel. The rocks on the sides were sharp. If she didn't control her flight path, she would get hurt.

Adrielle spread her wings and caught an air current. She was flying. The sensation was euphoric and freeing.

She tested shifting her course by lifting and lowering her wings and trying muscles she'd never used to control the wind currents passing through her feathers.

Manipulating altitude, velocity, and direction took a tremendous amount of concentration. She could barely control her heavy wings. Hovering in one spot was nearly impossible. It was easier to go fast, so she accelerated.

She didn't see any nooks or crannies to rest as the tunnel wall raced toward her. The darkness obscured the edge, and she narrowly missed a jagged rock.

Adrielle stared down the barrel of the long tunnel that seemed to be a sheer drop to an endless pit. A chill breeze wafted up to her.

She couldn't gamble going further down without a rest. Above her, the shell she'd been encased in hung like a discarded skin, supported by wiry intertwined fibers that seemed to go up for miles.

Adrielle flew up to the cocoon and slowed beside it to catch her choppy breath.

She was trapped in a dark pit, the only light projecting from her feathers.

The prospect of travelling back up to the passageway entrance and re-experiencing the lack of air along the route, was daunting. With exhausted wings, she couldn't hover much longer. Her muscles ached and cramped.

Her crest confirmed Haden was in the cave and she clung to the hope of finding him

She looked up and then down. Downward might give her much needed answers. Perhaps she'd be able to coast. Maybe maneuver a controlled downward spiral to save energy and regain strength.

Adrielle adjusted her wings to avoid a tailspin and dove downward.

She raced toward the bottom of this chimney-like shaft feeling like time itself was suspended. Then she felt radiating plumes of heat rising.

She thought of *Dante's Inferno* and hoped she wouldn't encounter any of the writer's imagined demons. But even so, how bad could that be? She'd faced Domenikos and he was as malevolent as they came.

A crust of hot material glowed in the distance. Adrielle plummeted toward it at an alarming speed.

The glow from the coals lit up the ground.

Adrielle aimed for a clear flat area as far away from the hot molten rock as possible and hit the ground with a thud. She tumbled, summersaulting, then smashed into something hard.

Her feathers did little to soften the blow.

Adrielle sat stunned. She looked down at her body. She'd morphed back into her human body.

How?

She slid her hands down her torso and limbs. No broken bones.

She stared at her luminous skin. *Were her eyes playing tricks on her?* She blinked hard. Her skin seemed to be lit from the inside.

She grabbed a handful of her long hair and brought it close to her face. The strands shimmered like thin fiber optic cables charged with a current.

Adrielle wiped the sweat from her forehead. Hot embers sprayed from a bubbling pool of molten liquids as it released an unfamiliar odor. Adrielle scooted toward the wall behind her.

She stiffened as she felt a presence. Someone or something was watching her. She jumped to her feet. She had to get out of here.

The stream of hot liquids feeding into the pool had to come from somewhere. And she was breathing, so air was funneling from somewhere too.

A musky odious odor made her dizzy as she walked, keeping clear of the hot walls.

The glowing embers cast shadows on the stone, revealing small etchings. They seemed to make a pattern, which Adrielle followed to a small opening in the wall.

She brushed her fingers along the stone. Coolness emanated from within the rock.

Adrielle studied the lines. Small, faded lines etched into a cavern could be easily missed or not have any meaning. But the consistency of the markings, the way the shadows danced off the pattern, weirdly reminded her of home. Of a home she'd never known and yet felt so familiar.

Adrielle closed her eyes and pressed her forehead to the stone. A wave of homesickness like she'd never felt, weakened her. She braced against the wall to keep from falling and inhaled a sharp intake of air. Another aroma filled her nostrils.

"Father? Are you here?" she cried This smell took her to her roots. To a time before she could walk. To a place that felt more a part of her than any other. Her father's den.

A nervous excitement fluttered in her chest and shook her to the core.

The wave of homesickness crushed her. She was alienated from everyone she loved and, despite the profound longing for family and home, she felt something wonderful was about to happen.

Chapter 61

Liz—In the memory tunnel— Back in time—Rome Italy 1504

LIZ'S SKIN WAS beginning to resemble a raisin, and she decided she'd waited long enough for Isabel to return. Time to take things into her own hands. She had to stop the wedding.

Liz stepped out of the tub, grabbed the towel from the wooden rack, and wrestled to wrap it around her chest. This over-sized handkerchief barely covered her torso. After much pulling and tugging, she was able to tuck in one corner.

She opened the door to the bathroom and stared at the stunning garland of freshly cut red roses that curved around the stairway handrail and went all the way down the hall to her room and downstairs.

Unfamiliar voices trailed up the stairs. Liz rushed down the hall and ducked into her room.

The trunk of dresses hadn't arrived. Her only choice was the wedding dress on the bed. She hated to put it on, but without the nightie Isabel had taken, it was either that or stay in the mini-towel.

The dress was beautiful. Francesco had impeccable taste, she'd give him that. The silk was the finest available, one of the perks of being the main silk merchant in Italy.

Liz slipped the dress on and felt like an extension of her body, like she was wearing nothing at all. It had no embellishments, no diamond studs or pearls to take away from the design lines. It was the most superbly cut dress she'd ever seen.

She wandered over to the night table and clasped on the necklace.

She went to the mirror. Staring back was Cinderella, on her way to happily ever after. She looked like the bride on the magazine cover, the one she never dreamed she'd be. Her knees weakened, and she dropped onto the bed.

Was Francesco her happily ever after? She'd thought he was, once. She loved him, sure. That's why she was here. But if what Leonardo told her was true, she couldn't commit to him. It also worried her she'd been so quick to believe there were other women.

A loud rap on the door shook her out of her reverie. Two handmaidens walked in.

"Oh good, you are dressed. We are late." They whisked her out of the room and led her outside, where a coach with two chestnut-colored horses and a footman waited.

Liz tried to object, but the handmaidens lifted her dress and said something indecipherable. They put their hands on her waist and applied pressure on her lower back until she climbed up into the box of the carriage. Liz flopped onto the seat, and they closed the door.

The coachman clicked on the reins and the horses moved forward.

People lined both sides of the street and cheered and tossed flowers onto the road. Others waved and waited for acknowledgement from her—*the bride.*

She thought of Prince Harry and Meghan Markle; their wedding wouldn't take place for another five hundred years.

Wow. This was a big deal. Liz waved so her hand could be seen through the window and crowds cheered louder. Some even whistled.

The carriage weaved through town and after some time, rolled to a stop in front of a stone cathedral with gigantic doors. Red rose petals were scattered up the front steps. The carriage rocked as footman got down from his stool. He opened the door to the box and held his hand out for Liz.

For a fleeting moment, Liz thought of running.

Isabel and the two handmaidens stood on the bottom church step. Somehow, they'd arrived before her. They wore mauve silk dresses with matching ribbons in their hair and were holding bouquets of red roses.

Liz stepped out of carriage, and Isabel handed Liz the largest bouquet. The two handmaidens lifted the train of her dress and gestured for her to begin the processional.

Liz gripped onto her bouquet of roses. She was going to tell him. She really was. But now was not the time.

Calm down, I'll fix this. She took a bold step forward to the longest and shortest walk of her life.

Chapter 62

Dave, Coco, and Eugene—
In the memory tunnel—
Back in time—Rome Italy 1504

THE CROWD OF onlookers were kept a respectable distance from the cathedral by several city guards.

Coco turned to Dave and gently squeezed his shoulder. "I'm sorry. No matter what we do, we can't get any closer."

Dave shook his head and averted his gaze from the footmen flanking the cathedral entrance. "This isn't how it's supposed to be."

Coco turned back to Eugene. "Stay close. Remember, we're your best bet for getting home."

"When exactly would that be?" Eugene said, his voice terse and curt.

Coco shrugged. "After the wedding. We'll get Liz and figure it out."

Figure it out? She really was an optimist. What they needed was Astraia. Dave scanned the sky but still no sign of her. He felt a slight jab in his ribs and turned, imagining for a moment it was Liz.

Coco pointed to a decorated carriage galloping toward them. "Looks like the bridal procession."

Dave felt gut punched. He and Liz had a standing plan to be each other's besties. The carriage drew closer, and Liz waved out the window, a smile pasted on her face.

"It's her fake smile. She doesn't want to do it," Dave said to Coco, feeling a crazed kind of happiness.

Coco stared back at him with her expression of pity.

"My best friend is getting married, and I've been cut off—" Dave burst into uncontrollable sobs.

Eugene pulled a handkerchief out of his pocket and handed it to him.

Dave blew his nose and handed it back.

Eugene shook his head. "Keep it. You need it more than me."

The carriage rolled by and Dave waved the handkerchief. "Liz, Lizzie, over here!" He watched the silk ribbons tied to the back bumper flutter in the wind.

The carriage stopped in front of the cathedral doors. A man dressed in an ornate velvet suit with a large floppy hat with a feather opened the door to help Liz down the carriage step.

"Liz! Liz, it's Dave. We're here." The roaring crowd drowned him out. Bodies pressed against him. He was stuck, crestfallen, as Liz and her entourage disappeared through the tall church doorway.

Coco sought out his gaze. "Maybe she won't go through with it."

But Dave knew better. He knew Liz so well, he believed if it had come this far, she was going through with it. Whether she wanted to or not.

<h1 style="text-align:center">Chapter 63</h1>

Adrielle–Inside the forbidden cave

ADRIELLE'S BODY GREW more and more luminous the further she ventured into the cave, and the markings on the wall deepened.

An intense burning swelled inside her and drew her in. Was it the result of her deep longing for something. For her life to make sense—call it destiny, purpose—whatever it may be?

The markings began to take the shape of text: ancient Achaean text. She read the script with effortless speed.

Deep within the earth lies the beginning of the fall. Tread with vigilant caution lest thou awaken the undead, for they lie dormant in these halls. If anyone pass with ill regard, the curse will befall you.

Adrielle reread the inscription. She inhaled a long breath and released it slowly.

Whoever carved this wanted to leave a message. But how long ago? No one spoke this ancient tongue.

Was the message from her predecessors?

Adrielle inspected the rockface as she continued further into the cave and discovered a fine crack in the stone. She placed both hands on the rock and felt a vibration.

A deep guttural rumbling shook the walls. Giant boulders crashed to the ground as it split beneath her feet and exposed a deep pit. Adrielle scrambled away from it only to be bit by crumbling rock from the ceiling.

Adrielle ran blindly into the dark as she pulled out the chain around her neck and clutched her chronometer. She could save herself by transporting to another time and place—breaking the first rule of the Achaean leaders, her father's rule.

But what about the countless soldier clones marching to the mirror, transformed into lethal killing machines …

Using her powers to save herself wouldn't stop Domenikos from stealing everyone's memories and destroying them. It wouldn't stop him from creating a future where human freedoms didn't exist. Humans might even be extinct.

There had to be another way.

Adrielle let the chain slip from her fingers and the weight of the chronometer hung heavily around her neck. The tumbling rocks now blocked any hope of escape. She was trapped. Buried thousands of miles below the earth's surface. No one would ever find her.

If this was her last moment, she'd fill it with memories. Good memories. She dropped to her knees and sank back onto her feet.

Coco's lilting laugh filled her ears. In her mind she saw the speckling of freckles across Coco's cheeks after they'd spent the day at the beach. Angelo's sun-kissed curls as he leaned in and gave her a first kiss. The warmth of his lips pressing against hers. Then she saw Haden, how handsome he'd been on their wedding day. He was beaming, though he knew she was marrying him to honor her father's wishes. She hadn't wanted to face the feelings she'd felt for him the moment she'd said, *I do.*

When Haden slipped the wedding ring on her finger, her hands were shaking. She'd felt happy. Unreasonably and undeniably happy.

Wait . . . She was confused. Were these real memories or was she delusional?

She felt lightheaded and pressed her hand to her forehead. All these years she'd thought she loved Angelo. Believed he was the only one for her. But Haden's firm grasp on her hand and his melting dark eyes that swore unending loyalty and love, brought more joy than she'd ever imagined.

She fought to breathe, and she opened her eyes. The falling rocks had stirred a thick cloud of dust. With much effort she wheezed in a breath.

She couldn't sit up anymore and curled up on the ground. She saw her father's eyes. Reassuring eyes that filled her with hope and love.

She remembered her father's rushed words as he approached their mother with his plan for co-habitation. "The Achaean Act is the only way humans and Achaeans can co-exist. It's possible for them to live side by side, in peace."

Her mother started to object, saying the majority of Achaean's would never agree to this.

"They must. If we continue to Time Travel and change human history, humans will not survive." His voice was rushed and unbending, but he took her mother's hand and kissed it gently.

"I love you. This means I must do whatever it takes to ensure your kind is safe."

Chapter 64

Liz—In the memory tunnel—
Back in time—Rome Italy 1504

LIZ'S RESOLVE WEAKENED with every step toward the large cathedral doors. She was ruining everything. Making a huge mistake. She'd dreamed of this day as far back as she could remember, and she'd never imagined marrying anyone without Dave as her maid of honor. Now here she was alone.

Veda would say it was doubtful this cross-time marriage could work. Dave would say impossible. She pushed the thought away and concentrated on the cheering crowd. She squeezed the stem of her rose bouquet and lifted her chin. This didn't really matter. This wasn't her timeline.

She walked the enormous doorway. The church pews were stuffed with hundreds of people.

Soaring arches rose higher than she could clearly see, since she'd refused to wear her glasses, but she could make out frescos with cherubs and clouds and heavenly images. At the end of the central nave stood Francesco, looking like a king in his velvet purple robes with gold cording.

The smile on his face reassured he loved her, and Liz felt a flutter. He looked happy as she marched toward him. He'd said she was the woman he'd always dreamt off, and here he was. Perhaps she'd been hasty in judging him.

Francesco sought out her gaze and locked onto it. His eyes were the guide wire pulling her in.

She reached the altar and stood beside him in front of the wedding officiant wearing a red robe. A cardinal? He made the sign of the cross and opened an old bible.

Nothing about this was right. Liz shifted her weight, and Francesco swung his gaze to her. His brown eyes were kind and held a promise of fidelity. To run now would be cruel. He didn't deserve that.

The officiant spoke in Latin, so Liz didn't understand what was being said. By the seriousness of his expression, they were sacred words.

Kate and her grandma would be impressed. They'd be happy for her. She glanced around the church and almost believed it could work. Francesco sought out her gaze again. His expression showed devotion. Love. And love could conquer anything—*couldn't it?*

Liz placed her hands on her stomach. She felt her abs through the thin fabric. In a few months, her baby bump would be showing. She was going to be a mom, have her own family with Francesco. What would Dave say?

The officiant said something, and the church grew quiet. Francesco turned to her and took her hands in his. They were strong, capable hands. He'd built an empire with them. Then a young boy brought Francesco the rings.

Francesco's expression took on a seriousness she didn't often see. He slipped a large diamond ring on her finger and then a simple gold band. He said he'd love her forever.

Liz felt a warmth stir deep inside her. This was the moment she'd always dreamed of. She felt a rush of tears and blinked them back. She gazed into his eyes and knew she would love him forever. "I love you Francesco," she heard herself say, the words spilling out of her heart.

The young boy handed her a simple gold ring. She went to slide it onto his finger, but her hands were shaking so hard she dropped the ring. Gasps echoed through the nave. Liz clasped her hands to her mouth, too mortified. The boy followed the ring and fell to his hands and knees.

Was this a sign? A bad omen? Could the universe be telling her this union defied the laws of physics? Her stomach squeezed and the contents threatened to spill out.

The boy held up the gold band over his head like a halo for all to see. A unanimous gasp of relief ensued and seemed to say, *all was well with the world, for today there would be a wedding.*

The boy went back to her side and handed her the ring. She slipped the ring onto Francesco's finger, and the priest clasped their hands together, Francesco's over hers, and lifted their clasped hands for all to see.

The crowd cheered. It was done. They were husband and wife till death do them part.

Liz had one permeating thought: *What about time? Was this marriage valid if they were separated by five hundred years?*

Chapter 65

Dave, Coco, and Eugene—
In the memory tunnel—
Back in time—Rome Italy 1504

AFTER AN INTOLERABLE amount of time, the cathedral doors swung open and crashed against the stone. Liz and Francesco walked through the doorway, their clutched hands raised high over their heads. The crowd roared and showered them with rice and flowers.

"Liz. Over here! Liz!" Dave shouted. He rose on his tiptoes and waved his handkerchief to attract her attention, but there were too many people. The expression on her face said she was happy. She wanted this.

Before he could reach her, the newlyweds disappeared into the carriage and galloped off. They'd imagined this day since grade school. Dave felt the crushing weight of his world collapsing. He was left behind, on the outside.

"You okay?" Coco asked. Her worried expression made him feel worse.

"Yeah," he said, turning away. This was Liz's moment, not his. "Let's find the reception and break her out." What worried him most was: *Liz might not want to be rescued.*

DAVE, COCO, AND Eugene followed the crowds to a mansion larger than Francesco's Florentine ranch. Tall Italian cypresses and an ornate wrought iron fence bordered the stone estate. Inside the periphery was a maze of manicured gardens surrounding the house. The gates were left open for guests, who were received by guards.

They stood outside, watching hordes of guests arrive.

"You expect us to go in there?" Eugene asked, alluding to his dirty coveralls and mud caked boots.

"You've got a point," Coco said, scrutinizing the trail of incoming guests. The men wore long capes, and the women were dressed in silk and velvet gowns, with jewels dripping from their ears, necks and fingers. "We'll be spotted immediately."

"Not if we're the help," Dave said.

"Now you're dreaming." Coco pointed to where a group of maids dressed in long black gowns with white aprons cinched at the waist, were coming out of a side entrance. "Maybe the smell of the gardenias is making you woozy."

"Wait, look." Eugene pointed to a horse-pulled cart that had just arrived at the same side entrance. It was loaded with large wooden barrels. "Wine. Must be the kitchen."

"Let's go," Dave called over his shoulder. He was already sprinting over to it. "We can help unload and sneak inside."

Coco and Eugene followed him across the vast gardens. Two men had started to unload the cargo.

"We've been asked to help," Eugene said.

The men glanced at his overalls and boots and nodded. They turned to study Coco.

"I'm on kitchen duty. And I'm late," she said, then curtsied. "See you on the inside," she whispered to Dave.

Before the men gave Coco the okay, she scurried inside.

Chapter 66

Liz—In the memory tunnel— Back in time—Rome Italy 1504

LIZ STOOD IN the center of the large ballroom, absorbing the celebratory buzz. The transformation was magical. Flowers oozed from every corner. Servants carried silver trays of canapes and food magically appeared, alongside bottomless jugs of wine.

A bustle of faces grazed her cheeks with kisses and shook her hands to congratulate and wish her well. Despite Liz's earlier reservations, she had a spectacular time. With the focus on her, what was there to complain about? She flitted from guest to guest, expecting to see Dave at any moment. It was unrealistic, she knew, because Dave had no idea where she was, but nevertheless entertained the hope.

Leonardo and Michelangelo were among the most revered guests, and the only guests she knew. They made several attempts to fire up a much deeper conversation.

"But, Lisa, are you fully prepared to live here, when you are accustomed to a life with more advanced innovations?" Leonardo asked.

Michelangelo was at his side, his intense stare waiting for her response.

Liz simply shrugged and smiled and sought out the next guest making their way over. She didn't want to think of anything so deep or responsible tonight. She tried her best to avoid Leonardo's and Michelangelo's efforts to engage her further.

A few hours later, while the party continued without letting up, Isabel took Liz to a much larger bedroom than the one where she'd been staying.

"This one is specially prepared for the newlyweds," Isabel said, then disappeared out the door.

The bedspread on the canopy bed had been pulled back and exposed the finest Italian linens. Bowls of fresh fruit, pastries, and bottles of wine sat on the night tables.

Liz hadn't decided yet whether tonight was the right time to broach the subject of how it would all work between them. She stepped out onto the balcony to enjoy the low hanging moon and give it some thought before Francesco came in.

She rubbed her arms against the chilly evening air and took in the sweet smell of gardenias and other flowers wafting up. This balcony was much larger and had chairs to relax in. The view of the manicured gardens below was grander with a maze of hedges and wondered if she'd get lost in it, if she took a stroll.

Liz heard the door unlatch. She turned and saw Francesco's attention was on an elaborately carved chest at the foot of the bed. Had Isabel not told her Francesco had ordered more silk dresses for her wardrobe as a wedding gift, she wouldn't have known about his surprise.

"Look at this chest. I wonder what could be inside?" he said.

She walked back into the chamber, knelt before the chest, and opened the lid.

She gasped in what she hoped sounded like surprised delight.

Seeing the joy on his face as she took out dress after dress was the real prize.

She reached the bottom of the trunk and Francesco pulled her to her feet and held her close.

She looked him squarely in the eyes, committed to discuss the baby and her plans to go back to the future. "Francesco, there's something I need to tell you."

He gave her three soft kisses on her neck and looked at her expectantly. Somewhere between his warm trail of kisses and the adoration in his eyes, she lost her nerve.

"What is it?" He led her to the bed and crushed his lips on hers. Liz felt absolute bliss. Until Leonardo's warning crept to mind.

She pressed her fingers to his lips. "Francesco, I heard rumors the night we were stranded. Of you keeping the company of other women."

"Women?" His expression turned angry. "Are you accusing me of cavorting with other women?"

"Is it true?"

He pulled away from her and shook his head. "Lisa, you are the most important person to me. I have given you my name."

That wasn't an answer.

"This is no way to start a marriage. We have barely taken our vows, and you are grilling me." Angry and without undressing, he lay down on the bed and turned his back to her.

Liz fought back hot tears. Why did she have to ruin everything? She'd only wanted to hear that it was a misunderstanding. That there was a reason for the women dangling on his arms.

  Montana Wakefield

Defiantly, the moonlight hitting the garden was the most beautiful she'd ever seen. She stepped out on the balcony and inhaled a shuddering breath. She swiped at tears rolling down her cheeks. Timing had never been her forte. Worst thing was, he hadn't answered. So, it was probably true.

Chapter 67

Adrielle—Inside the forbidden cave

ADRIELLE COULD HEAR voices, but the heavy cloak of sleep was enticing.

"Adrielle, Adrielle . . . wake up. She's not responding," a voice that sounded like Monika said.

"Touch the scepter to her crest and awaken her." Was that her father's voice?

"No, the choice must be hers and hers alone."

"Can she hear us?" Aaron asked. His voice was filled with uncertainty. "If she knew how important this is, she would awaken."

"What makes you so certain? Have you not put this poor child through enough?"

"She is no longer a child, but our leader. Within her lies the strength and courage the world needs to survive. She is their only hope."

"Then I'm doubly right," Monika said. "If she is to give up so much, the choice must be hers. Let her sleep the deep sleep. If she awakens on her own, then we can put the proposition before her,"

Adrielle heard the words but felt her limbs relax into the deep cavern in her mind where nothing mattered. She felt the warmth leech out of her body and her limbs grew cold. She shivered as the voices drifted into a chamber of nothingness.

SOMETHING SPARKED ADRIELLE to awaken.

A tapestry of feathers creating a shield in her father's den. Angelo in bird form appearing at her window as a child. The freeing sensation of flight, the rush of air beneath her wings as the expansive world spread below her. Coco's twinkling mischievous eyes coaxing her to join the rest of them—Liz, Dave, Kate, and Veda—for a party. Her mother's soft touch as she put Adrielle to bed.

Adrielle lingered in the deep sleep as her yearning of wanting to belong grew painfully strong. The desire to find her purpose intensified and burned within her.

Her father's voice pleaded for her to return. It filtered through the imagery and her hazy surroundings. The image of the box of ashes Domenikos held and swore contained Veda's and Kate's incinerated bodies. And then the crowning vision of Josh's lifeless body lying in a pool of red blood flashed before her.

"Adrielle, Adrielle . . . come back to us," her father begged. The sound was soothing and convincing and warm and full of inviting familial memories. Its steadfastness reminded her of the unfinished business she'd taken on.

A flash of Domenikos' smile appeared in her mind, his devilish snaggletooth provoking her to stop him, if she could. Or dared. He was on a mission to take over the world and make it his.

This stirring desire to put a stop to her brother's tyrannical conquest became so fervent, Adrielle snapped her eyes open.

She looked around in confusion. She saw she was lying on a bed of stone, surrounded by familiar and unfamiliar faces. Not many, but enough to cause her unease.

Adrielle attempted to sit up. A gentle hand pressed down firmly on her chest. She recognized the gold wedding ring, the three interlinked circles of the Trinity engraved in the band. She found solace in the strong fingers that had often interlaced with hers. They were her father's, Aaron.

"Lay still, my sweet Adrielle. You are weak. Death's stealthy grasp has drained your resources. Wait until you are stronger before you attempt to sit."

Adrielle shook her head and fought to inhale a rush of oxygen into her lungs. Her chest heaved hungrily. She'd wasted too much time. Her crest burned between her shoulders. She remembered her chronometer and felt a pang of panic until she wrapped her fingers around the gold jewel. She exhaled and sucked in another breath.

Why was she so weak?

Adrielle shivered, then a surge of tingles burst inside her chest and swam to her limbs. She tried to speak but no sound came out. Her voice was stuck in her throat.

Monika leaned over her face, her wrinkled skin hanging at the jowls. Her black eyes bore into her. "Adrielle, your life as you know it is over. You are at a crossroads with a hard decision to make."

"I need to go. I have unfinished work," she forced out through a dry and achy throat. She tried to sit but Monika pressed her down.

"Listen carefully. You have awakened the *undead*. There are consequences for this." The expression on Monika's face was frightening.

"The undead?" Adrielle searched out her father. She'd only seen the seriousness in his eyes during his final hours, as Domenikos tortured and burned him at the stake.

"Is it really you? And not some wild imagination of my mind?"

Aaron nodded. He clasped her hand in his and pressed it to his cheek. "It is me, my sweet daughter. I stand before you in awe of your will and determination."

"How is it you are here? Flesh and blood? I watched your body burn at the stake as my twin committed the heinous act."

"I am here. But I am not flesh and bone." He straightened, an expression of deep empathy on his face. "I stand before you as the undead."

"The undead? I don't understand." Adrielle caught a silent exchange between her father and Monika.

Her father clasped her hand firmly in his. The lightest brush of his thumb revealed the unspoken gravity of the situation.

"Adrielle, Monika is correct," he said. "You have awakened the undead. By coming here to seek answers, you have put yourself in a vulnerable position. You have come to the place of our origin. To the unspeakable depths of the earth, where no mortal has ever walked."

"I'm only half mortal, the other half is Achaean. You know this, you are after all my father."

"That I am," Aaron said, with a slight smile. "Because you are my daughter, you are armed with wit. Your aspirations and tenacity stem from my side of the family."

Adrielle smiled for the first time in a long while. "Coco's stubborn. Guess that's something she inherited from you, too. What's wrong? You look so serious and this is amazing. I'm so happy to see you. I've missed you *sooooo* much. I have so many questions. So much to catch up on."

"Adrielle," her father said, letting go of her hand. "You have an important decision to make, and not much time. I want you to know, whatever you decide, it is *your* will and not mine that should influence you."

"I understand." Adrielle glanced at a frowning Monika. She turned back to her father. "What is it?"

"This place is deep in the center of the earth. The air is so scarce it is not enough to provide substance for life. Not for a mortal."

"I'm ok, father. I'm breathing." Adrielle sucked in a long breath.

Her father held up his hand. "When you fell into the depths of this cavern, you passed a stretch of tunnel where there was no air to breathe. Do you remember this at all?"

Adrielle shuddered. "I do. It was scary. I must have passed out. When I came to, I was wrapped in some sort of cocoon. I escaped, thankfully. But it was terrifying."

"Adrielle . . ." He waited for her full attention. His expression was grave. "You were in your human form when you passed that stretch without air. That is impossible to survive—as a mortal."

"Luckily, I'm only half human. So, I made it."

Her father placed his hands on her arms and held her gaze. "Listen to me. You were in *human form*, as I was, when I burned at the stake." He paused. "You were whisked away to a future timeline for your own protection. Because you held the potential to become our true leader. The fog of travelling would remain intact as you grew up in Florida, until you were old enough to make your own choices. This was all accounted for. As part Achaean, you also held the capacity to morph into your true Achaean form." He shook his head. "But that's not what happened as you crossed the impassable stretch of earth. You remained in your human form. And because of that, your physical body did not survive."

"But I—I was in bird form. Navigating—" Adrielle remembered lying in human form at the bottom of the tunnel. "Did—did I—" She couldn't force the words out. "Am I dead?"

"The undead surround you."

There was that word again. "Am I dead or undead?"

Her father let go of her hands and extended his arms. "Look around, Adrielle."

Adrielle forced herself to look. To really look. Faces surrounded her bed of stone. Her breath hitched. Among those there, at her feet, were Veda and Kate.

Chapter 68

Liz—In the memory tunnel—
Back in time—Rome Italy 1504

FOR MOST OF the night, Liz sat in the balcony contemplating her dilemma. She gazed up at the blanket of blue covered with sparkly pinpricks and felt in awe. And small.

"Holy fudge sticks," Liz muttered, feeling crushing disappointment in herself. She'd wrecked everything. She'd made up her mind before the wedding to leave Francesco and live in present day Florida, but she'd been too afraid to stand up for herself.

Why, Why, why?

Because she was a coward, that's why.

She could almost feel the negative vibes of the confrontation, if she'd refused to marry Francesco a second time.

When she had poked her head out into the hall after the tub and saw everything decorated so beautifully—the wedding she'd always wanted—she'd gotten carried away. She'd been blinded by the glitz. The jewels. The opulent wedding bash. She'd sold out for the perfect wedding and the idea of being a princess for one day.

She'd thought she'd fix things later. But was there a fix?

If Adrielle showed up right now and whizzed her back to the diamond center, would anyone know she'd gotten married? Would she say anything?

People had kept darker secrets in the history of the world. But could she live with that? With herself?

She was terrible at keeping secrets. There was that. And this one had a ticking time bomb. She glanced down at her tummy and rubbed it.

She tiptoed inside and glanced at Francisco, sleeping peacefully like a baby. It wasn't his fault. She'd turned diva on him and gone for the glam.

He'd looked so happy slipping the wedding rings on her finger, as though he believed love would conquer all. But could it?

They hadn't talked about fidelity, nor discussed what it meant to each of them. Wasn't it a given you'd be devoted to only one person? He'd never said. And she'd never asked. The time to have broached this topic had long passed.

She watched Francesco for a long moment. She did love him. And she felt terrible. Had she taken advantage of him?

What about the baby?

Folded on the bench at the foot of the bed were her cargo pants and top. Careful not to wake Francesco, she slipped out of her nightgown and laid it beside her wedding dress, then dressed in her Florida clothes.

She unclasped her necklace and laid it on the night table beside Francesco. The moon beams reflecting off the jewels radiated throughout the room. He must have spent a fortune on it.

Her gaze drifted to Francesco's face. Something inside her fluttered. He was a good man. He looked like the happiest man on earth. Like he truly loved her. He wouldn't look so peaceful once she left him.

She was a poser. Seeing herself as an explorer, when she hadn't even had the courage to tell him she was pregnant.

She unpinned her hair and shook it loose. How could she have done this? He was the father of her child. Her heart raced. All this worrying and fretting—

She rushed to the French doors and stepped out onto the terrace. She yearned for her friends. For her life as it had been.

All her hopes and dreams swept away in one careless moment.

She closed her eyes to relive that carefree, innocent, twirl inside the diamond center, that inadvertently brought her to this distant time.

She lifted her chin to the sky, the cool breeze felt good against her skin. The moon stared brazenly at her.

She leaned over the iron railing to look out at the garden. Neat, manicured rows of bushes, roses, gardenias, and cypresses. Undeniably beautiful. The things of dreams.

As a child she'd read *The Secret Garden*. This is what she'd imagined. A lush paradise where anything was possible.

But that was a fairytale. She'd had the dream. And now came the consequence. She sucked in a deep breath and inhaled a sweet waft of gardenias that made her stomach swirl with nausea. She had no idea how to get home.

There was that.

She pressed her hands against her tummy. How long before she showed?

She was going to be a single mom. Voted most promising in their senior class and pregnant at eighteen. *Wow!* How easily she'd abandoned her dreams to raise a child.

Francesco's snoring drifted out. He was sleeping like a baby while a storm brewed inside her.

She looked at her wedding hand. To the fatty diamond that sparkled with life under the moon beams. She wiggled her finger, mesmerized by the sparkles reflecting into the night. The rays shooting out of the diamond resembled giant sunbeams and made her think of the diamond center. How irresponsible she'd been.

"I'm game," she'd said to Adrielle. "No way am I staying behind, I'm coming. I can help." *Sure you can.* She hadn't helped Angelo get his memory back. No, she was here alone, hundreds of years back in time, getting into all sorts of trouble.

Home. A wave of homesickness hit her so strongly, she almost lost her balance.

What if something happened to her friends, like it did to Kate and Veda? What if she never saw them again?

Tears streamed from her eyes. She stood transfixed, frozen in the moonbeam reflections of her diamond. She closed her eyes to wipe the tears away. When she opened them, the starry sky had disappeared. She was in the dark.

Chapter 69

Dave, Coco, and Eugene—
In the memory tunnel—
Back in time—Rome Italy 1504
Ten minutes before…

THE WEDDING PARTY was in full swing. After unloading the wine, Dave and Eugene slipped into the adjoining hall unnoticed. Coco was already there, waiting for them.

"How did it go?" Coco whispered.

"As well as unloading wine can. It was dope," Dave snarled.

Coco motioned for them to follow. "I've discovered a back stairway to the upstairs rooms."

With the celebration in the main ballroom, the three crept upstairs to begin searching for the bridal suite.

Artwork and doors lined the lengthy halls. They opened doors to seemingly unused rooms. They were grand and luxurious and overwhelming. After what felt like an eternity, they were no closer to finding Liz. They turned down the main corridor to an adjoining wing. A maid, carrying a tray of fresh fruit and a pitcher of milk, walked out of one of the rooms at the end of the hall. Dave, Coco, and Eugene ducked into another room and watched as she latched the door and disappeared downstairs.

They stood outside the door and listened. A rhythmic snoring came from the other side. Carefully, Dave opened the door ajar and peeked in.

A sliver of moonlight revealed Francesco was in bed, but there was no sign of Liz. Dave noticed tall, French doors opening to a veranda. He tiptoed in and saw Liz's wedding dress draped over a chair, her nightgown too.

He looked at the balcony. Liz was there, dressed in her Zara cargo pants. He felt a rush of emotion and suppressed a cry. He glanced at Francesco, relieved he was still asleep, and crept toward the balcony.

Before he reached her, Liz vanished into thin air.

Chapter 70

Adrielle–Inside the forbidden cave

THE STONE SLAB Adrielle was laying on was cold. The dark cavern musky and grim. Her father was watching her closely, his expression profoundly sad. She sat up. "If I'm *undead,* does it mean I can't die?"

"It's not that simple, but yes."

"Why are you sad then, skipping the dying part sounds great."

Aaron paused. "Adrielle, nothing is ever exclusively good or bad."

"Well, on the upside, I got to see you, father, and my friends." She stole a glance at Veda and Kate. "So, what's the downside?"

"Let's start with the obvious." Aaron extended his palm toward her. "You are half Achaean, so you still have a body. But it isn't the same as your human body, though it may look like it on the outside."

Adrielle ran her hands along her arms and legs. They felt solid, like before. She thought back to the arena in the future, where no one, including the Angelo clone, could see her. "Can people see me?"

"Only if you want them too."

Adrielle smirked. "Like when you time travel as a participant or as a spectator?"

Aaron raised an eyebrow and exchanged a look with Monika. "That's one way of looking at it. But there are serious implications. You will never age."

"Bonus," Adrielle said, turning to her friends. Veda and Kate wore deadpan expressions.

"Is it?" Aaron said.

A long silence followed, causing some of her optimism to wane. "What aren't you telling me?"

Aaron sighed heavily, his somber expression unwavering. "A cause as important as the peaceful cohabitation of mortals and Achaeans, has high stakes and grave consequences. As a half human, you understand humanity. And as the lead traveler, you have access to all the keys of your crest. Each of the feathers represents an ability—a power—if you will.

Adrielle nodded. "I'm not certain what the green feather does."

"Ahhh. The green feather represents death. And you have, in every sense, overcome death. You are undead."

"But what does *undead* mean?"

"Achaeans age slowly, and live thousands of years. A human's life is short but meaningful. As a hybrid, you had the benefit of both experiences. But now—you will not experience aging, what it means to be human. I believe it will be a source of great sorrow, for you. Your mortal friends will grow old and die, while you live on in this— undead state, in perpetuity.

"What about Coco? As half Achaean, will she die?"

"If she embraces her human side."

Adrielle felt the wind knocked out of her. To lose Coco meant an eternity of loneliness.

"And mom?"

Aaron nodded. "Your mother is mortal. The three of you are the first hybrids known. Our miracle, perhaps, because our love was so strong. If there was a way to spend the rest of eternity with your mother . . . But I cannot leave this place of our beginning and our end."

Never seeing sunlight was unfathomable. "Am I trapped?"

"No, you hold all the keys. Adrielle, you are the prophesized one in the *Book of Feathers*. The culmination of all light."

Adrielle glanced at Veda and Kate. "Why are they here?"

"They are what humans call *ghosts*. Their spirits are free to roam. You see them because you have earned the green feather of death."

"Do you know what's going on with Domenikos? I trapped him inside the scepter diamond, and he's gained access to the Time Vault through time tunnels in there. Now he's accessing real memories and destroying them. Changing history by stealing memories from humans and altering them to his warped delusional version. He's building an army of clones and re-depositing the changed memories into his clones. And he has Angelo—Angelo, for goodness sakes. The strongest and mightiest warrior—and he's been able to manipulate him."

Monika shook her scepter and smashed it hard on the rock floor. The sound resonated throughout the cave. "That is not the real Angelo."

"Relieved to hear that. I went in one of his buildings. At first, everyone could see me. But then, they couldn't. I was transparent. I don't know how it happened. Even the Angelo clone couldn't see me. His hands went right though my body."

"Adrielle, you *are* the light. You can absorb the light around you into your body, and it will give you tremendous power. You can appear as though you have vanished," Monika said.

"I can appear invisible?"

Monika nodded. "Among other things."

"Like?"

"It is not for me to tell you what you can do. You have the rest of eternity to discover yourself."

"I thought I had a grasp on banning time travel, but this is so far beyond that. Domenikos' goal is world domination." Adrielle curled her fingers around her chronometer, and Aaron's gaze was drawn to it.

"Banning time travel is only the beginning. Before mortals began compartmentalizing their life, time didn't exist for Achaeans. That's why we can travel without regard to it. That chronometer was built for you to account for time, to better safeguard the time continuum, and travel where you needed to. You are the link between our societies. The light that will save the world. Search deep within yourself and believe in your powers. A strange new light can be just as powerful and frightening as the dark."

Adrielle sighed. "Ok, lets circle back to this undead thing. So, I can become invisible, but I'm not invisible all the time—correct? People will still be able to see me?"

Aaron nodded.

"What about them?" Adrielle pointed to Veda and Kate. "Are they invisible to others?"

Monika nodded.

Adrielle walked up to her friends and swiped her hands through their midsections. "My hand goes right through, but you're really here."

"Yeah, we are," Veda grumbled. She didn't appear happy about it at all.

"Okay. I can change from bird form to human form, even though I'm undead. And my body will still feel solid? To others, I mean?"

"Yes. You will appear normal, though you are not. Humans will start to wonder why you don't age. You will have to learn how to deal with that," Monika said.

"And Haden? Why did I have such a strong feeling he'd be here?"

Aaron opened his arms to encompass the entirety of the space. "He is somewhere inside this forbidden cave. Try to remember there are different planes, and you have been searching for him in an altered level. He is not as deep into the earth as we are."

"You must go now," Monika said.

"But I have so many more questions. How do I change from bird form to human, and the other way—"

"Angelo and Haden can help. Astraia too," Aaron said.

"Oh, her," Adrielle moaned.

"Astraia can be of great help," Aaron said. "She is fiercely loyal."

Monika raised her arm high, the long velvet sleeve of her robe draping to the ground. "You have much to do and little time remaining, before you and the others will become trapped. You must go. Your exit is through there." She pointed.

"To the Time Vault?"

Monika nodded. "You accessed this cave through a time tunnel from the Time Vault. If you want the freedom to leave here, you must go now."

Adrielle turned to her father. "Can I come back to visit you? Will I be able to access this place through the Time Vault?"

"Each time you come, it will be more difficult for you to leave. Neither this place, nor the Time Vault, are places to access frequently. I warned you of the consequences." Monika shook her pointy red fingernail. "Each time you enter the Time Vault, history changes. You must find your way here through the forbidden cave. And find your way back without using the Time Vault."

Adrielle looked around at the dismal place. "I'm losing you all over again, when I've just found you. I hate leaving you here alone."

Aaron pulled Adrielle close and whispered in her ear, "You will never lose me. I will always be a part of you. And when the time comes for your mother's body to die, after she frees the prisoners and leaves the nether prison world, we will reunite here as husband and wife and be together as we once were."

Adrielle didn't want this for her mother. The thought of anyone being trapped here was terrifying. As much as she knew she would miss him, it terrified her to become trapped here. She wished she could close her eyes and be back with the others.

"Your mother will be a ghost, her father said, as if reading her thoughts. "She will be able to roam freely."

That brought Adrielle some comfort. She turned to Monika. "Uh, can you zap me back into the scepter diamond?"

"Use your chronometer," Aaron said. "It is, after all, your travelling tool. Concentrate on where you want to go."

"So, I don't have to go up through that shaft again?"

Monika shook her head.

Adrielle felt a huge relief. It seemed like a long time since she'd left Angelo. Enough time for him to have restored his memory. She'd find him first, then reunite with Coco and the others in the scepter diamond.

"Till we meet again," she said to her father and embraced him.

She cradled her chronometer. The second hand was making its way around the face. She had every intention of following her plan, but all she could think about was finding Haden.

Chapter 71

Dave, Coco, and Eugene—
In the memory tunnel—
Back in time—Rome Italy 1504

EUGENE LET OUT a loud yelp, and Francesco bolted up in bed and saw them.

Francesco grabbed the bell next to the bed and rang it as he yelled for the servants.

Within minutes three large men with angry scowls and needle-sharp swords charged into the room.

"Don't hurt us. We're here for Liz," Dave shouted and jumped behind Eugene who was much larger.

"Who?" Francesco howled as he looked around. "Lisa, Lisa? What have you done with my bride?"

"We're her friends," Coco said timidly. "Remember us?"

The three heavies moved closer. Their swords raised to strike.

<h1 style="text-align:center">Chapter 72</h1>

<h2 style="text-align:center">Adrielle–Inside the Forbidden Cave</h2>

ADRIELLE STOOD NEAR the entrance of the Forbidden Cave. Being pronounced *undead* had unforeseeable perks. Her mind was clear of the haze of confusion she experienced when traveling. A musky spicy scent seemed to rise up from the earth. And she could see the moon reflecting on the water outside the opening.

Adrielle went to the cave's opening. The drop down was heart stopping. She could barely see the rocks at the bottom, but she could hear the water crashing onto them.

Why wasn't she in the Time Vault?

She reviewed her final moments before leaving that ghastly cavern deep in the earth. *Oh, no.* She'd gotten sidetracked with Haden. She couldn't stop thinking of him and where he was.

Ugh.

An orange streak of light exploded across the horizon, and Adrielle felt a rush of joy. This was the most spectacular place on earth: the wide expanse of blue as far as she could see and the smell of the salty ocean with the waves crashing below. How she'd missed the light. She couldn't think of anything more oppressive than being trapped in darkness. Never seeing this place again.

She watched the sun rise until it was high above the horizon. She inhaled a long slow breath and gulped another greedily. She thirsted for oxygen. The air up here was pure and clean. Not that odorous stale and heavy stench below. It smelled of death. Yes, that was the smell she couldn't pin down while she was there. Death. Decay. She shuddered.

Poor father. Being trapped in there for eternity was suffocating. She pushed her spiraling thoughts away. She couldn't afford to look back. Only onward. Positive thoughts from here on out.

She turned back to the cave and Haden was quietly watching her.

"How long have you been there?"

Haden smiled. His expression said he loved her. That he wanted to take her into his arms and devour her.

A spark of joy flooded through her. Haden had never been good at hiding his feelings from her. *Thank goodness.*

Haden extended opened arms and went to embrace her, but Adrielle stepped away from him. "What happened to you? You went over the cliff's edge and vanished. You didn't stay to see Domenikos duped by the forgery of the *Book of Feathers.* I trapped him into the scepter prison."

As she said it, she wondered why she was so crabby when finding him was all she'd been able to think about since she'd left Domenikos' clone-making factory.

A confused scowl replaced Haden's heartwarming smile.

Adrielle crossed her arms.

They stood there, gazes locked, until Haden looked away.

"Truce." He raised his palms to her. "Your new position has made you sensitive."

"Sensitive? That's the most ridiculous thing I've ever heard."

"Is it?" He extended an arm, as if to say her agitated reaction proved his point.

Adrielle felt herself getting more and more irritated. "While you've been off doing god knows what, I've been trying to stop Domenikos from taking over the world."

"Isn't that your job?" he said, with a wry expression. "Aren't you our new leader?" He craned his neck to see the crest between her shoulder blades.

"Well, yes. Yes, it is." She moved away from the cliff's edge and shifted her stance to keep her back away from him. She looked him squarely in the eye. "Yes I am."

Now what. If this is your way of asking for Haden's help—Adrielle Maddox—you're doing a great job of muddling it.

Haden's cynical expression dissolved and transformed into an effortless grin. "Come here my stubborn, obnoxious wife. How I've missed you." He coiled his arms around her and chuckled.

"Wife? I'm not your—" Adrielle pushed away.

"Oh no? Seems to me we took our vows in front of all of Achaea. As a matter of fact, I have . . ."

Could this be possible? Had she suppressed this?

He dug into his breast pocket and pulled out a small platinum band. "If I'm not mistaken, this belongs to you." She held the ring up, and Adrielle was flooded with memories.

My god . . . he was right. She was married to him. Married! But did it still apply, in her condition?

Haden was watching her curiously. "What's wrong? Are you that surprised I still have it?" He held up his hand. "I'm wearing the matching band."

Adrielle gasped. She pressed her hands to her mouth.

He raised an eyebrow. "It has never left my finger since that day."

Adrielle dropped her gaze to the ground.

Haden kicked at a rock. "Well? *I'm* happy to see you. You look radiant. Why, you don't look like you've aged one day."

Adrielle felt like she'd been sucker punched. *No, no she hadn't aged. That wasn't about to happen now.*

Haden frowned. "You *do* remember, don't you, love? For better or for worse? Till death do us part, as you mortals say?"

Adrielle could only stare at him.

"That glorious reception afterward where Coco got so drunk your father had to cart her away."

Adrielle frowned.

"What's wrong? You look paler than usual." He grabbed her wrist and pulled her to him. He cupped her chin and raised it, then turned her face slowly. "You look like you've seen a ghost." His voice softened. "I'm not saying that lightly. That's a big thing with you—being so pale and all that." He searched her eyes. "Love, what aren't you telling me?"

Tears pricked Adrielle's eyes.

This was Haden, the fiercest, smartest, and most capable leader of the Achaean army. Her father entrusted the *Book of Feathers,* and her life to him— *her* Haden. The one she'd vowed to love all the rest of her days. He'd poured over the *Book of Feathers* for countless weeks at a time, searching through ancient script to find a way to save her life. To rescue her from her devious twin, who would think nothing of snuffing out her life, like he had their father.

Haden had always been honorable. Noble. She had no reason to mistrust him. He'd risked everything to propel her into the future at the time of the rebellion. He'd even taken a stab at Domenikos, to his own peril, when she'd confronted Domenikos with the forgery.

How could she tell him she had died? After all that? That all his efforts had been useless. That this was not her mortal body, but a new *undead* one. And when he asked, because surely, he'd ask what the hell that meant, she wouldn't know how to begin explaining it.

Adrielle's knees buckled, and Haden caught her.

"Haden . . . Haden, I'm—I'm . . ."

He bent down to kiss her, but she placed her fingertips on his lips. "We shouldn't. We can't. I'm—"

He searched her eyes. "What is it, Adrielle? You are acting so strangely I'm starting to panic."

"There's no easy way to put it."

"Say it," he demanded.

"I'm dead," she sputtered.

"Dead?"

Haden looked stunned. And then he chuckled.

"Listen to me. Haden, listen. I'm dead serious. I mean—I'm serious. I am dead. *Undead,* to be exact."

Haden coiled his arms around her and squeezed her so tight she had a difficult time breathing. She tried pushing him away, but he gripped even tighter and lay his head on her chest.

"Uh, Haden? You ok?"

Haden lifted his head. His face was wet with tears. The worried look on his face had been replaced with a joyful expression. "That makes two of us. Till death do us part no more. To the hereafter."

He slid the platinum band on her finger and held her gaze. "I love you, Adrielle Maddox. I will never let anyone hurt you again." Then he crushed his lips to hers.

Chapter 73

Dave, Coco, and Eugene—
In the memory tunnel—
Back in time—Rome Italy 1504

"YOU ARE LISA'S friends?" Francesco said and paused. "Yes, that's right." He remembered Coco and Dave, the—*he/she boy*—who hung on Lisa's every word. Who was the man they called Eugene?

Francesco barely stood up before one of his heavies lunged forward and thrust his sword at Eugene's chest. Eugene sprang backward, the sharp tip of the blade narrowly missing his heart.

A heavy fist landed on Dave's jaw and toppled him like a domino. Eugene tripped over him and tumbled on top. Coco shrieked as a black bird swooped in from the balcony and transformed into a magnificent black woman.

A collective gasp silenced the room.

Ping. Ping. Clash. Francesco's thugs dropped their swords and stood frozen.

Tension squeezed at Francesco's chest. He grabbed at it. "Ah. Ah. Ah . . ." This defied the laws of physics. Then he remembered Lisa's words.

I'm from the future, Francesco.

Impossible, he'd said.

No, it isn't. Believe me, we just appear. And disappear.

Lisa's expression was dire. She'd begged him to listen.

There are things about me you don't understand. About my friends, too. No one knows . . .

When she'd vanished without a trace, he thought she'd changed her mind. That she didn't love him. But then she reappeared one year later at his Florence home.

"What is going on here?" the bird/woman said.

Francesco took a step back. The bird woman was speaking. He slid his gaze to his men. They were paralyzed with fear. He was with them—the bird woman was terrifying. The transformation shook everything he believed in.

"Dave, why are you cowering under Eugene?" the bird/woman said.

Dave stood up and dusted himself off. He kept a safe distance from her too and seemed to be afraid of her.

Eugene muttered something unintelligible, and Coco extended him a hand. He stood up. "Dunno. Dunno what's happening."

"Time to go." The bird/woman hollered. Her dark eyes shifted to the door. "Let's go!"

They rushed out of the room with no resistance from his servants, the bird woman trailing at the back. Francesco followed.

The house was quiet now, the wedding celebration had died down. Dave led the pack down the stairs, and, *boom,* crashed head-on into Michelangelo.

Francesco was horrified. He'd invited Michelangelo and Leonardo to stay on for a few days after the wedding to rest, given the distance to travel back to Florence.

"Michelangelo. Thank God," Dave said.

"Dave?" Michelangelo said, steadying him.

Michelangelo's attention shifted to Coco, who was behind him. He glanced at Eugene and the bird/woman. "What are all of you doing here?"

"What are you—?" Dave slapped his forehead. "Duh, you're a guest, obviously. We came to find Liz. She—"

Michelangelo shook his head. "I know. She's made a mistake." He gestured to Leonardo who was standing beside him. "Leonardo tried talking her out of it."

"What?" Francesco said, his anger rising. *Marrying him was no mistake.*

"Has Adrielle lifted the levy on time travelling?" Leonardo asked. His voice was filled with anticipation.

Time Travelling?

"God, no," the bird/woman snapped. "The misfits are at it again."

Francesco couldn't believe his ears.

Chapter 74

Adrielle–Inside the forbidden cave

ADRIELLE TOLD HADEN everything that had transpired since she'd last seen him. He seemed particularly interested in Domenikos and his dominion, and creation of the soldier clones.

Haden vowed to help her put a stop to Domenikos' most heinous and wicked plan.

"We need to go. We're running out of time." Adrielle turned to the cave entrance.

Haden grabbed her hand. "Are you all right? Something is off. What's on your mind?"

"Everything," Adrielle said. "The whole thing with the mausoleum. I can't believe after all the work my father did, after fighting for everyone's freedoms, he ends up in such a terrible place. It's like a prison.

"It's the place we all go. The place of the Achaean beginning and end."

"This seems wrong." Adrielle tried to keep down her rising anger. "To think that Domenikos slaughtered him and sent him there prematurely."

Haden shook his head. "For us Achaeans, time doesn't exist. Not in the way you think of. It's humans who need to register time. We are here until we aren't. But as you're discovering, we never truly cease existing."

Adrielle frowned. "All those years you worked with my father . . . to see his only son betray him like that."

"He betrayed all of us." Haden clenched his jaw. "Don't worry, we'll work out a strategy to subjugate Domenikos and enforce the Achaean Act. But first we need to find a way to get into his head." He squeezed Adrielle's hand and sought out her gaze. "Don't worry, we *will* overcome Domenikos. I swear to you, we will."

She almost believed him. As head of the Achaean army, Haden understood Domenikos almost as well as her father had. But as his twin, she knew Domenikos better than anyone. The tie to him was undeniable, and she rebelled against it with all her might.

Her mother had told her they'd been close when they were young. No one sensed there was something devious in Domenikos until they were five or six. But she'd always known it. She couldn't believe they'd once shared the womb, knowing what she now knew about him. What he was capable of.

Haden squinted at her. "There's something else you're not telling me."

Adrielle shook her head. She didn't want to admit she hadn't told Coco Domenikos was their brother.

"I was supposed to meet up with Angelo in the Time Vault after his memory was fully restored. By now he's probably back at the scepter diamond with the others. Let's check in on them and catch them up to speed. Then we can find the exact point where Domenikos started shifting the history timeline. Where he began deleting memories in the Time Vault."

Chapter 75

DAVE, COCO, AND EUGENE–
IN THE MEMORY TUNNEL–
BACK IN TIME–ROME ITALY 1504

TIME TRAVEL? "STOP them! Seal the exits," Francesco hollered to his servants, even though he suspected there was nothing they could do to stop this magic that defied nature.

He grabbed a sword and ran upstairs to inspect his bedroom. Lisa's diamond necklace was on the night table. He swept it into his pocket. She had been telling him the truth. He should have believed her. She left him, or she wouldn't have left the jewelry. The love of his life was gone. Francesco doubled over; the realization a crippling blow.

DAVE FROWNED AS they wandered around the house. Guests were still partying, and servants were everywhere.

"Come with me. I am familiar with the manor's footprint. I'll take you to the furthest wing in the house." Michelangelo led the way back upstairs and almost collided with the thug servants.

Dave let out a breath of relief as the servants stepped aside, and Michelangelo lead them to what looked like a sitting room.

"Why did you travel back when Adrielle was adamant about stopping time travel?" Michelangelo asked.

"We were on a mission inside the diamond scepter. Liz accidentally fell through the diamond's edge into a memory tunnel, which led us back here," Dave said.

Leonardo exchanged a look with Michelangelo. "That's what Liz told me. The idea of time tunnels is fascinating. In theory, I understand the complexity and repercussions of changing history, but the entire possibility is riveting."

Francesco burst into the room. "Where is my Lisa. What have you done with her?"

"Francesco, we are at the center of a discussion," Leonardo said. "Dave, Coco, Astraia, and Eugene are trying to explain."

"That's right," Dave said. "We're not sure what happened. We tracked Liz to your bedroom, and she vanished before we got to her."

"Vanished? Like magic?" Francesco said.

"No, not magic. Time travel," Astraia said.

"How do we get her back?" Francesco said, clenching his fists and looking forlorn.

Francesco *did* love Liz. Dave leaned in and whispered, "She's not gone, just popped somewhere else. We'll find her."

Leonardo studied Eugene boots and overalls. "Where did *you* come from?"

Eugene wrinkled his brow. "Dunno."

"Are you saying you don't remember?" Coco said.

Eugene nodded.

Dave and Coco exchanged a look. Something was terribly wrong. Could his memory lapse be a part of the contagion?

Chapter 76

Adrielle and Haden—
Inside the scepter diamond

ADRIELLE AND HADEN popped into the center of the diamond and looked around.

Adrielle frowned. "They're gone."

Rainbows of colors exploded and glittered as the light reflected off the chiseled cuts inside the scepter diamond.

Haden's mouth was wide with amazement. "I always thought you were dazzling."

Adrielle looked down at her glowing body and followed the light trail from her body to the diamond cuts.

"Haden? Pay attention." She grabbed his arm and turned him to her. "This is serious. Something has happened."

"I'm trying to see, but this light is blinding. You're blinding."

"I know. I can't help it. I glow sometimes."

"I never would have imagined. I'm standing in the center of a diamond and . . . if you ever get the urge for me to buy you diamond ring, I'll just remind you to stop in here." He grinned.

"Listen carefully." Adrielle pressed her face to his and cupped her hands around his cheeks until he was focused on her eyes. "I'm not kidding around. Everyone was supposed to be here. I gave them explicit instructions not to leave. Not to do anything stupid. Was that too much to ask of them? To sit tight and wait until I came back?"

"Obviously."

Adrielle frowned.

"All right, all right. By everyone, w*ho,* exactly, are we talking about?"

"Coco, Liz, Dave, and Astraia."

"Astraia too? What was *she* doing here?" He tapped his forefinger to his lips and looked irritated.

"I don't know, Haden. She just was. She refused to let us come here without her."

"Hmmm."

"What do you mean, hmmm."

Haden frowned. "What do you mean by, what do you mean, hmmm?"

"Are you saying there's something I should be worried about with Astraia? Cause Dave has suspicions."

"Dave? That little twit?"

Adrielle planted her fists on her hips. "Look, if you're going to start calling my friends names—"

"Chill." He held up his hands. "Just saying."

"For your information, Dave happens to be the smartest person I know."

"Ahhh." Haden nodded. "Well, that explains it then."

Adrielle shot him a look.

Haden shrugged. "You said person. Now if you'd been including us Achaeans—"

"Stop." Adrielle shook her head. "Let's just forget it."

"Let's not." Haden narrowed his eyes. "*You* are supposed to have some loyalties to our kind."

"What is *that* supposed to mean?"

"Exactly that. Loyalties."

"I am loyal."

"Hmmph."

Adrielle grabbed his wrist. "Look, I don't want to fight."

Haden looked at her fingers wrapped around his wrist and raised his eyes to hers. "You are more assertive than you used to be. I like that."

"I'm loyal," Adrielle said.

"Then start acting like it. Astraia is one of us. An Achaean. And *you* are Achaean too."

"Partly. I'm also human."

"Not anymore. You're *undead,* like me. Which means—" He shook his head. "Forget it. I don't know what that means, exactly."

"Me neither," Adrielle admitted. "Listen, I didn't mean anything by it. I just don't know her. I'm not sure I can trust her yet."

"What's not to trust? She's the Achaean holding the black feather. You should know by now, since you hold that key, that she stands for truth and honesty."

"You're right. But think of who's holding the green feather."

Haden raised his brows.

"And all the Achaeans who followed him in the rebellion. Each one had abilities too."

Haden cocked his head.

"It's just that . . . Monika's bird, Arnadella, is her sister."

"What?" Haden looked surprised. "Monika's bird is Arnadella?"

"Yes. How did you not know?"

Haden shrugged. "She never said." He paused. "No wonder I haven't see her for a while."

"And we were all wondering—Dave and the others and I—if Astraia had anything to do with that. Dave thought she might."

Haden shrugged.

"And that's not all. Arnadella is stuck in bird form permanently."

Haden's eyes widened. "Good lord. How do you know that?"

"There was an exchange when they reunited." Adrielle waved her hand. "Anyways . . . no one dared ask how it happened. But Arnadella was pretty mad at Astraia when Monika came to zap us into the scepter diamond."

"I'm sure it's not related."

"Really?" Adrielle said. "'Cause that would make me feel soooo much better."

"No, I'm not sure. I just said it because denial is a natural reaction. Aren't *you* the one with the key to the black feather? Concentrate. And use your power."

Adrielle felt silly. He was right, of course. But he could be so annoying She closed her eyes, forcing her concentration away from Haden, considering whether Astraia had something to do with Arnadella's conversion or not.

She snapped her eyes open. "Omigod. Something terrible *has* happened to them."

"To whom?"

"I don't know for sure, but it has something to do with the *Book of Feathers*."

"You have to be wrong. The *Book of Feathers* is perfectly safe."

"What do you mean?" she asked.

Haden lowered his eyes.

"Haden, what have you done?"

"Nothing." He waved his arms. "I only stashed the book somewhere safe."

Adrielle was stunned. "Why? And where?"

"I didn't think it was safe in Florida," Haden said.

"Where did you put it?"

He looked at her sheepishly. "In Michelangelo's armoire."

"That's someplace safe?"

He shrugged. "I *thought* it was. It was safe there when you worked on the forgery."

Adrielle felt her anger rise. "Haden, you're not the keeper of the book anymore. You don't get to make those decisions. I had to go back and warn both Michelangelo and Leonardo not to meddle with the feathers. They're only human, they can't resist the temptation."

"That's why I never told them."

"Oh my god." Adrielle raised her hands.

"Calm down. Think about it. Who would find it in that house, with all of his books?"

Adrielle pressed her fingers to her temples and closed her eyes. "Oh my god."

"What? What do you see?"

"Nothing. I don't see anything, shhhh."

"Oh. I thought when you said, *oh my god* that meant—"

"No. I'm not a seer like Monika. I just feel. And I feel like someone has been tampering with the spells."

"Well, if you're right, then oh my god is right. Judging from what you've told me—that Domenikos has gained access to the Time Vault, and the Time Vault memory tunnels, then that changes everything. Let's just say your oh my god is not a hyperbole."

Adrielle turned to him. "How could you? And how did you? That means you must have travelled back in time. I don't need, nor want, to remind you it's against the rules. Sheesh—you know better than that. Another concern, and just as important, is how did *I* not know about it?" She collapsed into a lump on the floor and met his gaze. "I don't get it. My crest burns every time someone breaks the Achaean Act and time travels. So why didn't I know?"

"My guess is . . . that it doesn't work if you're *undead.*"

Adrielle felt a stab of panic. "What?"

"You heard me." He smiled. "It's too soon. You're in good shape, all things considered. Remember, we don't know the rules yet for the undead. And, by the way, you never asked how I became undead."

"I—You're right. I'm sorry. I guess with all that stuff I was trying to catch you up on." Adrielle felt awful. She'd been more concerned about losing her powers she'd only just gained.

"Don't worry. I'm not the hypersensitive one in this relationship." Haden extended his hand to help her up. Adrielle clasped his hand and pulled herself up.

"If you think back to when we were in the cave with Domenikos— during the forgery exchange, which by the way was genius." Haden grinned. "Domenikos lunged toward you, and I intercepted him."

"I remember." Adrielle lifted his shirt to look at his scar. "Where is it?" She pressed her fingers into his side. "I saw him stab you here, before you tumbled over the edge of the cliff. There's no scar." She raised her eyes to him. "How is this possible?"

Haden gazed at the ground.

"I remember Domenikos used his prized knife. The one with the twisted handle."

Haden sucked in a deep breath.

"The one he reserves for inflicting pain." Haden's reaction was irritating her. "I saw it go in deep. And then you went over the side of the cliff. I thought for sure you'd morphed into your bird form and flown away."

Haden looked up with a serious expression. "I couldn't. It was too late to morph. I'd lost too much blood while in human form."

"So that's how you died? Protecting me?"

Haden nodded. "There you have it. That's how I became—*undead.*"

"But it doesn't make sense. Why didn't you return to the crypt where my father is?"

Haden cocked his head. "Yeah. There's that."

"Haden."

"All right, all right." He sighed. "I poured over that book for months, trying to find a way to save you. I saw all sorts of things that might be of use."

"What are you saying?"

"I'm saying—" He raised his hands. "Go ahead and reprimand me. I confess. I used a spell I had memorized just in case."

"What? A spell? You used the spell of life?"

"Yes. There you have it. When I saw it, that first time, I couldn't be sure of the entire workings. But I was fairly certain I would continue living, if I ever died. And I couldn't very well protect you, if I was no longer living."

Adrielle was stunned.

"So, can you confirm if someone's been tampering with the book?" Haden asked.

Adrielle felt her black feather confirm, and she nodded.

"Then there's a very real chance that Domenikos has the *Book of Feathers.* And if he does, we're in real trouble."

Adrielle winced. "If I've lost my powers, we're all doomed."

Chapter 77

Liz–In the memory tunnel–
Back in time–Florence Italy 1504

LIZ GLANCED AROUND the darkened room. Where was she? Francesco was sleeping, and she'd been on the balcony, thinking of how much she missed Dave and the others. Also wondering how she was going to get back inside the diamond center to rejoin them. Then a profound wave of melancholy hit her. After that, everything went dark.

The moonlight illuminating the garden disappeared. Even the smell of gardenias was gone. Liz wriggled her nose. This room smelled stale, like it had been closed up for some time.

Liz stretched out her arms and felt her way around the darkened room. Ahead of her was something solid—a chair? A table? No, a sink, and across from it, the table. A kitchen? It was a kitchen. That was encouraging. She followed the counter and sensed her way to an arched door at the end of the room.

She opened the door slowly and breathed in the pungent smell of paints and solvents. She felt a rush of excitement. She had to be in Michelangelo's kitchen. This must be the door to the hall, leading to his studio.

The hairs on the back of her neck prickled. She'd spent so much time in this house, it was like coming home. But why was she here instead of in Rome with Francesco? Or Florida? Or the diamond center, where her friends were?

Liz tread carefully back to the kitchen, took the small lantern on the shelf where Michelangelo kept it, and lit it with the striker and flint next to it.

The room came alive, and the familiarity of the past welcomed her. The only thing missing were her friends.

She frowned at the sink. Someone had busted the window and boarded it up. She wondered if Michelangelo knew. If he didn't, there'd be hell to pay once he returned.

As much as she would have liked to linger in Michelangelo's house, she was feeling pressure to return to the Diamond center. She wished she could snap her fingers and pop back, but without Adrielle's feather, or an Achaean feather to time-travel, she had no idea how to get back there.

There had to be a stray feather kicking around somewhere. After all, Michelangelo wasn't the best of housekeepers. And they'd used plenty of Angelo's feathers to work on the *Book of Feathers* forgery. At one time they'd had baskets full of them.

Liz checked the studio and then the kitchen, the hall, the guest room. She came to Michelangelo's bedroom and felt terrible snooping through his stuff, but reasoned he'd never know.

Gosh, he had stacks of sketches lying around. There were even some in the trash bin. She took a bundle out and uncrunched them. These were fantastic. Didn't he know how much these would be worth one day?

If he didn't want them, she did. She rolled them up and bound them with her hair elastic and stuffed them in her cargo pockets.

She checked the Armoire. More drawings. And more books. Very little clothes. Except for—what was this? Pink fabric poked out of a drawer. Was this for real? She tugged . . . it looked like Dave's pink shirt they had got at the mall last month.

Fudge sticks! The drawer was stuck. She yanked harder and tried easing the drawer out by using her legs for leverage. One hefty wrench and the entire drawer slid out. She fell back on her butt, the contents of the drawer spilling onto the floor. She blinked. Along with Dave's shirt was the *Book of Feathers*.

What the what? She picked the book up and placed it gingerly on her lap. She was afraid to open it. It looked real. She ran her fingers along the worn leather. Yep, this was the real deal. But what was it doing here? With Dave's shirt?

She slipped Dave's shirt on and smelled his Dior perfume. Immediately she felt closer to him. If she couldn't have him here in person, she could have him in spirit.

She turned back to the book. There had to be a reason it was here in Michelangelo's armoire. She grinned, feeling the buzz of excitement. This mystery was exactly what she needed.

She opened the book to the first page. She remembered Adrielle saying it contained ancient secrets and magic spells. She couldn't read the ancient Achaean text, but she could follow along, tracing the letters with her fingers.

Was it her imagination? She could feel something stirring in the room. A presence.

Chapter 78

Angelo—Back in Time—Ancient Achaea

ANGELO STOOD IN the central chamber of the Time Vault. The jagged diamond in the golden bird's beak was the only source of light. Where was Adrielle? They'd agreed to meet up here after his memory was fully restored.

He walked around the chamber, mindful to stay away from the walls.

He had no idea how much time had lapsed. Time was difficult to decipher in a time tunnel.

After several minutes of waiting, Angelo decided to seek Monika's help.

He searched the nuances in the wall tunnels until he found the right opening, jumped into the entrance, and traveled along the memory tunnel to find her.

He came to the steps leading to the high tower and ran up them to the top. He found Monika as he remembered, wearing her purple gown with diamond scepter in one hand and black bird perched on her shoulder.

"Where is Adrielle," Angelo demanded.

Monika raised her scepter high and smashed it to the ground, which rumbled. The diamond released a piercing shaft of light within.

Monika beckoned him closer with the curve of her sharp pointy fingernail, and Angelo approached the diamond.

"Gaze into the stone," she said.

Angelo searched inside the diamond but all he could see was a myriad of glittering colors. "Why can't I see her?"

"Look deeper into the heart of the diamond." Monika rotated the scepter until shafts of light spilled out from the center gem and illuminated the room.

Angelo leaned in closer, his raptor vision targeting a single crimson feather drifting along a beaming stream of light. "I see a feather. Crimson. But only one."

"Yes, it is Haden's feather."

"Haden's? What is he doing?"

"He's trying to protect her."

"That's my job," Angelo said, his anger flaring.

"The skin of the fruit reflects the color of the feathers. You know as well as I, that you hold the silver feather, the one for military conquest. You are the best warrior. But Haden holds the red feather, standing for war. He is the leader of the Achaean army," Monika rasped. "Now listen carefully . . . the *Book* says: If you pass a beam of light through a prism, the light will split into all the colors of the rainbow. Adrielle is a prism now. Domenikos will try to diffuse her power by diffusing her light. He can't do this without the *Book of Feathers*. But if he gets a hold of it, she might never survive."

A spike of fear cut through Angelo's core. Adrielle was his reason for being. She was the only one guarding the sacred book, so why hadn't he seen her with it? Domenikos was inside the memory tunnels too. Wreaking havoc. If he found the book . . .

Monika snapped her fingers in front of Angelo's face. "Angelo, do you understand what I am telling you?" Her dark eyes searched his.

He pressed his hands to his temples. If his memories hadn't been fully restored, he might have believed this was an intense case of déjà vu. But this conversation with Monika was different from the last time he'd had it. Something was wrong.

He saw an urgency in Monika's gaze. "How long do I have?"

"Not long," Monika warned.

"And the *Book of Feathers?* Where is it now?"

Monika pointed to the scepter diamond, her crooked finger a red beacon.

Angelo pressed his face to the diamond surface. Deep within the diamond, plumes of smoke ignited and billowed. Gauzy images swirled into forms. He saw a city with a river running through it. A cobblestone street leading to an old house. A bedroom with drawings scattered. It had to be Michelangelo's. Then he saw an open armoire. Liz was there sitting on the floor, alone, leafing through the *Book of Feathers*.

Why was she there? He turned to ask Monika but her body was becoming a thin and wispy phantom.

"Wait," Angelo said.

It was too late. Monika had vanished.

Chapter 79

Domenikos—
in a chamber inside the Time Vault

DOMENIKOS FELT A jolt of energy pulse through him. Adrielle. He'd been expecting her for some time.

"She's close," he said to Brix. "Hurry, get me the spell."

He closed the *Book of Feathers* forgery and drummed his fingers on the leather cover. It angered him he had fallen for a banal trick. That he hadn't known the tooled leather cover was the handy work of a local tool smith. They would pay for their mockery. All of them.

Brix left the chamber and returned almost instantly. He handed Domenikos a page ripped out of the *Book of Feathers*. "Here's the spell."

"You tore this out?" Domenikos said, shocked.

Brix nodded, a triumphant sneer appeared on his face.

"You idiot. You should have brought me the entire book. Did anyone see you?"

"Only the girl with glasses. I took care of her though."

"How?" This Brix clone was not adept at thinking things through.

"I infected her with the virus from the future—the one we—"

"Yeah, yeah." Domenikos dismissed with a wave.

"She's paralyzed now. Won't be long before she's dead. I would have liked to see her expression in the last moments." Brix grinned. "But you said hurry."

"Getting a little chatty there? We'll have to nix that in your next cloned version." Domenikos turned back to the spell and eagerly devoured it. "You'll get plenty of satisfaction by seeing Adrielle fall to her depths."

"What does the spell do?" Brix asked, peering over his shoulder.

Domenikos raised his eyes to Brix. "How many times have I told you not to interrupt?"

Brix clamped his jaw shut.

"That's better. It will separate her prism light and render her powerless. Then I can bind her forever in the scepter diamond. With her trapped and out of the picture, I'll be free to build the new regime." Domenikos turned back to the spell and uttered the words.

"Uh . . . Dom, why not just kill her?" Brix said.

Domenikos sucked in a quick breath. "Because she's already dead, you idiot."

"Dead? How do you know?"

"I bear the pale green feather of her crest. Anyone dies, I know about it."

Chapter 80

Dave, Coco, Eugene, Leonardo, Michelangelo, and Francesco— In the memory tunnel— Back in time—Florence Italy 1504

"I WANT MY bride back," Francesco raged.

"It's complicated," Leonardo explained. "We might never see her again."

Francesco teared up and pulled a handkerchief from his pocket. He swatted at his eyes, and a diamond necklace fell to the ground.

Dave stared at it, stunned.

"It's Lisa's," Francesco said, seeing his reaction. He picked it up and held it to the light. "My wedding gift to her."

The sparkling diamonds drew everyone's attention.

"Those diamonds are huge," Dave said, moving closer. He'd never seen a necklace so grand. Francesco swiveled the necklace until the diamonds caught the light and an explosion of colors reflected from within the diamonds.

"How is it so bright?" Coco approached it.

Leonardo, Michelangelo, and Eugene also came closer. Dave felt the pressure of their bodies crowding together.

"What in the world?" Michelangelo gasped, his gaze darting around the room. "We're in my bedroom in Florence."

Dave screamed. Liz was passed out on the floor, wearing his pink shirt. The *Book of Feathers* open beside her. Coco was already at her side.

Chapter 81

Adrielle and Haden—
Inside the scepter diamond

FINDING THE RIGHT time tunnel was impossible, even with their faces nearly touching the diamond surface. They'd been at it for what felt like hours. Adrielle rubbed her eyes and blinked. The reflection of light was a killer on her sensitive eyes.

From her peripheral vision she saw Haden watching her. He had that same lovesick look he'd had when she'd agreed to marry him back in Achaea. She chuckled to herself.

Husband. Marriage. It bothered her she couldn't remember the actual ceremony. Was it the thump on the head from the Brix clone? Or was she another victim of Domenikos' memory lapse?

"Concentrate Haden," Adrielle scolded.

Haden turned back to inspecting the time tunnels. She didn't mean to take her anxieties out on him, but she'd never liked being the center of attention or be on the receiving end of lovesick adoring glances. They needed to focus on securing the *Book of Feathers*. Then finding Domenikos and putting a stop to his world domination.

They located the memory tunnel matching Florence, Italy 1504, and clasped their hands to cross the barrier together. Though she was technically dead, his touch made her feel alive.

Adrielle landed on a creaky floor and blinked at the scene around her. The chamber, which looked like a bedroom, was crowded not only with her friends, but Leonardo, Michelangelo, and Francisco. They were all fussing over something on the floor.

"She's out cold," Coco yelled.

Adrielle pushed her way through the group. Liz was passed out on the floor, and Coco was holding her wrist.

"What happened?" Adrielle asked.

"We're not sure. We barely got here," Coco said. "Her pulse is faint."

"Lisa," Francesco whined from behind. "Let me see my bride."

"Bride?" Adrielle turned to Coco.

"Apparently, yes," Coco said.

"They're married?"

Adrielle looked around. "Where's Angelo? Anyone see him?"

"I thought he was with you," Dave said, wiping his eyes and lightly tapping Liz's face. He looked freaked out. "She's not coming to."

Adrielle leaned in closely. "Liz, Liz, wake up. She's not responding to me either." She laid her head on Liz's chest and listened. "Her heartbeat is stopped. Dave, you know CPR."

"I'll try," Dave said shakily.

Adrielle scooted out of the way.

Dave got into position and pressed rhythmically down on Liz's chest.

"Harder, with the heel of your hand," Coco said. She was on the verge of tears.

"That's what I'm doing," Dave said, pressing harder.

"What is Dave doing?" Michelangelo roared. "Why is he hurting Lisa?"

"He's restarting her heart," Coco said.

Leonard shrugged. "I've never seen such a thing."

Adrielle saw Veda and Kate appear in the room. "What are you guys doing here?"

"We were in Rome, trying to get Liz back, and suddenly popped here—not sure how," Coco said.

"No—I didn't mean you, I meant them." Adrielle pointed to Veda and Kate, who had moved away to the corner of the room.

Coco glanced over, her expression confused. "There's no one there."

"It's Veda and Kate. They're ghosts," Adrielle said. "Haden, can *you* see them?"

"Yeah. It's your other two friends. The scaredy cat and the one who thinks she can outmaneuver me with her Tae Kwan Do skills."

Adrielle felt a surge of relief. At least she wasn't alone in this undead state.

"Wait, are we talking about Veda?" Coco asked.

Adrielle saw the *Book of Feathers* open on the floor next to Liz. "What's this doing here?" She picked it up. "A page is ripped out. Who did this? Who'd rip a page out?"

"Someone ripped a page out?" Coco asked.

"Brix," Kate said. "He did it."

"Brix is dead," Adrielle replied.

"Yeah, well, so are we," Veda said. "And here we are."

"*Who* are you talking to?" Coco asked.

Adrielle pointed "To Veda and Kate. They're right here."

"You see ghosts now?" Coco said.

"Apparently. I'll explain later," Adrielle said. She turned to Astraia, who was watching from near the window. "Astraia, where's Angelo?"

"He was with you, last time I saw him."

Adrielle didn't like her accusatory tone. "He was—until we found the opening to his memory tunnel inside the Time Vault. He left to restore his memory. The plan was to meet up, but I was jumped by Domenikos' clones."

"Clones?" Coco asked.

Adrielle nodded. "I got away, after I discovered Domenikos had gone to the future. He has cloning factories. The memories he's been stealing are implanted into these clones."

"What does he use them for?" Dave asked.

"To build his army."

"My God." Coco shuddered. "He *is* a monster. If we don't stop him soon . . ."

Adrielle wondered if she'd feel differently once she knew he was their brother.

"Liz's heart has started again." Dave sat back, looking relieved.

"What do we do now?" Coco said. She knelt and caressed Liz's face. "She feels hot."

"This whole thing could have been avoided if you'd followed the plan and stayed in the diamond center," Adrielle said.

"Liz fell through the side. We had to find her," Dave explained.

"Ouch." Francesco shot up from Liz's side. He pulled a syringe out of his leg. "What is this?" He inspected it closely.

"A hypodermic needle," Eugene said flatly.

Dave stared at the needle. "What if they injected her with a deadly virus?"

Coco pointed. "If that's what they used on Liz, we are royally screwed."

"Let's not get ahead of ourselves. Where did you find that?" Adrielle said.

"On the floor by Lisa. I felt the prick on my leeeeegggg . . ." Francesco toppled over, and the syringe rolled out of his hand.

"That's two down," Haden said. "Any bets on who's next?"

Adrielle gave him a stern look. "This is no time for humor."

Leonardo picked up the syringe and inspected it. "Interesting. It still has fluid inside."

"Careful. If Dave's right, it's probably lethal," Coco said. "Let's hope only the point jabbed Francesco."

"We don't know how much time we have before it kills her. Or him, "Adrielle said. "So, on top of everything else, we need to find the antidote to this."

"I'm getting Romeo and Juliette vibes," Kate said, from the corner. Veda jabbed her.

"That's not helping," Adrielle said, and turned to Eugene. "Who are you? And where did you come from?"

Eugene shrugged. "Dunno."

"Wait a minute. You don't know?" Dave asked .

"I'm not really sure?"

"Jeez. Now your memory is going?" Dave said. "Eugene, you told Coco about your family and now you can't remember where you came from? Or the year?"

"Eighteen—hmmm . . ." He shook his head. "No. I'm not really sure."

"Everyone, let's regroup." Adrielle motioned for them to gather around. "We know Domenikos is building an army of cloned soldiers, stealing memories and inserting them into their brains."

"That's possible?" Leonardo asked, looking incredulous.

Adrielle nodded. "Years from now, yes. He has Angelo—older—and Scarlett, working for him too. I'm not sure if she's real."

"Scarlett, I can believe. But why would Angelo? He's on our side," Coco said.

"He's not the real Angelo. At least I don't think so," Adrielle said.

"I agree. He'd never do that," Astraia added.

"So, you travelled to the future without leaving the diamond center?" Coco said. "Obviously, it isn't as secure as we once thought."

"No, it isn't. Domenikos has been wreaking havoc from *inside* the Time Vault. We need to seal the entry to the vault, so Domenikos stops accessing everyone's memories and changing the future," Adrielle said.

Dave raised his finger. "He's been doing a number with the history timeline too. Eugene is from the 1800s. And now he can't remember anything. Domenikos is not just changing the timelines, he's juggling them."

"I'd better find Angelo. The rest of you stay put," Adrielle said, glancing at Haden. He didn't look happy about it. She crouched down by Liz and placed both hands on her face. "Hang in there, Lizzie bear. I'll be back."

"What is that?" Dave pointed to Adrielle's ring.

"My wedding ring."

Dave slapped his hand to his forehead. "You got married too? Doesn't anyone invite friends anymore?"

"It's not like that. Haden's been hanging on to it all these years."

"Why?" Coco asked, her expression confused. "It's not like you two are married.

"We are."

Coco gave Haden a stern look. She turned to Adrielle. "No, Adie, you aren't. He's not your husband."

Adrielle felt her face grow warm. "I was married to him in the past."

"Adie, can't you remember? You're as single as I am."

"Actually, no, I can't remember. But Haden said its true."

Coco narrowed her eyes at Haden. "Don't believe everything someone tells you. Especially if it comes from an unreliable source."

Haden folded his arms and humphed.

Coco turned back to Adrielle. "Aren't you supposed to have the black feather? The feather of truth?"

"Yes, but I've lost my powers."

"How?" Coco said.

"Dear god. This now?" Dave said.

Astraia raised an eyebrow. "I can confirm you never married Haden."

Adrielle turned to Haden. "Why did you lie to me?"

Haden lowered his gaze. "We almost were. I wanted it to be true."

"That doesn't make it true." Adrielle felt like an idiot.

"Doesn't explain why you can't remember either?" Dave said. He searched her face. His expression concerned. "You're not looking so great. Are you ok?"

Aside from being undead? Adrielle pressed her hands to her temples. "I feel woozy." She walked to the bed and sat down.

Haden rushed over. "What's wrong?"

Adrielle was too weak to answer.

"Oh no, she was just leaning over Liz. Maybe the virus is airborne," Dave said, coughing.

Rays of white light radiated from Adrielle's body and separated into the colors of the rainbow. The more colors, the weaker Adrielle felt.

Angelo popped into the room, startling everyone.

"Your light is breaking up. It's a spell. I was just with Monika." He rushed to Adrielle's side. "Fight this, Adrielle." He squeezed her upper arms and pulled her in close to him.

"I—I can't."

VEDA AND KATE rushed to Adrielle's side. "What's happening?"

Haden didn't answer. He was more concerned with Angelo taking Adrielle in his arms.

"Adie, hang in there. Don't die on us now," Coco cried.

"That ship has sailed," Haden mumbled. He was worried about a fate worse than death. He glanced at Veda and Kate, and then at Angelo. He resented him taking Adrielle in his arms but wasn't about to protest.

"If Liz was awake, she'd put the puzzle pieces together. Let's see . . ." Dave held up a finger and wagged it. "Someone came here looking for a spell but only ripped one page out. Why didn't they take the whole book? It's full of spells. The missing spell must be what's hurting Adrielle." His face lit up. "I know. They were too stupid. It was probably a clone."

"Yes. It was Brix's clone," Veda and Kate said at the same time. They jumped and gave each other a high-five.

"That's a yes," Haden said. "The ghosts confirm they saw the Brix clone."

Dave waved an excited fist. "Yes! Liz must have surprised them. So, they stuck her with the needle. Which means . . . we have a fighting chance. Domenikos' clones must only have half a mind. That's why he needs memories. Snooping inside the diamond, he discovered memories are stored in the Time Vault." He pressed his fingers to his skull. "Jeez, no wonder there's a memory epidemic in Florida."

"The spell is blocking Adrielle's powers," Angelo said. "It's breaking them up by diffusing her prism light, her strength, into single colors. Divide and conquer, that's what Domenikos is doing. To combat the spell, we'll need to join forces. Use our corresponding feathers and share our powers with Adrielle so she can regain hers."

Angelo turned to Haden. "You have the red feather—war. I have the silver, for subjugation of power. And Astraia, your black feather is knowledge and truth. We're missing the feather for death. Domenikos' green feather. We need that to make her whole again."

"We have that feather. It's stamped on our shoulder," Kate said.

Haden turned to look. Kate lowered her shirt and showed him a green feather tattoo.

"I have one too," Veda said, showing him hers.

Haden searched his own shoulder. A small green feather had appeared on his shoulder too. "Well, I'll be," he muttered. He didn't have it until he became undead. He went to Adrielle and yanked on her shirt to examine her traveler's crest. The green feather on her wreath was brilliant.

"Whoa buddy. This isn't the time to gawk," Angelo said.

"No—look at the green feather. It's glowing. I have that one too." Haden showed him. "And so do they." He gestured toward Veda and Kate.

"Are you seeing ghosts too?" Coco said, appearing upset.

"Yes, I see them. We must have been branded with the green feather after we died," Haden said.

"Who died?" Dave said. He went to Haden.

"Veda and Kate," Coco said. "Apparently, they're both here."

"They're over there." Haden pointed. "Adrielle and I can see them because we died too. Makes sense why we have the green feather branding."

Angelo's face turned ashen. "You are both dead?"

Haden nodded.

"He's telling the truth," Astraia confirmed. She closed her eyes and concentrated, then opened them moments later. "Haden died trying to save Adrielle at the forgery exchange. When Domenikos stabbed him."

"That's why you disappeared? How are you here and not in the place we all return?" Angelo touched Haden's arm. "You feel like flesh and bones."

"Haden fell to his death before he could morph into his Achaean bird form. He died in human form. But he used an immortal spell to become undead," Astraia said.

Angelo turned to Haden with a shocked expression. Haden shrugged. "What can I say? I didn't trust Domenikos. I saw the spell while the book was under my care and memorized it. Adrielle died in the chamber in the earth's gallows. As the leading Achaean, she bears the green feather in her crest, so technically, she's undead. We both are."

"What does that mean? That you'll live forever?" Coco stared at them, beyond upset.

Haden nodded.

Coco placed a hand on his arm. "You'll take care of her, won't you, Haden?"

"Of course."

Angelo glanced at Haden. "You couldn't have planned it better," he muttered.

"Guys, hurry!" Dave said. "Adrielle's not looking good."

Haden turned. Dave was leaning over Adrielle on the bed.

"Quick. How do you share your powers with her?" Dave asked.

Chapter 82

The Gang—Inside Michelangelo's Bedroom—Florence, 1504

LOSING ADRIELLE TO death was Angelo's biggest fear. Finding out his brother was also undead, was a close second. Knowing they would share their lives together was crushing him.

Dave patted Adrielle's hand. "We need to restore Adrielle's powers."

Angelo pushed his pain aside and huddled with Haden and Astraia over Adrielle. They interlinked their arms.

"Concentrate," Haden said.

They hovered over her for several minutes.

Angelo pulled his arm away from Haden. "It's not working." He turned to Dave. "Quick, show me your phone. I need to search the *Book of Feathers*."

Dave fished his phone out of his pocket and tried turning it on. "Battery's dead."

"We can keep trying to strengthen her with our powers, but our feathers might not be strong enough to combat the spell," Angelo said. "A better option is to reverse the spell. And we won't know how to reverse it, until we see it."

Haden went to the *Book of Feathers*. "I'll check to see where it was positioned in the book, in case that gives us a clue."

"Good idea. Hurry," Angelo said. "There's another complication, aside from finding the antidote for Liz. We need to get back to the Time Vault and locate the exact point where Domenikos started messing with the timeline. Then restore it. Hopefully it will be enough to destroy Domenikos' warped future. If we don't, it could be our new reality. Once we seal the entry to Time Vault, no one else will be able to access it."

"Finally, a plan. But how do we do that? Find the antidote for Liz, *and* reverse Adrielle's spell?" Dave shook his head. "It's too much." He walked back to Liz's side.

Francesco was holding her hand. Dave knelt at Liz's other side. He picked up Michelangelo's hairbrush and ran it through her wooly hair. "Holy cow! Did you guys see that? Where did he go?" Dave pointed. "Francesco was just here."

"You seeing ghosts too? There's no one there," Coco said.

Dave shook his head. "Francesco vanished."

"Dave's right. I saw him," Angelo said.

Francesco popped back, holding the necklace. The ribbons of colored lights escaping Adrielle's crest merged into a single band of white light and funneled into the necklace diamonds. Before Angelo could get closer, Francesco was gone again. Then he reappeared.

"Stop." Astraia grabbed Francesco's arm. "How are you yo-yoing in and out?"

Francesco leaned back and stared at her with frightened eyes.

"I was admiring this—this necklace. Wishing Lisa was wearing it. Wishing this was only a dream, and I was back in my own bed. In my room. And then I wished I was with my Lisa. And here I am. And then back in my bed and—"

"We get it," Astraia said, letting go of Francesco's arm. She held out her hand. "Hand me the diamonds."

Francesco clutched the necklace. "No. It's Lisa's."

Astraia gave him a threatening look, and Francesco shuddered. He dropped the necklace into her palm. Astraia raised the necklace eye level. She singled out one diamond and studied the facets closely, then turned to Francesco with narrowed eyes. "*Where* did you get this?"

He scooted back. "From a travelling jeweler. I paid a hefty price." He tugged on his bed jacket. "These stones are the only ones of its kind."

"Let's hope," Astraia said, raising an eyebrow. She leaned into him. "What did this jeweler look like?"

"Green eyes, pointy tooth when he smiled." He made a sour face. "Pale— very pale. Francesco glanced at Adrielle. "He looked like her. Only with dark hair."

"I knew it!" Astraia said, turning to meet Angelo's gaze. "It was *him.* That's how he did it. He chiseled these diamonds from Monika's scepter diamond. And they have time tunnels channeling along the facets like the mother stone."

"WAIT." COCO SAID. "Who do you mean by *him?*"

Astraia folded her arms and tipped her chin. "Your darling brother, Domenikos."

"He's not my—" Coco staggered back. Her knees weakened, and she dropped into a chair. "How can this be? Adrielle never—" She gazed at Adrielle. Why hadn't she told her? She searched out Angelo's gaze for confirmation, but Angelo turned his eyes downward. Haden also turned away.

They all knew.

After a few awkward moments, Angelo took the necklace from Astraia. "If these diamonds are chiseled from the scepter, we should be able to access the time tunnel that funnels back to this room. Get back before the clone takes the spell, and reverse it, before it destroys Adrielle. He gazed into it with immense concentration. "I'll be back." He changed into bird form.

Angelo disappeared into the diamond in the necklace, as it dropped to the floor.

Francesco, wide mouthed, pointed at the necklace. "Did he just?"

"Yep," Haden said. "Get over it."

Across the room, Michelangelo and Leonardo appeared as awestruck as they had after the forgery exchange, when they watched Adrielle fly.

Coco went to Adrielle's side and took her hand. It must have killed her to keep this secret.

COCO WAS AT the foot of the bed, rubbing Adrielle's feet when Angelo popped back. He checked on Adrielle and then on Liz. Dave was hovering over Liz—wiping her forehead with a wet cloth. He glanced at Haden, who was leafing through the *Book of Feathers*.

Michelangelo and Leonardo were at the other end of the room in a deep conversation about time tunnels. They seemed oblivious Angelo was back. And Astraia was giving Francesco and Eugene the stare down.

"The ghosts were right," Angelo announced. "Domenikos sent a Brix clone. Apparently, Liz surprised him when he came for the spell, so he stuck her with the syringe. It must be part of their modern artillery, which is wrong on every level. I've seen the missing spell, but couldn't follow the Brix clone when he disappeared with it. I didn't want to give Domenikos the heads up on what we are up to. However, I heard them say the spell weakens the subject until they slip into a vegetative state."

Coco suppressed a shiver. "How do we stop it?"

Haden cleared his throat after a few moments. "The only way to reverse it is with a monumental sacrifice. Someone has to give up their life in exchange for Adrielle's. If they don't, she will remain a vegetable for the rest of eternity."

"Wowza." Dave wiped his brow with one finger. "That's one lethal book. It should be locked up."

"That counts me out. I'm already dead. And so are they," Haden said, pointing to where he'd said Veda and Kate were.

It annoyed Coco she couldn't see her best friends.

"I'll do it," Angelo said.

"No, no you won't," Coco said, standing up. "With Adrielle down, you're the only one who knows the way to the Time Vault. And we can't chance it not working and losing your feather power. You have the silver feather, and we need all the feathers to overcome Domenikos. We need Astraia's powers to guide us with the truth. Dave has the best knowledge of history, so, he'll be able to tell us when everything is historically correct. And Leonardo, Michelangelo, and Francesco are too important historically, to lose them. So is Eugene. Without him there's no Ghirardelli chocolate, which would affect a large percentage of the population. So that leaves only me. I'm the only one without a purpose."

Haden raised his eyes from the *Book of Feathers*.

"I wouldn't be so sure about that. Did you ever stop to think, that as Adrielle's sister, you are also half-Achaean? You have powers you haven't discovered yet," Angelo said.

Coco shook her head. "It's too late for me. I'll make the sacrifice. Maybe Haden could use that spell on me first. And I could be with Adrielle forever. The thoughts of not being with her . . ." Coco wiped her eyes.

Angelo put his hands on her upper arms. "Coco, we don't know that everyone continues living after they die."

Haden scoffed. "The correct term is undead. And I wouldn't be so sure about that. I used the spell on myself to become undead, and it worked for me. It will probably work on Coco, too."

"But you can't guarantee it." Angelo sounded agitated. "We are dabbling in things we shouldn't."

Astraia went over to Haden and gave him a pointed look. "Tell me, will it help my sister?"

Haden looked surprised. "Arnadella?"

Astraia nodded.

Dave turned his attention away from Liz and strode to them. "What's this? You turned your sister into a bird and now you want redemption?"

"No. It wasn't like that," Astraia said through gritted teeth.

Dave backed away. Astraia turned away and went to the window. She stared out it for a few moments.

"When Aaron first enacted the Achaean Act and stated we were to cohabit as humans," she said without turning away from the window, "Arnadella and I began practicing morphing into human form. Arnadella wanted to see what it felt like to fly with a mortal body." Her voice cracked with emotion. "She changed from bird form mid-air to human, and didn't morph back in time. She hit the ground—plunging from such a great height . . . We sought Monika's help, and she made Arnadella choose. 'Become my bird companion for the rest of your days, or remain paralyzed in human form forever,' she said."

Dave gasped. Coco felt the pit of her stomach drop. They'd mis-judged Astraia.

Astraia turned to Haden. "Monika is not someone to anger, so I've never confronted her. But perhaps there is still hope for Arnadella, in those spells."

Angelo turned back to Coco and held her gaze. "Dying for your sister is a noble sacrifice."

"I can use the spell if you want to become undead as Adrielle and I are," Haden said.

"This comes at great risk," Angelo said, squeezing Coco's hands.

"We're wasting time. Shall I use it?" Haden asked.

"Yes." Coco nodded, resolute in her decision.

"But we can't be sure the immortality spell will work," Angelo warned.

Haden snapped his attention to Coco. "I believe it will. But it is still a great sacrifice, and not to be taken lightly. Adrielle and I aren't sure what's entailed when you're undead. We know you will never age. And that everyone you love will die. It may sound good to you now, but there will be days when you wish you could end your life. And still, you will go on and on. Do you understand?" He held her gaze with intensity.

"I do. Give me the syringe."

Haden handed it to her.

Coco let go of Angelo's hands and held his gaze. "For the record, I love Liz like a sister too. And to save her, we need Adrielle to help find the antidote. We can't just let Liz die, when her life has just begun." She turned back to Haden. "Hurry. I'm ready."

Haden read over the immortality spell and chanted in a low murmur. Coco pressed the plunger flange into her arm and dispersed the poison liquid in the barrel of the syringe into her veins. It felt cold. She shivered and almost instantly, felt the poison swimming in her veins. Her knees weakened, and she lost her balance. The floor rushed toward her.

Chapter 83

Coco—
Inside the Deep Dark Cavity of the Earth

AS COCO DEPRESSED the remaining contents of the syringe, she fell into a pungent and humid tunnel. She plunged into a terrifying silence, couldn't even hear the sound of her heart beating or her lungs expanding. She pressed her arms to her sides to avoid the stone walls looming in the almost complete darkness.

After some time, she felt the impact of cold stone on her feet. Then everything went black.

"IT'S AARON'S DAUGHTER," someone whispered in a childlike voice. Coco opened her eyes. Round brown eyes stared back at her. The face belonged to a girl, tiny and pixie like.

"Go fetch him," the pixie girl said over her shoulder to someone. Her hair was pulled back into one long brown braid that hung over her shoulder.

Coco ran her hands along the cold slab she was laying on and shivered. She attempted to sit up, but her body was not co-operating. "Where am I?"

The pixie girl pressed a cold hand on her shoulder. "Try not to move. You are in the main chamber."

"Of what? A mausoleum?"

The pixie girl turned to someone beside her and scooted to make room for them.

Their eyes were kind and dark. Memories of her Achaean life flooded her mind. "Father?" It surprised her she'd had no recollection of him during her upbringing in modern day Florida.

He took her hands and squeezed, but she had no sensation. "It's all right. Everything will be all right.

Coco felt a burning tie to him, as though she'd come home. She attempted to sit up again. "I can't feel my arms and legs."

"Shhh . . ." he said.

Coco was drained of energy. Though she tried to stay alert, she slipped into nothingness.

After some time, she heard muffled whispers. Someone said it was unheard of for two Achaeans to lose their life at such a young age. And then they said she was only half Achaean.

Coco opened her eyes. Her father hadn't left her side. His clasped on hers loosened and a slight vibration in her chest swelled until it pounded hard against her ribcage. It was her heart. She could hear her blood swim in her veins and pulse in her ears. Then her lungs expanded with a jerk, and she sucked in a gulp of air, and then another. She remembered Haden had used a spell.

Coco shifted her attention to her father. He was studying her closely.

She was about to speak, when more memories of her prior Achaean life rushed back in one painful jolt. She pressed her hands to her skull. After a few agonizing moments, the pain subsided. She turned to him. "Father, I remember it all."

He closed his hand over hers, and it was cold like a corpse. She pulled her hand back.

"Don't be afraid, Coco," Aaron said. "The veil of forgetfulness we used to propel you into the future is gone now."

"What is this dreadful place? There's so little light here." She could barely see the pixie girl standing to one side.

"Darkness, true darkness, is the absence of light. As long as Adrielle lives, even in her undead form, there is light. She is our hope."

"You know Adrielle is undead?"

Without him speaking, she felt his sadness inside her.

"There's so much I have to tell you," Coco said.

As they talked, Coco felt a searing sting on her back. She went to touch it and felt something prickly between her shoulders, followed by a warmth sensation of peace and love. It became so intense she thought she might explode. Soon, a warm purple light illuminated the chamber.

"What is that?" she asked.

The pixie girl ran over and touched her. Coco felt a surge of energy leave her body from the point of contact, and a feeling of joy cycled between them. Others crawled from the surrounding stones to see and bask in the purple glow. Hope and acceptance were reflected in their expressions.

"What is happening? My back is burning," Coco asked her father.

Aaron turned Coco to see her back and sighed deeply.

"Is everything all right back there?" Coco asked.

"You have awakened your Achaean powers. The burning you feel is the purple feather seared into your back. If you use your power wisely, it will strengthen the world."

"Wait, are you saying I have powers?" Coco searched his eyes.

"Yes, Coco. As an Achaean, you do. Your entire being radiates love. You are glowing." He chuckled.

"How did this happen?"

"You earned it by giving of yourself. Losing your life for your sister is a great sacrifice." His expression reflected how proud he was of her.

An overwhelming wave of sadness struck her. "Something is wrong."

"Haden has used the spell of great sacrifice," Aaron said.

"How do you know this?"

"Because I understand the *Book of Feathers* better than anyone."

"Is that why you're sad?"

Aaron cupped Coco's chin. "No, my child. I am sad only for myself. The love in your heart is selfless and sacrificing. It means you can't stay here, with me. You must join the others in their efforts to strengthen Adrielle. She will need you and your feather to overcome the most loathsome of beings."

"How can I help? I'm a nobody."

"You are wrong. This love that is your power is what caused me to fall in love with your mother. It helped me see the importance of things beyond our kind. It is the core reason why I created the Achaean Act. We needed to change our way of life as a species, for humanity to continue."

"By loathsome beings, you mean Domenikos? I just learned he is my brother. Your son."

Aaron nodded. A single tear escaped his eye, and Coco brushed it away.

"He is my deepest pain. Perhaps with your powers, Domenikos will change and embrace the light. Go now and help the others."

The warmth inside her burned and she morphed into a tiny purple bird.

I have wings?

Coco circled around the chamber and flew upward into the dark tunnel.

Chapter 84

Everyone–Inside Michelangelo's Bedroom–Florence, 1504

"A PURPLE BIRD flew in through the window," Dave said.

They stared, stunned, as Coco morphed into human form in front of them. She brushed herself off.

"I'm back," she said, grinning. She met Haden's gaze. "Thank you."

Kate and Veda ran up to her.

"There you are, I've missed you guys." Coco tried to hug them, but her arms went through them. "At least I can see you now."

"So, I'm the only one that can't see them?" Dave whined.

"Guess so," Coco said.

"You've earned the purple feather," Angelo said, rushing to her side. He looked like he was going to hug her, but Haden intercepted him.

"I never doubted it," Haden said, extraordinarily pleased with himself. "The book explains every color and its powers. I just wasn't sure which one was yours."

"Love. I have *love. "* Coco beamed.

"Let's put it to the test, see if it helps Adrielle," Angelo said.

He extended his hand. Coco took it, and Haden took Astraia's hand. They formed a tight circle around Adrielle. She lay in the center, unmoving and rigid.

"Veda, Kate, come join our circle. We need your green feathers too," Haden said.

Veda and Kate took their place in the circle, on either side of Coco, and Haden recited the words of the spell. When he was finished, they held their breaths and waited.

The colors of their respective feathers seeped out and formed a tapestry covering Adrielle. After several moments, Adrielle glowed a dim white.

"Quick, bring the necklace," Astraia instructed.

Dave gave the necklace to her, and Astraia held it over Adrielle. The colored beams from their feathered tapestry shot out in all directions and reflected off the diamond facets. The beams funneled into a single piercing white light that struck Adrielle like a lightning bolt, absorbing the rays and shining as a clear prism.

ADRIELLE OPENED HER eyes and frowned at the tapestry of feathers covering her. "What happened?" She saw a purple light radiate from Coco. "You have wings?"

Everyone chattered at once as they filled her in on what happened.

"And Liz?"

"I don't think she's going to make it." Dave dipped a cloth in a basin of water and put it on Liz's forehead. "If the poison killed Coco, it's going to kill Liz too. Liz must have had a smaller dose, but she's going downhill fast."

"We can use the spell on her too," Haden said.

Adrielle frowned.

"C'mon, it worked for Coco and for me," Haden said.

"She's human. We won't know if it works until it's too late. The antidote is our best bet. There must be one," she said. "But first we need to find the exact point where Domenikos began altering the future. We'll have to split up."

"I don't think that's a good idea," Angelo said. "Look what happened when we were apart last time."

"It's our only choice. We're out of time," Adrielle said. "We'll go into the Time Vault together and then Angelo, you and Dave search the timeline for discrepancies. If the Brix clones are there, you'll have to destroy them."

"Might work," Dave said. "They're strong, but not smart."

"I'll show you how." Adrielle placed her hands on Angelo's temples and waited for Angelo to see the replay of her memory inside the future cloning building. Adrielle took her hands off Angelo's temples. "Did you see the future clone of you?"

"Yep. That's something I can't unsee."

"If you pretend to be your future cloned self, they'll buy it. At least for a while." Adrielle turned to Dave. "Can you help search the timeline?" Dave nodded. "Great. Then I'll secure the antidote. We'll meet back here. It must be inside that building. I can feel it."

"What about me?" Coco said. "I saw Father in that terrible place. I know Domenikos is our brother. You should have told me, Adrielle."

Adrielle winced. Coco only used her full name when she was upset.

"I meant to. I wasn't sure how to tell you. You're always so forgiving, and there can be no tolerance when it comes to Domenikos."

"And I'm coming with you." Coco folded her arms stubbornly.

"Me too," Astraia said, also folding her arms.

She couldn't very well refuse Coco, especially when she'd given her life for her. Or Astraia.

"What about Liz?" Dave said. "I can't leave her."

"We'll be here and take good care of her," Leonardo said, tipping his head toward Liz. "She already has a personal nurse."

Francesco was soothing her brow with the cloth.

"Kate, Veda, you two keep an eye on things here. Eugene, you're going home buddy. We'll pop you back into your correct time-line slot," Adrielle said.

"What about me?" Haden said. "You've given everyone an assignment but me."

Adrielle looked down at her ring and raised her eyes to him. "You tricked me into thinking we'd been married."

"Don't be mad all over again. We almost were. It's a technicality."

Adrielle shook her head and gave him a pointed look. "Don't lie to me again. I didn't remember, which means Domenikos must have altered my timeline. He has something big up his sleeve, and I don't know what it is. Let's hope I find out in time."

Chapter 85

The Gang—Inside the Time Vault

LIKE BEFORE, THE Brix clones guarded the entry to the Time Vault. *Two fierce sentinels looking for trouble,* Adrielle thought. They spotted Adrielle and watched her approach with angry scowls on their faces.

Adrielle concentrated on absorbing the colors around her and became invisible, like the prism that she was.

They stared in surprised and engaged in a heated discussion. Angelo swooped in and banged their heads together, knocking them out, and flew into the Time Vault.

Haden, Coco, Astraia, Dave, and Eugene rushed in behind him.

"Seal the entry," Adrielle ordered.

The sky became dark as a thousand birds came from all directions, swooping in with stones in their beaks and claws and laying the rocks on top of each other, until the doorway was covered.

Angelo led the way to the main atrium, while Adrielle and Haden followed from behind, to guard against an unforeseen attack.

None of the Brix soldiers were in sight. More troubling was the unpleasant smell of Sulphur that hadn't been there before.

"Can you smell that?" Adrielle said.

The others nodded.

"That's the after-effect smell of time travel. Domenikos must be here."

"What in the world—?" Eugene pointed to the diamond in the bird's claws, in the center of the room. He walked toward it.

Haden put a hand on his arm. "Nah-uh. Don't touch it if you want to live."

Eugene backed away and slithered to Dave's side.

Angelo inspected the time tunnels at the wall. "What year and city are we looking for?" he asked Dave.

"Let's go with San Francisco, 1905," Dave said. "That's when the Ghirardelli family sold only chocolate and mustard." He turned to Eugene. "You probably won't remember any of this, but I'd forget the mustard. Go all the way with the chocolate." He extended his hand and grinned. "You can never go wrong with chocolate."

"Found him." Angelo picked Eugene up like he was weightless and tossed him through the slot, then slapped his palms together. "One less mortal to deal with. Nothing personal," he said to Dave.

"None taken. Why would you want to be human, when you can do that?"

Haden grabbed the diamond from the clawed sculpture. He kneeled on one knee and held it up to Adrielle. "Will you marry me?"

"Give me that." Adrielle swiped for it, but Haden held it from her reach. "Haden. This is not the time to joke around."

"Who's joking?" Haden stood up.

A deep rhythmic rumble shook the room.

"Take cover. It's coming from the floor and the walls," Astraia said.

"It's the clones," Adrielle said. "Get ready, they're coming in droves from the other room. I have an idea. I think that mirror Scarlett uses is a portal to the building in the future. I'll head there now."

Astraia turned to Coco. "How are your fighting skills?"

"Not good," Coco said. "But I have the feather of love. I think I can use it to hypnotize them . . . should hold them back for a bit."

Adrielle smiled.

"Are you sure?" Astraia asked, taking the warrior's stance with Haden.

Coco shrugged. "No, but it's worth a try. This power must be good for something. You should be prepared, if it works, I may not be able to hold them for long."

"Let's roll," Adrielle said and entered the other chamber.

The line of Brix soldiers coming out of the mirror was endless. Adrielle used her prism light to get past them invisibly and worked her way around the soldiers to the mirror's surface. Her hunch was right. Instead of her reflection, she saw through the mirror into the future time, where Scarlett was beckoning the young boys from the cloning building into the mirror.

Adrielle penetrated the mirror's surface and gained access to the training room in the alternate future in Florida. She was elated. Her new ability to absorb the light was incredible, making it so much easier to get around when no one could see you.

As much as Adrielle wanted to shake the boys out of their trance and warn them to run as far away from this place as possible, she needed to find the antidote for Liz. She suppressed her craving to knock the wind out of Scarlett and left the main hall, where Scarlett was using her charm to lure the boys.

Adrielle made her way down the hall. *Where might they keep it?* She saw in her mind a door with a keypad.

Strange, the doors along this hall had windows, like in a high school. None of them had a keypad. But the one in her head did. It looked like a lab, a medical room with supply shelves and refrigerators with glass doors.

Adrielle kept going, the central room falling further away. She bumped into something and lost her concentration.

"What are you doing here? This place is restricted."

She stared into Angelo's face. "Uh, you can see me?" *Of course, he could.* She looked down at her hands and feet. She was no longer transparent.

"Where are you going?" Angelo asked, his tone combative, his green-flecked eyes studying her curiously. There was something unsettling about his gaze. The warmth and familiarity were gone. For the first time, Adrielle saw Angelo as his enemies did—a skilled warrior, one to fear.

He grasped her wrists and squeezed tightly.

"Ouch, you're hurting me." She wriggled her wrists, and his clutch tightened.

He lifted her like she was weightless and dragged her to a room with a numbered key lock.

Her breath hitched. This was it, the place in her mind. Instead of punching numbers he put his thumb print on the glass and the door slid open.

A fingerprint scanner?

She was inside what looked like a research lab. The walls were lined with shelves and glass front fridges—everything exactly as she'd seen in her mind.

Angelo dragged her to a metal table in the center of the room. She writhed, resisting him as best as she could. As he went to strap her in, his grip tightened.

It struck her, she had access to all the feathers. If she tapped into Coco's feather of love, she might be able to buy enough time to escape.

Adrielle used his grip as a channel to send a rush of memories to him of her feelings of love for the real Angelo. The Angelo clone stopped fighting and appeared disoriented. Dazed. Her gaze went to the fridge filled with rows of vials. One of them could be the antidote.

Adrielle wriggled from his grasp and snapped the arm restrains from the bed onto his wrists. She ran to the fridge.

Adrielle commanded her black feather to guide her through the hundreds of vials. The label marked with three Achaean symbols jumped out at her. She grabbed it and dashed out the door, only looking back for a second.

The Angelo clone had the same forlorn look Angelo had when she'd left him on the beach. She felt a familiar pang and pushed it out of her mind.

Adrielle returned to the Time Vault and found the entire chamber glowing purple. Coco was harnessing her feather's power to daze the clones with a mega dose of Oxytocin—the love hormone. Their disoriented gazes held no malice or spite. They smiled warmly at Astraia while Angelo and Dave worked to locate the exact point where Domenikos had shifted the history timeline.

Eugene was gone, returned to his rightful time.

"I'm back," Adrielle said.

"Did you find it? The antidote?" Dave asked.

"Got it. And you? Any luck finding where Domenikos shifted the timeline?"

"Got it," Angelo said. "I think we found where he sliced through your life-timeline, too."

Adrielle felt a rush of excitement. "Are you sure?"

"Looks that way." Angelo pointed. "Before this section here, they are intact."

"Where's the culprit? Have we found Domenikos yet?"

Angelo shook his head. "Haden's gone to look for him, but no." He stepped aside for Adrielle to see.

Adrielle pressed her face to the wall's surface. She followed her memory tunnel back along her lifeline. "It's my mother. She's in labor."

"Exactly," Angelo said, with a worried expression. "Now look at who's standing over her."

Adrielle pressed her face to the wall tunnel. Domenikos was next to her mother, wearing a cold and calculating smile. She hadn't noticed how much he looked like their father with none of his warmth.

Haden reappeared, his worried expression mirroring what she feared. If Domenikos was there at the time of her birth, he was planning to kill her when she was most helpless.

"We have to stop him!" Coco shrieked.

"I'm going in with you," Haden said.

"No. The only one who can go is Adrielle. Anyone else might alter something," Dave said.

Of course, Dave was right. One wrong move, and her existence would be erased.

Adrielle exchanged a look with Coco. It was him or her.

"Hurry," Angelo warned. "Your mother has just given birth to Domenikos. He's standing over her with a green scarf, and they don't even see him."

Chapter 86

The gang—Inside The Time Vault

ADRIELLE HAD EXACTLY one minute and thirty-five seconds to intercept Domenikos before she was born. It was a blink. An unforgettable amount of time that Domenikos had held over her, her entire life. He reasoned because he'd been born first, he should be heir and leader to the Achaean race on Aaron's demise.

"Quick, give me that rock," she said to Haden.

Haden tossed her the diamond from the bird sculpture, and she caught it mid-air. In the next second, she was in her birth room, in ancient Achaea, watching as her mother birthed her.

"Look who decided to join the party," Domenikos crooned. His eyes were cold daggers. He snapped the scarf in his hands and pulled tightly.

Rain pelted against the window with a vengeance that seemed to cry doom. For some reason, Adrielle had always imagined being born on a warm day.

The woman beside her mother held her hand. She was in her mid-thirties with flaming red hair. Adrielle gasped, recognizing her at once. She was the other Achaean leader Domenikos burned at the stake, along with her father.

"Don't do this Domenikos," Adrielle said.

"I have lived in your shadow all my days. This day changed our father forever. Changed our lives. Because of his stupid blind love for our mother, he punished the rest of us. We only wanted to live as we were meant to be."

"He did what was right. Time cannot be pierced without consequence to others," Adrielle said.

"You mean consequences to meaningless humans. We are a superior species."

"You're wrong. They love deeply. You should know this. You're half-human too. You've lost touch with that side of your being."

"Now!" the woman said. "Push now! The baby is crowning."

A baby's wail broke the silence. Domenikos lowered his scarf to the baby's neck.

Adrielle approached him and held up the diamond. "As the Achaean leader, I banish you, Domenikos, to the bowels of the Earth."

The diamond blazed white. Shafts of colored light shot out from Adrielle's crest, wrapped around Domenikos, and bound him immobile. Blinding rays of colors merged into white light and sucked him into the diamond.

THE PIXIE GIRL stood at the head of the stone. Iridescent light spun like glass from Adrielle's crest and secured Domenikos in a cage.

Domenikos seethed as he fought to escape, but he could not pierce the gilded cage. It was stronger than any shackles made from human bonds.

"What should we do with him?" the pixie asked Aaron.

"Take him to the pit," Aaron said, keeping his gaze averted. He could not bear to look at Domenikos. His son. He felt a sharp stabbing jolt through his heart.

Despite everything, his horrific acts, he still loved him. But he was a monster. And monsters couldn't roam free.

They drug him to the darkest of corners in the loathsome crevice of the earth. Two dragons with emerald eyes and breath of fire were posted as guards.

"Why is he here?" the pixie girl asked, as they left Domenikos in a place where no living thing had ever been.

Aaron sighed. "Everyone is hungry for something. Be it love, money, or power. Some will risk anything for it. Domenikos hungers for something that will never be his. Power and adoration that only comes from being a great leader. To be a great leader, you must be willing to sacrifice everything for the greater good, and Domenikos only thinks of himself."

ADRIELLE, COCO, AND their friends arrived back at Michelangelo's room.

Leonardo and Michelangelo stood at either side of the bed, watching Liz. Her face was pale and lifeless.

Adrielle rushed to Liz's side. She looked at the small vial and syringe in her hand. "I'm not sure how to—"

"Give it to me, I took that medic class for Doctors without borders," Dave said.

Dave filled the syringe and pushed it into Liz's arm.

"Will she be ok?" Coco whispered.

"Let's hope," Adrielle said.

They watched and waited, but Liz remained lifeless.

Chapter 87

The gang—Present day Florida

THE CATEGORY FIVE hurricane that blustered its way through Florida, left scars throughout the state. Roads were wiped out. Houses were blown to pieces. But Layla's house stood erect, with only minimal damage to the roof.

Coco switched off the TV and began straightening up the room. They were gathering in Coco's room in anticipation of their Friday night movie night. A celebration of victory after their journey through time. Everyone was looking forward to some form of normalcy.

"Who's coming?" Coco asked, picking up a pile of clothes from her floor and hanging them up.

"Everyone," Adrielle said.

"*Everyone* meaning . . . Haden and Angelo too? 'Cause Veda and Kate are always here."

"*Everyone* . . . meaning Liz and Dave. I'm not sure about Angelo or Haden."

"Of course, Liz and Dave. They're joined at the hip. God, can you imagine if Liz had died? Dave wouldn't know what to do with himself," Coco said, holding a white blouse in front of her full-length mirror. "And did you invite them? Haden and Angelo?"

Adrielle nodded.

"So, when are you going to choose?"

"Choose?"

"Yes, choose. They're both crazy about you." Coco looked at her, expecting an answer. "Out of the two, only Haden is undead. And Angelo will eventually die. So maybe you should choose Angelo, since his time is limited."

"Gee, Coco, that's a cheery thought." Adrielle switched the TV on. They needed a diversion. Coco was obsessed with being undead. It deeply affected her that everyone around would eventually die. "Don't forget that Achaeans live for thousands of years. We've got some time to deal with all that."

The news anchor was giving a rundown of the news. *Whew.* Nothing out of the ordinary. No memory lapse epidemic. No mass shootings. The best they came up with was gas prices were going up for the second time this week.

"We're here." Dave called from the entry. "Should we come up?"

"Yes," Adrielle hollered. "We could use a little livening up." She glanced at Coco who shrugged.

Dave walked in, holding a pizza, followed by Liz. He placed it on Coco's bed and plopped down. "What's wrong with her?" He tipped his head toward Coco. "She seems unusually down."

"She's still trying to deal with it all."

"Oh." Dave patted the bed, and Liz snuggled next to him.

"I'm fine. I was only asking if Adie was going to pick Angelo or Haden."

Adrielle shifted her eyes to her and scowled.

"It's a fair question." Coco shrugged. "You say you're not choosing, but you're still wearing Haden's ring. It must make Angelo feel terrible."

"Forgot all about it," Adrielle said as she spun it around her finger. As much as she didn't want to choose, she didn't want to take it off, either. She liked the idea of knowing someone else was going to be there for the rest of her existence. "Besides, why are you so worried about Angelo's feelings?"

"Liz is wearing her ring too," Dave said, raising her hand for everyone to see. Rays of light escaped the diamond and reflected throughout the room.

"Why haven't we seen that before?" Adrielle said, trying to get a closer look.

Liz put her hand behind her back. "It's so showy, I turn the diamond over so you can't see it."

Adrielle exchanged a look with Coco. She looked as surprised as she was. "Dave, did you know—?"

"Nah-uh," he said, biting his lip. "How about we keep me out of this."

"I'm starved. Can we eat?" Liz said, lifting the lid to the pizza.

Adrielle knew she was trying to deflect the conversation.

"I hate to ask, but are you back to binge eating?" Dave said. He turned to Adrielle. "Do you think she's okay? I mean—" His eyes drifted to Liz's tummy.

Liz threw the slice of pizza back into the carton.

"Don't be so sensitive," Dave said. "You're acting like—wait a minute. Are you?"

Liz nodded.

"Is that why—?"

"Yep."

"I see you two are back to your shorthand conversations. Finishing each other's sentences. I like that you're close, but do you mind clueing the rest of us in?" Coco said.

"She's pregnant!" Dave blurted, slapping his hands to his mouth. "It's bound to change the timeline."

"Pregnant?" Coco shrieked.

Liz reached into the pizza box.

Adrielle grabbed her hand. "That diamond is huge, Lizzie. Is this one of Francesco's diamonds? The ones he bought at the same time as the necklace?"

Liz blushed.

"The one we sealed in the Time Vault because it was clawed from the diamond scepter? Or—a knock off?"

"What's the big deal?" Liz said, pointing to Adrielle's neck. "You're wearing yours as a pendant."

Adrielle touched the diamond hanging on a chain beside the chronometer. Then she ran her hands along her chronometer chain. "The big deal is—it has time tunnels in the facets. If anyone else uses them. She shook her head. "Anyway, it's a quick shortcut for me if I need to access the time tunnels."

Liz spun her ring around until the diamond was hidden in the palm of her hand. "No one will ever know. I promise."

Liz's pleading expression broke Adrielle down. She didn't have the heart to take it away. It was Liz's wedding ring.

"Shhh." Coco turned up the television. "We've got bigger problems."

"Breaking news. Newly engaged couples are disappearing nationwide. Until now, authorities have kept this under wraps. Police have been working in collaboration with the FBI. This is turning out to be a major epidemic."

Montana Wakefield, author of the Adrielle Maddox series and other forthcoming books, her illustrated children's book series, *Squiggley Wiggley: The Magical Blue Bear*, and mystery novel, *Twist in Fate*, is a lover of life and has an unquenchable thirst for the next adventure. As an avid reader and writer, she's a firm believer that stories unite us all on a deeper level and will enrich our lives if we embrace the imagination within us.

Montana studied fine arts and writing at the University of Calgary, attended the Royal Conservatory of Music for classical guitar, paints, writes songs, and loves to play with her dog Scarlatti. This mother of three is happily married to her husband, close to all her siblings, is an avid TV binger, and is constantly surprised by life's turn of events. Her mission in life is to spread a little fun, love deeply, and stay true to her belief that each of us can reach unfathomable heights if we learn to believe in ourselves and each other.

Visit Montana's website: https://montanawakefield.com